Praise for *All About Us*

'Prepare ⟨…⟩ with this book.'
HELLO!

'Magical and beautiful.' **Josie Silver**

'An insightful, nuanced look at modern relationships, I LOVED it. *A Christmas Carol* meets *Love Actually*.' **Holly Bourne**

'A heart-warming and surprisingly feminist novel of "what if".' **Laura Jane Williams**

'Has all of the feels – the messy complexities of family and friends, the power of love and a sprinkling of magic. Gorgeous.' **Clare Pooley**

'Sharp, funny and poignant.' **Rachel Winters**

'A warm, cosy, Christmassy delight. It's SO honest, funny and sad, and most of all it is full of hope. It tugged at ALL of my heartstrings, and I loved it to bits.' **Cressida McLaughlin**

'Romantic and gloriously life-affirming.' **Rachel Marks**

'So captivating I couldn't put it down. A gorgeously festive story.' **Emma Cooper**

'An outstanding story about regrets, self-reflection and love, littered with relatable situations and fabulous humour. I LOVED IT!' **Roxie Cooper**

'A magical, compelling and thought-provoking story, full of depth and heart.' **C.J. Skuse**

'Clever, funny and romantic. I hope the Netflix adaptation comes swiftly after.' **Melinda Salisbury**

'Oh my gosh, it's wonderful! I cried so much!' **Polly Crosby**

Tom Ellen is the co-author of three critically acclaimed Young Adult novels: *Lobsters* (which was shortlisted for *The Bookseller*'s inaugural YA Book Prize), *Never Evers* and *Freshers*. His books have been widely translated and are published in 15 countries. He is a regular contributor to *Viz* magazine, and as a journalist he has written for *Cosmopolitan*, *Empire*, *Evening Standard Magazine*, *Glamour*, *NME*, *ShortList*, *Time Out*, *Vice* and many more. *All About Us* is his debut adult novel.

ALL About Us

TOM ELLEN

ONE PLACE. MANY STORIES

HQ
An imprint of HarperCollins*Publishers* Ltd
1 London Bridge Street
London SE1 9GF

This edition 2020

1
First published in Great Britain by
HQ, an imprint of HarperCollins*Publishers* Ltd 2020

ISBN: 9780008336035

MIX
Paper from
responsible sources
FSC™ C007454

This book is produced from independently certified FSC™ paper
to ensure responsible forest management.

For more information visit: www.harpercollins.co.uk/green

This book is set in 10.8/15.5 pt. Sabon

Printed and bound in Great Britain by
CPI Group (UK) Ltd, Croydon, CR0 4YY

To Carolina

Prologue

University of York, 5 December 2005

Running was a bad idea.

I can see that now. There was no need to run. It's a game of Sardines, not the Olympic 100m. Plus, they haven't even started looking for me yet. I can still hear them all outside the maze, shouting to fifty in unison. It sounds like a weirdly raucous episode of *Sesame Street*.

I could've taken my time, strolled about leisurely in search of the perfect hiding place, but no: drunk logic told me that fifty seconds was no time at all and that the best option would be to peg it into the campus maze at top speed until I was safely camouflaged. Now, as I slow down to a stumble in the darkness, I can feel six snakebite blacks, four sambuca shots and that doner calzone I split with Harv all roiling ominously in my stomach.

I stop for a second to catch my breath, which immediately explodes back out of me. I put a hand to the wall to steady myself, remembering too late that the wall is not actually a wall, but a hedge. I fall through it with the slapstick dexterity of a young Buster Keaton, miraculously avoiding being blinded

1

or castrated by a million scratchy branches. I try to get up, fail miserably, and then decide that this is probably as good a hiding spot as any.

The leaves settle around me. The counting has stopped now, and I can feel the maze bristle and creak as a dozen drunken bodies stagger into it, yelling, 'We're coming to ge-et you!'

I sit there in silence, trying to work some moisture into my parched mouth and listening to my heart galloping in my chest. I reach up to wipe my forehead, and my hand comes back covered in foundation and fake blood – souvenirs from tonight's stellar theatrical performance.

The play went about as well as any first-year uni play could be expected to, which is to say we probably won't be nominated for any Olivier awards, but no one fluffed their lines or vomited nervously on the audience. It was in the bar afterwards, though, where everything really kicked into gear: everyone gabbling at a hundred miles an hour about what we all want to write or direct or act in next. Maybe it was the adrenalin – or more likely the sambuca – but the world suddenly seemed alive with possibility, like I could actually see the future spooling out endlessly ahead of me, beckoning me in. Mad, really, to think that I can do anything I want with it.

It's funny, though. As weird and brilliant as tonight has been, I always thought it would be me and Alice's night. The night we finally got it together after a whole term of awkwardly not quite managing to. It's my fault, really: I've never been very good at 'making the move' (in fact, just the phrase 'making the move' makes me want to cringe so hard that my retinas detach). If I get even the slightest suspicion that a girl might be interested in me, my brain tends to immediately draw up a laundry list of reasons why she actually definitely isn't.

But with Alice, that list has been getting harder and harder to compile. Over the past ten weeks – ten weeks of private jokes and late-night chats and shared microwave meals – she's made it pretty clear that she likes me. And I like her too, I guess. She's funny and pretty and we get on really well, and I suppose I always thought that tonight – the night of the play, the last night before the Christmas holidays – there'd be enough booze and drama and emotion to give us the push we needed.

But then that Daphne girl showed up backstage and sort of knocked everything off track.

It sounds stupid when people say they just 'clicked' with somebody, but I can't think of another word for it. How else do you explain an hour of silly, funny, effortless conversation with a total stranger? Or that weird, tingly electricity in my chest every time I made her laugh?

So, maybe it won't happen for me and Alice tonight after all. Or maybe it will.

It definitely feels like *something* will happen tonight.

There's a flurry of whispers from somewhere nearby – two people bumping into each other in the darkness, forming a momentary alliance in their search for me. And then there's that whooping seal bark of a laugh that immediately identifies one of them as Harv.

I shuffle further back into the hedge, but somehow I'm sure he won't clock me. Call it intuition, or a sixth sense, or just being a bit drunk and horny, but I *know* that either Daphne or Alice will find me before anyone else does.

When we spilled out of the bar after Marek shouted, 'Let's

play Sardines!' I looked around to see both of them smirking at me. 'I think Ben should hide,' Alice said, and Daphne nodded her agreement: 'Yep. Ben seems like a natural hider.' I filed that statement away for further examination when I was less pissed, and then tore straight off into the maze.

Right now, just the idea of sitting here, hidden, with either one of them seems outrageously – *ridiculously* – exciting.

In fact, as I try to keep perfectly still, my heart going like the absolute clappers, I can't decide who I'd rather found me first.

Chapter One

London, 24 December 2020

'So ... are you coming, or not?'

'I mean, obviously I *can* come. If you want me to?'

Daphne breathes out heavily, but still resolutely refuses to make eye contact. 'Do you *want* to come?' she asks her reflection in the mirror.

I loiter by the bare Christmas tree, picking at stray needles. 'Well, if you reckon I should, then maybe. I guess.'

She snaps the brush back into her mascara bottle with impressive force. 'Ben, seriously. I'm starting to feel like Jeremy Paxman here. Can you just give me a yes or no?'

'Well, I don't know. Will they be expecting me? I came last year.'

'Yes, and what a great success that was,' she says to the ceiling, and there's a pause where we both remember what a great success that was.

'Listen ...' she says, pinching the bridge of her nose. 'It's Christmas Eve drinks at my boss's. *I* don't even particularly want to go, so there's no reason why I should drag you along too.'

'Well, like I say, I'm happy to come if you want me to.' She ignores this completely, so I add: 'But you clearly fucking don't.'

Finally she spins round to look at me. 'I want you to come if you're going to actually talk to people and try to have a good time. I don't want you to come if you're going to stand in the corner like a grumpy arsehole. OK?'

She snatches up her bag and walks out into the hallway.

Daff is of the opinion that fights are A Good Thing in a relationship. A Healthy Thing. Or at least she used to be of that opinion, back when our fights weren't really fights, but silly little flare-ups over nothing. I'd get sulky at her for taking too long to get ready, or she'd shout at me for farting or imperfectly folding a bedsheet. And then after a volley of yells, we'd break off, hugging and giggling at the idea that we'd caught ourselves bickering like a sad old couple.

But at some point during the last couple of years, something changed. That fun phoney-war play-fighting turned into this awful tight-lipped trench combat; each of us working doggedly to gain an inch of ground over the other, occasionally lobbing a passive-aggressive grenade into no man's land.

How did we get here? I wonder. From calmly discussing our evening plans to bitter, seething resentment in – what was it – a minute and a half? That's got to be some kind of spontaneous marital-spat world record. Because the truth is, everything seems to lead to a fight nowadays. Every nod or murmur or question feels loaded and potentially explosive, like it has to be patted down carefully for hidden meaning. I'm pretty sure this is my fault – in fact, I *know* it is. It's all tangled up with everything that's happened over the past couple of years, and my general sense of self-worth dribbling slowly down the plughole. I can see the problems clear as day, I just can't figure out how to fix them. Maybe they can't be fixed.

I follow Daff out into the hallway, where she's now yanking her long, curly black hair into a bun and fastening it with one of those Venus flytrappy things. 'Look, I'm sorry,' I say. 'I just always feel like such a spare part at these things. I can feel them all looking straight through me when I'm speaking.'

'Ben, that's not true,' she snaps. 'And if it is true' – which means she knows it is – 'then maybe it's because you make literally no effort with anyone.'

'I do make an effort,' I protest, but we both know this is bollocks. I stopped making an effort a long time ago. Not just with small talk – with everything.

She grabs her coat off the banister, and sighs. 'Look, don't worry, honestly,' she says. 'You know what these things are like. It'll just be boring work chat. If I go now, I can be back by ten.'

'OK, fine,' I say, and the look of relief that flashes across her face confirms something I've suspected for a while: that I've become a weight on her at these events. Or worse than a weight: an embarrassment.

Daff is a literary agent. She works for a big, important company and her clients are all big, important authors and screenwriters. Attending one of her work dos is like lowering yourself into a boiling cauldron of success – you're never more than six feet from a BAFTA winner or a Booker Prize judge. So I suppose I can't blame her for cringing slightly when I'm mumbling to these people about how I knock out the odd press release for a living. It doesn't make me feel great either.

The truth is, I've spent a lot of time lately wondering what Daphne is still doing with me, and at this thing tonight, I know everyone else will be wondering it too.

'Is you-know-who going to be there?' I ask, as she shrugs her coat on. 'The Big Man?'

I'm hoping this might make her laugh, just to prove I can still do *that*, at least. Even a sarcastic hollow chuckle would suit me fine. But instead she just rolls her eyes.

'Yes, Rich will be there. Is that honestly why you don't want to come?'

'No, of course not. I was only—'

'Because you don't have to talk to him, you know. You could try and talk to some new people.'

'No, I know. Well, he pretty much ignores me anyway, so ...'

'Maybe if you actually tried to be friendly, instead of sulking like a little kid?'

And yep. Back we go. Like I say: all roads lead to a fight.

Which is crazy, really, because Rich used to be one of our most reliable private jokes. A dependable classic we could always fall back on.

He joined the agency around the same time Daphne did, and since he looks like he's been laboratory-designed to worry insecure husbands, the idea of her copping off with him quickly became a running gag between us. If I burned the toast or something, she might sigh dramatically and murmur, 'I bet Rich is a *great* cook ...' Or if I went out for the night, leaving Daff home alone, I'd bid her goodbye with 'Tell Rich I said hi,' and she'd mime oh-shit-I've-been-busted as I walked away laughing.

But like all our other private jokes, this one seems to have curdled and hardened. Whether this is down to her actually starting to fancy Rich, or me just suspecting she might, I've no idea. He's definitely a major-league shagger (Daphne once told me, 'If Tinder was a computer game, Rich would have completed it,' which I found both hilarious and slightly intimidating), but I don't think there's anything between them. The idea that there might be does hit me occasionally, like a punch in the gut. I guess I just can't figure out why Daphne wouldn't be interested in him. Or maybe she is interested in him, but she's just not the kind of person who would do something about it.

I think suddenly about the messages from Alice, squirrelled away secretly on my phone. I'm exactly that kind of person, apparently.

When it comes down to it, I suppose that's the reason Daphne's still with me: because of the things she doesn't know. She doesn't know about Alice; she doesn't know about Paris. She knows about Mum, obviously, but she doesn't know the things I said to her before it happened. Things that still choke me awake in the middle of the night.

After fifteen years together, and four years of marriage, she doesn't really know me at all. If she did, then surely she wouldn't still be here.

She clicks open the front door, and makes to step out into the cold early-evening gloom. 'I'd better go,' she says, but she doesn't. She just stands there, frowning at the doormat. 'We can talk later. It's just … Work is so draining at the moment, and then I come back here and it's … even more draining, you know?' She breaks off and fixes me with her big hazelnut-brown eyes, and she looks tired and really – genuinely – unhappy.

And my insides freeze, because I'm suddenly sure she's about to say something: something big and awful and final.

But then she glances through into the living room at the Christmas tree, and shakes her head, as if remembering that this is not traditionally the season for big, awful, final announcements.

'Anyway, we can talk later,' she says again. 'And don't worry about the thing tonight – I'll think of something. Tell everyone you needed to put the decorations up, maybe.' She looks again at the naked tree. 'Actually, that wouldn't technically be lying, would it?'

'I'll do it as soon as you're gone, I promise. And the presents.'

She nods. Then she steps outside, shuts the door and she's gone. And even though nothing was actually said, I can still feel the storm clouds gathering inside my head. *We can talk later*. She said that twice. But talk about what?

The word DIVORCE stamps itself onto my brain, making me physically flinch. Is that what she wants? Could it even secretly be what *I* want? The thought of it makes my stomach lurch, but I don't know if it's the idea of losing Daphne, or the shame of being divorced at thirty-four.

Another failure to add to my already ridiculously long list.

But I can't think about this stuff right now. Daphne's parents, sister, brother-in-law and their kids are all arriving at midday tomorrow, and there's still a hell of a lot to be done before then. I should really head straight up to the attic to get the decorations, then sort the tree out and crack on with wrapping the presents.

That's what I *should* do.

Instead, though, I decide to go and get drunk.

Chapter Two

Christmas Eve is pretty much the only time you can guarantee that Harv will be available at short notice for a pint. On Christmas Eve, there are no swanky club nights to attend or Tough Mudders to endure, and presumably the dating apps are pretty quiet, too.

We meet in The Raven, a grotty little pub in Crouch Hill whose grottiness is trumped by its exact equidistance between my place in Harlesden and Harv's in Stoke Newington. It's already heaving when I arrive: packed to bursting point with rowdy office workers, all draped in tinsel from their Christmas lunches. I squeeze past an old bloke with a scraggly beard who is trying to flog an extremely unconvincing Rolex to a pair of drunken businessmen.

Harv is already at the bar, wearing a parka so large it resembles an unzipped sleeping bag. He waves me over with a tenner.

'You all right? What d'you want?'

'Just a beer. Whatever you're having.'

He wrinkles his forehead. 'I'm not having a beer, mate. D'you know there's two hundred calories in a pint of beer? You might as well have a Zinger Burger.' He taps his stomach, which looks impressively washboardy even through his T-shirt. 'I'm seeing this girl at the moment who's a fitness instructor,' he says. 'She's full of these facts and figures. We were talking last night about how drinking Guinness is literally like drinking a pint of lard.'

'Sounds like a very erotic relationship.'

'Yeah, the conversation can get quite boring,' he admits. 'But the sex is pretty great.'

I look again at Harv's perfectly flat stomach. I still can't get my head around how all blokes nowadays are suddenly insanely ripped. It seemed to happen pretty much overnight, about eight years ago, and I was apparently the only male on the planet who wasn't forewarned. When I met Harv at university, he was fifteen stone and subsisted entirely on Carling Black Label and chicken nuggets. Now he looks like Ryan Gosling's stunt double.

It's fine for guys in their twenties, who were raised on Instagram and *Love Island*; they don't know any different. But these mid-thirties blokes who suddenly become protein-guzzlers – they're old enough to remember the halcyon pre-David Beckham days, when young men were all pigeon-chested and Twiglet-armed. They're selling the rest of us out, I reckon.

I order a Guinness just to piss Harv off.

We sit down at a table by the window, him sipping his vodka and tonic and me slurping my black lard. Another office Christmas party comes barrelling through the doors, all wearing badly torn cracker hats.

'You going to your parents' tomorrow, then?' I ask Harv.

He nods. 'My sister's giving me a lift to Suffolk first thing. Are you round at your ...' He flinches and shakes his head. 'Sorry, man. Wasn't thinking.'

'No, no, don't worry.'

It's been two years now, and I still forget myself from time to time. I'll read some book or see something on TV and think, oh, Mum would like this, and then crumple as the realisation gut-punches me.

I wonder if that ever goes away. Probably not.

'Are Daff's lot coming to you, then?' Harv asks.

'Yep. I'm supposed to be doing the tree and the presents right now, but y'know …' I hold up my pint and take a big sip.

'Where is Daff?'

'She's at a work thing. I thought she wanted me to come, actually, but maybe not. She's always on at me to meet new people.'

'But you *hate* new people.'

'Exactly.'

We both laugh. It feels comforting to fall back into our old groove: me as the grumpy, shy one, Harv as the buoyant extrovert. It's a dynamic that's been in play since we first met at uni. Occasionally I worry that it's become a crutch; a performance we put on for each other because we don't have anything else to talk about. I wonder whether if we met today – stripped of all our shared memories and in-jokes – we'd have anything in common at all. But right now it feels nice to slip back into that tried-and-tested role play – like pulling on an old jumper or something.

Harv starts rambling on about work – he does something in social media, though I've never been exactly sure what – and I suddenly want to tell him everything. I want to spill my guts about Daphne and Mum and the messages from Alice, and how I'm starting to feel like my whole life has frozen on

13

screen and I've no idea which combination of keys will reboot it. But I don't know how to even start that conversation. I've known Harv fifteen years – he was my best man, for God's sake – but we never really talk about stuff like that. I don't think we ever did.

When I overhear Daff speaking to her female friends I'm always amazed at the sheer range of topics they cover. They can get from small talk to deep-and-meaningful within seconds. Whereas when I went on holiday last year with Harv and a couple of other mates, we spent all four days testing each other's knowledge of football and films and nineties hip hop. I'm not complaining; it was brilliant. I guess women see their friends as profound, complex human beings, while men see theirs as walking quiz machines.

Still, I'm half a pint of Guinness down and Harv has paused to look at his phone, so I decide to give it a go.

'Yeah, thing is, actually, Harv, I'm sort of feeling a bit … down at the moment, mate.'

He looks up at me. For some reason – possibly to cushion its emotional bluntness – I've delivered this statement in a comedy Scouse accent. I have never even been to Liverpool.

'Ah, don't be down, mate,' Harv says, mimicking my Steven Gerrard twang.

'Well … I am a bit,' I reply, still inexplicably Liverpudlian.

'Ah, mate …' He sips his drink. 'Don't be.'

This isn't really going anywhere. This is just two men having the world's dullest conversation in an accent neither of them can pull off.

But I suddenly, *desperately*, want to find a way to actually talk to him. Because it's too much, keeping all this stuff locked up in my head. It feels like a dam is about to burst somewhere inside me, and fifteen years' worth of suppressed emotions are about to stream out onto the table between us.

I'm mentally scrambling about for a decent inroad to this outpouring when Harv smirks and shoves his phone in my face.

'Look at this … Honestly, Mourinho is *such* a dick.'

I scan the news story, in which Mourinho does, to be fair, come off quite dickishly. Harv slips his phone back into his pocket and grins. 'OK, random one: d'you reckon, off the top of our heads, we could name *every* World Cup winner from 1930 on?'

I stamp a smile across my face, and manage to shove down all the sadness and guilt and grief that was about to come spilling out of my mouth. 'I reckon we could give it a go,' I say.

He thumps the table. 'Right. I'll get another round in first. Although technically, it's your turn …'

I hand him a tenner and watch as he squeezes through the crowd towards the bar.

And that's when I hear a gravelly chuckle from over my shoulder: 'Unlucky there, my friend. You were so close …'

Chapter Three

I turn around to see that the scraggly-bearded Rolex salesman is now sitting in the booth behind us.

He's wearing an ill-fitting electric-blue suit that has definitely seen better decades, and a tie covered in little cartoon reindeer. His box of moody watches is on the table in front of him, next to a half-drunk pint. He's spinning a beer mat on its side and grinning broadly at me through his rust-coloured tangle of facial hair.

'Sorry … what was that, mate?' I say.

He takes a sip of his beer. 'It just felt like you were right on the brink of opening up to your friend there. And then he walked off. Rotten luck.'

'Right, yeah. I mean, it was sort of a private conversation, but …'

The watch-seller shrugs. 'Oh, I wasn't listening or anything. Just couldn't help overhearing, that's all.'

He smiles at me again, blue eyes twinkling under his unruly coppery-grey hair. There's something familiar about him that I can't quite put my finger on. It's possibly the vaguely Bill Nighy vibe he gives off – all wiry and crumpled and mischievous. His age is impossible to place, though: he could be anywhere from fifty to about seventy-five.

Still, I've been cornered by enough pub bores in my life to know exactly how this conversation will pan out if I keep engaging. After a couple more pleasantries, this bloke will undoubtedly whip his chair round to our table and spend the rest of the night regaling us with long-winded anecdotes, while occasionally attempting to flog us a watch.

'OK. Well, fair enough,' I say. 'Have a good night, then.'

I start to turn back round, but the guy speaks again.

'Christmas is a time for reflection, isn't it? Getting things off your chest.'

I sigh. I'm not in the mood for a heart-to-heart with a total stranger – particularly not when I've just failed to initiate one with my best mate. But I also feel bad about leaving an obviously lonely old man hanging on Christmas Eve. So I turn back to face him.

'How d'you mean?'

The watch-seller is now wearing a thoughtful smile and drumming his fingers on the box in front of him. 'You start to wonder about the bad decisions you've made in life, don't you?' he says. 'Or the wrong turnings you might have taken.' He stops drumming and looks me straight in the eye. 'You start to wonder how things might have worked out differently for you. And whether – if you could go back and change things – you really would.'

I nod, now feeling slightly concerned that this bloke is some sort of mind-reader. I'm certain I've never seen him before, but for a split second I'm convinced that he knows me. That somehow he has access to my deepest thoughts and fears and secrets …

But then reality comes crashing back, and I remember that mind-reading watch salesmen don't exist.

I try to catch Harv's eye at the bar so that he hurries back quickly and gives me an excuse to end this conversation. 'Yeah, anyway, listen, mate,' I say. 'I'd better—'

'Is there anything you'd do?' the old man interrupts. 'If you could go back. Is there anything you wish you'd done differently?'

He's staring at me with a weird intensity now, those blue eyes almost fizzing in their sockets. Out of nowhere, all that confusion and guilt and regret I've just managed to push down comes rushing straight back up. I think of the things I said to Mum before she died – the things I'd do *anything* to unsay. I think of what happened in Paris. I think about that night in the maze at uni – the night I met Daphne. My throat is parched suddenly, and my face feels boiling hot. 'I guess … maybe there are things I'd do differently,' I find myself saying.

The old man blinks and nods, still watching me with that odd, unreadable expression. And then suddenly his face brightens, and he raps the box with his knuckles. 'So. Can I interest you in a watch, my friend?'

And there it is.

'No, honestly, I'm fine, thanks.'

'I notice you're not wearing one. I reckon this little number would suit you perfectly …' He opens the box and takes out a totally unremarkable wristwatch. No chunky silver frame or famous logo or complex features – just a plain white clock face with a black leather strap.

'Really,' I say. 'I'm fine.'

Harv finally catches my eye, and fails to suppress a smile as he watches me trying to fend off this aggressive entrepreneurial advance.

'Oh, come on,' the watch-seller says. 'How else will you know when the clock strikes midnight and it's finally Christmas Day?'

'Well, I could just look at my phone.'

He bats this suggestion away with his hand. 'Phone, schmone. Tell you what, I'll give it to you. An early Christmas present.'

I laugh. 'No, seriously, that's very kind, but you don't have to—'

He reaches across and slaps the watch onto the table in front of me. 'I just have,' he grins. 'Merry Christmas. Go on, try it on. It'll change your life, I guarantee it.'

There is clearly no way I'm getting out of this situation watchless, so I just decide to give the bloke whatever I can. 'OK, look ...' I take out my wallet and peer inside to see what I can offer. But when I look back up, he's already disappearing out of the door.

The watch is still on the table in front of me. I stare at it for a second and then fix it around my wrist. When I look closely, I spot straight away why he wanted to palm this one off: it's not even working. The hands are frozen at one minute to twelve. I fiddle with the winding mechanism, but they don't budge. His line about 'when the clock strikes midnight' suddenly makes sense: a little dig before he fobbed me off with a dud.

Harv returns bearing fresh drinks. 'So. Who was your mate?'

I blink up at him, feeling slightly dazed now, as if I've just imagined the whole conversation. I consider telling him about my weird gut feeling that the old man somehow knew me. But I don't want Harv to think I've totally lost the plot, so instead I just hold up my wrist. 'Not sure who he was, but he gave me the greatest Christmas gift I've ever received. A broken watch.'

Harv laughs. 'You get some proper weirdos in this pub.' He takes a sip of his vodka and claps his hands together. 'Anyway, let's do this. Every World Cup winner since 1930 … and no checking our phones.'

'All right, let's go.'

With that, I push every thought of Daphne or Alice or Mum to the back of my mind, and focus all my mental energy on meaningless football trivia.

And when we say goodbye two drinks later, having successfully managed to name every World Cup-winning team in history (with the exception of Uruguay in 1950), I definitely don't feel better. But I don't feel worse either.

And that's something, surely.

Chapter Four

I get home about half ten, and Daphne's still not back.

She hasn't texted, and my Guinness-addled brain immediately conjures an image of her and Rich stroking each other tenderly beside a roaring log fire, which has to be the least imaginative hypothetical adultery fantasy ever. Still, it does the trick: the thought of them at that party right now, drunk and flirting, makes me feel hot with anxiety.

I walk straight past the undecorated Christmas tree and into the kitchen, where I sit down and crack open the very expensive bottle of red Daphne bought specifically for tomorrow's lunch.

I pour myself a large glass and check Facebook. There's a new message. It's from Alice.

Hey! Found out that my conference thingy is DEFINITELY on for next week so I will be down in London! They're putting me up in the Hilton in Canary Wharf (fancyyyyy) so maybe we could meet for a drink there? Say, Tuesday 29th? Would be SO good to see you and catch up ... ;-) xxx

I take a big gulp of wine and think: is this how it starts, then?

Is this how *easy* it is?

When I was a kid, the idea of Having An Affair seemed like an incredibly elaborate, complex, almost Machiavellian thing to do. In my head, I built Dad up to be some sort of evil genius who'd spent months planning this dark, terrible scheme that would rip all our lives in two. But maybe I was giving him too much credit. Maybe he stumbled into it without thinking. Maybe he was just frightened and lonely and confused. If so, then I guess I've inherited those traits from him. None of his talent, none of his charm; just the cowardly, rotten, arsehole bits.

I pour myself another glass and stare down at the message, wondering how to reply.

The whole thing is just so ... odd. I hadn't seen Alice for years – not since Paris – until I bumped into her at Marek from uni's wedding a few months back. Daff wasn't able to make it, and Alice was on her own, too; she'd just split up with her fiancé in Manchester and was there, in her own words, 'to get as drunk and cynical as humanly possible'.

I'd been really nervous about seeing her again, but right from the off, she acted like nothing had happened. As if there was no reason for any awkwardness. She beckoned me across the lawn with a glass of champagne, and after three more, we were engaged in a lively debate about the ethics of switching dinner-table name cards. Before a conclusion had been satis-factorily reached, Alice had done it – 'Uncle Steve' was settling down oblivious on the other side of the marquee, and she was sitting in his seat beside me grinning like a mischievous kid.

Over salmon and chicken and endless white wine, we stead-fastly ignored our tablemates and huddled together revisiting the past, expounding on the present and then cringing at all the same bits in the speeches.

It wasn't just that she looked hot – though she very much *did* – it was how she made me feel as I talked to her: like I was nineteen again, like the past fifteen years hadn't happened and the future was still blank and inviting. It was just like in Paris: I loved the fact I could present an edited version of myself to her. I could prune away at the rudderless screw-up that Daphne has watched me become until a better man emerged.

And then later, right at the end of the night, something happened.

All I remember is that the music was winding down, and Alice must have been as wrecked as I was, because she dragged me off the dance floor and into the 'quirky' photo booth we'd spent most of the evening taking the piss out of.

We grabbed our ridiculous props – fairy wands and top hats – and at her insistence, we pulled a variety of stupid faces as the flash bounced off us: rictus grins and zombie grimaces and – for the last picture – air-kissing selfie pouts. I closed my eyes for that one, I remember that, and as I felt the flash echo through my eyelids, I realised I wasn't air-kissing any more. Alice's lips were pressed up against mine. I pulled away, obviously. But not as quickly as I could have done.

When I opened my eyes, she was shrugging and laughing like it was no big deal. Just a joke.

So that's what I've been telling myself it was. But jokes don't keep you awake at night, prickling with guilt.

When I got home the next day, I didn't even tell Daphne I'd seen her. Daff's always had a weird thing about Alice. I guess because Alice and I were so close during that first term at uni. Even now, she'll still make the occasional semi-joke about how Alice used to fancy me. Those jokes always leave me prickling with guilt too. So I didn't tell her when Alice messaged a few days later, and I didn't tell her when I messaged back. Daff and I were going through a particularly grim patch where we were barely even speaking; she was constantly busy with work, whereas I was fretting about how badly paid, boring and sporadic my employment situation was.

I'm a writer, I suppose, technically speaking. But that makes what I do sound much grander than it actually is. I always imagined I would follow in my dad's footsteps and write some great play or TV series or novel, but I could never quite sharpen those dreams down to anything specific. I used to think I lacked drive or self-confidence, but the truth is, I just don't have it in me. I never did. Paris proved that, among other things.

So at some point I downgraded my ambitions and worked as a staff writer for a pretty tawdry lads' mag. Then, when the dwindling print industry blocked off that career path, I started doing what I'm still doing today – penning press releases and travel brochures for any company that will pay me.

It's nothing to complain about, I know – I'm lucky to be working, full stop – but it's nothing to shout about either.

I remember Daff went through a period a while back of trying to light a fire under me. She'd introduce me to editors or other writers; encourage me to try and keep writing stuff I enjoyed, even if I never showed it to anyone. But I'd already given up on myself by then, so I couldn't really blame her for eventually doing so too.

I drain my glass, and as I pour another, the broken wrist-watch catches my eye. It was so strange, those memories popping into my head back in the pub. Particularly that game of Sardines in the maze at uni: I haven't thought about that in years. Daphne was the first one to find me, and we ended up snogging drunkenly in the thorny hedge, before Alice pulled the branches back, frowning, a few minutes later.

Deep down, I've always wondered what would have happened if Alice had found me first. Maybe she should have.

I read her message one more time, and then hit reply.

Hey! 29th sounds good – will be great to see you. Let me know what time works. Xx

As soon as I press send, I experience several contradictory things at once. Fear and excitement and guilt and self-pity, plus a weirdly thrilling sensation that I've set something huge in motion; crossed a line that can't be uncrossed.

Pathetically, though, the overriding emotion is that it's nice to feel wanted.

Chapter Five

After another large glass of wine, and a lot more staring blankly at my message to Alice, I discover – to my genuine surprise – that the bottle is now four fingers off empty.

Bollocks. That'll be another row tomorrow. Or later tonight, whenever Daphne gets back. It's coming up to half eleven now, and she still hasn't texted.

I feel knackered suddenly, but I decide to do the decorations before heading to bed, so as to provide myself with some passive-aggressive armour ahead of our next argument. I wobble to my feet, realising that my warm three-Guinness glow has now been replaced by a harsh, metallic red-wine drunkenness.

I trudge upstairs to the back attic, feeling the draught cut right into my bones as I open the rickety little door. The decorations are all the way at the back, of course, and to get to them, I have to navigate a treacherous obstacle course of cardboard boxes, suitcases and even an old skateboard (mine, not Daphne's).

I'm millimetres from the tinsel when I accidentally nudge a massive see-through crate full of Daff's stuff, which promptly smashes to the ground, spilling its contents everywhere.

'Fuck's sake …' I mumble.

I've dropped to my knees to start clearing up when I spot something among the debris. An old metal biscuit tin, its lid hanging half open to reveal a selection of random objects: a crumpled script, a torn-up ticket, a faded programme for a play and a bloodstained fake revolver.

And then it hits me. These objects aren't random at all.

Out of nowhere, a shiver runs through me; a ghost of that same feeling I felt in the pub, talking to that weird old watch-seller. The sense that this is more than just coincidence.

It's the gun I reach for first. Crazy how Daphne kept this. I never knew she had. I turn it over and over in my hands, feeling its cold plastic grooves, tracing the smudgy red finger-prints on the handle. I can picture her now, handing it to me. I remember it so clearly. The night we met.

The script, the ticket, the programme: they're all from that same night. The one that popped into my head earlier: the Sardines-in-the-maze night. I pick up the programme. The front cover reads: *UNIVERSITY OF YORK DRAMA SOC PRESENTS: THE CAROL REVISITED.*

The play was Marek's extremely cringeworthy – and surprisingly violent – modern-day reworking of *A Christmas Carol*. I only had a small part, but still, as I turn the programme over, there I am: allocated my own blurry black-and-white cast photo. I'm gurning toothily at the camera in what appears to be an impression of Wallace from *Wallace & Gromit*.

I stare down at the picture, and suddenly I cannot believe that this grinning nineteen-year-old kid and I are actually the same person. It's like looking at a photo of a stranger; I feel no connection at all. What is left of him now?

Obviously it could have been the snakebites and the sambucas, but that night in the maze – a week after this photo was taken – I remember feeling some strange, almost spiritual certainty that everything would turn out all right for me. That I was headed in a decent direction, that my dreams were achievable and the future was a blank canvas I was about to decorate beautifully.

And then – yeah. Look what happened. I took that canvas and filled it with mistakes and failures and wrong turnings. Bad decisions and lies and terrible things I can never, ever take back.

If there's ever a Ben Hazeley Wikipedia page – and unless someone who shares my name does something worthwhile with his life, there won't be, but just suppose there *is* – I can picture now exactly how it will look. Where other Wikipedia pages have headings like 'Career' or 'Legacy' or 'Filmography', mine will just say: 'Fuck-Ups'. It will be a long, detailed, heavily bullet-pointed list that will begin with the subheading, '1996: Dad Buggers Off' and end – next week – with '2020: Cheats On Wife'.

My head is getting heavier by the second, and I know I should crack on with the decorations, but for some reason I can't tear myself away from the items in this tin. It suddenly makes me angry that Daphne's kept all this stuff. I picture her sneaking up here from time to time, opening the lid and poring over these objects: physical reminders that she would have been better off without me.

Because that's it, isn't it? If your life is just a series of mistakes and screw-ups, then surely it would be best if you weren't around?

There's no photo of Daphne in the programme – she was drafted in at the last minute, after someone dropped out – but I can still see her exactly as she was at eighteen: this happy, funny, exuberant girl who gave everyone, friends and strangers alike, the full wattage of her amazing smile, as if she genuinely didn't realise its power.

And then I stepped in. Chipped away at her over the years, to turn her into the tired, angry, miserable woman in the hallway earlier. Surely her teenage self would be just as disappointed as mine at how things turned out? She must have imagined that by thirty-three she'd have a successful, supportive, *normal* husband. And kids. I know she wants kids, even though we haven't broached the subject once this year, despite lots of our mates starting to have them.

A weird memory hits me – not even mine, but something Mum told me when I was a teenager. I'd been eagerly pestering her for happy stories about me and Dad – positive that he'd soon be back in my life – and she'd finally caved and told me about how, when I was eight, I'd wandered in on him watching that Monty Python film, *The Meaning of Life*. Hearing the phrase, I'd repeated it, parrot-fashion: 'Dad, what *is* the meaning of life?' And he'd laughed and then replied: 'I suppose it's to increase the sum of human happiness.'

I loved that answer when I was fourteen, but now it strikes me as the most depressing thing I've ever heard. Because all I've done since then is subtract, subtract, subtract.

I squeeze the bridge of my nose, and my vision blurs at the edges. I look at my watch to see that it's one minute to midnight. One minute to Christmas Day.

And then I remember that the watch is bust. Still, that's

probably not far off the real time. Even a stopped clock is right twice a day ...

I pick up the programme again, and the fake gun, and hold them both steadily in the palm of my hand.

I've no idea how long I sit there staring at them before I fall asleep.

Chapter Six

Traditionally, I find that my hangovers wake up a few seconds after I do.

After a big night of drinking, I tend to get this lovely calm-before-the-storm moment as soon as I regain consciousness, where there's no pain yet, no regret, no violent urge to vomit. And then as soon as I open my eyes or move my head, all hell breaks loose.

I'm lying perfectly still with my eyes shut, enjoying this period of prelapsarian bliss as I try to fill in the gaps from last night. There are plenty of them. I remember the biscuit tin and the fog of self-pity, but I can't remember Daff coming home. I can't remember doing the tree. I can't even remember coming down from the attic.

Oh please God, don't let me have slept in the attic.

I experiment with turning my head very gently to the side. There's no blinding migraine or sudden desire to be sick, which is encouraging. I also seem to be lying on a comfortable pillow and mattress, which bodes well for the please-God-don't-let-me-have-slept-in-the-attic situation.

I decide to risk it and open my eyes. But it's not a headache that hits me – it's cold, hard terror.

I scramble upright, suddenly wide wide WIDE awake, my heart head-butting my ribcage.

Where the HELL am I?

It's like my brain is still a few seconds behind my eyes, struggling to process the information it's receiving. The bogey-green curtains; the scratchy Brillo-pad carpet; the poky brown cupboard that hides a grubby little sink and mirror within it.

I hear a low, slightly manic moan from somewhere, and then realise it's coming from my mouth.

This is ... this is *uni*. This is my bedroom in the first year at uni.

Have I gone mad? Is this what going mad feels like?

Or maybe ... maybe this is some kind of elaborate – *really* elaborate – prank. I suddenly remember an awful interactive theatre experience that Harv dragged me along to once, where the audience ended up as part of the show. We were led into the middle of this extravagant stage and forced to start shaping the plot by ad-libbing with the actors. Maybe this is something similar. If so, then whoever designed the set deserves every award going. It's literally *exactly* as I remember it.

I feel my head start to pound, the hangover kicking in now, but then I notice the door handle is rattling frantically and the thumping is actually coming from outside the room.

'Ben? You in there? Ben!'

The handle jiggles again, but it seems the door is locked.

'Benjaminnnnnnnn?' It's Harv's voice. Thank God for that.

I stumble to my feet, my heart still thundering, and notice that I'm dressed in a pair of jeans I don't recognise and my old Wu-Tang Clan hoodie. I thought I'd lost this thing years ago.

I open the door and immediately have to fight the urge to start laughing.

It's Harv, but it also … isn't.

It's like Harv has been gently inflated, or suffered some traumatic allergic reaction. His sharpened cheekbones and laughter lines are all gone, and his face is younger, rounder, doughier. I notice a solid pouch of belly hanging stoutly over his belt buckle. He has a can of lager in one hand and what appears to be a peanut butter and cheese toastie in the other.

'What the fuck are you doing here?' he says.

'I … have no idea,' I stammer, quite truthfully.

'Do you know what time it is?'

Instinctively, I glance down at my wrist. My watch says one minute to twelve. The watch I'm still wearing. I've woken up in completely different clothes, in a completely different place, and yet this watch is somehow still fixed around my wrist. My brain is poking fruitlessly at this fact when I realise Harv is snapping his fingers in front of my face.

'Hello? Hellooooo?'

He looks at me strangely, and then takes a large bite of his toastie. 'It's after six, man, you'd better get a shift on,' he says, stickily. 'Marek just called me. He's going mental. You weren't answering your mobile. They're all already at the Drama Barn.'

I shut my eyes for a second, hoping that when I reopen them I'll be back in the attic, nursing the mother of all hangovers, with Daphne glowering down at me.

But no. Inflatable Harv is still right there, swigging his lager and staring at me through narrowed eyes. 'Are you stoned or something?' he says. 'Or are you just being a twat?'

'No, I'm …' I have no clue *what* I am. I feel like I'm in some sort of highly advanced virtual-reality video game.

A door opens behind Harv and a small blonde girl emerges, smiling at us. Fuck. It's Geordie Claire. She lived opposite me in halls. I haven't seen her since … well, since uni. She waves two little red tickets at me. 'Good luck, Ben! Me and Stu will be front row.'

I squint at the tickets. They say: *DRAMA SOC PRESENTS: THE CAROL REVISITED.*

Suddenly I know where I am. And, more importantly, *when* I am. I have to grab the door frame to steady myself.

'Shit, Ben, are you OK?' Claire asks, rushing towards me.

Harv laughs and slips an arm round my shoulder. 'Must be first-night nerves. Come on, man, we'll have a quick drink and then I'll walk you down there.'

Claire looks slightly concerned, but just nods goodbye and heads out.

Harv leads me through to our corridor's shared kitchen, and the milky-cheesy-rotten-fruit stench that hits me is almost as strong as the déjà vu. I am now one hundred per cent *certain* that this is not a dream. Only reality could smell this bad.

I slump down into a plastic chair and take a few deep breaths (through my mouth, obviously). Harv shakes his head as he watches me gulping desperately for air.

'Mate, will you chill out,' he laughs. 'You'll be fine. It's not like you're the main part. What've you got, like, *three* lines?'

I'm barely listening to him. There's a *Nuts* magazine calendar hanging over the pasta-sauce-spattered microwave. Just above Michelle Marsh's partially exposed breasts is the confirmation I'm looking for, the confirmation I've been dreading:

DECEMBER 2005.

I've come back fifteen years.

Harv plonks a can of lager on the table in front of me. He's now talking into a little electric-blue flip phone. God, I remember that phone. He thought it made him look like someone out of *The Wire*. 'Yo, Marek,' he says. 'It's all right, relax, I've found him … Yeah, he's fine. Just a bit nervous … I know, three lines, that's what I told him. Anyway, we're on our way now, so don't panic … Cool. In a bit.'

He snaps the phone shut with a satisfying click. He used to love doing that. 'Well, Marek's officially losing his mind,' he announces. 'He thought you'd bottled it. Apparently the girl doing the props has also dropped out last minute. He's calling everyone he knows to find a replacement.'

I can't get my head around this. I know I should probably be crying or screaming or checking myself into an asylum, but all my brain seems capable of doing is compiling a list of every time-travel film I've ever seen. *12 Monkeys, The Terminator, Timecop*: they all involve people being sent back to kill somebody significant. Is that what this is? Does Geordie Claire turn out to be the next Hitler or something? She *is* vegetarian.

But then there's also *Bill & Ted, Back to the Future, Groundhog Day* …

'Harv …' I stare up at him blankly. 'What happens in *Groundhog Day*? I mean, like, why does he go back in time?'

If Harv finds this question at all random, he doesn't show it. He simply taps his can of lager against his teeth, thoughtfully. 'Er … isn't he, like, a weatherman, who's sort of pissed off with everything? And so he keeps reliving the same day over and over until eventually he … shags Andie MacDowell? Isn't that basically it?'

I nod dumbly.

He grins at me. 'Hey, d'you reckon we can name *every* Bill Murray film from *Groundhog Day* on?' He glances up at the clock. 'Nah, best not, actually. Marek would murder me.'

He downs his beer and pulls me up by the shoulder. 'Come on, man, let's go.'

Chapter Seven

As we tear across campus, I am hit by wave after wave of déjà vu.

Our poky little college bar, the run-down Kwiksave, the cocky squads of ducks that waddle up from the lake to shit on the walkways; all of them appear as we sprint past, as if daring me to doubt how real this is.

Because it clearly is. Real.

But still, as I chase Harv across the rickety red bridge by the English block, I feel almost like I'm watching this whole thing from above. Like it's happening to someone else. Maybe that's the best way to deal with it: forget the whys and the hows and the what-the-actual-fucks and just go with it until it's over.

We finally stop running when we reach the Drama Barn – or the Drama Closet, as we rechristened it: a tiny fifty-seater venue right in the middle of campus. There's already a line of people outside queuing to get in.

'Fucking hell,' Harv pants, mopping his forehead with his sleeve. 'I need to start doing more exercise.' He nods at the entrance. 'Well, go on then, dickhead. Break a leg and all that. I'll see you afterwards.'

Still on autopilot, I walk past the queue and approach

the bloke sitting by the main door, taking tickets. I vaguely remember him; a second-year, I think, fully kitted out in the unofficial Drama Soc uniform of black turtleneck, black jeans, black trainers.

'Sorry I'm late,' I tell him. 'Can I, erm … come in? I'm in the play.'

He grunts but doesn't look up from his phone. 'What's your name?'

'Ben Hazeley.'

He starts scanning a list on the table in front of him. 'Any relation to Patrick Hazeley?'

And even in my stupefied state, I still feel it. The sense that I've been instantly reduced to a little kid; that I exist only as a footnote in the life of a man I barely know.

'Yeah, he's my dad.'

The second-year looks up at me; I'm suddenly interesting enough to warrant his full attention. Interesting by birth. Interesting by proxy. 'Shit, is he really your old man?' he says. 'I *love* his stuff. Seriously, *Earth Weight* was the first play I ever saw. Fucking … brutal. Incredible writing.'

'Yeah,' I say.

He moves aside to let me through. 'Good luck anyway, mate. See you after, probably.'

I slink into the venue, which is still dark and empty at this point. I remember that the dressing room is right at the back, but I feel like I need a few minutes alone before I have to do any more actual interacting, so I duck into the little toilet behind the lighting rig.

I should really have been expecting it, but seeing my reflection in the mirror makes me genuinely jump. If Harv's been inflated, then I've been whittled down. It's the face I saw in the programme last night. I push my bony nineteen-year-old cheeks right up to the glass to find soft patches of nearly-stubble in place of wrinkles, and no sign yet of a widow's peak retreat in my thick dark brown hairline.

I splash my face with cold water and as soon as I come out of the toilet, I hear a voice behind me.

'Marek is going to KILL you!'

Alice is right there, smirking up at me. She looks … To be honest, she looks almost exactly the same as when I saw her at the wedding. Which is to say that she looks a bit like a blonde Phoebe Cates in *Gremlins*, except she's now sporting more of an Uma Thurman in *Pulp Fiction* haircut. She looks good.

'Come on, the audience will be in any minute.' She beckons me through to the dressing room, which is stuffed with bodies: people wriggling into shiny suit jackets, having their faces frantically powdered, yelling out lines at random across the uproar. I spot Marek – who hasn't changed much either; same beard, glasses, wild hair – in the corner, muttering into his phone. He sees me, mimes throttling someone (presumably me) but doesn't break off the call.

'He's found somebody to do the props, I think,' Alice tells me. 'Some mate of Jamila's. He's just speaking to her now.'

I nod as I feel the beginnings of a thin film of sweat on my brow. Because I suddenly know where all this is heading. I know that I'll see her in – what will it be – ten minutes? And then it'll be much, *much* harder to pretend this is all happening to someone else.

'Audience is coming in!' somebody hisses, and suddenly the noise level in the room sinks to a nervy murmur.

The next few minutes are a total blur. I'm helped into my costume – a cheap black *Reservoir Dogs*-type suit – and then slapped about gently by a girl with a powder brush.

The play has started by now – I can hear Marek on stage, hamming it up – and its finer details begin to tumble back into place in my mind.

The Carol Revisited. 'Dickens meets Tarantino' is how Marek pitched it to us at the first rehearsal. Six months from now, he will be openly dismissing it as 'crude and underdeveloped', but at the moment, I can hear him giving it his absolute all as he bellows, 'Humbug, motherfucker!' at the presumably bewildered audience.

Marek was – is – Drama Soc chairman, and therefore also was – is – a massive show-off. Not content with writing *and* directing, he's also playing the main part: Vinny Scrooge (seriously), a meth dealer who is near-fatally shot by a hitman and then guided through his past experiences by a mysterious ghost.

I'm playing the hitman, I remember that much. And the ghost—

'Ben, dude, they want us backstage.'

I turn around to see a stark-naked man standing in front of me, a stoner's grin smeared across his face.

Bloody hell. Clem Matthews. Third-year, I think. Not what you'd call a natural actor, but apparently the only student on campus willing to get his knob out in public. I suddenly wonder what he's doing nowadays. Porn, presumably.

Quite why Marek insisted on the ghost being fully nude, I can't remember now. Something to do with spiritual realism and shocking the 'boring old farts' in the drama department, I think.

'Come on, let's go,' Clem says.

The costume girl stops me. 'Hang on, are you keeping that watch on? You weren't wearing it in rehearsals.'

I stare down at my watch, still stuck firmly at a minute to twelve. I forgot I had it on. Why *do* I have it on? How the hell is it still here when everything else has disappeared?

'It's fine,' Clem breezes. 'Hitmen obviously wear watches. They don't want to be late for their murders, do they?'

He grabs my arm, and I follow his bare arse cheeks out behind the wobbly set. We both stand in silence, waiting to go on.

'How you feeling?' he whispers. 'Nervous?'

I suddenly recall how awkward this always was in rehearsals, having to make small talk as I tried very hard to ignore Clem's dangling penis.

'Bit nervous, yeah,' I whisper.

He shrugs. 'You've only got, like, three lines. You'll nail it.'

Three lines. Why is everyone so obsessed with this three-lines thing? Then it hits me: I have *no idea* what these three lines are. It's been fifteen years since I looked at this script. I'm about to walk out on stage with no clue what to say when I get there.

I've just decided to make a run for it when I feel a light tap on my shoulder.

'Hey, are you Ben? This is yours, right?'

Daphne smiles brightly as she holds out a plastic fake revolver.

Chapter Eight

I was expecting to see her, but still.

For a second, I am caught so completely off guard that I can't even move. Daphne has to lift my hand up and press the gun into it.

'They told me: "Ben's the one who's not naked",' she whispers. 'So I'm guessing that's you?'

I nod, dumbly. I can't believe it's really her. My heart feels like it's trying to punch its way out of my chest.

Even in the almost pitch darkness I can tell her smile is on full beam. Her curly hair is pulled back into a ponytail that drapes halfway down her shoulder and she's dressed in the regulation backstage outfit of tight black top and black leggings; a combination that makes her look a bit like a ballerina or a strangely sexy cat burglar.

I'm vaguely aware that I am just staring openly at her, which is probably coming across as more than a little creepy. But I can't help it.

When this moment first happened, fifteen years ago, I'd be lying if I said it was a fireworks-in-the-sky, love-at-first-sight revelation. As she handed me the gun, I'm pretty sure all I thought was: 'Huh, the new props girl is quite hot.'

But now – *somehow* – I'm standing here looking at the girl who'll become the woman who'll become my wife. I've spent the past fifteen years with her. I know her inside and out. Or at least I *think* I do. Either way, I have no idea how to treat her like a total stranger.

This weird, silent trance is shattered by the sensation of Clem's penis bopping me gently on the thigh as he leans across to introduce himself.

'I'm Clem,' he whispers, offering his hand. 'I'm the one who *is* naked.'

Daphne nods and shakes it. 'OK: naked, not naked,' she says, pointing at him, then me. 'I think I've got it. And I'm Daphne, by the way.'

Clearly, both of them are now finding my slack-jawed gawping slightly awkward, because Daphne dials her smile down and looks away, and Clem starts massaging my shoulders.

'Ben's a bit nervous,' he mouths at her. 'Even though he's only got three lines.'

That brings me back down to earth with a jolt.

'I don't know what they are,' I splutter. 'I don't know my lines.'

Clem laughs without smiling. 'Good one.'

'No, seriously … I can't remember them.'

Clem is now looking at me like *I'm* the one with his tackle out in a public space. But Daphne just raises her index finger and says: 'Give me one sec,' then disappears into the darkness.

Clem starts muttering something at me, but I'm not paying attention; I'm just listening to Marek out on stage telling Tiny

Tim to go fuck himself, and before I know it, Daphne's back again, bearing a script and a key-ring torch.

'Right, what's your character's name?' she whispers, flipping through the pages.

I look at Clem blankly.

'Are you fucking *kidding* me?' he hisses. 'Have you been hit on the head or something?' His laid-back stoner persona seems to have completely evaporated over the past thirty seconds. 'He's called Jimmy the Hat,' he tells Daphne.

'Jimmy the Hat ...' she repeats slowly. She shines the torch at me. 'Shouldn't you be wearing a hat, then?'

'Marek says it's an ironic nickname,' Clem explains, through gritted teeth. 'Like Little John in *Robin Hood*.'

'Ah, right, gotcha.' Daphne nods. 'Such a fine line between ironic and just ... confusing.' Her expression is thin-lipped, earnest, perfectly deadpan, and despite everything, I have to put a hand to my mouth to muffle my laughter.

She finds the page in question and stabs it with her finger. 'OK, got it ... Jimmy the Hat ... Right, so you walk in when the lights go out. Then the lights come up, and you say: "Scrooge, you son of a bitch, I thought I might find you here."' She looks up at us. 'Isn't this set in Scrooge's house? Obviously he's going to find him here.'

This makes me start laughing again, and for a second I'm worried I won't be able to stop, and that I'll be shoved out on stage still giggling like a lunatic, until the men in white coats arrive to take me away.

'This is not the time to start dissecting the fucking script,' Clem whispers, but he's smiling now too.

'OK, OK ...' Daphne looks back at the page. 'Scrooge

44

says: "Jimmy the Hat, what the fuck do you want?" And you say, "Where's the dope, Scrooge?" And he says, "Fuck you, Jimmy!" and you say, "Eat lead, cocksucker!" and then you shoot him.' She gives me a conspiratorial glance. 'This is great stuff. Dickens would be so chuffed.'

I lean over and stare at the page under the torchlight, trying to burn the words into my brain. And then suddenly the stage lights go out, and I feel Clem grab my shoulders and bundle me roughly through the gap in the set.

When the lights come back up, they are bright white and searing intensely into my face, and I'm staring out at forty or fifty bored-looking audience members. I turn to look at Marek, who is lying in bed with a rictus grin on his face, his eyes begging me to say something.

'Er ... Scrooge, you ... son of a bitch,' I stutter. 'I thought I might find you here.'

I see Marek wince at my robotic delivery, but he's instantly back in character.

'Jimmy the Hat!' he bellows. 'What the *fuck* do you want?'

'Where's the dope, Scrooge?' I enquire, with slightly more emotion this time.

He jabs a finger at me. 'Fuck you, Jimmy!'

'Eat lead, cocksucker!' I shout back. And the relief that I've actually *done* it – I've managed to deliver my three lines without ruining the whole play – is so overwhelming that I almost start laughing again.

But then, nothing happens.

The audience are all still staring at me blankly, like they're expecting something more. I think I can see Harv in the back row, although I can't be sure, as he's got both hands over his face. I turn to look at Marek, who is now beetroot red and visibly shaking. He's glaring down at my hand, for some reason. Or, no, not my hand; the gun in my hand.

'Ah, right, yeah,' I murmur. And then I point the revolver at him and squeeze the trigger.

There's a loud bang from up in the sound booth, and Marek is suddenly screeching in over-the-top agony, his white night-shirt covered in what is quite clearly tomato ketchup.

I stumble backwards, past Clem, who is emerging nakedly onto the stage and muttering, 'Mate, seriously, what the fuck?' as he passes me. I grope my way back into the darkness, where Daphne's smile is still waiting for me. She raises her hand for a high-five and leans in so close I can feel her breath on my cheek.

'And the Oscar goes to ...' she whispers, and we both dissolve into silent laughter.

Chapter Nine

I spend the next hour in the dressing room, alone for the most part, trying and failing to make sense of what the hell is going on.

The thing I keep coming back to is that nothing – *nothing* – is playing out the way it did first time around. Obviously, fifteen years ago, I didn't forget my lines or gawp at Daphne like a creepy oddball, and she didn't have to go and find me a script or high-five me as I came offstage.

I have no idea whether any of this matters. But I do remember reading some sci-fi story when I was a kid about a time traveller who crushes a butterfly and ends up killing off the dinosaurs as a result. And if there's any truth in that logic, then I'm starting to seriously wonder what sort of knock-on effects all these new developments will have.

But then maybe, I consider, as I stare at my insanely youthful face in the dressing-room mirror, maybe that's the point of all this. I think back to the attic, which already seems like days ago: didn't I drunkenly imagine what might have happened if tonight had gone differently? And that old man in the pub. The watch-seller. When he asked me if I would change anything, tonight was one of the memories that flashed into my mind. That strange feeling rushes through me again – the unsettling sense that the old man *knew* me somehow. I stare down at the watch he gave me, its hands still frozen at one minute to twelve, and make a concerted effort to wrap my brain around what is going on.

Before I can manage it, though, the rest of the cast are stomping back into the dressing room, dragging me back out on stage for the curtain call.

I blink into the white light again as the audience claps half-heartedly at us, and then we're all back in the dressing room together, shouting and laughing and hugging.

If Marek bears me any ill will for turning his gravely serious near-death scene into a ridiculous farce, he doesn't show it. He squeezes me just as tightly as he does everyone else, gushing about how *amazingly* the whole thing went, and seeming particularly pleased that several audience members walked out during a flashback in which Scrooge slits a rival drug dealer's throat with a guitar string.

'Did you see the looks on their faces?' he yells. 'They just couldn't fucking handle it!'

We all spill out of the Drama Barn into Langwith College bar next door, and as my feet cross the ominously sticky threshold, the déjà vu is humming away stronger than ever. God, I remember this place *so* well. I can't count the number of nights I spent in here, feeding my student loan into the pool table, fifty pee at a time.

The bar's lime-green walls are reverberating to the sound of 'I Bet You Look Good on the Dancefloor', and my butterflies-and-dinosaurs theory begins to flounder slightly, because everything starts slotting neatly back into place, exactly as I remember it.

Daphne has disappeared, just like she did all those years ago, and I recall the sharp pang of regret nineteen-year-old me felt as I scanned the bar and couldn't spot her. Harv turns up and starts forcing sambuca shots on everyone, and then Alice sits down next to me, just as she did first time round.

She's pink-cheeked, fresh from scrubbing off her stage make-up, and she looks lovely. I watch her down her shot, and wonder if maybe *this* is where things will really start to change. If maybe this time Daphne won't show up at the bar at all, and tonight will become what I always imagined it would: me and Alice's night.

She drops the tiny glass back onto the table and grimaces. 'Well, thank *God* that's over.'

'What, the shot?'

She laughs. 'No. The play.'

'Oh, right. Didn't you enjoy it?'

'Yeah, no, I did. It's just I've been so nervous about it for weeks. It's nice to be able to finally stop worrying about it.'

Alice had a much bigger part in *The Carol Revisited* than I did – although to be fair, the same could be said for literally every other member of the cast. She was playing the second lead – Marie, Scrooge's fiery moll – and as I recall, it required a ton of line-learning and late-night rehearsing.

'You were great,' I tell her.

She shrugs. 'Thanks. It *was* pretty fun. But tonight's what I've really been looking forward to.' She smiles at me for a second before adding: 'The cast party, I mean.'

I smile back and find myself wondering if she always imagined this would be our night too.

She picks up two shots from the tray in front of us and says: 'Here, come on. Let's get very, very pissed.'

I smile and nod, feeling exactly as torn as I did all those years ago; part of me enjoying the feeling of being flirted with by Alice, the other part desperate to see Daphne again.

We do another grimace-inducing sambuca shot each, and then Alice squeezes my arm and gets up to say hi to somebody else. And as I scan the room again, Daff is suddenly there, right on cue.

She's standing at the bar with her best friend, Jamila, and a few of her other mates. She gives me a grin and a wave and then turns back to them.

Under the bar's garish strip lighting, I can finally see her face properly, and my heart starts pulsing in my chest. It's stating the blindingly obvious to say that she looks younger – a little bit redder and rounder in the cheeks – but the really big difference is in the way she carries herself. There's this lightness to her that I remember being immediately struck by when I first met her – a goofy, playful silliness that I honestly haven't seen in years.

Probably because I've managed to gradually grind it out of her.

She's listening to Jamila tell some story, and as she nods along, she nibbles absent-mindedly at the rim of her plastic pint glass. That's a trait I remember thinking was a cute little nervous tic, until I later learned it was a tactical ploy to hide her top lip.

Daff's always had a weird thing about her top lip. She hates the little scattering of light brown freckles that run across it – which, to be honest, I've always thought were really cute. But some boy at her school once teased her about them in Year 8, and it's stuck with her ever since.

And now here she comes, walking towards me, smiling awkwardly, and I have to pretend I don't know any of that. I have to pretend I don't know *anything* about her. That she's some random girl I've just met.

How the hell am I supposed to do this?

'Hey!' she says. 'Not-Naked Ben.'

'Not-Naked Daphne. Hi.'

She pulls out Alice's chair, and before I can tell her that it's Alice's chair, she's plonked herself down in it. She raises her pint glass to me. 'Congratulations again on your stellar performance.'

I hold my hands up and force a laugh. I'm still finding normal conversation with her too much to handle, to be honest. Plus, I've become so keenly aware of my tendency to stare that I'm now doing the exact opposite – making barely any eye contact at all. Which is probably just as weird.

'I thought you'd headed off,' I tell her left shoulder.

She shakes her head. 'No, I was supposed to be meeting some friends off campus, but I brought them back here instead.'

'Ah, right. Cool.'

Alice is now back at the table, holding a tray loaded with pints of snakebite and black. I see her glance pointedly at Daphne as she slides one towards me and then goes off to find a free chair next to Marek down the other end. I feel a twinge of guilt, as well as something else I can't quite put my finger on. Regret, maybe? But there's no time to dwell on it, because Daff is leaning back in.

'So is this your thing, then?' she asks. 'Do you want to be an actor? Because I have to say, I'm not a hundred per cent sure you're cut out for the hitman business.'

'You're right,' I say, nodding. 'The best hitmen do tradition-ally remember to kill their victims.'

'Well, maybe you could be a sort of pacifist hitman,' she suggests, her smile widening, 'who's trying to bring down the industry from within.'

'A non-violent hitman. Yeah. I'm into it.'

'The Gandhi of assassination.'

I snort a laugh at this, and it draws another glance from Alice.

Harv materialises behind us, clutching another fresh crop of sambuca shots. He sinks one himself and then thumps another down in front of me. 'I didn't get you one,' he tells Daphne, 'because I don't know who you are.' He sticks his hand out. 'Let's remedy that *right* now. I'm Harvey.'

'Daphne,' she laughs, shaking his hand.

'OK. Daphne. Now that we're old mates, I'll go and get you a shot.'

She's still shaking his hand and laughing. 'No, no, honestly, I'm fine. Thanks.'

'You sure? Final answer? All right. Nice to meet you, anyway. This is the longest handshake *ever*.' He breaks off and slumps down into a free seat at the other end of the table.

I really can't face this latest shot. I'm feeling extremely light-headed as it is, and I suspect that inexplicably travelling into the past is a bit like operating heavy machinery: you probably shouldn't be pissed when you do it.

'Do you want this?' I whisper, nudging the sticky glass towards Daff. 'Because I definitely don't.'

She grimaces and slides it back. 'Ugh. No way. Can't stand sambuca. It was the first drink I ever got sick on. Bad memories.'

'That's so true,' I say. 'The first drink you get sick on will always be undrinkable. Mine was peach schnapps. Still can't go anywhere near it.'

She laughs, wrinkling her nose. 'Peach schnapps. You must have been a classy kid.'

'Oh yeah, big time. We were about fourteen, I think, down the park one Friday night, and Ross Kennett turned up with a bottle of it that he'd nicked out of his mum's cabinet.'

'Classic Kennett,' she says.

'Exactly. Textbook Kennett. I think I only had three shots, but even now, just the *smell* of it makes me feel sick. I must've thrown up underneath that slide for about fifteen minutes straight.'

'Well, that's a lovely image, Not-Naked Ben. I'll keep it with me always.' She takes a sip of her pint. 'So, hey, you never answered my question before – is acting actually what you want to do?'

'No, no, not at all,' I say. 'I just did this for a bit of a laugh, really.'

When she asked me this question first time round, I vaguely recall launching into a long, boring spiel about how what I *really* wanted to be was a writer. I think I trotted out the standard monologue I'd memorised for when trying to impress attractive girls, which was full of painfully crowbarred references to Franz Kafka.

This time, though, I decide against trying to conjure up some non-existent self-belief, and ask her a question instead.

'What about you?' I say. 'Do you want to get into theatre stuff?'

She shrugs. 'Well, I was only helping out tonight as a favour, really. But yeah, I do enjoy it. I don't know, though … I'm definitely not an actor, and I don't think I'd be much of a writer or director, either.'

'Gun-handler?' I suggest. 'Last-minute script-finder?'

She laughs. 'Yeah, exactly. Or maybe … I don't know. Maybe producer? I like the idea of being someone who helps to make good stuff happen, you know?'

I nod, and the difference between us at this age suddenly seems staggeringly clear. I was a pretentious knobhead, full of unrealistic dreams and unfounded confidence; Daff was modest, humble and obviously bound for success.

She shoots me another one of her wide, bright, amazing smiles – the kind I see so rarely in 2020. I don't know if this is the exact same discussion we had first time round – probably not – but the general feeling I'm getting is the same. That fluttering excitement at the knowledge that I'd definitely met someone special – someone I'd still be thinking about long after this conversation finished. But also, a strange sense of ease and comfort – like I'd known this person for years, and conversation just flowed effortlessly between us.

She says something else, which I don't quite catch, because as I glance over at the bar, I see a face I recognise.

A scraggly rust-coloured beard above a tie covered with cartoon reindeer. Two twinkling blue eyes that meet mine as he shoots me a wink …

I launch up from my chair, nearly spilling every drink on the table.

'Are you OK?' Daphne laughs.

I'm craning my neck to see through the mass of people surrounding the bar. But he's not there. I must have imagined it. After all, I've just come back fifteen years: why would he look exactly the same and be wearing the exact same tie?

I must be losing it.

'Sorry. Just thought I saw someone I knew.' I slump back down, but Daphne's attention is focused on the other end of the table. Marek is now aggressively drunk and sounding off so loudly that everyone is forced to turn and listen.

'I'm honestly *glad* that people walked out,' he shouts. 'The truth is, you can't produce a truly great work of art that is also commercially successful. It cannot be done. The two things are fundamentally incompatible.'

Everyone around him nods in solemn agreement, and I suddenly remember *exactly* how this bit goes.

Daphne puts down her glass, clears her throat and then asks him, quite earnestly: 'Do you think that's definitely true?' Fifteen heads turn to look at her.

Marek is used to holding court without any interruptions whatsoever, so he's now staring at Daphne like she's just poured her pint over him.

'Er, yeah,' he snaps. 'I do.'

'Oh, OK then. Fair enough.' She nods and says nothing more. Marek clearly feels the need to reassert himself, though. 'You *don't* think it's true, then, I'm guessing?' he says.

'Well, no.' She shrugs, apologetically. 'I think there are lots of good writers who are also commercially successful.'

'Go on, then,' Marek smirks. 'Would you care to enlighten us with some examples?' Daff opens her mouth to speak, but he shouts over her before she can get a word out: 'Because, to be honest, I'm not sure I'd even *want* to be commercially successful anyway.' She tries again, but Marek is way too loud for her. 'Anything of any real artistic merit has always been scorned or ignored by the masses,' he proclaims. 'Like, look at the Dada movement, right ...' – and at this point, I stop listening and focus on watching Daphne.

She doesn't seem particularly cross at being interrupted; she just sits there looking at Marek with one eyebrow raised, and it hits me again that I haven't seen this playful, feisty spark in her in years. If we hadn't got together – got married – maybe she'd still have it.

'But isn't that the ultimate dream?' she says, when Marek finally breaks off for a swig of snakebite. 'To make something really good that also resonates with lots of people?'

Marek slaps his glass down. 'Not achievable, I'm afraid, because most people are idiots. I mean, seriously: can you name *one* decent writer – in any genre – who's also commercially successful?'

Daff takes a deep breath and starts counting them off on her fingers. 'Nora Ephron, Stephen King, Sue Townsend, Armando Iannucci ...' She puffs her cheeks out. 'That's four, for a start.'

There's a beat of embarrassed silence while we all watch Marek consider arguing that these good and successful writers are not good and successful. In the end, he gives up and reaches for a *Big Lebowski* quote: 'Well, that's just like ... your *opinion*, man,' he drawls.

Daphne holds up a fifth finger. 'Ah, yeah, and the Coen brothers. Thanks. That's five. Or six, if we're counting both of them.'

There are a few laughs at this, and Marek takes out his phone and starts jabbing at it to indicate that the conversation is over.

'Sorry about that,' Daphne murmurs to me, not looking in the least bit sorry. 'I hope I didn't upset your friend.'

'He's not really our friend,' Harv whispers, leaning across. 'He's more a bell-end that happens to live on our corridor.' Daphne laughs hard at this, and Harv stands up to address the whole table. 'Right, I'm getting more shots. Who's in?'

'Fuck shots,' says Marek, snapping his phone shut and assuming leadership once again. 'Let's play Sardines!'

Chapter Ten

A dozen chairs scrape backwards noisily, and the cries of 'Yes!' and 'Let's do it!' instantly drown out the Kaiser Chiefs' riot predictions on the stereo.

I can feel beads of sweat starting to prickle on my brow, so I excuse myself and barge through the last-orders throng at the bar, towards the bathroom.

I slip into a cubicle and slump down on top of the toilet lid, my heart pounding in my chest. Playing Sardines in the campus maze was an end-of-term Drama Soc tradition, one that Marek had always insisted we should keep up tonight. But this evening's game represents something way more significant than a bit of random boozy fun: it was the first time Daphne and I ever kissed.

I take a deep breath and try again to make some sense of the situation. I've spent the past half-hour being reminded of how brilliantly Daff and I once got on; how right we once seemed for each other. But while I may not have a clue why this is all happening, one thing I *do* have is hindsight. And that means I now know *exactly* how we'll end up. How far we'll eventually drift from our hopeful, happy, seemingly perfect-for-one-another teenage selves.

Fifteen years ago, it was just a random quirk of fate that Daphne found me first in the maze. And that quirk has gone on to define the rest of our lives. So maybe this time … will it be *Alice who* finds me first instead? The idea makes my heartbeat instantly double its speed. Will I get to see what my life would look like if she and I had got together tonight?

There *was* always something between us, and over the years, it's like fate has constantly found ways to bring us back together. There was Paris, then Marek's wedding, and now this drink we've arranged back in 2020. Maybe this – tonight – is where it was all supposed to start? But instead, Daphne found me first during the game of Sardines, and all three of our lives were sent spiralling off in the wrong direction …

I must be breathing pretty heavily as these thoughts ricochet around my head because the bloke in the next cubicle thumps the wall and shouts, 'You all right in there, mate? Tactical chunder?'

I unlock the door and splash some cold water on my face. As I walk out, still dripping and borderline hyperventilating, I bump straight into Alice on her way to the ladies'.

'Bloody hell,' she laughs. 'You look like you've just done fifty lengths. You all right?'

I nod.

'Oh-kay.' She tilts her head at me. 'Hardly chatted to you all night, Benjamin. Impossible to tear you away from the sexy props girl … who clearly fancies you, by the way.'

Telling me that random girls clearly fancied me was something Alice did quite a lot over this first term. I would estimate that ninety-eight per cent of the time it was utter bollocks, but still, it always made me feel pretty good. Probably because, even at nineteen, I realised that 'so-and-so clearly fancies you' can usually be translated as '*I* clearly fancy you'.

'I'm not sure about that,' I tell her.

'Soooo modest.' She rolls her eyes, mock dramatically, and gives me a coy smile. For a second, it's like I'm right back at that wedding with her, feeling the words *WHAT IF?* burn themselves onto my brain.

'What's her name again, the props girl?' Alice asks, fiddling with her fringe. 'Daisy?'

'Daphne.'

'Daphne, right.' Getting Daphne's name wrong was something Alice did quite a lot from this night onwards. 'Well, anyway, if you can tear yourself away from Daphne, maybe me and you can hang out a bit later?' She grins and nudges my trainer with hers. 'I feel like I've hardly seen you recently, what with having to rehearse all the time. And tomorrow it's the holidays, so I won't see you for, like, three weeks, you know?'

I nod, dumbly. It's odd to think now, but throughout this whole first term, Alice was probably the person I hung out with most. More than Harv, even. We were next-door neighbours in halls, and since we were both doing artsy degrees, with precious few contact hours, our daytimes would mostly be spent cooking sausage sandwiches in the shared kitchen and then retreating to the bar to play pool and talk bollocks. We were pretty much inseparable for those first ten weeks. And now – just like in Paris, just like at the wedding – I'm starting to remember why. She was funny and clever and I liked who I was when I was with her. And as the term wore on, I have to admit I enjoyed the heady sensation of knowing something *might* happen between us, but not knowing exactly when.

'Hanging out later sounds great,' I tell her. It briefly crosses my mind to suggest that we sack off Sardines altogether, and head straight back to the corridor, just the two of us. But before I can weigh this idea up properly, Alice says, 'Cool, see you out there,' and slips past me into the loos.

When I step out of the bar, everyone is huddled up in coats and scarves, their breath billowing out in smoky speech bubbles. Harv slides an arm around my shoulder and starts gabbling about something or other, but I can't concentrate on what he's saying. Everything is zoning in and out of focus, feeling real and unreal at the same time.

Alice comes out and loops her arm straight through mine. I'm not sure if Daphne sees this, because she's at the front of the pack, chatting to someone else. Marek shouts, 'Let's go!' and starts to lead our chattering, giggling group down the walkway and over the bridge behind the English blocks, where the campus maze looms out at us through the darkness.

A couple of the group have no idea what Sardines is, so Marek's explaining it to them: 'Someone goes to hide, right, and then we all look for them. When you find the hider, you hide with them, and it goes on like that until everyone's hiding and there's only one person left looking.'

'So who's hiding first?' someone else asks, as we arrive at the entrance to the maze. I look round to see Daphne and Alice both grinning at me.

'I think Ben should,' Alice says.

'Yep.' Daphne nods. 'Ben seems like a natural hider.'

I feel the sudden urge to just drop onto the damp grass and adopt the foetal position until this dream or nightmare or vision or whatever the fuck it is is over. But something propels me forwards, and before I know it, I'm bolting into the maze while they all start counting to fifty behind me.

I'm nowhere near as drunk as I was first time round, but still, I have absolutely no clue where I'm running to, or where I originally hid. I'm just sprinting mindlessly, turning corners whenever I feel like it, my footsteps keeping time with my heartbeat, the sweat cold and clammy on my temples.

The counting has stopped now, and I can hear them all bundling raucously into the maze after me. I slow down to a standstill, clutching the throbbing stitch in my stomach, and claw my way into the nearest hedge. I flop down painfully among the prickly branches, and try to picture Alice climbing in beside me.

But what happens if she does? We kiss? And then what?

Do I *stay* here, in this new reality? For how long? For the rest of my life?

I try to decide whether I would actually – genuinely – want that. Whether it would be better for everyone, Daphne included. But I can't. The concept is just too massive to properly process. My head throbs with confusion and doubt, and I realise the only thing to do is let fate take control, exactly as I did last time.

I hear Harv's whooping laugh float around the corner as he bumps into somebody in the darkness. I remember this happening first time round too, and wonder idly if I've somehow ended up in the exact same hiding spot as before. Just as they did originally, the two pairs of trainers bounce right past without stopping.

And then, almost immediately, I hear another crackle of feet on twigs. I crane my neck to see someone else rounding the opposite corner and beginning to emerge through the leaves. I squint to try and make them out …

And as I do so, something even stronger than déjà vu slaps me hard across the face. A sense memory so vivid it makes my head spin.

All these years I've been telling myself the story of what happened in this maze. And I realise now I've been telling it *wrong*.

It was Alice who got to me first.

I see her now through the gaps in the hedge, creeping past just as she did back then, scouring the branches for any movement. The precise thought I had at the time flashes suddenly into my brain: *I could make a sound now. I could let her know where I am.*

But I found that I didn't want to make a sound. I didn't want her to find me.

Alice squints right through the branches, and for a second I'm certain she's looking straight at me. But then she draws back, turns and keeps walking.

I breathe out shakily, because it's all coming back now and I know exactly what will happen next. I'm not sure how I could have forgotten it – the booze, I guess, or just the gradual erosion of the intervening years – but the memory is now crystal clear in my mind.

Right on cue, Daphne appears, peering gingerly into the hedge opposite. And without thinking, I do exactly what I did fifteen years ago: I reach up to bend one of the branches above me until it snaps cleanly in two.

She jumps at the sharp sound and turns in my direction, a smile playing on her lips.

It wasn't random chance at all.

I wanted her to find me. I *made* her find me.

She gets nearer and nearer until she's standing right over me, grinning down through the leaves.

'So,' she whispers. 'Not a great hitman, not a great hider.'

I just about manage to croak a laugh.

'Is there any room in there?'

I lift the biggest branch and she climbs under it and sits down opposite me, cross-legged. Our knees are already overlapping, but then she has to lean forward to readjust her position, which brings our faces so close they are practically touching.

'Oops,' she whispers. 'This is a bit, erm …'

She lets the sentence hang there, unfinished, as we look into each other's eyes. My heart is thumping so hard that I'm sure she must be able to hear it. But I can't help it. My head is suddenly filled with the memory of this moment, fifteen years ago: our first kiss. How *right* it felt, as I leaned forward and touched her lips to mine. The way she smelled, the way she felt, the way she tasted.

She tucks a stray curl back behind her ear and smiles at me. And *God*, I want to kiss her again.

She tilts her head slightly, and without thinking, I reach up and touch her face, very gently. She smiles again, and the tip of her nose brushes my cheek as her lips find mine. And as we kiss, everything around me seems to fizzle and dissolve, until there's only the two of us left.

Chapter Eleven

I'm not sure how long we stay like that, lost in that kiss.

I must have kissed Daphne a million times over the past fifteen years, but I can't remember any of them feeling *this* perfect. It's like my whole body is being lit up from inside. I don't want it to ever end.

But then, suddenly, it does.

There's a sharp crackle of leaves, the branches are pulled back, and there's Alice, staring straight down at us.

Daff pulls away, and the look on Alice's face brings me right back to earth with a jolt. It's exactly as I remember it: the initial flinch of confusion that melts instantly into a kind of embarrassed disappointment. She sucks in her bottom lip, glances down at the grass and mutters: 'Sorry.'

Daff shoots me an ugh-this-is-awkward grimace, but I have no idea what to say or do. The moment is so insane and unreal it feels like it's happening to someone else.

Thankfully, I don't have to *do* anything. Marek and a couple of others materialise out of nowhere, right behind Alice, giggling like idiots. They barge into our hiding place, and suddenly there are enough bodies in the hedge to muffle the awkwardness.

I'm doing everything in my power to avoid eye contact with Alice – which is not difficult, really, since the space is now so crowded that my face is pressed directly into Marek's armpit. And even though I feel sick with guilt about Alice finding me and Daff together, I'm still thrumming with the exhilaration of that kiss. I can't help it. It's all coming back to me now: the way I felt at this moment, fifteen years ago. The ballooning sense of excitement in my stomach. The tingly feeling that this might be the start of something really good. The absolute certainty that there was no way in hell I could wait the whole Christmas holidays before I saw Daphne again.

Finally, after what seems like centuries, the last person finds us and the game comes to an end. We all scramble out of the hedge, and start traipsing back out of the maze. I lag behind, right at the back of the pack, trying to figure out what I'll say to Alice when I get out.

But it turns out I don't need to worry. By the time I step out of the maze, Marek is already leading the charge back towards the bar for last orders. Everyone is staggering drunkenly after him, and I can't see Alice anywhere. I linger by the maze's entrance and watch the bodies disappear into the night, terrified that Daphne might have disappeared with them …

Then, suddenly, she's right beside me in the darkness.

'Not sure I'm up for another drink,' she says.

'No, me neither.'

'So …' I feel her hand brush gently against mine. 'I guess this is goodnight, then …'

The first time around, it was. We were still surrounded by people, so we just exchanged a brief, awkward 'See you later', and then I headed off for one last beer, before stumbling back to my room to lie wide awake in bed, reliving the memory of that kiss.

But this time, I don't want the night to end. I still can't make head or tail of what is happening, but I know for absolute certain that I don't want Daphne to leave.

'Do you want to …' I begin. But I can't think of a way to add 'come back to mine' without sounding like a massive sleazebag.

Daff must pick up on this dilemma, because she tilts her head at me playfully. 'Not-Naked Ben, are you asking me back to your room?'

I laugh. 'Well, yeah. But for entirely innocent reasons, I promise.'

She still looks dubious – which is fair enough, really. I don't know how to communicate that I am actually telling the truth. As amazing and electrifying as that kiss was, the idea of us going any further honestly hasn't crossed my mind. I just want more time with her – with *this* Daphne. This happy, funny, carefree girl who is so different from the woman I live with in 2020. I want to get to know her all over again.

'A cup of tea,' I say. 'That's all, I swear. If you fancy it?'

She sizes me up with her big brown eyes. And then that amazing smile spreads across her face. 'OK, yeah. I could murder a cup of tea, actually.'

We wind our way slowly back to my hall of residence. And with every step, I can feel the excitement rising in my chest. Daff loops her arm through mine and shoots me a grin that makes me think she's feeling the exact same thing.

But then we get to the entrance, and I come face to face with a bulky locked door, and a numbered entry panel beside it.

'Oh. Shit.'

My heart sinks right into the pit of my stomach.

'What?' Daphne asks.

For the hell of it, I punch in 1-2-3-4. No joy. We could be here a while.

'How drunk *are* you?' Daff laughs. 'Can you really not remember your own door code?'

'No, hang on, don't worry ... It'll come to me ...'

But obviously it won't. I'm about to pull my phone out and see if Harv is still awake when I hear someone shout 'WAHEY!' at a deafening volume behind me.

I turn around to see Geordie Claire standing there, grinning drunkenly, with her massive rugby player boyfriend next to her. Both of them smell strongly of tequila and chilli sauce.

'Hey, Ben!' Claire slurs, dragging me into a wobbly hug. 'So, we both *really* enjoyed your play. Really, really, really. It was very, erm ... original.'

'Yeah, top work, mate,' says her boyfriend, whose name escapes me. 'You were ... great.'

'He was, wasn't he?' Daff nods, somehow managing to keep a straight face. 'He's a natural hitman.'

Claire punches in the entrance code, and we all troop up the stairs together. We say goodnight to the two of them at the end of the corridor, and as we do, I find my voice dropping automatically to a whisper. It's not even half eleven – still early for a freshers' dorm on the last night of term – but I'm suddenly keenly aware of the fact that Alice's room is right next door to mine. I have no idea whether she went on to the bar with the others, or whether she's in there right now, just one paper-thin wall away from us.

By some miracle, my room key is in the pocket of the jeans I was wearing when I woke up, so I let Daff in before heading into the kitchen to make the tea. I flick the kettle on and stare at it hard, willing it to boil faster. I don't know how long we'll have together tonight – I have no idea if I'll find myself back in 2020 at any moment – so I want to make the most of every second here.

Once the kettle's boiled, I dart straight back to my room with the two steaming mugs to find Daff kneeling on my bed, peering closely at the bookshelf next to it. I spent *hours* arranging that bookshelf in preparation for precisely this moment: a hot girl peering closely at it. It was chock full of wilfully obscure, borderline unreadable paperbacks, all designed to make me look much deeper and more intellectual than I actually was.

I feel a little shiver of exasperation at my try-hard teenage self as I hand Daff her cup of tea.

'Here you go,' I say. 'Milk, one sugar.'

She wrinkles her brow. 'How did you know?'

'I, er … Lucky guess.'

'Very lucky. So, you're doing English, right?'

'Yeah.'

'Me too.' She takes a sip from her mug. 'Mmm, good tea.' And then, with a little smile, she adds: 'You know, I've actually seen you in lectures.'

'Oh, really?' I'd definitely never seen her before this evening.

'Yeah. You and Marek,' she says. 'You always seem to be the last ones to arrive. The lecturer starts talking, then the door slams and everyone looks round, and you two come swanning in in your long flappy coats, looking like you've just got out of bed.'

I can't help laughing at the memory of it. 'Oh God. We don't mean to always be late,' I start. 'We just—'

She interrupts me with a grin. 'I reckon you both like the attention.'

She's right, of course. We loved it. God, we were a pair of knobs.

It's so weird, thinking back to what I was like at this point. So full of ill-founded confidence, so desperate to appear cool and interesting at all times. For this whole first term, I saw Marek as a bit of an aspirational figure, I guess. Like Alice, he was clever and funny and sarcastic, and he seemed to have stepped straight out of *Withnail & I*, chain-smoking roll-ups in his moth-eaten pea coat. I'd bought one in the exact same style – I can actually see it now, through the gap in my wardrobe.

By second term, though – once I'd met Daphne – the Marek effect started to wear off. I began to realise that Daff and Harv were much more fun to hang out with. Mainly because when I was with them, I didn't have to try so hard to be someone I wasn't.

Daff shifts round to face me and sits cross-legged on the bed. She's slipped her shoes off already, and she tucks her stripy-socked feet underneath her. Her curly hair is starting to wriggle free from her ponytail, and as she reaches up to retie it, she pushes her shoulders back and tilts her head, and for a moment, she looks so beautiful I can barely think straight.

This is just ... mad. I mean: this is *Daphne*. I've known her fifteen years. Why the hell am I so nervous?

I plonk down opposite her, nearly spilling half my tea.

'So, you've already got me figured out, then, have you?' I say.

'Yup.' She grins. 'Always late. Reads highly pretentious books. Bad at hiding in mazes. Good at making tea. That about sums you up, I reckon.'

'Oh, great. Thanks a lot.'

'No worries.' She stretches her leg out and pokes me gently in the thigh with her big toe. It's a gesture that's so familiar – so relaxed and comfortable – that I'm suddenly seized by the idea that she *knows*. That this isn't 2005 Daphne: it's 2020 Daphne, and she's inexplicably jumped back through time, too.

But as soon as that idea forms, it dissolves. Because the truth is: she was always like this. Right from the start. I remember it even on our first date. I made her laugh at one point, and she reached across and squeezed my hand. She was so intimate; like we'd known each other our whole lives.

She cranes her neck round to look out of the window, but she doesn't move her leg away. She just leaves it there, with her foot still resting lightly on my thigh. She can't possibly know the effect this is having on me – or at least I hope she doesn't. It's like a cement mixer has just been switched on in my stomach. All I can think about is leaning forward and taking her in my arms again.

'You got so lucky with your view,' she murmurs, staring out of my grubby second-floor window. 'You can see the lake and the ducks and everything. My room looks out onto the bloody staff car park.'

'Trust me, it's not lucky,' I say, remembering the racket the ducks used to make. 'Listen to this lot.' I lean past her, catching a scent of her perfume as I do, and crack the window open. The sound of hooting and quacking comes floating in, along with a blast of bitingly cold wind. 'They're like this all night,' I say. 'Honestly, I barely sleep in here.'

71

She laughs, her brown eyes twinkling. 'So *that's* why you're always late for lectures. The ducks.'

'Exactly. Blame the ducks.'

She glances out of the window again. 'They're probably hungry ...'

She jumps up and bolts out of the door. When she comes back in a few seconds later, she's swinging a half-empty bag of sliced bread. There's a Post-it note stuck to it that reads: *MAREK'S – DO NOT TOUCH*. For a self-styled anarcho-communist, Marek always had surprisingly conservative views on food-sharing.

'On a scale of one to ten,' Daff says, 'how pissed off will Marek be if we nick two slices of his bread?'

'I'm going to say eleven,' I tell her. 'But let's do it anyway.'

She drops back down on the bed and hands me a slice. We both poke our heads out of the window into the freezing night air. And as we lean out, shivering, we're pressed right up against each other, arm to arm, so close that her loose curls are spilling onto my shoulder. We start dropping the bread.

'This is not doing anything for the noise levels,' I say over the excited honking.

Daff laughs, and nudges her shoulder into mine. 'Yeah. Plus it's absolutely freezing.' She dusts her hands off and watches as the crumbs rain down. 'Come on, let's go back in.'

We retreat inside and shut the window again. She recrosses her legs, and wraps both hands tightly around her tea mug to warm them up.

'It's crazy how quickly this first term has gone,' she says. 'Before we know it, uni will be over.' She shakes her head at the idea. 'We'll be twenty-one. We'll be actual adults.'

'We are technically actual adults now, you know,' I say.

She gives me a perfectly deadpan look. 'Ben, we've just spent the last hour playing hide-and-seek in a hedge.'

I laugh. 'Good point.'

She takes another sip of tea, and shuffles backwards on the bed until she's leaning up against the headboard. She stretches her legs out again, and without thinking, I lift her foot back into its previous position on my thigh. If she finds this at all weird or forward, she doesn't show it. She just smiles at me and says: 'It's crazy to think about, though, isn't it? Once uni's over, we'll have no one telling us what to do any more. We'll actually have to decide what to do with every day of our lives.'

'So what do you *want* to do with them?' I ask her.

She laughs, and wriggles back against the headboard, trying to get comfy. 'I just want to … be happy, I suppose. Enjoy life. Have good friends. Be a good friend. Do something for a living that I love.' She pauses for another sip of tea. 'First up, though, I want to go travelling. Bit clichéd, I know, but when you grow up in a tiny village where you know everyone, the idea of visiting the other side of the world seems quite appealing.' She shrugs. 'That's the plan, anyway. But I bet I never get round to it.'

'I bet you will,' I say. Because I *know* she will. She and Jamila will spend five months backpacking around South East Asia and Australia straight after uni, while I work night shifts in a pub in Ealing, missing her like mad.

It's crazy to think about that period now. We'd been going out for two and a half years at that point, but it still felt fresh and new and exciting. I was still so caught up in her; so hopelessly head-over-heels. I couldn't believe that this funny, sexy, incredible girl was actually with *me*. It's a feeling that's starting to sink back in again right now – it has been ever since that kiss in the maze.

What's happened to that feeling in 2020? When did it get lost along the way? How did we turn into this bitter, sniping couple, constantly at each other's throats?

We sit in silence for a few seconds, at opposite ends of my single bed, just smiling and looking into each other's eyes. And suddenly it's like I really am nineteen again, my brain fizzing with the excitement of having met someone *this* brilliant. Someone I feel an instant, inexplicable connection with.

Daff yawns and stretches her arms behind her head. The urge to lean forward and kiss her grips me tightly again, but I content myself with another large slurp of tea.

'What are you doing for Christmas, then?' I ask.

'I'll just be at home,' she says. 'The usual stuff: stockings, presents, turkey. My mum's not actually that big on Christmas, though. We tend to do all the proper, extended-family stuff on January the first.'

I nod. 'Greeks are all about the new year, right?'

She freezes with the mug halfway to her lips. 'How did you know my mum's Greek?'

Oh God. This is a minefield.

'Erm … just another guess,' I stammer. 'You kind of … look Greek?'

Which is true, to be fair. She narrows her eyes at me. 'Are you sure you haven't been stalking me on Myspace, Not-Naked Ben?'

The mention of Myspace makes me laugh out loud. If I ever doubted that I am genuinely in 2005, *here* is the conclusive proof.

'So, what about you?' she asks. 'What are you up to for Christmas? At home with your mum and dad?'

'Well, I ...' I have to stop suddenly, because the thought of Mum almost makes me choke up. But I take a deep breath and manage to keep it together. 'My mum goes mad for Christmas, so it'll be the full whack – turkey, all the trimmings, tinsel everywhere ...'

'What about your dad? Is he into it too?'

I shrug. 'He's not really in the picture, actually.'

She looks down at the duvet. 'Oh. Right. Sorry.'

I shake my head. 'No, don't be. I mean ... hopefully, some day, that might change.'

She looks at me fondly, and then yawns again. As she stretches, a few more curls escape and tumble gently around her shoulders.

God, she looks *amazing*.

'I feel knackered suddenly,' she says quietly.

And this time I can't stop myself. I move in to kiss her again. She leans forward to meet me, and we're locked into each other once more, kissing hungrily, her hands on the back of my neck, my hands tangled in her long black curls.

And then she breaks away.

'Ben, I don't know if I want to ... you know?' she says. 'We've only just met ...'

'Yeah, no, of course! Of course not. I mean, if you want to head back ...'

She shakes her head. 'I don't want to go.'

She pulls me gently towards her, and we both lean back slowly until our heads are resting on my squashy foam pillow. For a while, we just lie there, fully clothed, on top of the duvet in my tiny single bed, looking into each other's eyes and smiling. And then I shift round and wrap my arm around her, so that her head is resting on my chest. Her hand finds mine and our fingers interlock. She lets out a tired, contented sigh. And despite all the madness and chaos that this day has brought, I feel totally at peace. Calm and happy and in control. Like I'm exactly where I'm meant to be.

'Almost midnight,' Daff mumbles.

I glance up at the clock above the door. It's not far off the time that's frozen on my watch. I think suddenly of that piss-take sales line the old man gave me: *How else will you know when the clock strikes midnight?* A flicker of that strange feeling I felt in the pub passes through me, but I'm too tired to properly examine it.

Daff nuzzles further into my neck. 'This should feel weird,' she says, sleepily. 'I mean, I hardly know you. But it doesn't.'

I feel my eyelids starting to droop. 'Yeah,' I murmur. 'The fact that it isn't weird is, in itself, weird.'

We both laugh softly. I pull her even closer and gently kiss her forehead.

And before I know it, I'm asleep.

Chapter Twelve

I must have been dreaming about that kiss in the maze, because now, as I stir suddenly awake, it's like I can still hear the rustle of the leaves around me. I can almost taste Daphne's lips on mine.

For some reason, I feel dizzy and slightly winded, like I've just been flung from an out-of-control merry-go-round. I didn't even feel that drunk last night, but I guess those pints of snakebite were stronger than I thought.

With my eyes still closed, I groan softly into the pillow and flip it over to the cold side. I lie groggily under the duvet, still half asleep, feeling a weird combination of things: warm and fuzzy and happy after what happened last night, but also – somewhere in the pit of my stomach – fraught and scared and anxious. Because as right as it felt – as perfect as we seemed for each other – I know exactly how things will pan out. How sour our relationship will eventually become.

I nuzzle my face further into the cold pillow, wishing I could get my head around what's happening. I half open my eyes, remembering that at any moment now, Harv will be pounding my door down, demanding one final bacon-heavy fry-up before we head home for the Christmas holidays.

I reach across instinctively for Daphne. But she's not there.

I open my eyes fully and squint at the daylight streaming in through the curtains. The first thing I focus on, propped up against the lamp on the bedside table, is an advent calendar. Nearly every window is already open on the front of it, but rather than revealing badly drawn images of the infant Christ, they contain cut-out magazine pictures of an actress I used to have a major crush on: Larisa Oleynik.

For the second time in as many days, I shoot bolt upright in bed, suddenly wide awake and breathing heavily. I stare wildly around the room, which is much more instantly familiar than my university dorm, but feels far less comforting to be waking up in right now.

Clothes are strewn haphazardly across the frayed carpet, a PlayStation 2 is buried under a molehill of games in the corner, and the walls are decorated with ragged Blu-Tacked posters: a mixture of scowling New York rappers and gurning mid-air skateboarders.

Daphne is gone, and I'm in my bedroom at home. *Home* home. The home I grew up in.

I have jumped forward this time, instead of backward, and thanks to the single unopened window on the advent calendar, I know *exactly* which date I've landed on.

This must be December 24th, 2006.

I squeeze the bridge of my nose tightly, and a shard of sunlight bounces off my watch. I'm still wearing it. I am now naked except for a pair of boxer shorts I don't recognise, and yet I am *still* wearing this watch. The hands are stuck in the exact same place – one minute to midnight.

The watch-seller's weirdly cryptic line about the clock

striking midnight flashes into my head again. I looked at the watch last night, just before Daff and I fell asleep. That must have been when it happened: last night, when the real time matched up with the time on my watch … that must have been when I 'jumped' again! I guess I was already asleep by then, because I definitely don't remember it.

I feel a momentary burst of pride at having potentially figured out the logistics of this time-hopping madness – although it's quickly buried under a fresh heap of confusion as I remember I have no idea how this is happening, or why.

With my heart still thudding, I reach over to pick up the advent calendar. I remember it so well, though I have no idea where it is back in 2020. It's a cheapo supermarket thing with a ruddy-cheeked Santa Claus grinning maniacally on the front. But Daphne customised it especially for me; ripped the cardboard back panel off and replaced it with a whole new collage of photos. A few months into our relationship, we'd been watching the stone-cold classic Nineties romcom *Ten Things I Hate About You*, and I'd confessed to spending my post-puberty years obsessing over the film's star.

And so, just before the first term of second year ended, Daff presented me with this calendar, full of hidden pictures of Larisa.

'Now you can take your one true love home for Christmas,' she deadpanned as she handed it over.

I pick open the final window, which is much bigger than the others, and it reveals a surprisingly realistic composite of Ms Oleynik and myself standing next to each other, smiling. It has to be said, we actually make a pretty good couple.

I drop the calendar back onto the table. It takes me a couple of seconds to figure out the significance of this date. If my maths is right, then Daff and I have now been going out for just over a year, and today – Christmas Eve 2006 – is the first time she ever came to my house. In fact, it's the first time she ever met my ...

I hear spoons tinkling and cups clinking downstairs, and my stomach instantly turns in on itself. My chest knots so tightly that for a second I think I might pass out, and there's a sudden hard, hot pressure thundering behind my eyeballs.

'Benjamin!' Mum yells up the stairs. 'Will you please – *please* – get your backside out of bed and come and help your poor mother?'

And the next thing I know, I am crying so hard I can barely breathe.

Chapter Thirteen

Mum died on November 26th, 2018.

It was a Monday – a grey, drizzly, nothingy Monday – and I was coming back from work when I got the text.

I was temping at a travel agency at the time, spending forty hours a week knocking out press releases about Pacific cruises for the over-sixties. It was around 7 p.m., the end of yet another mindless, monotonous day, and I felt my phone buzz in my pocket as I stepped off the Tube. I remember staring down at the name on the screen. My uncle Simon, Mum's brother. That's weird, I thought. I don't think Simon's ever messaged me before.

All it said was: *Are you at home?*

I texted back: *In about 20 mins – why?* But there was no reply.

As soon as I got in the front door, I called Mum to see if she knew what was up with him. It went straight to voicemail, her cheery voice ringing out in my ear: 'So sorry, but I can't come to the phone right now …' Even then, I didn't make the connection. It didn't even cross my mind. Why would it?

When Simon knocked on the door a few minutes later, my first thought was that he'd had an accident. His shoulders were hunched, his eyes red raw and his face twisted like he was in agony.

I asked him what was wrong, but he walked past me and said, 'Let's go in and sit down.' And when we were sitting at the kitchen table, he just came out with it: 'Ben. I've come from the hospital. I'm so sorry, but something terrible's happened. Your mum's died.'

And that was it. Just like that, the world ended.

Simon told me later – months later – that the nurse had instructed him to say it that way. Direct and to the point. No beating around the bush. Like pulling off a plaster.

I didn't believe him at first. I thought it was a joke. Some weird, dark, sick joke. But then his voice broke as he said it again. And as he started to cry – these horrible, heavy, jagged sobs – the truth ripped through me like a blade.

I remember just sitting there, gasping like I was drowning. The shock was so severe – so insanely violent – that it took the wind right out of me.

The only thought in my head was that I would do anything – *anything* – for this not to be true.

I sat, paralysed, as I listened to Simon explain what had happened. An aneurysm. A weak blood vessel in her brain. No warning, nothing anyone could have done. She'd been on her way back from the shops, and she'd fallen right there in the street. Dead at fifty-eight. Gone forever.

There's a blank space after that, where my memories should be. The last thing I remember is hearing Daphne's key in the door, and the scrape of Simon's chair as he stood up. Crazy how your brain just slams the shutters on things it can't cope with.

I have a half-formed memory of Daphne standing over me in the bathroom later that evening, when Simon had gone, trying to pull my hands away from my face. And I couldn't understand why until I looked in the mirror and saw the bloody red tracks my fingernails had been leaving.

But the rest of the night is a blank. Which is strange, because I know I didn't sleep. The next thing I really remember is the sound of the rain on the window the following morning. By then, the shock and violence had given way to a kind of numb, broken emptiness, and I lay on the sofa, feeling like I was underwater, while Daff called the travel agency to tell them I wouldn't be coming back in.

I went round to Mum's house a couple of days later. The house I grew up in, the house I'm in right now. I don't know why. I just had to. Daff didn't want me to go alone, so I lied – told her I was meeting Simon there.

As soon as I opened the door, I knew it was a mistake. The place smelled of her. How could her *smell* still be here, when she wasn't?

I didn't get further than the hallway before I broke down. Above the hall table, there was a photo of the two of us. We're on the beach at Whitley Bay, near Newcastle – one of Mum's favourite places on earth. I'm fourteen or fifteen, mugging at the camera from beneath an unfortunate Britpoppy fringe. Mum has her arm wrapped tightly around me, and her blonde hair is whipping about wildly in the sea wind. But through it all, you can still see her bright smile and her blue-green eyes, sparkling with laughter and life.

I pulled the picture off the wall and crumpled onto the floor, my back pressed up against the front door. I don't know how long I sat there staring at it, crying so hard that my entire body was shaking. Because it hit me then, quite suddenly, that this was *real*. That this nightmare was actually happening. That my mum was gone, and something inside me was broken and might never be fixed.

Her phone was still on the hall table – she was always forgetting to take it out with her – and I sat there calling it over and over again, crying harder and harder each time her voicemail kicked in. She sounded so real, so *alive*. How could she be gone? It didn't make any sense. It still doesn't.

The days after that were a blur. There were forms to fill in – endless fucking forms. There were trips to the funeral director's office. I would sit there next to Simon in that bleak little room on Ealing High Road and think how absurd it seemed to be discussing things like flowers and food at a time like this. Mum was dead, the ground was cracking beneath me, and here I was talking about whether I preferred lilies or chrysanthemums. What the fuck did it matter? What did *anything* matter now?

The funeral itself I remember in random stop-motion snatches. The unreal horror of the coffin behind the podium. The way Uncle Simon's face seemed to collapse as he stood up to give the eulogy. I was supposed to speak, too. I was meant to read a poem – a Walt Whitman thing, one of Mum's favourites. But a couple of days before, I'd decided I couldn't do it, for fear of breaking down in front of everyone.

I've always regretted that.

I remember staring around the church while Simon was speaking, to see if my dad had bothered to show up. I'd been so certain that he would. That he would step back into my life today, when I needed him most.

But no.

When the service finished, even through the blinding misery, I felt a violent stab of anger at him for that. Of all the shitty things he'd done to her – to *us* – that seemed to be the shittiest.

The weeks and months after that all bled into each other to form one long, airless vacuum. I pushed everything inwards: tried to nail a brave face on and keep moving. I guess I thought that by going through the motions, things would eventually get back to normal. But they didn't.

Daff tried to help, to get closer to me, to console me. I lost count of the nights she came home early, or the days she took off work. She'd grip my hand and pull me close, and beg me to talk to her – or talk to someone else: a friend, a therapist, a bereavement counsellor. But every time, I just pushed her away. I didn't see how talking could change anything. Talking wouldn't bring Mum back.

I went back to temping. A different office, but equally dull and monotonous. And every night, after eight hours of typing and smiling and making small talk, I would go into the grotty public toilets by the Tube station near work and cry until my throat was raw.

Because I think it was only then, in those weeks that followed, that I really started to process it all. Mum had been the one constant in my life. She had always been there, and now, suddenly – inexplicably – she wasn't. She was my only real family. And she was gone.

I never even got to say goodbye. Or, more importantly, to apologise. Because the last time I'd seen her … well, it didn't even bear thinking about. That was the worst thing – the thing I never told anyone, not even Daphne. The last things

I ever said to Mum were so horrible, so childish, so spiteful. And when she died, I wished with every fibre of my being that I could take them back. But I couldn't.

So instead I buried them, deep down inside me, and left them there to fester.

'Ben?'

Mum's voice breaks in again, drifting up from the kitchen, and I realise I'm still crying.

I can hear her feet starting to pad softly up the stairs. 'It's after eleven! Daphne will be here any minute!'

Chapter Fourteen

Without thinking, I leap out of bed and sprint across the corridor into the bathroom.

'One second,' I gulp, as I lock the door and duck my hot, streaming face under the cold tap.

'Well don't be too long,' I hear her shout over the rushing water. 'She'll be arriving any time now.'

I let the water run and run, and then sit on the edge of the bathtub for a bit, staring blankly at the wall, my mind too frazzled to work properly. When my eyes have finally dried and lost their puffy redness, I go back to my room and put some jeans and a T-shirt on. I have no idea how I'm going to deal with this. But I know I can't stay up here hiding forever.

I take a deep breath, then walk downstairs with my heart hammering.

The house looks like a Santa's grotto has exploded inside it: holly and ivy hang from pretty much every wall, and tinsel curls down the banister like an exotic silver snake. Mum always took Christmas *very* seriously.

With every step, the déjà vu gets more intense. Every inch of the house conjures some long-forgotten memory: the photos of me and Mum that line the staircase; the deep dent halfway down the banister rail (a result of my decision to slide down it wearing rollerblades, aged nine). And then there it is: the picture of us at Whitley Bay, hanging next to a faded photo of Mum's dad – my grandad Jack – as a young man, a broad grin stretching out beneath his twinkling blue eyes.

I feel a strange shiver run through me – something I can't quite define. This place was home. And back in the present – in 2020 – it's someone else's home. Uncle Simon and I put it up for sale a few months after Mum died. We got a fair bit less than the asking price, but I didn't care. I just wanted the whole thing over with as quickly as possible; it was too painful to keep setting foot in this house with Mum gone.

So now another family lives here, filling it with their own memories.

I push open the kitchen door. Mum is standing with her back to me, arranging bits of smoked salmon into a neat pattern on a plate. 'Finally,' she says, brightly. 'I thought I was going to have to entertain the poor girl on my own.'

She turns around and smiles, her eyes crinkling softly at the sides, and it takes everything I have not to fall apart again. There's less grey in her hair, but aside from that, she's exactly as I last saw her. She's wearing black trousers and a smart button-up velvety cardigan thing, and even with my extremely limited fashion knowledge, I can tell this is one of her 'special occasion' outfits. I feel a powerful rush of love for her.

'Now, I've done some little salmon bits to start with,' she says. 'And the beef's in the oven. But, you know, I forgot to check with you whether she actually eats meat. Because more and more people don't these days. You know Hiam's son, Henry, well, he's become a "pescatarian", and …' She breaks

88

off, her finger quote marks still hanging in mid-air. 'What's the matter, darling? Is something wrong?'

I realise I am clenching my jaw painfully, twisting my mouth into a shape that's supposed to resemble a smile. Clearly it's not having the desired effect.

'Oh God,' Mum sighs, dropping her hands to her hips. 'She's a veggie, isn't she? I knew it.'

I can't take it any more. I rush forward to hug her.

'Blimey,' she laughs. 'What's all this?'

She pats my back gently, and I speak into her shoulder, my voice thick and muffled. 'I'm sorry, Mum,' I mumble. 'I'm so sorry ...'

'Don't be stupid, darling,' she says. 'I can easily do her a macaroni cheese.'

There is so much I want to say to her that I don't know where to start. I want to apologise for all those terrible things I haven't even said yet; to tell her I won't mean them when I say them, and that she's the best mum in the world and I'm a useless, pathetic excuse for a son. And I want to warn her about what will happen in – what will it be? – twelve years' time.

There are a million things I want to say, but I don't get the chance to say any of them. Because the doorbell interrupts me.

Mum breaks out of the hug and claps her hands together: 'Right, you let her in, I'll go and get the baby pictures.'

She laughs at whatever expression I'm currently wearing, and then adds: 'I'm joking, I'm *joking*. We can do the baby pictures *after* lunch.'

She nudges me out of the kitchen. At the end of the hallway I can see Daff's silhouette through the stained glass on the front door. Oh God. I'm just about getting a handle on seeing Mum again, and now I've got to open the door to a nineteen-year-old Daphne. I take a deep breath and try very hard to compose myself.

Through the glass I can see Daff fiddling with her hair, and when I open the door, she stops and smiles at me.

'Hey.'

'Hey … you look amazing,' I say. Because she really does.

A whole year has passed since 'yesterday', but she looks pretty much exactly the same: young and happy, albeit with a touch more nervous energy about her. The cold air outside seems to have coloured her entire face – her cheeks and the tip of her nose are a soft pastel pink and her big brown eyes are bright and glistening. She's wearing a black knee-length coat with smart blue jeans and a plain white shirt underneath. Just visible under the collar, winking in the sunlight, is the diamond necklace her parents bought her for her eighteenth.

She leans forward to give me a hug, and when she pulls back, she looks at my chest and laughs. 'Great to see you've made an effort too.'

I follow her gaze downwards. The T-shirt I picked up at random from my bedroom floor turns out to have the slogan *PERVERT 69* emblazoned across the front.

'Shit, sorry … I'll change.'

Behind her, I can see a little brown car pulling out and disappearing up the road: Daff's dad, Michael. I'd already met him and Daphne's mum by this point – they'd come up to uni for a weekend at the end of first year.

'Isn't he coming in?' I ask her.

She shakes her head. 'No way, I sent him packing. Way too

stressful to have the parents meeting each other as well. Maybe he can say hello later when he comes back to pick me up …'

She breaks off and grins over my shoulder. Mum is wandering through from the kitchen behind me, doing a frantic double-waving routine that is bordering on jazz hands and is presumably intended to waft away any meeting-the-mother awkwardness.

'Hello! Hello! You must be Daphne!' she beams as she dances towards her.

I'm sure I was absolutely mortified by this the first time round, but now it just makes me love Mum even more. She's clearly nervous and desperate to make Daff feel welcome: I've spent the past few months talking about her pretty much non-stop, so Mum knows how big a deal this is.

'Hello! Hi! Yes! You must be Rosie!' Daff is doing the jazz hands back at her now, making them look like some kind of 1920s musical hall double act. Despite everything, I can feel a bubble of laughter rising to bursting point in my chest. I start doing the jazz hands too, and suddenly all three of us are laughing together.

'It's so lovely to finally meet you,' Daff says, sticking out her hand for Mum to shake. Mum looks at it for a second, clearly thinks about taking it, then swats it away and pulls her in for a hug.

'Sorry, sorry, embarrassing mother,' she says, squeezing her tightly. And as Daff squeezes back, she shoots me a sideways glance that is pure excitement and happiness.

'Anyway,' Mum says, letting go of her, 'come on through!'

Chapter Fifteen

We sit around the kitchen table, and I eat the salmon while they talk.

I'm not even particularly hungry, to be honest, but stuffing my face seems like a good excuse for not speaking, and right now, forming coherent sentences is proving to be way beyond my grasp.

I'm doing my best to keep it together, but the whole thing is just so insane. I thought I would never see Mum again, and now here she is – *somehow* – sitting centimetres away from me, chatting and laughing and telling me to please, for God's sake, leave some salmon for everyone else. For the first time since I've been back here in the past, the confusion and fear is outweighed by sheer, mind-melting joy.

Mum was – is – an English teacher at the local secondary school. And at times like this, you can really tell. She bombards Daphne with questions about the English course at uni – which writers does she like best, which modules has she enjoyed most – and pretty soon the conversation blossoms to cover not just books but telly and music and whatever else. It's a bit like watching a dream first date unravel in front of me, because they agree on literally everything: from Charlotte Brontë to Bob Dylan, Alan Partridge to Adrian Mole.

'We're doing medieval poetry this term, which is a bit of a slog,' Daff says, as talk returns to uni. '*Sir Gawain and the Green Knight*; all that sort of stuff. It's a bit like being bored to death in a language you don't fully understand.'

Mum laughs. 'I see the exact same thing with my Year Elevens, groaning their way through Chaucer. You just know you're putting them off reading for a good ten years. I almost want to slip a *Hitchhiker's Guide to the Galaxy* into their bags to try and restore their faith. I mean, reading is supposed to be fun, for goodness' sake.'

Daff nods. 'I've started sneaking Patricia Highsmith books into lectures, just to keep myself awake.'

Mum's eyes light up at this. 'Oh God, Patricia Highsmith! She's *brilliant*, isn't she? Mad as anything, but still: brilliant. Have you read *Deep Water*?'

Daff shakes her head, and Mum leaps up from her seat and darts into the living room, sending her voice back through in her absence. 'It's my absolute favourite, this one. There's a chap whose wife is sleeping around on him, and so he starts … Well, no, I won't spoil it. You'll have to read it yourself.'

She comes back in, waggling a tattered copy of *Deep Water*.

'Here, Daphne, take it with you now. I insist. Early Christmas present.'

Daff laughs. 'Are you sure? That's so nice of you.'

'Yes, yes! I can buy another copy.' This is typical my-mum behaviour. Most mothers force clumps of foil-wrapped food on their guests; she forces paperbacks.

She sits back down and smiles at me fondly. 'Ben steadfastly refuses to read anything I give him. He's far more keen on his mardy books.'

This comment has the effect of making me want to simultaneously laugh and cry, and I have to stuff another salmon square into my mouth to ensure I don't do either. 'Mardy books' was a running joke between Mum and me: the books being the gloomy novels by Kafka and Jean-Paul Sartre that began to line my shelves around this time, and the 'mardy' being a hangover from her childhood. Mum was born and raised in Sheffield, and when she was in particularly high – or low – spirits, the Yorkshire slang would come tumbling out.

'Mardy books,' Daff repeats, grinning at me. 'I love it. That is Benjamin's taste exactly.'

Secretly, of course, I preferred non-mardy books. I still do. *Adrian Mole* and P. G. Wodehouse and *Hitchhiker's Guide* and all the other funny, silly novels I fell in love with as a fourteen-year-old. But as a posturing, insecure twenty-year-old, I was tirelessly working to rebrand myself from 'funny and silly' to 'moody and interesting'. And the best way to do that, I reasoned, was to have a mardy book poking out of my jacket at all times as I swanned around campus. Who exactly this was supposed to impress, I have no idea. Possibly Marek and Alice (who, to be fair, did seem quite impressed). Definitely *not* Daphne (who on one occasion removed a Kierkegaard paperback from my pocket and whacked me over the head with it).

Mum and Daphne are both smiling at me fondly now, giggling at my purported mardiness. I imagine that when this moment happened first time round, I probably found it slightly patronising – like I was a dog that had just performed a trick for them or something. But right now, it fills me with a happiness so intense that I almost feel drunk on it.

The two of them always got on well, right from the start. They spoke on the phone more and more regularly over the years, chatting away about books and telly and things. Now, as I return Daphne's smile, I suddenly find myself wondering how Mum's death must have affected *her*. She loved Mum too, I know she did. And yet after she died, I don't think I ever even asked Daphne how she was coping or if she was OK. I didn't once try to go through the grief *with* her; I just let it push us further and further apart.

Mum turns to Daphne and asks: 'Has Ben let you read any of his own stuff?'

'Not yet, no,' Daff says. 'I'm always on at him to.' She shoots me a mock-pissed-off glare, and I'm not quite sure how to respond to it. I was always a bit shy about people reading my stuff, even in the early days. Probably because, deep down, I was worried they would compare it – unfavourably – to my father's.

Mum's giving me the mock-annoyed look now too, her mouth set squarely in a pouty frown. 'Oh, well you *must* read some of it at some point,' she tells Daphne firmly. 'He's brilliant, just brilliant.'

Even through the insane joy of seeing her again, I feel a familiar prickle of irritation. Firstly, I'm *not* brilliant, and secondly, Mum hasn't read a single thing I've written since about Year 10 at school.

This was something that really got to me over the years: Mum's pig-headed insistence that I was something more than mediocre. I always wondered what on earth she based it on.

The fact that I'd won a couple of creative writing competitions at school? Maybe it's just a trait all parents have; you can't accept that your kid is no good, because that would mean there's something wrong with you too. Even after all the rejection letters I received, and my so-called career spiralling down the toilet, she would still tell me again and again how brilliant I was. It used to infuriate me.

In fact, it's what led me to say those terrible things to her before she died. She was just being supportive and kind, and I threw it all back in her face. I feel the guilt of it churning in my chest again, and I have to bite the inside of my cheek to stop the tears coming back. I took it completely for granted that she would always be there: my mum, fighting in my corner. And then one day she wasn't, and everything seemed to collapse as a result.

I guess at this point, though – 2006 – I didn't need anyone fighting in my corner. I was still pretty confident that I was some kind of genius-in-waiting. If I remember rightly, I was spending all my non-seminar hours writing a long, sprawling, entirely plot-free novel that was so meticulously ripped off Samuel Beckett it might as well have been labelled 'fan fiction'.

Not that I realised it at the time. The future still seemed bright and full of possibility, and I knew that even if this book didn't make things happen for me, sooner or later something else would. Back then, I assumed I had enough of my father in me to be sure of that.

I watch Daphne smiling as she flicks idly through the Highsmith novel. I can't remember how much I'd told her about my dad at this stage. Not that much, I don't think.

She'd asked me about him, of course, and she knew he wasn't around. What more was there to say? He'd left when I was ten, and the number of times I'd seen him since could probably be counted on the fingers of one hand. I guess I didn't talk to Daphne about him because I didn't want to seem wimpy and pathetic: a twenty-year-old man who still hadn't got over his dad leaving. I didn't want Daff to pity me.

Obviously, though, she knew all about his work. Pretty much every student on our course did. While he wasn't quite established enough to be an actual part of our modules (that would've been too awful to imagine), he was still regarded as one of the coolest modern British playwrights around. In Sunday supplements, his name was thrown about regularly as a potential successor to Pinter and Tom Stoppard, so any reference to him in a lecture or seminar would send every head turning my way.

They weren't to know, I suppose, that I had no sort of relationship with him at all.

Looking back now, I can see that that's what all the mardy books nonsense was really about. Throughout this whole period – late teens, early twenties – my idea of him was in constant flux. One minute I hated him for leaving; the next I desperately wanted his approval. Just before I left for uni, I'd come across an interview with him in a newspaper in which he cited his five favourite books – every one of them unmistakably mardy. Without even thinking about it, I'd ordered the lot. I still can't explain why. Did I really expect to bump into him randomly in the street, with one of them poking out of my pocket? Probably not. But it was always a possibility.

Mum clears the plates away and then starts rifling about

noisily inside the fridge. 'Right,' she says, 'it's after midday, it's Christmas Eve …' She turns around cradling a large bottle of cava. 'I think we are obliged to start drinking.'

'Hear, hear,' says Daphne.

I get up to fetch some glasses, realising yet again that everything – right down to the cartoonish squeal Mum makes as the cork pops – is happening exactly as I remember it first time round. And as incredible as it is to be with Mum again, I can't help thinking: what is the point?

What is the point of seeing her again and then having her torn away from me a second time? What is the point of seeing how right for each other Daphne and I once seemed, only to end up drunk in our attic again thinking about Alice?

What is the point of any of this? It just feels like the universe rubbing my face in the mistakes to come, and I can't for the life of me work out why.

Mum opens the oven to check on the sizzling beef, and then – just as I could have told you she would – she remembers that we don't have any mustard, and orders me out to the shops to get some.

I shrug my coat on in the hallway and open the front door, feeling the crisp winter air hit me full in the face. Digging my hands into my pockets, I start trudging up towards the high road, confusion and anger still doing battle in my brain.

I'm not even halfway to the shops when I spot a little wooden barrow stall parked on the corner of the street, with a man standing behind it. The stall is decorated with tinsel and twinkling lights, and there's a sloppily painted sign above it that reads: *HOT ROASTED CHESTNUTS!* Why its owner thinks that a suburban street corner in Acton is the best place to flog his wares is beyond me. But one thing's for sure: he was *not* here on this day originally.

I'm almost at the cart now, but I still can't see the man's face – it's hidden beneath the tinsel-strewn awning. His tie, though …

'Ah, there you are!' he cries, and as soon as I hear his gravelly voice, my stomach back-flips.

He pops his head out, and sure enough, two bright blue eyes are twinkling at me through a tangle of rusty grey hair.

'Can I interest you in a bag of chestnuts?'

Chapter Sixteen

This at least I didn't see coming.

I stand rooted to the spot for a moment, gawping at the watch-seller. I can't believe he's actually here! My brain is a blizzard of questions, but for some reason the first thing that tumbles out of my mouth is:

'You're ... still wearing the same tie?'

The old man frowns down at the cartoon reindeer. 'Don't you like it? I know novelty neckwear isn't to everyone's taste, but I think it's rather jolly.'

I have a go at formulating a more sensible question. 'Who *are* you?' I splutter.

The old man takes out a metal spoon and starts prodding chestnuts around the grill. 'Oh, let's just say I'm a concerned bystander. I only wanted to check in and see how you were doing. I imagine all this must be rather disconcerting.'

I stare at him. 'Rather disconcerting? I've spent the past twenty-four hours wondering if I've lost my mind!'

He chuckles. 'Let me reassure you that you very much haven't. I was going to pop over and say hello back in the bar at York, but you looked rather busy talking to that young lady.'

'That *was* you in the bar? I thought I'd imagined it.'

'It was indeed.' He wrinkles his nose slightly. 'I was glad to get out of there, truth be told. The smell of sambuca was overpowering.'

'I can't believe this,' I murmur.

There's something so familiar about him. Something I can't quite put my finger on.

'So … you remember meeting me in that pub on Christmas Eve?' I ask.

'Oh yes. Christmas Eve 2020.'

'But that hasn't happened yet,' I hiss. 'That's fourteen years from now!'

'Mmm. It is indeed.' He pops a chestnut in his mouth and chews thoughtfully. 'Needs more salt.'

I take a deep breath and try to compose myself. 'Look, I don't mean to be rude, but would you mind please just telling me what is happening?'

The old man purses his lips as he sprinkles salt over the chestnuts. 'I noticed you were at something of a crossroads that night in the pub. You were feeling lost and confused. And I wanted to help.'

'Right. And your method of helping was to give me a time-travelling watch?'

'That's about the long and short of it.' He grins and taps the grill with his spoon. 'Did you want a chestnut?'

I exhale and squeeze the bridge of my nose. 'What happens if I eat one? Do I get whisked back to the Renaissance or something?'

He bursts out laughing. 'The Renaissance! Very good. No, these are just your average common-or-garden chestnuts. Well, above average, actually. Extremely tasty, in fact.' He holds one up to me, but I shake my head. 'Suit yourself,' he shrugs. 'I'm sure you're full of questions and we haven't got long. So, fire away.'

That 'haven't got long' remark makes me think of the time frozen on my watch. I hold it up to him. 'Why is it stuck at one minute to twelve?'

A crumpled smile cuts through his scruffy beard, and his blue eyes sparkle at me. 'I think you've already worked that out, haven't you?'

'Because one minute to midnight is when my time here is up?' I say, slowly. 'It's when I … jump again?'

The old man beams and nods, like a teacher who's just coaxed the correct answer out of a particularly dim student.

'So, I *will* jump again, then?' I ask him.

'It's highly likely.'

'Where to?'

The old man sighs. 'That, I can't tell you.'

'Why not?'

'Because you already know the answer.'

'Trust me, I don't.'

He jabs at the chestnuts with his spoon. 'I'm confident it will come to you.'

I lean my head back in frustration. 'Look … I get that being vague and mysterious is sort of your thing. But I could really do with some proper, concrete answers right now.'

He laughs through his nose. 'The most important thing to ask yourself is *why* you might be revisiting these particular moments. Perhaps after experiencing them a second time you might feel differently about them. Or perhaps you won't.'

'But … will I get back to the present at some point?'

He opens his mouth to answer this, but a voice rings out behind us.

'Excuse me?'

I turn around to see three old ladies smiling at us. 'Sorry to interrupt,' one of them says. 'We were after a few chestnuts.'

The watch-seller claps his hands and grins at them. 'Finally! Some paying customers.' He looks back at me. 'You'd better be on your way.'

'But … hang on,' I stammer. 'I need to know—'

He cuts me off by raising his hand and checking his own watch. His eyebrows leap up into his scruffy hair. 'It's getting on a bit. Time to head back to your mother's.'

'What?' I ask, confused.

He looks me straight in the eyes, suddenly deadly serious. 'Trust me. Time to go. I know you have more questions, but don't worry, you'll see me again. I guarantee it.' He turns back to the women, smiling again. 'Now, ladies. Will it be three bags of chestnuts, then?'

'I do like your tie,' one of them says, and the watch-seller gives me a what-did-I-tell-you smirk.

I turn and start walking, feeling possibly more confused than I did before. I am still no clearer as to what is happening, or why. But something about the firmness in the old man's voice when he said 'Time to go' keeps me moving forward. I glance back over my shoulder, half expecting him to have disappeared, but he's still there, nattering away cheerfully with the old ladies.

It's only when I get back into the house that I remember why I left in the first place: mustard. I take my coat off and hang it on the banister. It's only me who likes the stuff anyway; I'll just tell Mum that I'm fine with gravy.

I walk back towards the kitchen, still feeling so dazed that it's like I'm on autopilot. The door is half open, and I can hear Mum and Daphne chatting away over the rattle of pans and the thwack of the knife on the chopping board.

'My sister is the worst,' Daphne is saying. 'All the Christmas presents she buys us are just presents for herself. Last year, she got into Wicca …'

'What, as in basket weaving?' Mum asks.

Daphne giggles. 'No, I wish. A basket would've been quite nice. I mean Wicca with two c's. As in witchcraft.'

'Gosh. Right. How interesting,' Mum says, giggling now too.

'She's a massive hippie,' Daff says. 'I unwrapped her present to me last year, and it was two tiny bells to be used, in her words, "to mark the differences between ritual ceremonies". I said to her: "Kat, seriously, do you think I'll be doing enough ritual ceremonies to need special bells to distinguish between them?"' I hear the potato pan clattering as Mum shakes with laughter. 'And then when she left on Boxing Day, she just picked them up and took them with her, saying, "Well, if *you're* not going to use them …"'

I'm about to push the door open and walk in when Mum stops laughing and says: 'You know, I'll never forget the present Ben got me the Christmas after his dad left.'

The chopping noises die out suddenly, and I wonder if Daphne has broken off to give Mum her full attention. My heart starts thumping. I hardly ever heard her talk about Dad. As a kid, it was always me that seemed to bring him up. It feels odd hearing her even mention him.

'He must have been … what was it? Ten?' Mum continues.

'And everything was a bit up in the air at that time. Things were quite tough, really, on both of us. Anyway. In the run-up to Christmas, I started to notice things going missing around the house. Only little things – like my stapler, or the Sellotape, or the pad of Post-its I kept by the phone; stuff like that. But I didn't think anything of it, because there was so much else to think about. And then, come Christmas morning, there were three presents for me under the tree from Ben. I unwrapped them, and there they were: my stapler, my Sellotape, and the pad of Post-its.'

There's silence for a second, and then both of them burst out laughing.

'Oh my God,' Daphne says. 'OK, I think you've trumped me there. That's worse than the bells.'

'I know.' Mum snorts. 'But you know, the funny thing was, I was genuinely really pleased to see them. I told him, "I've been looking for these *everywhere*!" and he was so delighted with himself. I hadn't been expecting him to get me anything – he was only ten years old. I suppose he was just trying to cheer me up, and that was the only way he could think to do it. It's silly, really. But it made me laugh and feel genuinely happy at a time when I honestly didn't think I was capable of either.'

There's another silence, and then I hear Daphne say, very quietly, 'That's really sweet.'

'And this is probably reading far too much into it,' Mum adds, 'but years later, I started to wonder if those presents were Ben's way of telling me that we could get along fine without his father. Almost as if he was saying: "We've already got everything we need here. We just have to remind each other of that from time to time."' The pans begin clattering again.

'Anyway. Gosh. Sorry, Daphne, listen to me: one glass of cava and I start boring you with all this old nonsense.'

'No, it's not nonsense at all,' Daff says softly. 'And I take it back now, by the way. My bells were a much, *much* worse present.'

They both start laughing again. And as I step away from the door, I realise I need another spell under the cold tap before I can go back in and join them.

Chapter Seventeen

The rest of the afternoon passes in a warm, pleasant, vaguely unreal blur.

Mum is delighted to learn that Daphne is not in the least bit vegetarian, and once we've all made a serious dent in the beef, and the bottle of cava, and then a bottle of red wine, we stumble woozily through to the living room and slump onto the sofas in front of the fire.

For the first time in a long time, I actually feel good about myself, even if it's for something I did when I was in primary school, and which – let's face it – essentially amounted to stealing some stationery and then giving it back again.

Daphne nuzzles into my shoulder on the sofa, and at this moment, everything between us feels so good – so *right* – that it's hard to believe it will ever go wrong.

The watch-seller's comment about questioning why I've come back to these particular moments keeps swirling around my brain. I missed that conversation between Mum and Daphne originally. Daff never even told me about it. Is that why the old man was so adamant that I went straight back home; so that I'd overhear them, and remember that I wasn't always a screw-up of a son? Mum shoots me an affectionate glance from her armchair, and I decide that now is not the time to analyse it. I'd rather just bask in the way it made me feel.

Unfortunately, though, I don't get long: within a few minutes of us sitting down, the doorbells rings.

Daff stirs and sits up. 'That'll be my dad.'

My stomach clenches tightly, because I suddenly can't bear the thought of her leaving. I want to stay like this, just for a little longer. I want to pause everything and remain in this weird, perfect bubble, before the future happens and everything between us warps and fractures and turns rotten.

But of course, I can't.

Mum leaps up to answer the door, and we follow her, and there's lots more wild flapping of jazz hands as she pulls Daphne's bewildered-but-pleased-looking father in for a hug.

While the two of them swap animated pleasantries across the doormat, Daff sneaks a kiss onto my lips and smiles. 'Today was great,' she whispers. 'Really great.'

'Yeah, it was brilliant.'

'I'll call you tomorrow.' She squeezes my hand. 'Merry Christmas.'

She kisses me again, and then she's gone – down the path and into the car. And I've got no choice but to watch her go, not knowing where – or when – I'll be the next time I see her.

Mum shuts the door, and turns to me with a grin. 'Right then, young man,' she says. 'I think it's high time I thrashed you at Monopoly.'

The ultra-competitive Christmas Eve Monopoly marathon was always a tradition in this house. I can't even remember when it started, but it dated back a long way – to when Dad was still around. I was always the dog, Mum was always the ship and he was always the top hat. Those were the unwritten rules. No idea why, but we stuck to them rigidly. And as a result, the top hat in our Monopoly set hasn't left the box since Christmas 1995.

Mum fetches another bottle of wine and stokes the fire while I get the game out of the cupboard behind the sofa. And as I do, I spot something else nestled there – something I'd completely forgotten about.

'Oh my God,' I laugh. 'Is this the full collection?'

I pull out a little wooden rack stacked with cassettes, each one wrapped in its own carefully hand-written track list.

'Of course,' Mum says proudly. '*Now That's What I Call Long-Distance Car Trips*. I've still got every one we ever made.'

I stare down at them, feeling a lump start to work its way into my throat. These tapes were another family tradition, although this one began *after* Dad left, when I was about twelve. Before every long car journey – whether it was a summer holiday or a weekend visit to see Nan in Sheffield – Mum and I would compile a tape for the trip. The track list would alternate back and forth: one song for her, one song for me. As a result, they are perhaps the only compilation albums on earth in which gentle folk rock weaves consistently in and out of hardcore gangsta rap.

We'd spend hours making these tapes, sitting cross-legged in front of the hi-fi together, scribbling the lists, doodling designs on the covers, taking the mick out of each other's song choices. It's weird: sometimes I almost enjoyed those afternoons more than the holidays themselves.

I spot the one from August 2000 – the trip to Whitley

Bay where that photo in the hall was taken. The lump in my throat doubles in size, but I manage to swallow it. 'Can I put this on?' I ask.

Mum's sitting on the carpet, dealing out Monopoly money like a Vegas card shark. 'Well, we're not technically on a long-distance car trip,' she says. 'But it *is* Christmas. So go on.'

I slide the tape into the stereo and the opening strains of her first selection – 'California' by Joni Mitchell – begin to rise softly out of it.

'Right, come on then, let's have you,' Mum says, patting the carpet. I sit down across from her, and she rolls the dice onto the board.

She taps her ship onto Pentonville Road and starts peeling off banknotes. 'So …' she says. 'Daphne seems utterly fantastic.'

I pick up the dice and roll. 'Yeah. She is.'

'I was a bit worried, you know,' Mum says. 'I mean, you do realise she's the first girl you've brought home since The Ghastly Tish?'

That really makes me laugh. Leticia Middleton – aka The Ghastly Tish – was the closest thing I'd had to a proper girlfriend before Daphne. She went to the incredibly posh girls' school near my sixth-form college, although she did everything she could to disguise her immense poshness by swearing like a trooper and dressing like Gwen Stefani from No Doubt. We went out for about three months when I was seventeen, and towards the end of it, I got so sick of Mum nagging me to invite her over that I finally caved.

'I don't think The Ghastly Tish even made eye contact with me once,' Mum chuckles.

'Mum, she was probably shy!'

'Shy! The girl dropped the F-bomb about ten times during dinner!' She rolls the dice, and then starts laughing again. 'Oh God, d'you remember when she got that bit of pasta stuck in her lip ring? Poor girl, mustn't laugh …'

But neither of us can help it. The memory is just way too absurd: Mum bombarding Tish with jolly politeness while Tish swore at the clump of spaghetti trapped in her piercing.

Suffice it to say, she didn't come back again.

When we've both stopped laughing, Mum says, 'So. I'd say today was a little more successful than that.' She taps her counter round the board again. 'You and Daphne are wonderful together.'

'Yeah …' This comment touches so sharply – so *precisely* – on everything I've been worrying about over the past twenty-four hours that I can't help picking at it. 'Do you really think so?' I ask her.

'Of course.' She looks up at me. 'Don't you?'

I shrug. 'I feel like we're good together *now*. But I mean … how do I really know that we're right for each other? In the long run?'

She shakes her head and laughs. 'For God's sake, Ben. You're only twenty years old. All that matters right now is: do you make each other happy?'

'Right now we do, yeah.'

'Well, there you go, then.' She nudges the dice back across to me. 'You can think about the long run later. But the truth is: if you want a relationship to work, you have to *work* at it. And to me, you and Daphne seem to have a relationship that's worth working at. I don't know why, but I've got a feeling about you two …'

I roll the dice, and out of nowhere, I hear myself say: 'But you must have had a feeling about you and Dad too, at some point.'

She's halfway through counting out a wad of banknotes, but that stops her in her tracks. I've never said anything like that to her. Ever. I don't really know anything about her relationship with my dad, except for the way it ended: with him running off with another woman. We never talked about it beyond that. I don't know why. Maybe I was waiting for her to start the conversation, and she never did. But I suddenly, desperately, want to find out more about it. For some reason, I've been given this insane chance to see her again, and I'm burning with the desire to actually *talk* to her. To ask her the things I always wanted to, but never got the chance.

I can tell she's taken aback. There's a beat of awkward silence, which, helpfully, our car tape steps in to shatter, as Joni Mitchell's mournful guitar is rudely smothered by the clatter of NWA's 'Fuck tha Police'. We lock eyes and start laughing.

'A perfect edit from us there,' she murmurs.

I reach over to turn Ice Cube down slightly, and Mum rolls the dice and starts moving her counter. For a second, I think she's going to pretend she didn't hear what I said. But then she rubs the bridge of her nose slowly with her thumb and forefinger, and says: 'The truth is, Ben, I don't know if I ever *did* have that feeling about your father and me. Even after we got married. Even after we had you.'

My heart starts pounding like a kick drum. She looks up at me, her mouth crinkling softly at the sides as she smiles. 'I know I was ... *taken* with him,' she says, rolling her eyes at the idea of it. 'He was very charming and talented and all that. But we hadn't known each other long before we got married. Six months, something like that. And I suppose in the back of my mind, I did always worry that he was more interested in himself than he was in me. That his ambitions and his career meant more to him than anything else.' She exhales slowly through her nose. 'And he proved me right there, in the end.'

I feel my face getting hot, and that lump starting to work its way back into the bottom of my throat. 'But what about you?' I say, trying to keep my voice steady. 'What about *your* ambitions?'

She swats my comment away with her hand. 'I had ambitions too, thank you very much. I always wanted to teach, and that's what I did. I love doing it. And I'm OK at it, I think.'

'You're *brilliant* at it,' I say. And as I do, I realise that I'm exactly mirroring her comment earlier to Daphne, about my writing. She always supported me, without question, one hundred per cent. And in the real world, in 2020, she's gone. At one minute to midnight, all this will disappear, and she'll be ripped away from me all over again. I don't know if I'll be able to handle that.

God, I've missed her *so* much.

'Ben? Are you ... Oh, darling, what's wrong?'

I swipe my hand across my cheek to stop the tears that are suddenly spilling down it.

'I'm so sorry, Mum,' I mumble.

'Ben, don't be silly! What's got into you? You've got nothing to be sorry for.'

But I do – she just doesn't realise it yet. I'm sorry for the awful things I'll say to her before she dies. I'm sorry for the screw-up of a son that I'll become. But I don't know how to tell her these things, and it's only making the tears fall faster.

I speak into her shoulder, my words coming out thick and muffled. 'I'm going to let you down, Mum. I know I am. I'm going to let everyone down.'

She grips me even tighter and says, 'Ben, you couldn't let me down. It's just not possible.'

I dissolve, then. Everything liquefies.

Some time passes, I'm not sure how much. But when we pull away from each other, Mum is red-eyed and damp-cheeked as well.

'Look at the state of us,' she says, wiping her face. 'You've got me going too. This is hardly very Christmassy, is it?'

I laugh and sniff. 'Sorry.'

'Anyway, come on. Enough of this. We've got a game to finish.' She points down at my dog counter, which is sitting on Pentonville Road. 'And don't think all this crying is getting you out of *that*.' She holds her hand out, grinning. 'You owe me rent, young man.'

The Monopoly game grinds to a halt pretty quickly after that. I find I can't concentrate on my fictional property portfolio when I know that my time with Mum is slipping away, second by precious second.

So instead, I put on two more of our long-distance car tapes, and spend the next three hours asking her all the things I've never thought to ask before. I hear about her childhood, her school days, university. Her early twenties, when she worked on a kibbutz in Israel. All this crazy stuff I never knew. She even tells me about the night she met my dad. It was at the opening of an N. F. Simpson play at the Royal Court. Their interval drinks orders got mixed up, they got talking, and the rest was history.

'What's got into you this evening?' she chuckles at one point. 'You've never showed the slightest bit of interest in my life before, and now you've turned into Michael bloody Parkinson.'

It's meant as a joke – I think – but the truth of it stings me to my core. I never did show any interest. I was completely self-absorbed. I just thought of her as Mum, rather than a real person with hopes and fears, who'd had adventures and made mistakes.

Finally – after a lot more laughing and drinking and story-telling, all soundtracked by our excellent folk/hip hop compilation albums – we pack the Monopoly set away and slump in front of the TV.

The closing moments of some Seventies James Bond film flicker before us, and despite everything, I feel exhaustion bite right into me. The emotional whirlwind of the last few hours – not to mention the copious red wine – is beginning to take effect.

I glance over at Mum as she watches Roger Moore prancing about on the screen, and feel so full of love for her. I don't want this moment to end.

But it will. The clock above the telly reads ten to midnight. Which means I have exactly nine minutes before all this evaporates and I find myself in another place, at another time.

I know I should be grateful that I got even one more day with Mum, but I can't help it: I want more.

I sit up straight and take a deep breath. There must be a way to make it happen. There has to be some kind of loophole. The watch-seller told me I'd jump again at one minute to midnight – but when it happened last night, I was asleep. Maybe the jumps can *only* happen when I'm asleep?

Maybe, as long as I can keep my eyes open, I'll get more time with Mum ...

I have no clue if it'll work, but it's worth a try. Unfortunately, at that exact moment, she tosses the remote control over to me and stands up.

'Right. I'm bushed.'

'No, wait ... Don't you want to stay till the end of the film?'

'I think I can guess what happens,' she yawns. 'Roger gets his end away after delivering an appallingly sexist one-liner.'

I stand up too. I'm suddenly desperate not to let her go. 'Well, we don't have to watch the film, then ... We can just talk or play another game or something.'

She laughs. 'Ben, it's late. I'm exhausted.'

'I know, but ... Let's stay up a bit longer. Please. Just a few more minutes.'

I make a decision on the spot: I'm going to tell her. I'm going to tell her what's happening to me! It'll sound *insane*, obviously – 'The thing is, Mum, I appear to be travelling back through time' – but I'm sure I can convince her. And then, once I have, I can apologise properly. I can tell her I won't mean all the awful things I'll say to her in the future. Maybe there's even a way to *change* the future. To stop what will happen to her.

My heart leaps at the thought of it. There's still time!

'Let's just stay up until midnight, OK?' I say. 'Just till Christmas Day.'

Mum glances up at the clock. 'Well, that thing's slow anyway. It might even be midnight already.'

She pulls out her phone to check. And that's when everything goes black.

Chapter Eighteen

The feeling is one of being hurled backwards with extreme force.

One second I'm standing upright, the next I'm lying flat on my back on a soft mattress, the entire room shaking around me.

I try to sit up, but I can't. My head is spinning and I'm gasping for air.

And then, suddenly, the shaking stops. Through the window opposite, I can see exactly what caused it: an orange-and-white Overground train, now thundering off into the distance.

I look around me, and with a sickening jolt I realise that the living room is gone – *Mum* is gone – and I'm somewhere else entirely.

I shoot bolt upright, my heart hammering like crazy.

Was that it? Is it over? Was that the last time I'll ever see her?

A tight, cold panic seizes me. There was so much more that I could have said. That I *should* have said.

The watch is still fixed firmly around my wrist. Clearly, there is no loophole. Asleep or awake, I will jump at one minute to midnight, and there's nothing I can do about it.

Regret begins to swell painfully in my chest, but there's no time for it to properly take root, because as I stare wildly around the room, I suddenly realise: I know where I am.

This is Dalston. 79 Kingsland High Road, Dalston. The flat Harv and I rented together after we left uni.

I stagger out of bed, still trembling like mad, my eyes darting from one side of the room to the other. It's all exactly as I remember it: the fire extinguisher slumped in the corner by the wardrobe, the laminated safety codes stuck to the back of the door, the horrible strip lighting on the ceiling that – when activated – gave everything in the room a sickly yellowish tint.

Both floors of the flat had previously been the offices of an Albanian law firm, but at some point the Albanian lawyers had given up trying to wage their legal battles over the constant roar of the London Overground, and the landlord had taken the opportunity to rebrand the place as a 'bijou apartment space'. He'd not even bothered to redecorate – just squeezed in a couple of cheap single beds and a sofa, and left everything else as it was, right down to the jaundiced lighting and the fire safety accessories.

The room starts quivering again as another train bursts out from behind the building, making the window panes chatter like wind-up teeth.

If I remember rightly, Harv and I had allocated who got which bedroom by playing an extremely competitive game of FIFA, which he had won. Both rooms were ridiculously loud, but the one Harv chose, at the front of the flat, picked up only random, sporadic street sounds – the howl of a fox, the scream of a drunken argument, the glassy explosion of a car window. And Harv apparently preferred all that to the meticulously scheduled sleep deprivation of the back room – my room – which had the train tracks running literally right beside it.

We were in this flat for just over three years, and I don't think I ever slept more than four hours consecutively in that whole time.

Which suddenly makes me wonder: what date have I landed on now? We lived here from, what … 2008 to 2011? So I might just have jumped five years in the blink of an eye.

The thought makes me drop weakly onto the edge of the bed.

My head is ringing with confusion, but I can't exactly stay sitting in this room forever. I start getting dressed, picking up clothes at random from the floor. Harv's bedroom door is shut, so I creep downstairs, nostalgia prodding me sharply with every footstep. I pass our boxy living room and spot the grimy fish tank next to the TV that contains two goldfish we named after members of the Wu-Tang Clan, though right now I can't remember exactly which ones.

I open the kitchen door and walk in. There is an incredibly attractive girl standing at the sink, sniffing an open carton of milk with a look of pure disgust on her face. She's wearing only a baggy grey T-shirt, which ends just above the knees on her long, tanned bare legs, and her sandy-blonde hair is pulled up into a messy topknot.

The shock of seeing her is enough to make me flinch. 'Oh my God! *Liv!*'

She looks up, her nose now wrinkling at me instead of the dodgy milk.

'Er, yeah? Hi?' she says, in her ridiculously plummy accent. The bewilderment that floods her face tells me I've made a big mistake here. We definitely met for the first time while I was living in this flat. So is *this* it? Is right now the first time that I'm meeting her?

'I'm Ben, Harv's flatmate,' I explain quickly, but her beautiful face remains puckered and wary.

'Right, OK. I'm Olivia. Liv. But you already know that, apparently?'

'Yeah, sorry, that was a bit random, coming in like that and just … shouting your name out.'

'It was a *little* bit, yeah.' Like a caricature of a posh person, Liv actually pronounces 'yeah' as 'yah'.

'It's just that I've, erm, heard so much about you from Harv, that's all.'

An indignant voice comes from behind me. 'What? No you haven't!'

I turn around to see Harv appearing through the kitchen door in his T-shirt and boxers, glaring at me.

'I've barely mentioned you,' he says to Liv, who – quite rightly – doesn't look convinced by this statement. She knows full well that she's the kind of girl men *do* mention to their mates. 'I mean, no, that sounds bad,' Harv gabbles on, his neck starting to turn bright red. 'I mean, I probably did say something about you, in passing. But only that we work together or whatever. It's not like I'm just going on about you all the time, is it, Ben?'

Thankfully, Liv interrupts this torturous monologue by pouring half a pint of thick, gloopy white liquid down the sink.

'Nice to meet you,' she says to me, unsmiling, as she slaps the empty carton back down on the counter. 'You guys need milk.' She squeezes past us and walks out, back up the stairs.

'Mate, what the *fuck*?' Harv hisses at me. 'What are you doing telling her I can't stop talking about her? Are you insane?'

'Sorry, I just—'

'I've liked this girl for ages, man, and then you start …' His eyes suddenly light up and a smile splits his face in two. 'Ah, no, screw it. I literally, *physically*, cannot be angry at you right now.' He drops his voice to a whisper. 'So, last night, right. Work Christmas party. We finally … Yeah. And it was, like …' He slaps both hands on my shoulders, puffs his cheeks out, rolls his eyes and exhales slowly into my face.

'What does that mean?' I ask. 'Exhausting?'

'What it means is, we had actual sexual intercourse. And it was really quite something, Benjamin.' He gazes up at the ceiling and shakes his head. 'It was *really* quite something.'

He looks so joyously, heartbreakingly happy that I'm not sure what to say. I mean, what *can* I say?

Olivia Woodford is, without a doubt, the worst thing that will ever happen to him.

From the start, their relationship was so dangerously unbalanced that I could hardly believe it lasted six weeks, let alone four years. Four whole years of Harv jogging along a few steps behind her, never being quite rich enough, or cool enough, or … *anything* enough for her.

They met at this music marketing company where Harv had a low-level admin job. Liv was employed there – as far as I could understand – on the sole basis that her dad had been in the same university drinking club as the CEO. After weeks of me listening to Harv moon on about her while we played PlayStation, they finally hooked up at the office Christmas party.

And that was it. I pretty much lost him for the next four years.

It was partly because I didn't much like Liv, to be honest. She seemed to have that thing a lot of ridiculously hot people have, where they assume their ridiculous hotness is an acceptable excuse for extreme unfriendliness. Talking to her was a constant battle for eye contact; she always seemed to be looking over my shoulder for someone more interesting. But more than that, I didn't like who Harv became as their relationship intensified.

In an effort to fit in with Liv and her rich hipster mates, he became colder and harsher and more sarcastic. He seemed to lose all the things I'd liked about him at university: his self-deprecating humour, his goofy charm, his infectious excitement for life. He was besotted with her – 'besotted' really is the perfect word – and in her presence he would dial his confidence up and his self-awareness down. To me, it always seemed obvious that he was trying so, so hard. And I guess I've always thought that real love is about not having to try at all.

But then look where that's got me.

Anyway. Over the next four years, Harv drifted gradually away from me until he was completely absorbed into Liv's friendship group. We'd almost lost touch altogether by the time everything came crashing down around him.

He found out that Liv had been cheating on him with a stupidly handsome start-up millionaire who'd appeared in one series of *Made in Chelsea*. They broke up, and I naïvely assumed I would get my best mate back. But he didn't magically change back into the bloke he once was; instead, he seemed to move even further away from him. He became suddenly and terrifyingly fitness-obsessed; I guess out of concern that his slight chubbiness had been the reason Liv had gone off with the *Made in Chelsea* guy (who, as I recall, was built like Zac Efron).

It strikes me now, watching Harv bogle around the kitchen in post-coital bliss, that I never talked to him about any of this at the time. We fell slowly and cautiously back into friendship, but I never once properly checked whether he was OK. I never once offered anything beyond the cursory 'Ah, buck up, mate, plenty more fish' platitudes. I probably told myself this was because we were blokes, and blokes didn't really talk about that stuff. But that's bollocks, really. I was too wrapped up in myself, and my own problems.

I think back suddenly to Christmas Eve 2020, in the pub, feeling that disconnect between us – that inability to ever talk about anything real, anything important. It all started here, really; this was the period when our friendship first began to unravel. Not just because he hooked up with a girl I couldn't stand, but because I was too self-involved to be there for him when it all went to shit.

Maybe that's what today is all about, then. Maybe that's why I'm back here, on this specific day. Am I supposed to tell him what will happen in the future? Surely he wouldn't believe me even if I did?

Harv interrupts my thought process by opening the fridge and asking, 'Have you fed Ghostface and Raekwon?'

I stare at him. 'The … Oh, right, the goldfish?'

'No, the Staten Island-based rap duo. *Yes*, the goldfish.' He clicks his tongue. 'What is wrong with you this morning, man?'

'Sorry, I'm just feeling a bit … off, I guess.'

'So, is it a yes or a no to the feeding?'

'It's a no.'

'Right.' He takes the fish food out of the fridge and glances up at the clock. 'Aren't you going to work?'

God. Shit. Maybe I am. I find myself just staring blankly at him again, with absolutely no idea what to say. Since I've no idea *when* exactly I am, I also have no idea *what* exactly it is I do.

'It's your office Christmas thing tonight, isn't it?' he reminds me. 'Y'know: "Ain't no party like a lads' mag party".'

And then, finally, everything slots into place. I know exactly what day it is. And I'm not looking forward to reliving it one bit.

Chapter Nineteen

Within a few seconds of leaving the flat, my assumption is confirmed.

A quick scan of the newspapers in the shop downstairs tells me that today's date is 16 December 2010. I remember quite clearly what happened on this day, although I have no clue why I am being forced to go through it again. It was, in pretty much every respect, an absolute shit-show.

It briefly crosses my mind that I don't actually *have* to go through it again. I mean, it's not like anyone's forcing me to do anything. If I wanted, I could go full Ferris Bueller: ditch work completely and spend the whole day lip-synching to Beatles songs, or whatever it is Ferris does with his freedom.

My heart stutters as I realise I could even go back and see Mum again. She's still here, just a few Tube stops away, alive and well.

But I keep coming back to what the watch-seller said at that chestnut stall. I must have landed on this particular date for a reason. And as much as I'm dreading what this day will bring, I'm also eager to find out if I'll see something or hear something or remember something new. It happened in the maze, it happened at Mum's house: will it happen again here?

The best way to find out, I figure, is to live this day exactly as I did originally, and keep my eyes peeled for anything I might have missed.

With that in mind, muscle memory kicks in efficiently and I find myself mechanically retracing the steps I walked every weekday for three years. They take me to the bus stop at the end of the street, where I wait a few minutes for the 243 to arrive. When it does, I find a seat on the top deck, and slump my head against the juddering window as we start to weave our way slowly south through Bethnal Green. Garish Christmas decorations adorn pretty much every tree and lamp post and shopfront we pass: constant reminders of what tonight will bring.

I feel a buzz in my pocket, and take out the phone I didn't even realise was in there. It's an early iPhone, which to my 2020 eyes looks clunky and quite cute – like a kid's toy. There's a message glowing on the screen. It's from Daphne.

My stomach flips as I open it.

Hey, hope this eve is OK! I'm sure it'll be fine – will be thinking of you. Just see it as a field trip. It's research: you're like David Attenborough, observing the LAD in his natural environment. David Lad-enborough? Doesn't quite work. Anyway, see you later maybe, love you xx

I slide the phone back in my pocket and watch my breath fug and unfug the grimy bus window. It's so weird, thinking back to a time when Daff and I didn't live together. When I didn't see her every single day. Back then, the idea that I'd be meeting her after work, or getting to wake up with her, seemed like light at the end of the tunnel: a reward for getting through a tough day.

After uni finished, we both decided it was too soon – or maybe too boringly grown-up – to live together straight away. So I moved in with Harv, and Daff found a place in Balham with Jamila and some other mates. But about a year from now – at the end of 2011 – we will finally pool our meagre earnings and rent our first flat together: a poky little fifth-floor apartment in Shepherd's Bush.

As the bus winds its way down through Barbican, it all comes rushing back to me: the giddy thrill we felt picking up the keys from the estate agent; how amazing our first night there was. We sat giggling on the floor, surrounded by cardboard boxes, like kids playing at being adults. Which, to some extent, I guess we were. We watched *Dazed and Confused* on my laptop, and ate takeaway curry with plastic forks because neither of us owned any actual cutlery. It strikes me now that that night was probably one of my happiest ever. Back then, it felt like we could do anything together. Like we had it all ahead of us.

I scrub the fugged-up bus window with my sleeve and peer up at the towering brutalist buildings above me.

Yes, at this point in my life – the tail end of 2010 – everything still felt just about possible. For a start, I was finally writing for a living. Well, sort of. After months of desperately emailing and cold-calling magazine editors all over the country, and hearing nothing back, I'd spotted an advert for a newly launched lads' mag that was on the lookout for 'young 'n' hungry' staff. The magazine was called *Thump* – and from the brief description of it in the ad, it was clear that it was to be the kind of publication built predominantly around topless women, Jason Statham films and pictures of botched tattoos.

But I was pretty desperate by now – and sick to death of pub shifts and office temping – so I'd applied for a fortnight's work experience. I got it, and when it ended – to my immense surprise – I was offered the job of editorial assistant.

There was a fair amount of photocopying and note-taking and tea-making to be done, but I was also getting to do the odd bit of writing, as well. Mostly, though, my three years at *Thump* were spent trying desperately to ignore the near-constant stream of casually sexist and homophobic 'bants' that washed back and forth between the other staff members. A stream that tonight, at the Christmas party, will be in full flow.

Still, none of that really has anything to do with why today ended up being so terrible. No, the real terribleness was all down to that email. I try to remember now: what time did I receive it? It must have been late afternoon, I reckon. I spoke to Daphne just after it landed in my inbox, and everything just spiralled downwards from there. The idea of experiencing it all over again makes my stomach clench with dread.

The bus is approaching my stop now, and as I stand, I examine the ghost of my reflection in the window. I'm still insanely young-looking compared to my thirty-four-year-old self, but the four years I've just skipped over have definitely left their mark. There are the beginnings of two sharp lines at the edges of my mouth, and the skin around my eyes seems a little darker and looser than it was 'yesterday' in 2006.

I hop out at Holborn station and make my way through the back streets towards Covent Garden, past the theatres all decked out in festive red and gold. I find I can still perfectly recall the short walk to the office: a grubby, iMac-filled basement in a huge grey nondescript tower block.

I'm the first to arrive – it's 9.15, still early in media terms – and I sit down at my desk and switch on my computer. I have absolutely no idea what I'm supposed to be working on, and suddenly, the idea of muddling through a whole day in this office seems laughably impossible. I found it difficult enough to fit in at this job when I *wasn't* inexplicably travelling through time, so God knows how I'm supposed to interact with my colleagues with any degree of normality now. I resolve to just do exactly what I used to do: shut up and keep my head down.

There are a few documents scattered across my computer desktop, so I click on one at random. The headline screams: *FRANKENSTEIN'S WAG!*

Ah, yes. I remember this masterpiece quite clearly. A photo-montage feature in which the best body parts of the UK's top WAGs were cut-and-pasted together to create a Mary Shelley-inspired hybrid monster that would represent the Ultimate Footballer's Wife. Hallowe'en was a good six weeks ago, but our editor, Graham, hadn't let that stand in the way of such an outstanding and ground-breaking idea.

My job, I remember as I scan the Word document, was to write fifty words apiece for each selected body part. Half a dozen short, exclamation-mark-heavy odes to Cheryl Cole's lips, Danielle Lloyd's breasts, Louise Redknapp's legs, Abbey Clancy's buttocks, and so on.

I wince at the sentences in front of me, and close the file. Next to it on the desktop, though, is another one that makes me wince even harder.

There it is. My novel. Well, actually, 'novel' is probably being slightly too kind: it's more of a grotesquely bloated short story. There are forty-thousand-odd words in that document, and yet if you asked me what the actual plot was, I would struggle to tell you. I'd spent the last two years chipping away miserably at this pretentious, rambling mess, giving up countless nights and weekends when I could have been out having fun with Daphne or Harv.

Then, a couple of weeks prior to today, I finally got the nerve up to send it out to an agent. And later this afternoon, I will hear back from her.

I'm wondering if my stomach is strong enough to try reading a bit of it when a deep voice booms out behind me.

'Fuckin' hell, you're in early, mate. Or did you sleep here?'

Jonno – the features editor of *Thump*, the creative genius behind Frankenstein's WAG – stomps into the office, removing an expensive-looking pair of Oakleys, despite the fact that the sun is a no-show outside. Jonno is in his mid-thirties, with a shaved head and a permanently self-satisfied smirk. He's wearing combat trousers, a black parka jacket and a bright red Kasabian T-shirt.

'I'm all right, thanks,' I say. 'How are you doing?'

He nods. 'Yeah, chipper as fuck, mate. Chipper. As. Fuck.'

I'm guessing I've been in this job about six weeks at this point, but I'm still not entirely sure that Jonno knows my name yet. If I remember rightly, he tended to address me exclusively as 'mate', 'buddy' or, on special occasions, 'fella'.

He plonks himself down at his desk and starts removing various cables and wires and headphones from his rucksack. 'Had an early one last night in preparation for tonight's shenanigans,' he says, adopting a wonky Irish brogue on 'shenanigans'. Jonno speaks as if he's constantly hosting the Radio 1 Breakfast Show: loud and brash and irritatingly chirpy, with a strong Cockney inflexion despite originally hailing from Chichester.

'You're out with us tonight, right, buddy?' he asks me. 'Christmas piss-up?'

'Yeah, think so.'

'Oh, mate …' He runs a hand over his stubbly head. 'It's going to get messy. Trust me. Honestly, the girls at Archie's are absolute filth. Mingers, mostly, but they're up for anything.'

'Oh. Right. OK …'

Throughout my entire three years at *Thump*, I was never quite sure how to respond to comments like this. Obviously I didn't want to start spouting a load of sexist cobblers right back, but I also knew that saying I found these conversations at best mildly distasteful and at worst aggressively hateful would just result in being told: 'Chill out, mate, it's just a bit of banter!'

So for the most part I just used to stay quiet.

Jonno starts making himself a cup of tea, while launching into a long, powerfully depressing monologue about an unattractive stripper he'd encountered on a recent stag do. I'm guessing that when this story unfolded first time around, I just sat here laughing along and feeling like shit inside. But right now, I honestly can't deal with it. I used to tell myself that if I wasn't *actively* contributing to the belittlement of women or gay people or everyone who wasn't straight and male, then I could still consider myself a decent person. But in hindsight, you know you've got problems when you're employing the same case for the defence as a World War II collaborator. The truth is: I left this job in 2013 with a fair chunk of my self-confidence missing. And it was all because I didn't have the guts to stand up to a load of idiots.

Without offering any explanation, I get up and walk out

to the corridor. I'm suddenly hot with anger, and I have the worrying urge to boot the wall as hard as I can. The truth is, I was miserable here. Totally miserable. And my misery was compounded every day by the fact that I wasn't brave enough to quit. I suppose I was too scared of being broke again, back doing pub shifts and spending my nights endlessly trawling the *Guardian Jobs* website. I also thought – deep down – that this job might eventually lead to something more interesting if I stuck with it. It never did.

I take a deep breath and reach instinctively for the phone in my pocket. I think about calling Daphne, but I'm not sure if I'm ready to speak to her yet. I scroll through my contacts until I get to Harv, and before I can think what I might say to him, I'm dialling. He answers after one ring.

'Yo. What's up?'

'Nothing. Just … Sorry. Just calling to say hi, I guess.'

'Oh. Right.'

Calling to say hi is not something Harv or I have ever done in fifteen years of friendship.

'So … what are you up to?' I ask.

'Playing FIFA. Still reeling from last night.'

'Is Liv still there?'

'No, she's gone into the office, but I've got the day off. What are you up to?'

'I'm just …' I breathe out heavily and rub my eyes with the heel of my hand. 'I'm wondering what the hell I'm doing here, to be honest.'

'I thought you said the job was going all right?'

Had I said that? Probably. It's not like Harv and I were having any particularly deep or honest conversations at this point. I answer his question by outlining the basic premise of Frankenstein's WAG.

He snorts down the phone. 'Yeah. OK. Well, you're unlikely to win a Pulitzer for that. How detailed *is* this feature, though? Are we talking internal organs as well? Like, Victoria Beckham's small intestine?'

I laugh. 'Coleen Rooney's gall bladder.'

'Good name for a punk band.' I hear him shuffling about on the sofa. 'Look, honestly, man, don't worry about it. Obviously they're not your kind of people, but you're not gonna be there forever, are you? And we're twenty-four years old, for fuck's sake. We're not supposed to be sorted yet. Who's sorted at twenty-four?'

This strikes me as a pretty good point; one I wish I could've grasped properly at the time. But it stings a little when I remember that I will be even less sorted at *thirty*-four.

Still, though, this is the deepest conversation I've had with Harv in a long, long time. And it definitely didn't happen on this day originally. I feel a sudden rush of affection for him – my best mate, my future best man – and I wonder if I *can* actually change what's about to happen to him.

'Hey, so, Harv,' I say. 'You know Liv?'

'I'm aware of her work.'

'Well, I just … I dunno. This sounds a bit weird, but I wanted to say that I think you two should, sort of … take things a bit slowly.'

There's a long pause, and then the phone is flooded with laughter. 'Mate, what are you on about?'

'No, nothing, I just … She might not be as perfect as you think she is, that's all.'

'Have you *seen* her?'

'Yes, obviously she's very hot. But I'm just saying, maybe ...'

I kick at the carpet in frustration. I can't think of any way to do this without telling him the truth, which would obviously make me sound like an utter lunatic. I'm about to try another tack when he grunts and says, 'Look, I've got to go anyway, man. My toast's burning. But have fun tonight.'

The phone line rustles, and before he hangs up, he adds, 'Say hi to the naked ladies for me.'

Chapter Twenty

If there is a more depressing sight than a Christmas tree in a strip club, then I've yet to see it.

It sits there forlornly in the corner of the dark mirrored room, beside a stage on which a pneumatically breasted woman is grinding listlessly against a greasy pole. I'm not sure what it is about the tree's presence here that's so jarringly awful. Possibly the fact that everything Christmas is supposed to represent – family, love, kindness, joy – seems totally alien in a place like this, where blokes are essentially paying large sums of money to forget those concepts exist.

I've whiled away most of the day sitting silently at my desk, either moving exclamation marks around at random on Frankenstein's WAG or checking my phone to see if the agent's email has arrived (it hasn't). But now it's 4 p.m., and I am walking into Archie's Strip Club in Shoreditch with the ten other members of the all-male *Thump* team.

The overpowering blend of cocoa butter and sweat fills my nostrils as soon as we step past the bouncers. The Archie's design team have really gone all out on the Christmas theme in here: as well as the sorry-looking tree, there are also silvery scraps of tinsel draped across the L-shaped black leather sofas, green and red baubles dangling limply above the bar, and a few of the dancers are even wearing Santa hats.

This was my first visit to a strip club – the second came during a stag weekend for an old school mate a few years later – and I have to be honest, I still cannot see the attraction. I mean, obviously, objectively, it's nice to look at naked women. But doing it in a place like this requires a level of self-detachment – maybe even self-deception – that I just don't seem capable of.

In a weird way, I find it more interesting to watch the customers than the dancers. These hunched, baggy-faced men in bad suits, who still manage to look desperately unhappy while smiling. The horrible, hungry glint in their eyes that makes you feel vaguely ashamed to be the same gender.

We all walk past the bar, where five women in silky underwear are smiling coyly at us and attempting to make eye contact. I remember arguing the case once to Daphne that *this* is what men actually come to these places for: the feeling of being wanted. It's not really about the boobs and bums and simulated sex, I told her: it's about experiencing the simple, mind-blowing novelty of a beautiful girl trying to catch your eye. Because for the average bloke, that just does not happen in the real world.

I don't think Daff was convinced, to be honest. She just laughed and said that whatever the reason was, it was pathetic. Even so, she wasn't particularly angry about me coming here today. I think she just felt sorry for me because she realised how much I didn't want to go.

I think again about her David Attenborough text, and suddenly feel a very strong urge – a physical *need* – to see her.

I desperately want to turn around, walk straight back out of the door and go and find her. But Jonno thwacks me on the back and keeps me moving forwards.

The team flops down collectively onto one of the big oily couches next to the main stage. Jonno remains standing in front of us, chewing his bottom lip and gyrating his hips to 'Hot in Herre' by Nelly. The strip club is so clearly Jonno's natural environment that it's hard to believe he wasn't raised in one.

'Here we go, boys!' he shouts over the music. 'Here. We. Fucking. Go!'

'Shots?' someone else yells, but Jonno's already up at the bar ordering them, his arm snaked around a scantily clad redhead.

A very tall, Viking-esque woman wearing only a see-through nightie approaches me and squats down by the edge of the sofa.

'Would you like a dance?' she asks. Her accent is eastern European, and weirdly, even though I haven't thought about this moment in ten years, I remember her straight away.

'No, honestly, I'm fine, thanks,' I tell her, adding, 'I don't think I can afford it,' because it seems a simpler excuse than 'I'm ideologically opposed to it.'

She shrugs. 'You can just buy me a glass of champagne, and the dance will be free.'

'How much is a glass of champagne?'

'Forty-five pounds.'

'Right. No, thanks, honestly, I'm fine.'

First time round, I tried – unsuccessfully – to engage this woman in a highly patronising conversation about her hopes and dreams, and how she'd ended up in a place like this. It was partly to assuage my guilt about being here, but also – if I'm totally honest – probably to indulge some lame knight-in-shining-armour daydream, in which I could imagine my words compelling her to quit this awful job immediately and start flirting outrageously with me – but because she actually *wanted* to, not because I'd just bought her a glass of horrifically overpriced champagne. And let's face it, that makes me just as pathetic as every other bloke in here.

I don't bother with my patronising interrogation this time, so the Viking girl just wanders off to find another punter. I'm left sizing up my disgusting tequila shot and watching as Jonno and another *Thump* staff member get wriggled on by two near-naked blondes in front of me. Strangely, they seem to be looking at each other more than at the actual girls; swapping child-like grins and thumbs-ups every time a nipple comes within a few centimetres of their faces.

I feel a buzz in my pocket, and find myself hoping that it's Daphne. But it's not. It's an email from Clare Rodway, at Rodway Cohen Associates.

'Just got to check something,' I announce, standing up and waggling my phone about. But no one's paying the slightest bit of attention to me. I smile at the murderous-looking bouncers as I walk past them and step back out into the dying afternoon light on Shoreditch High Street.

The email is just as I remember it. I don't bother to read the whole thing, just scan it to make sure the general gist is the same. *Thank you so much for sending … Shows great promise, but unfortunately …* And then the killer blow at the end: *I think you're Patrick's son, is that right? Pat and I go WAY back, so I'll mention you next time I see him!*

I put the phone back in my pocket and think about how I reacted to this email first time round. Not well, is the answer. I felt utterly broken and desperate: like a total failure. Daphne called me as I stood outside this very club, and when I told her what had happened, she came straight back from work to meet me at my place. We then spent a dreary evening together dissecting what might have been wrong with my manuscript.

Now, looking back, I honestly find it hard to believe that I was such a jumped-up, overly melodramatic *dick*.

Like Harv said, I was only twenty-four years old. Did I honestly expect that the first thing I wrote would get published? Who the hell did I think I was?

The answer to that seems staggeringly obvious now. I thought I was my dad.

The first play he wrote was staged at the Young Vic theatre when he was twenty-four – though obviously I found that out from Wikipedia rather than him. And I suppose I thought … Well, what *did* I think? That if I performed the same trick, he might reach out to me? That he might get back in touch once he realised how similar we really were? I don't know. It sounds stupid, obviously. But despite him leaving, despite what he did to Mum, he's still my dad. I guess I always imagined that at some point we'd be close again. If I'm honest, I still do.

I watch the furry white sun disappearing gradually behind Liverpool Street station, and wonder for the zillionth time why all this is happening. I look down at my watch and find myself wishing that the watch-seller was here. He told me he'd see me again: 'I guarantee it.' Well, where is he now? There's so much more I need to know …

I unfasten the watch strap absent-mindedly, half expecting to be whizzed straight back to the present as soon as it's off my wrist. But nothing happens. On the back of the face, though, I spot something I didn't notice before. A block of worn-off lettering. An address: *15 Foster Road, Bloomsbury, WC1A*. That's central London …

An idea flashes into my head, but before I can properly weigh it up, my phone starts buzzing. I take it out to see Daphne's name flashing on the screen. Despite everything, I feel a burst of happiness as I slide my finger across to answer it.

'Hey,' I say.

'Hey! Just calling to see how your lads-lads-lads thing is going? Have you done a shot in your eyeball yet? Are you wearing fake breasts? Have you gaffer-taped someone to a lamp post?'

'Doing all three as we speak.'

'Excellent, glad to hear it.'

'I actually … Daff, I actually just got an email from that Clare Rodway woman.'

There's a pause, and then she says, 'Oh …?' And the hope that she fills that one syllable with is genuinely heartbreaking.

'Yeah, no, she said it wasn't for her in the end.'

There's a blustery crackle on the other end of the phone as Daff sighs heavily. 'Oh, Ben. I'm so sorry. Well, look … Do you want me to come round in a bit, and we can talk about it?'

The thought of ruining her evening all over again with my boring, self-pitying bullshit makes me actually wince with embarrassment. 'No, seriously, don't worry,' I tell her. 'I feel all right about it, you know. She was probably right to knock it back; I don't think it's very good after all. But it'd be great to see you tonight, if you still want to meet?'

'Yeah … OK,' she says, brightly. 'I've kind of got this work thing. But it'll be done by seven, I reckon.'

'What's the work thing?' About six months prior to this day, in summer 2010, Daff started in a junior role at the agency she still works for today, in 2020.

'It's nothing. Just, they do these Rising Star awards every year in the office, and this year they've kind of … chosen me.'

'Shit, *what*? Why didn't you tell me?' I'm racking my brains, but I have no memory of this. Yet it must have happened that same night; the night Daff spent listening to me bore on about my rejection email.

'Well, you've just been so caught up with all your book stuff,' she says. 'It's only a stupid in-house thing anyway. It doesn't mean anything.'

I feel myself flush with shame. She gave up this whole night – this awards ceremony – for me. Instead of being publicly honoured for being brilliant at her job, she chose to come home and comfort and support me when I was down. Words start clogging up my throat, rushing to get out.

'Daff … Fuck … OK, I'm sorry. I've been a selfish fucking idiot. This is *so* great! It's so exciting. Well done!'

'Ben, calm down,' she laughs. 'Like I say, it's not a big deal.'

'It's a massive deal! So, shall I come and meet you once it's all finished? I could be outside your office at seven?'

'Yeah, that sounds great. But can you leave your work thing? Won't it look bad?'

'I really, honestly don't care.'

She laughs again. 'OK. Cool. See you here at seven.'

I hang up the phone, suddenly feeling alive with purpose. Seven o'clock gives me just under three hours. Plenty of time to try and get some unanswered questions answered ...

I'm about to head off in search of the nearest Tube when Jonno steps outside, bringing with him a powerful stench of cocoa butter. The perspiration is glistening on his forehead as he grins at me and lights a cigarette.

'You had the right idea ducking out here, fella,' he says. 'I shit you not: there is a bird on that stage right now whose tits are literally down to her waist. Told you there were some munters in this place.'

'Jonno,' I say, before I lose my nerve. 'Obviously I can't change your weird, angry, backwards world view. But I would appreciate it if in future you saved your more mindlessly twattish comments until I was at least out of earshot.'

He stands totally still, staring at me, his cigarette dangling limply in his mouth. He looks like I've just punched him in the face, and for a second I wonder if that's now what he's about to do to me. But then he bursts out laughing, leaving a cloud of thick grey smoke floating between us. 'Chill out, mate!' he says. 'It was only a bit of banter.'

I walk off, feeling giddy at having scratched a ten-year-old itch, and head straight for 15 Foster Road, Bloomsbury.

Chapter Twenty-One

Harv takes a large bite out of his 12-inch Subway Meat Feast and stares at the block of terraced houses in front of us.

'Pretty weird place,' he says, finally.

As an architectural summary, it's bang on. While the other buildings on Foster Road are all identikit immaculate white rectangles, number 15 appears to have been dropped onto the street by mistake. It's a squat red-brick affair with an uneven roof and a precariously wonky chimney. It looks like one snaggled tooth in an otherwise perfect mouth.

'So …' Harv takes another chunk out of his sandwich. 'Why are we here again?'

I hold my wrist up. 'I told you: I bought this watch a couple of days ago, and it's not working. So I'm going to try and have a word with the guy who sold it to me.'

He nods. 'Right. And you need me here because …'

To be honest, I'm still not totally sure why I called him. I think I just wanted someone else with me. This is my first ever visit to what could potentially be a time-travelling watch outlet, and I figured it might be nice to have a bit of backup. Or at least a witness.

I point at the posh-looking tinsel-strewn pub across the

street. 'I thought we could get a pint after I've sorted my watch,' I say. 'Two birds with one stone.'

Harv shrugs and takes another bite. 'Fair enough.'

We walk up the little staircase and pause in front of the bright purple front door, its gold number 15 glinting in the dying sunlight. On the Tube over here, this seemed like a brilliant idea. But now the doubts are starting to creep in. I mean: what if this is just somebody's house? How will I even begin to explain what I'm doing here without sounding like a total lunatic?

It's only the building's strong Harry Potter vibe that's keeping my scepticism at bay. If I was a time-travelling watch salesman, this is *exactly* the kind of place I would live.

Harv looks over at me as I stand dithering on the doorstep. 'The normal procedure is to knock, man.'

He pounds the door three times with his non-sandwich hand.

For a few seconds, nothing happens. I almost feel relieved. I'm on the verge of suggesting we leave when suddenly I hear muffled footsteps, and the clunk of a heavy lock. And then a familiar scraggly-bearded face emerges.

'Ah!' The watch-seller beams. 'You found me, then!'

A minute later, Harv and I are sitting at the old man's kitchen table while he makes tea at the stove. And if I thought this place had a strong Potter vibe from the outside, then the inside makes it look positively conventional.

Wooden beams jut out at bizarre angles across the ceiling, and there are clocks covering almost every inch of the walls. They're all different shapes, styles, colours and sizes, and their combined ticking sounds like the hooves of a hundred tiny stampeding horses. Cogs and watch faces and straps and springs are scattered across the kitchen counters, nestled among dozens of notebooks and pieces of paper, all of them teeming with strange diagrams and illegible scrawls. Next to the old-fashioned stove, there's a sink big enough to bathe a St Bernard in, which sends out a howling clanking sound as the old man spins its rusty faucets. He is still wearing the same ill-fitting blue suit and reindeer tie, and his unruly copper-grey hair flaps wildly as he flits about taking mugs out of the cupboards. There's something *so* familiar about him.

Harv is gazing around the room, looking understandably bemused. 'So you … sell watches, do you?' he asks.

'Among other things.' The old man chuckles. 'In fact, I was selling chestnuts fairly recently.'

He shoots me a wink and I nod back, dumbly. Even though I was expecting to see him, that now-familiar sense of confusion and nervous excitement is thrumming once again in my chest. There's so much I need to ask him.

The old man plonks three mugs of tea down next to Harv's half-eaten sandwich, and settles in the chair opposite me. 'So, I told you we'd meet again, didn't I? What's on your mind this time?'

I look back at Harv, who's blowing the steam off his mug of tea as he stares around him. The idea of bringing him along now seems utterly, obviously insane. I mean, how am I supposed to have this conversation in front of him?

The watch-seller reads my mind. 'Don't worry about your friend here,' he says. 'Back in the present, he won't have any memory at all of this encounter taking place. It will be like it never happened.'

'Er … what was that, mate?' Harv says.

The watch-seller grins and glances down at Harv's belly. 'You've filled out a little since I last saw you.'

Harv's mouth forms the 'W' of 'what', but no sound comes out. Despite everything, I find I'm quite enjoying the novel sensation of not being the most bewildered person in the room.

'What is going on, Ben?' Harv demands. 'Seriously, who is this dude?'

The watch-seller answers for me. 'In the year 2020, I gave your friend here a wristwatch that allows him to revisit various moments in his past. He's reliving one of these moments right now, and I assume he's here because he wants my advice.'

Harv continues to stare at him blankly, his mouth a perfect straight line.

'It's true, Harv,' I find myself saying. 'It sounds mad, obviously …'

Harv sniffs and takes a gulp of his tea. 'Look, if you're both gonna be twats, I'll just go to the pub.'

I turn back to the old man. 'Will he really not remember this?'

The old man shakes his head.

'So, nothing I do in these moments will have any effect in 2020?'

'Not directly, no.'

'What. Is. Going. On?' Harv thumps the table with every word, making the mugs rattle. 'Is this some kind of prank? Are we being filmed or something?'

'Do you really not remember?' I ask him. 'When we talked about time travel, the night of Marek's play at uni? Before we played Sardines in the maze? You came with me to the

Drama Barn because I was so late. And before that, we talked about *Groundhog Day* in the kitchen.'

Harv narrows his eyes. 'No … that's not what happened, Ben. I only saw you later, after the play. And we definitely didn't talk about *Groundhog Day*. I would remember if we did, because I bloody love that film.'

The watch-seller nods. 'Great film.'

I try to process this new information. So, nothing I do in these revisited moments will be remembered by anyone but me? All this new stuff – Daphne getting to accept her award, us falling asleep together in my room the night of the play – it will be like none of it ever happened when – if – I finally get back to the present?

That means I can't change anything. I can't affect the future in any way. The Monopoly game with Mum flashes suddenly into my head. I had the idea that night that I might be able to stop what happens – that I might be able to stop her dying. And now I find out that I can't. A throb of anger surges through me.

'What's the point of all this if I can't actually change anything?' I mutter. 'Nothing I do here even matters!'

'On the contrary,' the old man says. 'It matters very much. Other people won't change as a result of all this, but *you* might.' He leans towards me, pressing the tips of his fingers together to form a triangle. 'Maybe you'll end up with a clearer understanding of what you really want.'

'Will I get back to the present eventually, then?' I ask.

He breathes out through his nose, and I see his moustache hairs wriggle. 'That's complicated. It … depends.'

This time it's me who thumps the table. 'Can you *please* stop being so bloody vague?!' I suddenly don't even care that

Harv is still here, staring at me as if I've completely lost my mind. 'I need to know why this is happening to me!'

The old man just sighs. 'You already know. Think back to that night in the pub: all the things you wanted to say to your friend here, but couldn't.'

'What things?' Harv snaps.

It all pours back into my mind: Mum, Daphne, Alice. The regrets I've managed to accumulate over the years. That terrifying feeling that my life had ground to a halt and I didn't know how to restart it.

'But why is this …' The words dry up, and I put my head in my hands. 'What am I supposed to do?'

'Just keep going,' the old man says softly. 'You'll get there. That's all I can tell you at this point. And now …' He looks up at one of the many clocks on the wall. 'You'd better be off. After all, you've got a date, if I'm not mistaken?'

His blue eyes twinkle at me again, and with a sudden jolt, I realise who it is he reminds me of: my grandad Jack. Mum's father.

He died when I was twelve, so my memories of him are pretty sketchy: mainly based around that faded photo in the hallway at Mum's house. But I do remember his hearty laugh, his bright blue eyes and his kind, crumpled smile: three things the watch-seller also possesses. His wild face fuzz makes it hard to pinpoint any further similarities, though: Grandad Jack was always clean-shaven.

The old man stands up from the table. 'Time to go,' he says. 'But don't worry: I'll see you again.'

*

Harv and I stand blinking on the doorstep of 15 Foster Road. It's dark now, and the street lights are flickering on, sending our shadows stretching down the steps to the pavement.

'So,' Harv says, 'whenever you're ready to explain what the hell just happened, I'm all ears.'

I puff my cheeks out. 'He's, erm … he's a theatre bloke. Immersive theatre. My editor at *Thump* is thinking about interviewing him for the mag, and he wanted me to go along and check him out first. So you were sort of our guinea pig. Hope you don't mind.'

Harv scratches his nose as he takes this in. 'Right. OK. Well, I wouldn't bother with the interview. He was rubbish. It didn't make any sense. You were quite good, though.' He thumps me on the back. 'You've definitely come a long way since Marek's play.'

I laugh.

'I was genuinely freaked out back there for a second,' he adds. 'You're lucky I've just hooked up with the hottest girl on the planet, or else I'd be pretty pissed off with you right now.'

He can't help grinning as he says it, and it breaks my heart. I look at him – my best mate – standing on the threshold of a relationship that's going to snap him in two. That's going to bend him out of shape and change him completely. And now I know there's nothing I can do about it. I can warn him, but it won't make one bit of difference. No matter what I tell him in this moment, things will turn out exactly the same.

'I'm sorry about earlier,' I say. 'On the phone. What I said about Liv. I'm happy that you're happy.'

He nods, and I carry on. 'I just … Whatever's going to happen will happen. But I want you to know that I'll always be here for you, man. I promise.'

I'm not quite sure why, but at that moment I pull him towards me into a tight hug. I feel his body tense up in my grip. But then he laughs and squeezes me back.

'All right, cheers, man. Bit weird, but ... cheers.'

We break out of the hug, and he points at the pub across the road. 'So, what you saying, then? Pint?'

I look down at my watch, forgetting that it's frozen. One minute to midnight: that's when this day will disappear forever. But I can't think of a better way to spend the next hour than by reconnecting with my pre-heartbreak, pre-Ryan-Gosling-six-pack best mate.

'Yeah, why not?' I tell him. 'I've got time for a quick one before I go and meet Daphne.'

Chapter Twenty-Two

It's just after seven, and I'm standing in the middle of Soho holding a huge bunch of red tulips.

I'm pretty much clueless when it comes to flowers, so I've chosen these purely because they were Mum's favourite. But now, as I stand here opposite Daphne's office, on what might be the busiest corner in central London, I'm starting to realise that as romantic gifts go, flowers are actually incredibly impractical. The delicate red bulbs are being constantly knocked this way and that by the shoulder-barging throng of pedestrians storming past me. There is no way these things are going to survive the whole evening.

Still, it's the thought that counts, isn't it? Hopefully.

Because midway through my pint with Harv, I made a decision. I decided that even though I don't know what will happen in the future – even though I don't know if Daff and I are really meant for each other – I can still make tonight right. In the real world, I ruined this special evening for her with my own stupid self-pity. So at least, in this alternate reality, I can try and make up for that. I can give her the night she deserved – even if she'll never remember it.

The revolving doors start spinning and I see Daff emerging

from the building with a few other people behind her. They all seem in pretty high spirits: laughing and back-slapping and hugging goodbye. I can see from here that Daff is clutching a chunky glass block that must be her Rising Star award. I give her a wave from across the crawling traffic, and she waves back, grinning.

The four years we've just skimmed over seem to have done nothing at all to her face; she looks just as young and fresh and happy as she did back in 2006. She's wearing a smart dark blue shirt and tight black velvet skirt; and weirdly, I remember the outfit exactly from this night ten years ago. When she arrived at my flat, my first thought was to ask what she was so dressed up for. But then my own selfish problems squeezed that question straight back out of my head.

They must have given her the award the next day, as she muttered some excuse about why she hadn't been able to stick around. I clasp the tulips tighter as I feel yet another spasm of resentment towards my egotistical twenty-four-year-old self.

Daff is walking across the road now, doing a mock-overwhelmed are-those-for-*me*? mime as she spots the flowers, which get even more crumpled as I pull her into a hug.

'Well done! Daff, this is so great.'

'Thank you.' She breaks out of the hug and smells the tulips. 'And thanks for these.'

'They're already pretty much destroyed. Sorry about that.'

'No, don't worry. They're beautiful.'

She's smiling from ear to ear and her flushed cheeks suggest she's already had one or two celebratory drinks. She looks amazing.

'So, what happened, then?' I ask. 'I want the full details.'

'Well, it was all pretty embarrassing, really. I had to get up and make a speech and everything.'

'I hope you went full Gwyneth Paltrow?'

'Oh yeah. I was weeping, dedicating it to my parents, thanking God ... No, I just mumbled "Cheers for this" and then ran straight back to the wine.'

I take the award off her, feeling its weight. 'Seriously, this is so brilliant, Daff. Well done. I can't believe you didn't tell me.'

She shrugs. 'It's not that big a deal. You know I've been out seeing tons of plays lately, and I mentioned a couple of the playwrights to Sarah, and she's ended up taking them on as clients. So I guess they think I'm showing some promise, or whatever.' I can almost hear the speech marks around 'showing some promise'. Daff has always been so modest. Too modest.

I hand the award back. 'You're doing absolutely amazing.'

She frowns at me. 'Are you *sure* you're OK about that email? You're being a bit weird about it. I thought you'd be a lot more upset, to be honest.'

'So did I. But as it turns out ... I'm not.'

She nods back towards her office. 'You know, I could always give your book to the fiction team at work. They could take a look at it.'

'No, honestly. I don't want to talk or think about the book at all tonight. I just want us to do something fun' – I tap the award – 'to celebrate this.'

'Something fun,' she repeats. And then her eyes sparkle and her mouth twists up at the corner. 'I can think of something fun.'

Half an hour later, we are sitting in the cheapest of cheap seats in the Leicester Square theatre, our view partially obscured by a concrete pillar, watching a man I vaguely recognise from *EastEnders* scamper across the stage dressed as Aladdin.

'I cannot believe this is your first ever pantomime,' Daff whispers, her mouth half full of Revels. 'I should report your mum to social services.'

'I can't believe this *isn't* your first pantomime,' I say, as the *EastEnders* guy gets his cheeks tweaked by Widow Twankey, being played here by the orange bloke off *Bargain Hunt*.

'Dad used to take us every year when we were little,' Daff says, passing me the chocolates and taking a sip of her beer. 'Family tradition.'

'Since when is Widow Twankey Aladdin's mum?' I ask.

She rolls her eyes. 'Since forever.'

'They don't even look alike. Plus, Twankey doesn't sound like a particularly Arabic surname.'

'You know, Ben,' she deadpans, 'I'm not sure that realism was at the forefront of the production team's mind here.' With perfect timing, a former *Big Brother* runner-up covered entirely in blue paint emerges from a giant smoking lamp in front of us.

'If only your colleagues could see you now,' I say, smiling. 'The great Rising Star, eating Revels and watching Ian Beale run around in a pair of MC Hammer trousers.'

She elbows me in the ribs. 'Oi! I love panto. Best thing about Christmas. Just because something's considered lowbrow doesn't mean it can't also be brilliant and fun and entertaining.' She laughs. 'Hey, d'you remember, I had pretty much this exact argument with Marek on the night we met?'

'Yeah,' I say. 'I do, vividly.' We join the audience in col- lectively alerting Ian Beale to the fact that someone is behind him.

Daff is giving the stage her full attention now, but her mention of the night we met – the night I've only just relived – makes me want to double-check what the watch-seller told me. 'Hey, so you recall that night,' I say. 'The play at uni?' She nods, her eyes still fixed on the stage. 'Do you remember when I forgot my lines? And you had to go and find me a script?'

She turns to me. 'No I didn't. Did I?'

'Yeah ... And I totally fluffed it when I was on stage? Forgot to shoot Marek?'

She's looking at me like I've gone mad. 'No ... I'm pretty sure that's not what happened, Ben.'

'Oh, OK. Doesn't matter. Maybe I've remembered it wrong.'

She turns her attention back to the panto, still frowning slightly. So it's definitely true, then. Nothing I do here has any knock-on effect whatsoever.

I try to work out how all of this makes me feel, but before I can come to any definite conclusion, Daff nudges me gently in the ribs. 'Benjamin. Too cool for audience participation?'

I snap out of it, and smile at her. And then I'm yelling, 'Oh yes you have!' along with everyone else.

Chapter Twenty-Three

It's pitch dark and freezing by the time we troop out of the theatre.

The Revels and beers have sharpened our appetites, so we stroll through Covent Garden hand in hand in search of a place to eat. Daff has the flowers poking out of her backpack like some strange alien antennae. I'm carrying the award for her, occasionally holding it up to random passers-by and announcing, 'Rising Star coming through,' before she slaps my hand down. As we wander towards the river under the never-ending cascade of Christmas lights, everything feels absolutely right with the world.

It strikes me suddenly that this is the complete opposite of our last theatre trip together. That was a total and utter disaster.

It was on September 25th, 2020: Daff's thirty-third birthday. We'd gone to see one of her clients' new plays at the Lyric Theatre. It was only a few weeks after Marek's wedding – after I kissed Alice (or Alice kissed me) in that photo booth. My head was still swimming with that moment: guilt and regret mingling with daydreams of what life would have been like if Alice and I had actually got together. All mixed in with a side helping of dark thoughts about my non-starting career, and even darker thoughts about Mum. I got sulky when Daff left me on my own to go and chat to Rich at the after-show drinks, and when it was just the two of us later, at dinner, things got even worse. We spent the entire three courses snapping at each other, and at the end of the night, Daff sighed heavily as we stood up and said, 'Well, thanks, Ben. This has *definitely* been a memorable birthday.'

Looking at her now as she bounces alongside me, so happy and carefree, it's impossible to imagine that we'll turn into that couple one day. And it might be the alcohol swimming to my head, but I can't help thinking: maybe I should just forget that we will. Maybe, just for tonight, I should forget about the future, and all the shit that will come with it, and try to make the next few hours as perfect as they can possibly be.

When we get down to the Thames, we find that a festive-themed cluster of food vans have been set up next to Waterloo Bridge. I buy two large turkey baps packed with smoking hot stuffing and cranberry sauce, and two paper cups full of steaming cinnamon-laced mulled wine.

Daff and I sit on a bench eating and drinking, huddled together for warmth, and even though we've been going out in this reality for nearly five years, it honestly feels like a first date. A really, *really* good first date.

I tell her about waking up this morning and seeing Harv and Liv in our kitchen, and how worried I am about it all going wrong between them. Daff just shrugs and says, 'Yeah, well, what can you do? Have you actually said anything to him?'

'Yeah, I sort of did on the phone earlier. I don't think he wants to listen. But I just *know* she's wrong for him.'

She swallows a bite of her sandwich. 'How do you know? You can't *know* someone's wrong for someone.'

'Why not? You can know someone's *right* for someone.' I'm not sure where this comment comes from, but clearly Daff thinks it's about us, because she leans into me and says, 'Smoooooth.'

A brightly coloured boat full of loud pissed people in tuxedos and ball gowns floats slowly past us on the river. When it's finally out of earshot, Daff turns to me and says, 'I think I knew you were right for me pretty much straight away.'

I look at her. 'Seriously? How come?'

She shuffles even closer to me on the bench. 'Because I couldn't stop thinking about you.' I laugh involuntarily at that, as it's the sort of statement you tend to hear in films rather than in real life. But Daff just shrugs and continues. 'I know it sounds cheesy, but honestly, it's true. D'you remember our first date?'

'What, at the cinema?'

She nods, and the memory comes trickling back. After that night in the maze, I spent the entire Christmas holidays moping about at home, wondering if I should text her, wondering why she hadn't texted me, and generally counting the days until uni restarted and I'd be able to bump into her. And then, two days into the new term, I did bump into her. We chatted for a while outside the library, and she mentioned that she fancied seeing that Keira Knightley *Pride & Prejudice* film that had just come out. Seeing my chance, I told her I was desperate to see it too, and, hey, why didn't we go together?

'I took the bus into town to meet you at that pub first, d'you remember?' she says. 'And it sounds weird because we'd only actually met once at that point, but I'd thought about you a lot over the holidays, and I was really nervous about seeing you again. So I started daydreaming on the bus, thinking about that kiss in the maze, and what might happen tonight. And in the end, I got so caught up in these stupid daydreams that I completely missed my stop.' She breaks off and laughs into the steam rising from her cup. 'I ended up in Clifton bus depot. That's when I knew you were probably more than just a crush.'

I'm laughing now too, and despite the bitter cold, I can feel a warm glow spreading gradually through my body. 'So *that's* why you were late that night?' I say. 'You told me your washing machine flooded!'

'Well, what was I supposed to say? "Sorry I'm late for our first date; it's just that I was thinking so hard about you I ended up in a different town." I didn't want to come across as a total psychopath.'

I shake my head. 'I remember getting so stressed in that pub, waiting for you. I genuinely thought you weren't going to show. The barman even gave me a free half-pint because he assumed I'd been stood up.'

'What?' She nudges my elbow with hers. 'You told me you'd arrived late as well! You said, and I quote: "Don't worry, I've only just got here myself."'

'I was trying to play it cool! I got there bang on time. I think I was even early.'

She laughs and takes a sip of mulled wine. 'Well. It's all coming out now. What a revelation.'

'Yeah,' I say, 'and here's another one for you: I'd already seen the film. My mum dragged me along over the Christmas holidays.'

'You're joking?' She purses her lips in mock-outrage. 'So why did you pretend you hadn't seen it?'

'Because you wanted to see it. And I wanted to see you.'

She sighs and leans into me, linking her arm through mine. 'So underhanded. So deceitful.'

'So *romantic* would be another way of looking at it.'

'True,' she says. 'True.'

We sit for a while in silence, watching the boats drift by lazily on the river. And even though I'm not speaking, my heart is galloping like mad, because that first-date story has set something running, and my mind is suddenly alive with memories of all these fun, silly, happy times in our relationship that I honestly haven't thought about in years. Ever since Mum died, it's like all these moments have wilted away, as if they never even existed. And now, sitting here on this bench – feeling that strange warm glow spread right to the tips of my fingers – it's like a door reopening. It's like light flooding back in.

Daphne tucks a stray curl behind her ear and smiles up at me. Without thinking, I say: 'I love you, Daff.'

Because here, in this moment, it feels true. It *is* true. I love her so much. But what am I supposed to do? I know how we'll be ten years from now – bitter, unhappy, arguing the whole time. So how *can* we be right for each other? When it comes down to it, aren't we just as wrong as Harv and Liv?

'I love you too,' she says, nuzzling into my shoulder.

'Daff, can I ask you something?'

'Yeah?'

'Why do you put up with me?' She laughs at that, but I keep going. 'No, I mean, seriously. I've been such a dick lately, about all the book stuff. Or maybe I've been a dick the whole time we've known each other. But either way—'

She tilts her chin up and kisses me gently on the mouth. 'You haven't been a dick …' she kisses me again, 'the whole time.' She tastes of cranberries and chocolate and cinnamon, and it's a delicious combination. 'The thing is, Ben,' she says, 'I'm in love with you. And don't get me wrong: I'm not happy about it. I'd rather be in love with someone who was less of a twat. But unfortunately I don't have much choice in the matter. I fell in love with you, and now you're stuck with me whether you like it or not.'

Later – much later – we're lying in bed, in Daff's tiny shared flat in Balham.

She's on her side, snoring lightly, and I'm snuggled right up against her warm bare back, my naked body curved neatly around hers.

And still that sentence keeps running over and over in my brain. *I fell in love with you, and now you're stuck with me whether you like it or not.* I can't get it out of my head. The firework of happiness that shot through me when she said it. I remember something else, too; something Mum said during that Monopoly game yesterday. *All that matters right now is: do you make each other happy?*

Right now, I feel the happiest I've felt in a very, very long time. I honestly think Daff does, too.

All I wanted to do tonight was to make up for what happened on this evening first time around. To change my memory of it from a grim, shameful one to a good one. And I think I've done that. But I never planned to end the day like *this*.

I never imagined that after the long, rumbling Tube journey south, Daff would close her bedroom door and kiss me so passionately, so hungrily. And that I would feel my whole body pulse with excitement because I knew *exactly* what was going to happen next ...

I can't even remember the last time we had sex back in 2020. And whenever it was, it definitely wasn't like this. I forgot we could be like this together. I forgot that we fit so perfectly, that I can lose myself so completely in the moment with her.

And now she's lying fast asleep beside me, and I can feel exhaustion weighing down on me too. There's no clock on her wall, and my phone is somewhere in the jumble of clothes on the floor, so I have no idea how much longer I have here. But it must be nearly midnight by now.

At any second I'll find myself somewhere else, on some other date. Maybe I'll even be back in 2020.

But God, I wish I could stay here. Just for one more day.

I nuzzle further into Daff's neck, and she murmurs softly. For her, it will be like this night never happened.

But as I lie here next to her, I know that I'll never forget it.

Chapter Twenty-Four

Dear Ben,

(That felt quite formal, didn't it? 'Dear Ben'. But then this whole writing-a-letter thing is weirdly formal anyway. So what the hell, I'm sticking with it. I'm owning it. DEAR BEN.)

I know we said no messaging and no speaking over these next few months, but we never said anything about no letter-writing. And we definitely didn't say anything about no Christmas cards. And since this is very obviously a Christmas card (see reindeer picture on front), that means I'm not technically breaking any rules, am I?

So: Merry Christmas! I hope this actually gets to you in time for Christmas Day. As I write, it is December 17th in New York, so SURELY that's enough time, even if the entire French postal service is on strike. Which — let's be honest — they probably are.

How is Paris, anyway? Is your French still sub-GCSE level? Have you figured out when to say 'tu' and when to say 'vous'? Everything is OK my end. I am basically a native New Yorker these days – I live solely on pretzels and always shout 'I'M WALKING HERE!' every time I step into a road. But no, seriously, it is fun. The work is hard, but it's really interesting and I'm getting to meet lots of new people. I definitely think it was the right thing to come here.

I really hope you're OK out there. I hate to think of you all alone on Christmas Day. I hope you're doing something fun.

I don't know why I'm writing, really. I suppose it's just to say that I miss you. A lot, actually. But I still think it's a good thing that we're spending this time apart. I keep thinking about what you said after Jamila's wedding. It really freaked me out, because we've been together nearly ten years now and I guess I thought we wanted the same things in the long run.

But maybe we don't. I know that sounds horrible, but

I stop reading then, and lay the card back down on the table.

I'm not sure I need to reread the whole thing. I'm not sure I'm up to it.

Instead, I sip my bitter machine-made coffee and stare out over the rusty iron railing of the tiny eighth-floor balcony.

Opposite me, squatting solemnly under the cold, cloudless blue sky, are the huge white domed towers of the Saint-Sulpice church. The bells inside them are ringing loudly again now, sending clouds of pigeons fluttering out of the trees below.

It was those same bells that exploded around me an hour ago, as I sat up to see that Daff had disappeared, and I was definitely not in Balham any more.

My stomach lurched sickeningly when I realised where I was – *when* I was – but maybe, somewhere in the back of my mind, I always knew this might be one of the moments I would revisit. Even though I won't actually see Daff today – there's currently about three thousand miles and the Atlantic Ocean between us – what's about to happen changed everything.

I pick up my coffee cup and lean over the railing, looking down on the square below. From up here on the eighth floor of number 39 Rue Étienne Marcel, the whole of Paris sprawls out in front of me, its spires and chimneys and iron roofs looking postcard-perfect. Down in Place Saint-Sulpice, tourists wrapped in long coats and thick scarves are milling about cheerfully around the edge of the huge three-tiered fountain, or taking selfies in front of the giant Christmas tree behind it.

Four years have flown by in the blink of an eye, and now I'm here: 25 December 2014. A day I've spent the past six years trying to forget, sometimes because of burning regret, other times because I feel guilty at how much I enjoyed it.

Last night is still so clear in my head. I just wanted one more day there, in that reality. But no: from the happiest moment I can remember with Daphne in a long, long time, I've been dumped here, right into the thick of one of our worst, bleakest, most desperate periods. A period in which – technically – we weren't even together.

I swallow the last grainy dregs of coffee, and look back down at the card. One sentence jumps straight out at me, making my skin prickle with guilt: *I hate to think of you all alone on Christmas Day.*

Whatever I was on this day originally, I definitely wasn't alone.

I pick the card up and step back inside the tiny, freezing

apartment. The bare parquet floorboards squeal irritably beneath my feet, and I can hear muffled yells from the married couple upstairs. I wonder what it is about the French language that makes even bickering sound eloquent.

I slump back down onto the iron-framed single bed and stare up at the ceiling. And all I can think is: what the *hell* am I doing here?

First time around, the answer to that question was pretty straightforward. That stupid argument after Jamila's wedding.

It happened a few months before today, in August 2014. Daff and I were both a bit pissed, coming back from the reception on the Tube, and she made some innocuous comment about 'when *we* get married …' And without thinking, I blurted out the truth: I wasn't sure I'd ever want to.

It seems mad now that we'd never had that conversation before. But even though we'd been going out nearly a decade by then, we were still only twenty-eight. We were still so young.

The argument was all my fault, as usual, because I didn't explain myself properly. I just grunted and shrugged and said I didn't really see what the point of getting married was. 'It's a waste of money … It's just a piece of paper' – all that sort of rubbish. Because the real reason felt too stupid and childish to admit: that ever since my dad left, marriage had been clearly marked as A Bad Thing in my head.

I'd lost count of the times I'd come back from school to find Mum sobbing at the kitchen table, or overheard her crying on the phone to her friends at night, and thought to myself: I'm never getting married.

I guess deep down, I was terrified it would flick some

invisible switch inside me. That the minute a ring was on my finger, I would turn into a cheat, just like my dad had.

But of course, I didn't tell Daff any of that: I thought it would make me sound weird and screwed-up and weak. So instead, I clammed up. I let her think it was about her, rather than me and my parents and my stupid, muddled brain.

Basically, I took her for granted, just like I always do. And then, a month or so later, she told me about New York – how she'd been offered the chance to spend six months working in her agency's Manhattan office – and suggested that maybe we should use that time to 'take a break'. Not split up, exactly, but not stay together, either. Just spend some time apart, with no contact, and have a think about what we really wanted.

So that's what I was supposed to be doing here. Thinking. Not making a mistake that still keeps me awake at night six years later.

But then ... *was* it a mistake? The watch-seller told me to think about why I'm revisiting these particular moments. Over the past couple of years, as things have gone from bad to worse between me and Daphne, I've thought about this one a lot. I've always wondered what would have happened if I'd stayed in Paris, instead of running straight back to London ...

With comically perfect timing, the intercom screams out by the door. I sit bolt upright in bed, and my stomach begins to squirm. She's here.

I get up and walk across the flat, the floorboards complaining noisily beneath me again. I pick up the little plastic phone by the door, and a female voice speaks.

'*Joyeux Noël!* Are you ready to go?'

Chapter Twenty-Five

I am not, as it turns out, ready to go. In fact, I am nowhere near.

I am wearing only a hoodie and a pair of Queens Park Rangers pyjama bottoms. And my heart is suddenly hammering so hard I can feel it in my legs.

'*Joyeux Noël!*' I splutter into the intercom. And then: 'Er … Can you just give me ten minutes?'

'OK,' she says. 'I'll be in that café across from the church.'

I open the wardrobe and start pulling on clothes, my chest clenched with the anticipation of what's to come. What am I supposed to do here? It's not like I can change what originally happened. So what is the point of coming back – just to remind me what might have been? To set me on a path I've often wished I could've explored further?

By the time I'm fully dressed, these questions are still pinballing around my brain, resolutely unanswered. I give my face a sizeable cold-water splash, and then sprint down the eight creaky flights of stairs. I shoulder-barge the huge courtyard door, and step out into the freezing fresh air. The Saint-Sulpice church bells are at it again, singing out into the clear blue sky, sending another flock of pigeons spiralling upwards towards the summit of the giant Christmas tree. The stark, cold sunlight bounces off the crunchy brown carpet of leaves on the ground. The whole square looks idyllic.

And then, across the street, sitting at an outside table sipping something warm, I spot her.

She's wearing a long, stylish dark brown coat, and a scarf that's almost completely obscured by her thick chin-length hair. It's a blonde version of that bob Audrey Tautou had in *Amélie*, and it suddenly strikes me as perhaps the Frenchest hairstyle in existence.

The waiter approaches her and she smiles up at him. Dark eyebrows, dirty-blonde hair and deep-red lips: dramatic flashes of colour on her otherwise pale heart-shaped face.

For a second, I think about just turning and walking away. I don't know what to do.

But then she spots me, and beckons me over, just like she did at Marek's wedding. And before I know it, I'm at the table.

'Hey, Alice.'

'Hey!'

She stands and offers me her cheek to kiss. The scent of her perfume wraps itself around me like a flowery headlock. '*Ça va?*' She nods behind me, at my apartment block. 'Ben, I can't believe you live *right* on the square. You know this is, like, one of the poshest parts of Paris?'

'I know …'

'How did you find this place?'

'My mum,' I tell her. 'It's her friend's flat. A very loaded friend. He's away for four months, so I'm house-sitting.'

Alice raises an eyebrow. 'Bloody hell, you're so lucky.'

She's right, really: I was. This whole Paris thing was Mum's idea in the first place. She didn't react well to the news that Daphne and I were taking a break ('That girl's the best bloody thing that's ever happened to you' were her exact words). And so, when this Saint-Sulpice flat-sitting opportunity came up, she practically insisted I take it. It would be a breath of fresh air, she said: a chance to properly clear my head and come to my senses, instead of rattling around our London flat on my own while Daphne was off in New York.

It seemed like a good idea. And since I was freshly unemployed at the time – *Thump* having folded, unceremoniously, in April – I even got it into my head that I could live out a clichéd writer-in-Paris fantasy here: spend four months having another crack at penning something that was actually publishable.

That was the plan, then: write a masterpiece while re-evaluating my relationship. Simple. But then I bumped into Alice, and that simple plan became *much* more complicated.

She sips her hot chocolate, and reaches into her bag for a packet of Gauloises. At uni, she only ever smoked roll-ups, and I remember being quite impressed at how sophisticated – how *French* – she seemed to have become.

'So,' she says, lighting a long, thin cigarette. 'Are we doing today in English or in French? You did say you needed to practise. *On pourrait au moins essayer?*'

'Erm … *Je* …' I give up instantly. This whole situation is confusing and surreal enough in my native language. There's no way I can possibly stagger through this minefield of a day in French. 'Sorry … can we just stick with English for the moment?'

She sighs in mock disappointment. 'Honestly, Benjamin. Call yourself a Parisian?'

I can't help laughing. 'Not really, no.'

'Well, you've only been here three months, I suppose,' she says, ashing her cigarette. 'Give it time.'

'You've been here, what ... two years now?'

She wrinkles her brow. 'A year and a half. I told you last week.'

'Yeah. Sorry. You did.'

She takes another long drag on her cigarette as she looks at me. 'I still can't believe you're here, Ben. That we're here together, on Christmas Day. It's mad.'

As I meet her eyes, I feel a flicker of the excitement I felt on this day originally. 'Yeah. It really is.'

It was four days earlier that I'd bumped into her. I was sitting outside another café in the Marais, trying to cure my crippling writer's block by taking my laptop out of the apartment for once. But all I could focus on were the irritated glares the waiter was throwing me, possibly due to the fact that I'd only ordered one small coffee in four hours. I was on the brink of calling it a day, snapping my MacBook shut and heading home, when I heard a familiar voice from across the street.

'No way ... Ben!'

I looked over, and there she was. Alice from uni.

I hadn't seen her since we'd left York in 2008. We'd been so close during that first term, but once I started seeing Daphne, we'd gradually drifted further and further apart. By third year, we would barely even exchange a nod if we passed each other on campus.

But the truth is: I still thought about her. As the years passed, I checked in on her Facebook from time to time – which was pretty pointless, really, as she barely ever posted. I'd seen she was working for some big-time marketing company, but she hadn't mentioned anything online about living in Paris. So when I saw her across that street, grinning from ear to ear and looking even hotter than I remembered, the shock quickly gave way to heart-pounding excitement.

I guess it was partly because I was having such an awful time at that point. I was missing Daphne like mad and getting zero work done, in a city where I knew literally no one. I was lonely and confused and miserable, and suddenly here was a friendly face I hadn't seen in years.

The odds of randomly bumping into her must have been millions to one. It felt like fate.

It still does.

The waiter approaches our table, tapping his notepad with a pencil.

'*Bonjour, monsieur. Qu'est-ce que vous voudriez?*'

I clear my throat and decide to have a go at wheeling out my rusty French. '*Oui, bonjour. Er, je voudrais un chocolat chaud aussi, s'il vous plaît.*'

He smirks and rolls his eyes. 'Do you want whipped cream?'

'*Non, pas pour moi,*' I say, refusing to cave in.

'What about marshmallows?'

'*Non, pas de …*' I look at Alice.

'*Guimauves,*' she says, smiling.

'*Pas de guimauves pour moi,*' I tell the waiter firmly.

'OK, one hot chocolate, no whipped cream, no marshmallows, coming up.'

'What am I doing wrong?' I ask as he walks away. 'No matter how hard I try, they always reply in English.'

'Your accent's a giveaway,' Alice says. 'Even when you speak French, you still sound like Hugh Grant.'

'How come you've nailed it so perfectly? You sound like Thierry Henry.'

She laughs and her Amélie hair bounces gently above her shoulders. '*Merci beaucoup. Je vais prendre ça comme un compliment.*'

God, she looks good.

It's all coming back to me now: how knocked out I was to see her again. She had changed so much since uni. Not in looks, particularly, but in the way she carried herself. She was more confident, more self-assured. At York she'd been funny and outgoing, but there was always an air of self-consciousness about her. Even when she flirted with me, I could sense it was slightly guarded; she'd hold just enough back for it to not be awkward when nothing happened. Maybe that was why we never got it together at uni – neither of us was bold enough to make the first move.

Whereas now – here in 2014 – she's like a different person. I remember thinking at the time that it must have something to do with her new job. She told me all about it in that first café – how she'd seen off four other colleagues to get this promotion to her company's Paris office. She didn't mention money, but I remember sensing that she was probably earning truckloads. Despite knowing nothing about fashion, I can tell that her clothes must have cost an arm and a leg.

She had transformed from this self-deprecating hoodie-clad girl I used to cook sausage sandwiches with to a Gauloises-smoking businesswoman who could speak fluent French with a ridiculously sexy accent.

And, honestly, it knocked me for six.

I suddenly realise that I am openly staring at her. But rather than looking away, embarrassed, like the old Alice probably would have, she's looking right back at me, with a wide smile on her face. I snap out of it and feel my cheeks start to redden as I glance down at the pavement. 'So, what's the plan for today?' I ask, just to fill the silence. 'Are you going to show me how real Parisians do Christmas?'

I can remember precisely what the plan for today is. Every single step. And the thought of how it ended first time around makes my skin prickle. I can't even tell if I'm excited or anxious. Probably both.

'Oh, I've got it all laid out, don't worry,' Alice says, finishing her hot chocolate. 'I've sorted a full Christmas itinerary for us.'

She turns her smile up a notch, and as she shifts her feet under the table, I feel her ankle brush against mine. I smile back, and try to remember exactly what I was feeling at this moment six years ago.

I was missing Daphne something rotten – I know that for certain. But if I'm brutally honest, I was also enjoying the feeling of flirting with this new, confident Alice.

Maybe it was because Daff and I had been together nearly a decade at this point, so nothing felt exciting or new. Or maybe it had been starting to dawn on me back then that I was twenty-eight years old, and yet I'd only slept with two women: Daff and The Ghastly Tish. Harv, on the other hand, had just split up with Liv, and was masking his obvious unhappiness by waking up in a different bedroom every morning, thanks to a newly launched app called Tinder. Maybe that's another reason why the marriage conversation had freaked me out so much. I was wondering if I should have woken up in a few more bedrooms.

Despite all that, though, spending Christmas Day with Alice was not something that had even crossed my mind until she had suggested it four days earlier at that first café.

She'd joined me at my table, and within minutes, we'd slipped effortlessly back into our first-term banter. It was strange how easy and comfortable it felt: as if we were picking up exactly where we'd left off nine years ago.

We spent an amazing hour laughing and reminiscing, and I couldn't stop thinking how sad it was that we'd lost touch when we got on so brilliantly.

As we were getting ready to leave, I asked if she had any good Christmas-Day-in-Paris tips. I'd told Mum I couldn't afford the Eurostar back to join her at Uncle Simon's, but in truth, I was worried that being home for Christmas would make Daphne's absence feel more palpable. Maybe my mawk-ish, self-pitying side had even relished the romantic idea of being alone in Paris on Christmas Day. I don't know.

As soon as I mentioned it, though, Alice's green eyes lit up. She told me she had to work on the 27th, so she would be here too. In that instant, it was decided: we would spend Christmas Day together. Her excitement at the idea was infectious. She started throwing together a plan right then and there: how she would sort out a surprise Christmas itinerary for us; how she'd show me the *real* Paris I'd been missing out on while I was cooped up in my flat, writing.

It was properly thrilling.

As Alice gushed about how much fun we'd have, though, my mind went straight to Daphne. Technically, we were on a break, but I couldn't shake the feeling that spending Christmas Day with Alice would be overstepping the mark somehow. Crossing a boundary I shouldn't be crossing.

I'm brought back to reality – if right now can legitimately be called that – by our waiter rocking up to our table and plonking my hot chocolate down in front of me.

'*Merci beaucoup*,' I tell him.

'You're welcome,' he replies.

This gets a chuckle out of Alice, and I have the sudden urge to throw the drink at the waiter's back as he saunters off.

'When you've finished that,' she says, nodding at my cup, 'we should get going.'

'What's the first stop?' I ask, taking a sip, already knowing the answer.

She smiles. 'Le Dodo Manège.'

Chapter Twenty-Six

When I experienced this day originally, I think I was pretty surprised that Le Dodo Manège was Alice's first stop on our Christmas itinerary.

I thought I had her pegged as this big-shot marketing executive whose idea of a good time probably involved sipping Instagram-friendly cocktails in some exclusive members' club. And yet here she was, leading me through the beautiful Jardin des Plantes, just a stone's throw from the banks of the Seine, towards what appeared to be a children's fairground ride. It was a nice surprise, to be honest: it made me realise that no matter how much she seemed to have changed, she still had that fun, silly streak I'd been so attracted to at uni.

That said, though, Le Dodo Manège isn't just *any* children's fairground ride. I later learned that it's a bit of a Parisian legend: a Victorian-era carousel on which, instead of the usual brightly painted horses and carriages, there is a cavalcade of exotic, endangered or extinct creatures. Huge lifelike models of giant pandas, sabre-toothed tigers, various kinds of dinosaurs, willowy gazelle-like things and, of course, a plump, slightly angry-looking dodo.

'*Voilà!*' she says, as we push through the iron gate and it appears before us in all its glory. 'Le Dodo Manège.'

I nod, and then remember that I am supposed to be seeing it for the first time. I quickly feign excitement and surprise.

'Oh, yeah! Wow! It's incredible!'

Alice wrinkles her brow. I may have slightly overdone it. It's only a merry-go-round, after all, not the Hanging Gardens of Babylon. But then she gives me a smile, apparently convinced that a) I've never seen it before, and b) I am suitably impressed. 'It's cool, right?' she says. 'Come on, let's get on.'

The carousel is already pretty much full as we arrive – heaving with excited kids and their weary-looking parents. As we clamber up onto the main platform, I see there are only two riderless creatures left. The first is a pretty striking golden mountain lion, which Alice immediately hops up on and straddles, looking vaguely Napoleonic. The other is a giant turtle – fat and squat and about ten inches high – whose seat is basically a small trench that's been hollowed into its enormous shell. I attempt to retain some dignity as I lower myself into it, but after kneeing myself painfully in the face, twice, I'm not totally sure I manage it.

The plinky-plonky music starts up, and the ride begins to turn slowly. The air is suddenly thick with the delighted squeals of French toddlers. Up above me, Alice is rising and falling gracefully on her mountain lion, and for a few minutes, among the twinkling lights and the soporific music and the gentle spin of the carousel, I actually switch off and lose myself entirely. It's like my brain fades into sleep mode. It's actually quite a relief not to have to think about anything for a few minutes.

But then the ride begins to slow, and the music stutters to

an end, and I remember that in just a few hours, I will have a huge decision to make. And I have no clue what I should do.

We dismount our charges and wander to a nearby stall to buy hot, sticky Nutella and banana crêpes.

'So, what d'you reckon to the Manège?' Alice asks, as we watch the next load of customers pile onto the platform, the children all squabbling over who gets to ride which crazy creature.

'It was great,' I say. 'The perfect start to Christmas Day.'

'Don't worry, there is more.' She pops a slice of banana into her mouth. 'So. What would you have been doing today if we hadn't bumped into each other?'

'Well, I definitely wouldn't have been sitting in a giant turtle.' I take a bite out of my own crêpe, managing to smear Nutella across half my face. 'I don't know, really. I'd probably be back in the apartment, writing.'

'Of course,' she says. 'How is the writing going?'

If I remember rightly, the writing was going pretty bloody terribly at this point. High on the thrill of seeing Alice again at that first café, I think I'd bigged myself up as something of a budding experimental novelist. I even have a dim recollection of using the term 'Kafkaesque' – although I really, *really* hope I'm misremembering.

The truth is, I spent the past couple of months here starting, and then almost immediately abandoning, a dozen different projects. A TV sitcom script, a dystopian sci-fi story, a truly awful one-man stage play: all of them fell quickly by the wayside.

Paris was supposed to be my last chance to actually give the whole 'proper writing' thing a go. And when I failed at it – when I came back to London in January with nothing of any merit on my laptop – it was like a door finally slamming shut in my face. I gave up on that dream right there and then.

Still, I'm sure when Alice asked me this question first time round, I probably tried to style it out; made out that I was effortlessly bashing out page after page of sparkling prose. But now, for some reason, I don't have the strength to pretend. 'The writing is … not going very well, to be honest,' I sigh. 'I think the chances of me actually getting anything published are pretty slim.'

She shrugs. 'Ah, well. Who cares about getting something published? You enjoy writing, that's what counts.'

'I don't really enjoy it at all, actually,' I say blankly.

Alice swallows a bite of crêpe as she considers this. 'If you don't enjoy it, then why are you doing it?'

I stare at the Dodo Manège spinning gently in front of us. Last time around, I was trying so hard to impress her, mentally triple-checking everything I was about to say before it came out of my mouth. I was dead set on appearing cool and successful, rather than lost and confused.

Right now, though, I feel an impulsive desire to tell her the truth: to just lay everything out and see what she says. It's partly the unreality of the situation – the whole thing feels like a strangely vivid dream – but also partly because I know that, whatever I say here, she won't remember it back in 2020.

'I don't know why I keep writing,' I tell her. 'Maybe because I think my life will suddenly magically get better if I succeed at it. Maybe because I want to … reconnect with my dad.'

As I say it out loud, I realise how ridiculous it sounds.

'Sorry. That sounds stupid.'

Alice shakes her head and smiles. 'No, not at all. I get it.'

Weirdly, it feels like she really *does*. I remember sensing this a lot during the first term – that Alice instinctively understood me. That we understood each other.

'Anyway, I'm not sure my dad would care either way, to be honest,' I say quietly. 'He left when I was ten. I haven't seen him in years.'

She balls up her napkin and drops it into the bin beside us. 'I remember you saying. At uni.'

I look at her. 'Did I? When?'

She laughs softly. 'We were pretty close that first term, Ben. I guess you forgot. Remember the last day of freshers' week? We stayed up all night in my room, talking and drinking that horrendous Swedish liqueur we found under the sink. You told me about your dad then. Not much: just how you weren't really in touch at the moment, but you hoped some day you might be.'

I shake my head. I'd completely forgotten about that night. The minute I met Daphne, it was like all these moments with Alice were just erased from my brain. But she's right: there *was* a connection between us. I told her stuff that night that I've only ever gone on to tell Daphne.

I thought about kissing Alice so many times during that first term. What would have happened if I'd got up the nerve to do it? What would my life look like now?

She studies me closely for a second, and reaches into her bag for her cigarettes. 'I don't know,' she says, as she lights one. 'I'm not sure you should really care what your parents think about your life anyway. I mean: what do they know? I feel like mine have always wanted me to be someone I'm not.'

'How d'you mean?'

She exhales a plume of smoke as she considers this. 'Well, my dad's OK. He's a management consultant, so: boring. But my mum's an artist. My sister's a graphic designer. And they've always been like this little clique, the two of them. I think they were disappointed I wasn't more … arty, like them. Maybe that's what doing all those plays at uni was about. I was trying to be someone I wasn't.' She takes another drag. 'I don't know. I sometimes feel like they look down on me for wanting a proper career, a decent salary. I mean, I was so chuffed to get this job out here – it was a really big deal for me, this promotion. But my mum and dad don't get what I do, so it was like they barely even noticed. My sister had just had a baby, and that sort of stole the limelight, somehow.' She shakes her head. 'Sorry. I'm the one sounding stupid now.'

'No. Not at all. I get it.'

She looks up at me and laughs. 'We both sound stupid, and we both get it.'

I grin. 'We're a perfect match.'

I'm not sure where that comment came from, and there's a moment where it hangs awkwardly in the air between us. But then we catch each other's eye and start laughing. I'm not even sure what we're laughing about.

It all feels so good. So easy.

Is this why I've come back, then: to remember all this? Is Alice supposed to be my future? Should we have been together all along?

I watch as a new batch of passengers clamber onto the merry-go-round, and then I ask: 'You don't want any of that stuff, then? Marriage? Kids?'

'I don't know.' For a second, she can't quite meet my eye, and it's like the eighteen-year-old Alice is back – all self-conscious and guarded. 'Maybe I do want those things,' she adds, 'if I find the right person. But it's not my priority at the moment. There are other things I want to do first.' She ashes her cigarette and turns to me. 'What about you? Do you want kids and stuff?'

'I thought I did,' I say. 'But now … I'm not sure.'

Daff and I were actually going to start trying for kids a few years back. It was soon after we got married, just after she turned thirty. Even though my career was still stop-starting, it seemed like the right time. And back then, it was something we both definitely wanted. We would text each other horrifying Face Swap mash-ups of ourselves accompanied by *This is what our kids will look like haha* messages. We even sketched out a date that Daff might come off the pill.

But then … Well, then Mum died and everything went dark. And the conversation never properly reignited after that, despite the fact that all our mates seemed to be starting families around us.

It became this weird unspoken thing between us. We'd go and visit friends with their new babies, and even though I oohed and aahed in all the right places, I honestly felt … nothing. Which was scary, because I used to genuinely love the idea of being a dad. I would even experience something close to broodiness whenever I passed a smiling young couple swinging a toddler between them in the park. It would send me spiralling straight into a daydream about Daff and me doing the same thing. But after Mum died, it was like something fused inside me. There didn't seem to be any point to anything any more. All sense of excitement about the future just fizzled and burned out. I'd suddenly realised that the people you loved could just get torn away from you, at any moment, for no reason at all.

The worst thing was that Daff and I never talked about it. I could tell she didn't want to pressure me – that she knew how much Mum's death had messed me up. As the months dragged on though, I worried she was starting to resent me. That she wanted to find someone else, someone she could actually build a future with, but that she would feel too bad about leaving me. Sometimes, in the middle of the night, it would occur to me that she might never have children because she'd wasted her thirties with me.

That was the worst feeling in the world.

I look over at Alice, who doesn't seem particularly bothered by the fact that I've zoned out of the conversation. She's focusing all her attention on the cloud of grey smoke she's just sent drifting into the air above us. I'm not sure why, but I feel the need to fill the silence, to vent the thoughts that are building up in my head. Thoughts I've never really vented before. I clear my throat, and say, 'I guess when I was younger I liked the idea of having kids just because I wanted to prove that I wasn't my dad, you know? That I had it in me to be a decent father. Or at least to make a better job of it than he did.'

Alice nods. I can feel my face getting red, and the words starting to thicken in my throat, but I keep going. 'But the older I get, the more I think it'll just be the same story over again. It really feels like I've inherited everything bad about him. He cheated on his wife and walked out. I'll probably end up doing the same.'

I realise as soon as I say it how awful this sounds. But I genuinely believe it. Daphne and I weren't technically together on this day originally, but still, I've never told her what happened. And back in reality – in 2020 – I have arranged to meet Alice for a drink behind Daff's back. A drink that I know full well could turn into something more.

I am *already* following in my father's footsteps.

Alice brings me back down to earth by asking: 'Are you still with Daphne, then?' She digs at the grass with her foot as she says it: a gesture that seems rehearsed in its attempt to convey nonchalance. As if asking this question is no big deal.

I try to swallow, but my throat suddenly feels very tight. 'We're … No. I guess not, at the moment. She's in New York for her job.'

'Oh. Right. OK.' I can hear the forced breeziness in her voice. She stubs her cigarette out. 'Well, at least we're both in the same boat.'

'What d'you mean?'

She shrugs. 'I had a thing with a guy out here, but it ended a couple of months back.'

'Oh. I'm sorry.'

'No, don't be. I'm not sure about French men, in the end. Too short. I think I'd be better off with a British guy.'

She nudges my shoulder and smiles up at me. It's a move that's straight out of the first term at uni: flirty, but cushioned just enough that it could still be taken as a joke.

It doesn't feel like one, though. I'm instantly transported back to Marek's wedding: the two of us huddled together drunkenly at the dinner table. I know it's pathetic, but it was so exciting to feel … wanted. To feel like someone fancied me. I haven't felt that from Daphne in such a long time.

Alice's phone starts buzzing and she pulls a face as she looks at the screen. 'Sorry, I'll just be one sec.' She puts the phone to her ear and wanders away.

I'm left watching the Dodo Manège and realising that this – everything we've just been talking about – is entirely new territory. We never spoke about any of it originally, I'm sure of it. And it makes me wonder: will it affect what happens later? After all these fresh conversational twists and turns, will everything still pan out the way it did first time round?

The thought of how this night ended originally makes my stomach churn. I want to do the right thing – I really do – but I have no idea what that is. Because, as shameful as it is to admit, I *have* thought about this night a lot over the past six years. Half the time it comes back to gnaw guiltily at me as I lie beside Daphne in bed. But the rest of the time, it makes me wonder what might have been. How my life could have turned out if I'd stayed here.

My head is throbbing suddenly. I close my eyes and press my hand against them, enjoying the coolness of my palm. When I open them again, my gaze falls on the little wooden hut next to the crêpe stand. It's a cutesy Christmas stall, decorated haphazardly with tinsel and fairy lights, selling all sorts of cheap, touristy festive gifts. And then I spot something I recognise.

The snow globe.

I walk over to the stall and pick it up. I bought this thing for Daphne first time around. It must have been at this exact moment, when Alice was on the phone. I thought it would make a funny, cheesy Christmas present – a nice thing to send back in reply to her card. I had no idea that I'd be posting it three days later feeling sick with guilt about what had happened tonight.

I give it a gentle shake, and hundreds of tiny snowflakes begin swirling gently around the miniature Dodo Manège. It's a tacky little thing, really. I wonder where it is now. I wonder if Daphne kept it.

'*C'est combien?*' I ask, without looking up.

A gravelly voice replies, 'Oh, you can have that one on the house!'

I glance up, and almost inevitably, there are two bright blue eyes twinkling back at me.

Chapter Twenty-Seven

'Bloody hell …'

I stare in disbelief at the old man's crumpled smile, half hidden inside his scraggly grey-gold beard. 'You gave me the shock of my life there. Although I guess I should have been expecting it.'

The watch-seller laughs. 'You should indeed, young man.' He smoothes down his reindeer tie, and leans towards me conspiratorially. 'I think I make rather a good French souvenir salesman, don't you? People seem to be buying it, anyway. Which is more than I can say for the souvenirs themselves. Haven't shifted a single bloody thing all morning.' He starts whistling 'Good King Wenceslas' as he rearranges some Arc de Triomphe-branded oven gloves.

My brain is still frazzled from the conversation with Alice, and I find I don't really have the patience for the watch-seller's trademark enigmatic cheeriness right now. 'What are you doing here?' I ask bluntly.

'I just wanted to stop by and wish you a merry Christmas,' he says. 'It's all part of the service.'

'And what exactly *is* this service?'

He gives a throaty chuckle. 'Oh, I can't go into that at the moment, I'm afraid.'

'Right. And I'm guessing you still can't tell me why all this is happening, or when it will end, either?'

The old man tosses a Louvre-shaped paperweight into the air and catches it. 'You guess correctly, young feller-me-lad. Even if I wanted to, we wouldn't have time.' He nods over at Alice, who is still circling the Dodo Manège with her phone clamped to her ear. 'Your friend there is going to be walking back over in approximately' – he checks his watch – 'one minute twelve seconds.' He stops juggling his merchandise and looks at me. 'All I really wanted to do was check in and see how you were getting on. I realise this experience can be somewhat … overwhelming.'

He tilts his head and gives me a kindly – almost paternal – smile. That faded photo of Grandad Jack flashes back into my head again. The similarity is actually pretty eerie.

I'm on the cusp of bringing it up – asking if we're somehow related, maybe – when the old man says, 'So, come on: how are you coping, then?'

'I, erm … OK, I guess.' I shrug. 'I mean, it's not difficult to figure out why I've come back to this particular day. Something … happened here, first time around. It's something I've thought about a lot over the years. I was actually thinking about it in that pub in 2020, when I met you. I was wondering whether I'd made the wrong decision today, whether I ended up with the wrong person. And I guess, since I've come back here, maybe it means that I did.'

The old man scratches at his beard with a miniature Eiffel Tower. 'Hmm. That's one way of looking at it.'

'Is it the right way or the wrong way?'

'Well … that's not for me to say.'

I groan loudly, and he laughs again, his blue eyes sparkling. 'You'll figure it out,' he says. 'Just give it time. And speaking of time ... I'm afraid ours is up.'

He taps his watch and glances behind me.

I turn to see Alice approaching, and as I turn back, the watch-seller is delivering an enthusiastic sales pitch to a passing couple in what sounds like perfect French.

I slip the snow globe into my jacket pocket just as Alice reaches my side.

'Sorry about that,' she sighs, dropping her phone back into her bag. 'My boss won't even leave me alone on bloody Christmas Day. I'm the only one in the office next week, so there's tons to do. Anyway ...'

She loops her arm through mine, just like she did all those years ago when we were heading to the maze. The watch-seller breaks out of his sales pitch to shoot me one last crumpled, twinkly grin.

'Come on, then,' Alice says. 'We're going to be late for our next stop.'

Chapter Twenty-Eight

We *are* late.

We arrive at the tiny Champo cinema on Rue des Écoles almost ten minutes after the film has started. We edge our way down the aisle towards the only free seats, muttering '*Excusez-moi*' and '*Je suis desolé*' at the disgruntled people standing up for us.

The cinema screen is lined with tinsel, and it's showing the same film we saw first time round: a schlocky Christmas romcom called *The Holiday*, starring Cameron Diaz. As we sit down, I remember that it's dubbed into French, so I'm expecting to pick up exactly as little of it as I did originally.

'Shit, sorry, I thought it was subtitled,' Alice whispers. She nudges my elbow. 'Good practice for your French, though, right?'

'Yeah, exactly. No worries.'

I sit there in the darkness watching Jude Law gabble incomprehensibly in someone else's voice, my hand almost touching Alice's on the armrest. I remember so clearly how excited I felt at this moment the first time around. It wasn't only the mystery agenda; it was also the fact that this was starting to feel like a proper date, rather than two old friends spending Christmas together because they didn't have anyone else.

The difference this time, though, is that Daphne and I aren't on a break. We're married. We might be in a bad place in 2020, but we're still together. Did I think about her at this moment originally? I must have done, surely. She's out there, in New York, at this very instant. I wonder if she's thinking about me too.

Alice interrupts this train of thought by nudging my arm. 'Are you following what's going on?' she whispers.

'Yeah, yeah. Totally.'

She cups a hand round my ear. 'Cameron and Kate Winslet have done a house swap, and now Cameron fancies Jude Law, who is Kate's brother.'

I can feel her breath tickling my skin, and despite everything, certain parts of my body begin reacting fairly predictably. That was another reason this moment felt so exciting first time round: I was realising just how much I fancied her.

I get the sudden urge to turn my head so that we're face to face. I could kiss her right now. It scares me how much I want to.

But instead I just nod and whisper, 'Yep, crystal clear, don't worry.'

She smiles and turns back to the screen.

After an hour or so, the film finally comes to an end. As we shuffle out, I agree strongly with Alice that it was 'super romantic', despite having picked up roughly seven words throughout.

By the time we're back on the street, it's freezing cold and the sun is already starting to set. We make our way down to the banks of the Seine, where twinkling red-and-white Christmas lights are strung delicately through every tree along the river.

We walk slowly, side by side, taking it all in. Alice is talking about her job now, and I can't help cringing slightly as she throws around terms like 'brand awareness' and 'synergy' with an entirely straight face. She's definitely much more earnest than she was at uni. I think I was quite impressed by this the first time around: I was swept up by how hot she looked, and how confident and sophisticated she seemed. But now, as she starts venting on her 'useless' boss and 'annoying' colleagues, I can sense a sharpness – a bitterness – I don't remember her having before.

I can't help thinking about Daphne: a superstar at her job, too, and yet still kind and modest and funny.

Alice must read my mind somehow, because she switches tack completely as she pulls out another cigarette. 'You know, I always thought it was such a shame that you and I lost touch after uni.'

'Yeah.' I nod. 'Me too.'

'Or even before that, really,' she says. 'We did everything together in the first term, and then when you came back after Christmas, it was like things had changed.'

I scratch the back of my neck. 'I know … I'm sorry. I don't know what happened.'

Alice shrugs. 'No, it was fair enough, I guess. You and Daphne had just started going out, so you had other stuff going on. I was just sad that we didn't get to hang out together any more. I … missed you.' She laughs suddenly, as if to soften the impact of that last statement.

'I missed you too,' I tell her, although I'm not sure if it's out of honesty or politeness. I'm trying desperately to remember if we had this conversation originally, but I'm drawing a complete blank.

Alice coughs and fiddles with her fringe. She keeps her gaze fixed straight ahead as she says, 'It sounds stupid, but I always felt like Daphne had a weird … thing about me. That maybe she didn't like me very much?'

I try to work some moisture into my mouth. 'No … I don't think that's true.'

Alice just nods, but she doesn't look convinced. I can't think of anything more to say, so I just keep quiet. A boat full of rowdy tourists in Santa hats drifts past, and I scour my brain for a change of subject.

Before I can find one, she carries on: 'So, how come you guys split up, then? If you don't mind me asking?' That same studiedly casual tone has slipped back into her voice, as if we're talking about a two-week fling rather than a nine-year relationship.

I try to keep my voice as steady as hers. 'Well, we didn't really split up. I mean, technically we're not together right now, but—'

'Something must have changed, though?' she cuts in. 'If she's in New York, and you're here?'

'Yeah. I guess. It's … complicated.'

'Mmm,' she says. 'Yeah, it sounds like it.' Her face is blank – totally unreadable. But then she stops in front of a big flight of stone stairs and turns to smile at me. 'Anyway, here we are. Next stop.'

Thankfully, all talk of Daphne dries up after that.

We head up and onto the Left Bank, where we eat the same incredible steak-frites at Le Relais de l'Entrecôte restaurant in Montparnasse. And after that, we retreat to the same crowded little piano bar in Denfert-Rochereau, where we huddle up at the same corner table and see off what is almost certainly the same bottle of house red. I just sit there, feeling increasingly drunk, listening to Alice talk about her co-workers, occasionally pouring scorn on them with an acidity I definitely don't recall from the first time around. Everything is beginning to blur at the edges now, starting to feel scary and unreal. Because I know what will happen once we leave this restaurant, and I have no idea what I should do when it does.

Even though Alice has stopped grilling me about her, I still can't get Daphne out of my mind. Something Mum said to me during that Monopoly game comes back suddenly: *you and Daphne seem to have a relationship that's worth working at.* That's what I was supposed to be doing here in Paris: working at it. When really I was sitting in this bar doing the exact opposite.

And then it hits me … *Mum.*

She's out there too, in this reality. She's still alive.

As soon as the thought enters my head, I'm up and out of my chair, mumbling an excuse to Alice behind me. My heart is thudding in my chest; I'm suddenly desperate to hear her voice. I step out into the freezing cold and press my phone against my ear, thinking: please, please, please pick up …

'Hello, darling!' she trills. 'Merry Christmas!'

The winking Christmas lights on the lamp posts begin to dissolve in front of me as the tears blur my vision. I have to bite the inside of my cheek hard to keep it together. 'Hi, Mum, merry Christmas!' I'm trying to keep my voice steady, but I'm not totally sure I'm succeeding.

'I was going to call you later, when I got back from Simon's,' she says. 'Is this costing you an absolute fortune? I can call you back if you want?'

'No, no, don't worry.' God, it is so good to hear her voice. She sounds happy – and more than a little tipsy – and I'm suddenly overwhelmed with gratitude for this chance to speak to her again.

'I just wanted to say that I miss you,' I mumble. 'I wish I was there with you.'

She drops her voice to a whisper. 'Trust me, you don't. I spent the whole of lunch sitting next to your cousin Lucy's incredibly dull new boyfriend. The man talked about nothing but *Top Gear* for an hour and a half. I am now the world's leading expert on Richard Hammond. I think I know more about Richard Hammond than Richard Hammond does.'

I am half laughing and half crying now, receiving some very concerned looks from people walking past.

'So, what are you up to?' she asks. 'Please tell me you're not moping about on your own?'

I take a deep breath and try to pull myself together. 'No, don't worry. I'm spending the day with a friend, actually.'

'Oh, that's nice. Where do you know him from?'

'Her, actually. She's an old friend from uni.'

'Oh. Right.' There's a pause on the other end of the line. And then I hear Mum clear her throat stiffly. 'And have you heard from Daphne today?'

'Yeah. Well, I got a Christmas card from her yesterday.'

'Yes, I got one, too.' There's another pause, and she adds, 'She's such a lovely girl, honestly.' I can feel the prickle in her voice.

'I know,' I say.

'I hope you do. You bloody should.'

I was never totally honest with Mum about why Daff and I were taking this break. I just told her it was because Daff was going to New York; I didn't mention anything about my marriage freak-out; it was way too closely intertwined with her and Dad.

For a second, I consider telling her about it now. But then I hear a muffled voice behind her. 'I'll be right in,' she calls to somebody. And then: 'I'd better go, love. We're about to do presents.'

I feel a spasm of panic rip through me. If I let her go now, I don't know if I'll ever get to speak to her again. But then what can I do? I can't exactly spend the rest of this evening standing out here chatting to her.

I stare dumbly at the pavement, feeling my throat constrict so tightly that I can't get any words through it. Luckily, Mum speaks for me. 'It feels rather odd, not being with you today,' she says. 'Not having lunch together, not giving each other our presents in the morning.'

'I know ...' I swallow the lump in my throat, and then remember the conversation I overheard through the kitchen door. 'Hey, do you remember that Christmas when I was a kid, and I nicked your Sellotape and stapler and then gave them back to you as a present?'

The line is flooded with her laughter. 'God, I'd forgotten all about that! What a little cheapskate.' She breaks off and sniffs. I wonder if she might be crying, too. 'You know,' she says quietly, 'that was actually one of my favourite gifts you've ever got me.'

'I love you, Mum,' is about all I can manage.

'Love you too, darling,' she says. 'I'll speak to you soon. Merry Christmas.'

'Merry Christmas.'

I take a deep breath as I blink wetly into the night air. All I can think is: God, I hope I get to see her again. Just one more time.

My phone tells me it's now 10.47 p.m. There's just over an hour before all this ends and I find myself somewhere else completely.

Through the window of the bar, I can see Alice flagging our waiter down, signalling for the bill.

Once we've paid, we stumble back out, and Alice slips her arm through mine again as we wander tipsily through the near-deserted streets of the 14th arrondissement.

Occasionally we pass someone – usually another tipsy, looped-armed couple – and exchange a friendly *Joyeux Noël*.

We walk in silence for the most part. Alice is now seemingly all talked out, and I can't conjure any words either. My brain is just white noise, like a scrambled TV. It feels like I'm on a conveyor belt; aware of where I'm heading, but not sure what will happen when I get there.

I glance down at my watch, its hands still stuck at 11.59. I'm about to check the real time on my phone when Alice stops outside a big blue doorway.

'Here we are, then.' She punches in the entrance code and looks me straight in the eye. 'So … do you want to come up?'

I stand there dumbly, just as I did six years ago, feeling excitement and terror do battle in my stomach.

And then I tell her: 'Yes.'

Chapter Twenty-Nine

On the face of it, Alice's place is not much different to mine: a low-ceilinged two-bedroom flat halfway up a creaky seven-storey apartment block. Even the floorboards squeak in the same way – though I can't hear any explosive marital disputes coming from above.

Alice chucks her coat onto the baggy brown sofa and asks if I'm OK with more red wine. I tell her that I am. And as she goes into the kitchen to find a bottle, I take the opportunity to have a proper look around.

She must have been in this place for two years now, but it looks like she's only just moved in. The walls are bare – no photos or posters – and there are no books or magazines or DVDs in sight. The whole place has a slightly furniture showroom feel to it: everything spotlessly clean but not very … homely.

The only concession to the time of year is a small, undecorated Christmas tree about the size of a toaster, which sits glumly on the windowsill.

I slump down onto the sofa and try to remember what I was feeling at this exact moment last time. Nervous. Excited. Those were definitely the two overriding emotions, with horny probably bagging third place on the podium. Despite that, though, I don't think I felt particularly guilty at this point.

Daff and I were supposed to be on a break: that was what I kept telling myself. And even though we hadn't set any rules, or mentioned the idea of seeing other people, *she* was the one who had initiated the whole thing. Plus, I couldn't escape the idea that this entire evening felt like fate. I mean: what were the chances of randomly bumping into the girl I'd once had a major thing for? It seemed like it was meant to be.

Or maybe I felt no guilt because at this point I still didn't think anything would actually happen. From the minute we stepped through the door of the flat, I kept expecting Alice to yawn and sigh and tell me it had been a fun day but she was knackered and maybe I had better go. I think part of me would have been relieved if she had. But she never did.

Instead, she came back from the kitchen, sat down on the sofa, and kissed me. I kissed her back, and then we went through to the bedroom, leaving our wine undrunk behind us.

I don't know what I was thinking, really. As soon as we kissed, it was like I stopped thinking altogether. My brain took a back seat and – with pathetic predictability – other parts of my body stepped in to take control.

So it wasn't until afterwards that the guilt came.

It flooded my veins the next morning as I lay frozen in Alice's bed listening to her snore softly beside me. The sunlight was peeking in through the curtains, and the gravity of what I had done was fifty times more crushing than my hangover. At that moment – miserable, sweating, in the vice-like grip of regret – I don't think I've ever missed Daphne more.

I missed everything about her: the feel of her, her touch, her smell. The way we lay together afterwards, our bodies curled like speech marks. The way we seemed to fit so perfectly.

I feel hot suddenly, and as I shrug off my jacket, the snow globe spills out of the pocket. I stuff it back in, and take a deep breath to try and settle my roiling stomach. I pull out my phone to check the time, but the battery's dead.

Alice walks back in from the kitchen holding two very large glasses of red wine. She passes me one, and settles down on the sofa next to me.

'So,' she raises her glass, '*Joyeux Noël. Santé.*'

'*Santé.*'

We clink glasses and drink.

'Thanks for today,' I say. 'It was great. The best day I've had since I've been here.'

'No worries. I had fun too.'

I take another sip. The wine scorches my throat as it goes down. 'Do you know what time it is?' I ask.

Alice frowns. 'My phone's in the kitchen. Why – were you thinking of heading back?'

'No, I just—'

'Good. I was kind of hoping this wouldn't be the end of the night.'

There's a little pause during which we both look at each other, not saying anything, and my heartbeat starts behaving very irregularly indeed. Because, God, she looks incredible.

She leans forward and puts her glass down on the coffee table. When she leans back again, she's very slightly closer to me. She lays her hand on my thigh and, almost automatically, I lay mine on hers. I close my eyes, and feel the touch of her lips on mine. And despite certain parts of my body screaming

YES!, my head is suddenly full of Daphne. I instinctively pull away.

'I'm sorry,' I say quietly.

Alice looks at me blankly. She doesn't seem particularly embarrassed or pissed off. She just seems like she's waiting for an explanation. The best I can do, though, is stammer the word 'sorry' a few more times.

'Is it Daphne?' she says finally.

I nod. 'Yeah. I guess.'

She picks her glass back up and takes a sip. 'I thought it was over between you?'

'I don't know if it is or not, to be honest.'

'But you're not together right now, you said?'

'We're ... on a break.'

She laughs, and then holds a hand up in apology. 'Sorry, that was just very Ross and Rachel. Remember how pissed off you used to get at uni when I wanted to watch *Friends*, and you wanted to watch *The Wire*?'

'Yeah, I remember.' My head feels heavy suddenly. I have no idea what I should do.

Alice sighs and shuffles closer to me. 'Look, I don't want to fuck things up with you and Daphne. But I guess I always thought there was something between us. And maybe, if it's not going to work out with her in the long run ...' She tails off and swirls the wine around her glass. 'I mean, you don't exactly know what she's doing in New York right now, do you?'

It's true: I don't. I never asked Daphne if anything happened in New York, just as she's never asked me about Paris. I guess we both took it as read that the other had stayed faithful.

Guilt stabs me sharply in the chest, and all of a sudden

I think I understand why I'm here: why I decided to come up to Alice's flat. In 2020, I've arranged to meet Alice for a drink at her hotel. And this is how it will feel if I go. This is how it will feel to be on the brink of cheating on my wife; to be on the brink of knowing I'm about to lose Daphne for good.

Am I really prepared to go through with that?

Alice puts her glass back down and stands up in front of me. Without saying a word, she holds her hand out.

I stare at it for a second, trying desperately to decide whether I should take it. And that's when everything disappears.

Chapter Thirty

'Ben … Ben?'

I groan and roll over. I can feel someone rubbing my arm gently.

'Ben, wake up. We need to get going.'

The feeling is the same every time I jump: dizziness, motion sickness, and a dull pain in my chest like I've just had the wind thumped out of me. My eyes flick open, and as I take in my surroundings, the first thought that enters my still-fuzzy brain is: I'm back.

Daphne is perched on the edge of the bed beside me, stroking my shoulder. But this isn't the twenty-three-year-old Daphne I fell asleep with two nights ago in Balham. This looks more like the thirty-three-year-old Daphne I'm married to in the real world. In 2020. I inhale sharply, and glance around me. This is our flat. The flat we bought together. The flat we currently live in.

This madness is finally over. I'm back in the present.

The relief is so overwhelming that I scramble up and pull Daphne towards me, hugging her tightly. 'Oh my God, Daff …' is about all I can manage to say.

She hugs me back even tighter, her fingers tracing through

my hair. 'Shh, it's OK … I know, I know … Everything's going to be all right, I promise.'

I pull away to see that her eyes are red and glistening with tears. There are dark circles underneath them, as if she hasn't slept properly in days.

The relief freezes inside me, turning instantly to cold, clammy fear. There's something wrong here.

Was the watch-seller lying? Has the present changed after all? Maybe Daphne somehow knows about what happened in Paris.

'We'll get through it,' she mumbles as she wipes her eyes. 'Everything will be fine.'

My mind is fizzing and spluttering, trying to comprehend what's going on.

And then, behind her, I see it. The black suit.

It dangles limply on the back of the bedroom door like an invisible man hanged for some terrible crime.

Daff puts her head in her hands and starts crying: hard, heavy, jagged sobs. And with a sickening jolt, it dawns on me. This madness isn't over at all.

It's about to get much, much worse.

Ten minutes later, I'm sitting at the kitchen table, staring at the green and white wreath by the door. Lilies. That was the decision in the end: lilies.

Tulips were Mum's favourite, but apparently they weren't suitable for the occasion. I can't remember who said that – the funeral director, maybe, or Uncle Simon – but it was decided one way or the other.

I sit here in silence, watching the steam curl up from my

undrunk coffee and feeling a dark, scary anger start to uncoil inside me at the thought of going through this again. Daff is standing by the stove, stirring a saucepan of porridge and intermittently pressing a tissue to her eyes.

She's already dressed in her smart black outfit, her curly hair pulled back in a neat ponytail. Despite her tired eyes and worried frown, she still looks beautiful.

I, on the other hand, must look anything but. I'm still wearing the T-shirt and pyjama bottoms I woke up in. I just couldn't face getting changed yet. Putting that suit on would make it all seem real somehow, and I'm not sure I'm ready to believe yet that it is. So the suit's still upstairs, on the back of the bedroom door, waiting for me to climb into it and relive one of the worst days of my life: December 10th, 2018.

Daff plonks a steaming bowl of porridge down in front of me and attempts a smile.

'Here you go. Please eat something.'

She kisses me on the top of the head. Not the kind of kiss you give a husband or a lover: the kind you give a child. Then she mutters something about going to put on some make-up, and leaves the room.

I try a mouthful of porridge. It's blisteringly hot, and I wince as it scalds the roof of my mouth. But, weirdly, the pain feels good – sharp and alive – in stark contrast to the numbness in my chest.

I swallow another spoonful. My watch is still stuck at one minute to midnight, but the clock on the wall says 10.35 a.m. I woke up much earlier on this day first time around. I'd thought I wouldn't be able to sleep, but I had, somehow.

I remember having a dream in which Mum was still alive. I had those dreams a lot in the months after she died.

She was always still alive, too, in those first few hazy seconds after I woke up, blinking and yawning and becoming increasingly aware that something big and awful had happened but not quite able to put my finger on it yet. And then I had to remember all over again, and sometimes the pain of remembering was so intense it was actually physical, bending my body at odd angles, or curling my hands into claws as I lay there crying silently into the mattress, trying not to wake Daphne.

She comes back in and stands in the doorway, looking at me. The shadows under her eyes are now hidden under a layer of foundation, but she doesn't look any less miserable. 'Simon will be here soon,' she says quietly. 'You should go and get changed.'

I stare down into the porridge. 'I'm not sure I can do this,' I hear myself say.

'Oh, Ben …' She sighs and runs a hand across her forehead. 'I'm not sure I can either. But we have to.'

'No, I just …' I don't know what to say. How can I explain it to her? How can I tell her that I just physically *can't* go through this again? This day nearly broke me the first time. It will break me this time. I know it will. So why do I have to relive it? What the *fuck* is the point?

I suddenly want to see the watch-seller again. I want to demand an explanation for why this is happening, for what I could have done to deserve this.

I look down to see tears dropping steadily into my porridge bowl.

Daff rushes across to me and wraps me in her arms. 'Ben,

we can do this. We can get through this day together, I promise you we can.'

The tears are starting to roll down her cheeks too now, spoiling her fresh make-up. I didn't even try to get through this day *with* her, originally. I barely took any notice of her grief because I was so caught up in my own. I just shut her out completely and retreated inwards; I didn't even realise I was doing it.

Maybe this is why I've come back, then: so that we can go through this terrible day together, as a team. I have to relive these next few hours; I've got no other choice. The only thing I can do is to try and make them better than they were before.

I can already think of something I've always regretted about today. Something I was supposed to do but didn't. My stomach twitches with nerves at the thought of it, but I suddenly know I have no choice but to do it.

I wipe my eyes on the sleeve of my T-shirt. Daff goes to kiss me again, on my forehead, but I lift my chin and kiss her on the lips. She smiles in surprise – an effortless reflex smile – and a surge of strength shoots through me. That's what I need to do, I realise: I need to let her in. To lean on her, and let her lean on me. That's the only way it will be OK.

'You're right,' I tell her. 'We'll get through this together.'

She touches her lips to mine again, and then nods. 'You'd better go and put your suit on.'

'I will. But first, can you help me find something? You know that book of Walt Whitman poems …?'

Chapter Thirty-One

'Are you sure about this, Ben?' Uncle Simon gives me a concerned glance in the rear-view mirror. 'You know you don't have to do it. No one's expecting you to. No one will think any less of you if you don't.'

He looks back at the road as he guides the car onto the dual carriageway. I can understand why he's dubious. Three days before the funeral, I pulled out of reading Mum's favourite poem during the ceremony. I just completely lost my nerve, terrified that I would break down in front of everyone. The programmes even had to be reprinted to remove the mention of my reading. So the fact that I've just told Simon – at the very last minute – that I've changed my mind *again*, and I now want to do it, must seem more than a little disconcerting.

But it's like that kiss in the kitchen cleared the fog inside my head. It not only gave me a weird sense of courage and confidence; it also made me see how ridiculous it was to have spent this day entirely wrapped up in myself. I bottled out of reading the poem because I was scared of looking stupid or pathetic if I started crying. But really, who cares how I look? The most important thing is making the effort. Trying my best to do Mum proud.

'Don't worry,' I tell Simon, touching the dog-eared book in my jacket pocket. 'I'll be fine. I promise. I really want to do this.'

Simon glances back at me, and nods. In the passenger seat next to him, his wife, my aunt Chrissie, sits with the wreath of lilies perched carefully on her lap. And beside me in the back of the car, Daff reaches across and squeezes my hand, giving me a tearful smile. Our fingers interlock, and our wedding rings clink gently against one another. Mine has been missing from my finger over these past few days, since I was revisiting moments when Daff and I weren't yet married. I never even noticed it was gone. It seems strange that I've only realised it now.

It's even stranger to think that I'm here with her now, when only last night I was in Paris, in Alice's flat. What would I have done, I wonder, if my time hadn't run out? If the clock hadn't reached one minute to midnight?

I honestly don't know.

I stare out of the car window at the trees and houses whizzing by. It was on the Eurostar back from Paris that I decided I would ask Daphne to marry me. The thought popped into my head totally at random, and at first it seemed crass and embarrassing: a knee-jerk response to the guilt I felt over sleeping with Alice. An over-the-top way of making amends for what I'd done. But the more I thought about it, the more I knew that it wasn't any of those things. I was in love with Daff. That was the only fact in my life I was really sure of. The idea of losing her was genuinely terrifying; what had happened with Alice had only served to make me realise that.

It was as if all my worries about marriage and what it had

done to my parents had suddenly dissolved, because I knew now for absolute certain that I wanted to spend the rest of my life with Daphne. But to come to that realisation, I'd had to do something that could easily break us apart for good if she ever found out about it. So I quickly came to the conclusion that she never, ever would.

I'd slunk out of Alice's flat early on Boxing Day morning, refusing her offer of breakfast with a few grunted monosyllables. I knew how shitty it was – how rude I was being – but I couldn't help it. I felt like I was suffocating in there; I needed to get outside and clear my head.

Three days later, when I'd decided to go back to London early, I messaged Alice to tell her I was sorry; that I was heading home, and maybe I'd see her soon. She never replied.

Daff came back from New York in February 2015. Obviously, I didn't propose to her straight away; we were still technically on a break, so immediately popping the question would have seemed at best optimistic and at worst utterly insane. All I told her was that I wanted to try again. To make it work between us. Luckily, she agreed – and for those next few months, it did work. We had fun again. I started pursuing boring but lucrative temp work as a copywriter, and gradually I pushed what had happened in Paris into a corner of my mind so remote that it only emerged very occasionally, creeping out in the middle of the night to remind me what might have been.

I finally proposed in summer 2015, during a holiday in Greece, and we were married a year later, on August 18th 2016, at Islington Town Hall. Nothing very fancy: Daff didn't want some massive posh do, and neither did I. We just wanted our families and our best mates and a fun, memorable day.

I was nervous, obviously, but only about the practical things: speeches and seating plans and whether Harv's DJ set would contain anything at all for the elderly relatives to dance to (it very much didn't). I certainly wasn't nervous about the bigger, existential concerns I'd always imagined would rear their heads on my wedding day: all the scary is-this-really-what-I-want-type questions. As Daff walked up the aisle towards me, beaming from ear to ear, I knew for certain that this was exactly what I wanted.

I remember how happy Mum looked, too. She didn't stop smiling all day – laughing and joking with friends of mine she hadn't seen for years. At the end of the night, once Harv's drum 'n' bass onslaught was over, we danced together tipsily to one of her favourite songs – an old doo-wop track called 'Life Could Be a Dream' – and when it finished, she clasped me by the shoulders and told me, 'I'm so proud of you, love.' The memory bites so hard that I have to physically shake my head to remove it. I can't let myself break down before I even get into the church.

We're nearly there now: the car is purring slowly down the high street. Every single shop window is screaming with Christmas decorations: manic grinning elves and jolly pot-bellied Santas. I remember noticing this stuff first time around, too, and thinking how jarring it all seemed. It just didn't make any sense to be surrounded by brightness and festivity on such a miserable, desperate day.

Finally, the car slows and comes to a stop. Up front, Simon takes a deep breath and meets my eyes in the rear-view mirror.

'Here we are then,' he says.

The funeral is taking place at the little church a few streets over from Mum's house in Acton – a church that Mum and I had never even been into before today.

My stomach is churning and my throat is parched. I'm desperate to just get inside and get it over with, but there's already a little crowd of people gathered by the church door. They're family members, mostly, and a few of Mum's friends too. They move towards me one by one, and I let them take my hand and tell me they're sorry, or pull me into tight, breathless hugs. I let this weird, pointless procession of tears and apologies play out in front of me as if I'm not even part of it; just a spectator, watching from behind a screen.

Then, with a jolt of surprise, I spot Harv through the crowd. I'd totally forgotten he would be here. He's standing by the big wooden door, hands jammed in the pockets of his suit jacket, looking uncharacteristically awkward and shy. He was away on holiday when Mum died, and even though we spoke briefly on the phone, this was the first time I'd actually seen him since it happened.

He's changed a lot since 2010. The weight has dropped off him, and his face is all cheekbones and laughter lines. He looks like present-day Harv again. He catches my eye for a split second, then sort of grimaces and looks away. He clearly doesn't know how to react, or what to say, and I can't really blame him. There are no guidelines for this kind of situation. I don't think either of us ever imagined we'd have to help the other through a day like this.

Our friendship – like most male friendships – has been built primarily on ripping the piss out of each other. For more than a decade, it has been nothing but banter and trivia and talking bollocks. And now, suddenly, Harv is standing outside a church, waiting for my mum's coffin to be lowered into the ground, and trying to figure out what the hell he should say to me. I watch him squirming on the spot, wrinkling and unwrinkling his brow, and feel an intense rush of affection for him. Because despite everything, he's still here for me. He's always been here.

I walk towards him and he yanks his hands out of his pockets and wrings them together. He stares down at the ground, shaking his head and muttering, 'Mate ... Fuck ... I just ... Fuck ...' like a malfunctioning foul-mouthed robot.

And then, almost violently, he pulls me towards him and hugs me. This must have happened last time, but like everything else, I suppose I blocked it out. I hug him back, and feel the tears start to prickle in my eyes.

'I'm so fucking sorry, man,' he whispers. 'I'm just ... so, so sorry.'

And then he sniffs loudly and lets me go, shoving his hands back into his pockets again, and not quite meeting my eye.

When it's finally time to go in and sit down, I take the exact same seat in the middle of the dark brown pew at the front.

Daff sits on one side of me, her hand clamped tightly in mine. Simon and Chrissie and my cousins sit on the other side, taking it in turns to shoot me sad, concerned glances.

It's strange, once the service starts, the things I notice that I didn't first time round. Originally I blanked out everything the vicar was saying; my brain was just white noise as I stared at the coffin behind him. But this time I find myself listening closely to his every word. Mum wasn't in the least bit religious, so to hear him talking so earnestly about how she is 'with God now' just makes me angry. Because what kind of God decides to randomly rupture an aneurysm in the brain of a fifty-eight-year-old woman as she's walking home from Tesco on a Monday afternoon?

I'm suddenly struck by the image of her falling – what she must have looked like laid out in the middle of the high street. I feel Daff pull me towards her, because all my steel and self-control is faltering now, and I'm starting to gulp and heave. Hot, salty tears are running down my face and I can feel Daff's whole body shaking as she kisses my soaking cheek and whispers, 'It's OK, it's OK.'

But it's not OK. I am so angry, and I don't know if I will ever not be. I am angry about what happened to Mum. I am angry at the injustice of it. I am angry at my dad for leaving us, for not giving a shit about us, for not even bothering to show his face today. But I am also angry at myself, for the terrible things I said to Mum before she died, which I've never told anyone about. And it's so tiring being angry all the time, and not knowing if it will ever end.

Uncle Simon is at the podium now, telling everyone that I'll be coming up to read a poem, and for one awful second, I think the tears will completely overwhelm me.

But then Daff grips my hand tightly, and presses her forehead against mine and whispers, 'I love you.' And somehow, I find that I'm in control again. Just.

Simon looks over at me, his brow furrowed with concern. But Daff gives my hand one more squeeze, and I think: I can do this. If I know she's here, I can do it.

The walk to the podium feels like a hundred miles. The only

sound in the church is my echoing footsteps. I look out at the sea of gloomy faces, but the only one I focus on is Daphne's. I feel unsteady on my feet, and my stomach is roiling like crazy, but slowly, I start speaking.

'I wanted to read one of Mum's favourite poems,' I say into the microphone. 'It's called "Song of Myself" by Walt Whitman. Mum was always on at me to read it when I was younger. She was always on at me to read a lot of things but, being a typical moody teenager, I never listened to her. And then, a week ago, Simon and I were going through stuff at her house, and I spotted this on one of her bookshelves.' I take the tatty Walt Whitman paperback out of my pocket and hold it up. 'It's not exactly in great condition, as you can see. And as everyone here will probably know, that's typical for one of Mum's books. Pretty much every book she ever owned has a cracked spine and dog-eared pages and is full of scribbled notes in the margins. She was proud of that. She used to say to me: "That's how you know they've been properly read."'

There's a warm ripple of laughter at this, and for a moment it drowns out all the sobs and sniffs. I keep going.

'A week ago I finally read this poem, and I can see that I should have listened to her all along. Because she was right: it's brilliant. She was always right, really ... about everything.' I feel myself starting to falter, and I have to grip both sides of the podium. 'I'm not going to read the whole thing, because it's far too long. But the last stanza was where Mum had done most of her underlining and scribbling, so I thought I'd read that. So, here goes.'

I take a deep, wobbly breath. And as I lay the book open on the podium, I spot him.

The watch-seller.

He's sitting in an empty pew right at the back of the church, his blue eyes fixed straight on me. The rest of his face is unreadable beneath his wild grey-gold facial hair. He's still wearing his shabby suit, with the jacket buttoned right up and his reindeer tie just about visible underneath. He nods at me solemnly, and without thinking, I nod back. A sad smile cuts through his scruffy beard, and I'm reminded again of Grandad Jack. It's weirdly comforting, like there's another member of my family here, spurring me on.

In the front row, Daphne is smiling encouragingly too. Three rows behind her, Harv is doing the exact same thing.

For some reason, I don't feel angry at being back here any more. I don't need an explanation. I understand.

Trying to keep my voice steady, I open the book and focus on the words in front of me:

The spotted hawk swoops by and accuses me, he complains of my gab and my loitering.
I too am not a bit tamed, I too am untranslatable,
I sound my barbaric yawp over the roofs of the world.
The last scud of day holds back for me,
It flings my likeness after the rest and true as any on the shadow'd wilds,
It coaxes me to the vapor and the dusk.
I depart as air, I shake my white locks at the runaway sun,
I effuse my flesh in eddies, and drift it in lacy jags.
I bequeath myself to the dirt to grow from the grass I love,

If you want me again look for me under your boot-soles.
You will hardly know who I am or what I mean,
But I shall be good health to you nevertheless,
And filter and fibre your blood.
Failing to fetch me at first keep encouraged,
Missing me one place search another,
I stop somewhere waiting for you.

I look up. The sea of faces is now completely blurred by my own tears. But I got through it. I didn't let her down.

People are clapping now as I walk back to my seat, and Uncle Simon grabs my shoulder as I pass and whispers, 'Well done.' And as I reach Daphne, she stands and takes me in her arms, and I just feel so pathetically grateful that I was given this second chance.

When the ceremony is over, my cousins and I carry the coffin outside while Mum's all-time favourite track, 'A Song For You' by Gram Parsons, echoes around the church's wooden beams.

I look around for the watch-seller, but I can't see him. The whole congregation gathers as the coffin sinks down into the earth, and I remember what happened at this point last time. I just walked out: told Daphne I needed some time to myself before I joined everyone else at the wake, and spent the next hour wandering the streets alone, fizzing with misery and anger and horror at the idea of living the rest of my life without Mum in it.

This time, though, I take hold of Daff's hand and ask if she minds if we stay here a little longer, just the two of us. I tell Simon and Harv we'll be right behind them all, and before long the graveyard is empty, and it's just me and Daphne, sitting in silence on a bench in front of Mum's grave.

'I'm so glad you did that reading,' Daff says. 'Your mum would've been so proud.'

'I'm glad, too,' I tell her. 'Though to be honest, just before I got up to do it, I thought I was going to lose it completely. I'm sorry.'

She shakes her head almost angrily. 'Ben, are you crazy? You don't have to say sorry. You *should* be losing it. You don't ever have to apologise for that.'

'I do, Daff. I wish I'd told her … I wish I could have said sorry to her.'

'Don't be so silly. What would you possibly need to say sorry for?'

And so, finally, I decide to tell her.

Chapter Thirty-Two

It was a Sunday night, eight days before she died.

Daphne and I were supposed to be round at Mum's for dinner, but Daff had been called to some last-minute film screening in Soho. So in the end, it was just Mum and me.

And that felt weird for a start, because at that point I hadn't actually seen Mum, just the two of us, for a while. Whenever we met up, Daff was usually there too – the old clichés about hating your mother-in-law being totally untrue in our case – and her presence always softened the edges, made the conversation flow more easily. Not just because she was upbeat and fun, in contrast to my usual mardiness around that time, but because she actually had stuff going on in her life. She had things to talk about. She'd tell Mum about whatever exciting project she was currently working on, or whatever gossip she'd heard about such-and-such actor or writer. Mum loved all that.

But I had nothing going on, nothing to say. So when it was just the two of us, the room felt smaller somehow, the silences harder to fill.

And on that particular Sunday night, they felt even harder than usual. I was in the middle of an arid spell work-wise, staring down the barrel of another entirely blank week, so

I arrived at Mum's in a pretty rotten mood. And over the course of dinner, it got steadily worse, despite the deliciousness of her beef-and-Yorkshire-pudding Sunday roast. We small-talked our way through the meal, and when the plates were cleared away and soaking in the sink, Mum made coffee and set a slab of the posh Waitrose dark chocolate she liked on the table between us.

'So, what time will Daphne be home tonight?' she asked.

'No idea.' I shrugged.

Mum tutted and broke off a chunk of chocolate. 'Poor girl. They work her far too hard at that place.'

'She's all right. She enjoys it.'

'Yes, well, it's brilliant that she's doing so well.'

I shrugged again at this, tore off some of the silver foil from the chocolate wrapper and curled it into a tight, tiny ball between my fingers.

Mum gave me a look that fell somewhere between exasperation and pity. 'Come on, love. It won't be like this forever. I'm sure things will calm down at some point, and she'll be around more.'

'I know, it's just … I barely ever see her these days. She was in the office all weekend, and out most nights last week too.'

'Well, like I said, she's doing well. That's a good thing. You should be proud of her.'

'I am,' I muttered, but clearly it wasn't very convincing, because Mum snorted into her coffee and said, '*Please* don't tell me you're having a ridiculous macho crisis because your wife makes more money than you do?'

I flicked the little foil ball into the middle of the table. 'No, Mum. Of course not.'

'Good. Because I thought I'd raised you better than that,' she said huffily.

'It's not about money,' I snapped. 'Money's got nothing to do with it. I'm happy she's doing something she's good at and she loves. It just reminds me that I'm *not* doing it, that's all.'

Mum sighed through her nose and fiddled with her necklace. I remember it struck me then that she was the only person I could really talk to about this kind of stuff: frustration with work and the feeling that Daphne was leaving me behind or getting sick of me. I couldn't speak to Daff about it, for obvious reasons, and I never found a way to broach it with Harv or any of my other mates either. Mum was my only real lifeline for this stuff. She always knew the right thing to say. But that night, I didn't want to hear the right thing. I just wanted to lash out.

'Work's not going well, then?' she said finally.

I responded to that by rolling my eyes and stuffing my mouth with chocolate.

'Well, you just need to keep at it, and it'll all come good. Or try something new. Remember' – she raised a finger, mock-serious – 'everything will be OK in the end. If it's not OK, it's not the end.'

'Mum, you've gone into teacher mode again,' I muttered. 'Where d'you read that, on a fridge magnet?'

'No.' She half smiled at me. 'Saw it on Facebook, actually. Rather good, I thought.'

She was trying to cheer me up, make me laugh, but I wasn't in the mood. 'Yeah, well, I don't need meaningless slogans. I'm not revising for my bloody GCSEs. This is actual real life.'

I could feel myself degenerating into a sulky teenager

– something I often did when I was back here – but I couldn't snap out of it. I was pissed off and frustrated, and I wanted someone to take it out on.

Mum took a sip of coffee. 'Well, what about your own writing?' she pressed.

I stared at the kitchen table. 'No. I've given up on all that. I wasn't any good at it.'

She pinched the bridge of her nose, and then looked at me sadly. 'I wish you could see yourself the way I see you, love. You're so hard on yourself all the time. You've got so much talent. I just wish you had a bit more self-belief. You've got it in you to do great things, I know you have. But you give up too easily.'

I opened my mouth to speak, but nothing came out.

Mum kept going. 'I'm not talking about making millions of pounds or being world famous. I'm talking about doing something that makes you happy, that makes other people happy. Leading a good life.'

I said nothing again, but inside me, everything was churning and whirring. I felt we were suddenly on the cusp of talking about something we hadn't properly talked about *ever* at that point: Dad.

He was on my mind already that day because I'd spotted something online about his new play, which was opening soon in New York. And now I could feel it all boiling up in my chest: the years of us avoiding the subject, the anger I felt at him leaving, at never making the slightest effort to get in touch.

'I don't know …' I began. I could feel the words gathering pace in my head, and before I could decide whether I really wanted to say them, they were spilling out of me. 'Maybe if

Dad had stuck around, he might have rubbed off on me a bit more. I might have had a bit more ambition, I might have learned from him. I might have actually *achieved* something.'

Mum looked down at the table and rubbed the back of her neck. I couldn't see the expression on her face.

'But I guess there was something wrong with me,' I added. 'Or with us. We weren't enough for him, in the end.'

She looked up at me then, her forehead wrinkled. 'Have you ever considered that it might be a good thing that your father left?' she said softly. 'That maybe it's better he didn't rub off on you? That life might have been worse if he'd stuck around?'

'I don't see how life could be any worse,' I muttered. And in eight days' time, the universe would show me.

Mum sighed heavily. 'When you were growing up, I always tried not to bad-mouth your father in front of you, because no matter what he'd done, he was still your father. But the truth is, Ben, he was a shit.'

The shock of hearing her use that word nearly snapped the anger right out of me. I almost started laughing. I don't think I'd ever heard her say anything worse than 'bloody' before. But then she carried on: 'All these years, you've hung onto this idea of him as this' – she flapped her hands in the air, trying to pick out the right word – '*great* guy, who's had all this success, but trust me, it's a good thing you're nothing like him. You don't know him. Not really.'

'And that's the whole problem, isn't it?' I said, my voice rising as the resentment poured back into me. 'I never got the chance to know him. When I was growing up, every time I wanted to get back in touch with him, you put me off. You always warned me against it.'

Her voice rose to meet mine. 'Because I didn't want you to get hurt! It broke my heart in the year or so after he left, when you tried to arrange to meet him, and he always cancelled or couldn't be bothered. You were eleven, twelve years old, Ben! It shouldn't have been *you* making the effort. It should have been your father.'

I shook my head, my throat tightening and my cheeks getting hot. 'I don't know … He was still my dad, and it always felt like you were trying to keep us apart. Maybe we *could* have had a relationship, if you weren't always getting in the way.'

I regretted it as soon as I said it. Of course I did. It was stupid and spiteful and I didn't mean it in the slightest. But I said it anyway.

Mum put down her coffee mug on the table, and I'll never forget the way she looked at me. Straight in the eyes, her smile dissolving slowly as the shock gave way to sadness.

She ran her hand gently across her forehead, as if she was trying to soothe a tension headache. And I wanted to take it back, to walk straight round the table and hug her, but I didn't. I still don't know why. She shook her head and picked at some fluff on her sleeve. When she spoke again, her voice was so quiet I could barely hear her. 'Well, if that's the way you feel, then … I'm sorry.'

That's what she said: 'sorry'. When I should've been the one apologising, *she* said 'sorry'. That will always stay with me.

And that was it. It didn't end dramatically. It wasn't some *EastEnders*-style bust-up, doors slamming and plates smashing. It just ended with me standing up and saying, 'Look, I'd better go,' and Mum saying, 'Yes, OK, all right.'

We didn't hug at the door. I thanked her for dinner and

we both just mumbled goodbye. And that was the last time I ever saw her.

As I walked back down the path, I thought: fuck it. I'll call her later and apologise.

I didn't call her later. I let eight days slip by without calling or seeing her. And then she was gone.

Chapter Thirty-Three

I finish telling Daphne all this and find that I'm suddenly exhausted.

It's as if the secret has been holding me upright these past two years: woven right through me like the stake in a scarecrow. And now that it's out, it takes all my concentration not to just flop limply into a heap.

I slump back against the bench, my eyes still fixed on Mum's gravestone, and expel a deep breath. Daphne studies me carefully for a second or two and then pulls me forcefully towards her. 'Oh, Ben ... I'm so sorry,' she whispers.

I pull back and look at her, confused. 'Sorry? Did you not ... Daff, *I'm* the one who should be sorry. The things I said to her ...'

She shakes her head and smiles at me sadly. 'It was just a fight. We all have fights. They don't mean anything. You fight and then you make up. That's what happens. But you didn't get to make up.' She cups my face in her hands and kisses me gently. 'And I'm so sorry for that.'

I feel something buckle inside me, and wipe a hand across my eyes. 'I never got to tell her that I didn't mean it.'

'Ben, look at me,' she says firmly. 'She *knew* you didn't

mean it. Blurting out a few stupid, hurtful things when you were feeling down can't possibly undo everything you went through together. You must know that. She was your *mum*, for God's sake. She knew you loved her. Of course she did. Nothing you said that night could possibly have changed that.'

'You really think so?'

'I know so.'

I close my eyes, and feel the relief flow through me like water. I've kept the secret of that night locked in my head for more than two years, letting it gnaw at me, make me hate myself a little more each day. And now, hearing Daphne say those words ... it's like being washed clean. I'll always regret that that was the last time I saw Mum – always – but Daff is right: it doesn't have to define the rest of my life. I don't think Mum would have wanted it to.

Before I can properly bask in this thought, though, my mind snags on something else.

'But what if ...' I clear my throat to stop my voice trembling. 'What if the stress of the fight – the stuff I said – what if it caused what happened? She might still be here if I hadn't said those things to her.'

Daphne looks at me with her mouth set firmly and her brown eyes blazing. 'Ben. Listen to me. The doctor told us this was completely random. This wasn't about stress or unhappiness or her worrying about some stupid fight you had. It was about a weak blood vessel in her brain. That's all.' She shakes her head again and squeezes my hand. 'It's a terrible, *terrible* thing, but it wasn't your fault. You mustn't think that.'

I lean forward and touch my forehead to hers. 'I don't think you'll ever understand what it means to hear you say that.'

We stay like that for a while, forehead to forehead, as the afternoon wind whips around us. It's so strange to feel good – *happy*, even – on today of all days. I just wish so badly that I'd had this conversation with Daphne the first time around.

I wrap an arm around her and she nestles into my jacket. 'I'm glad I told you that,' I say.

'Of course. You can tell me anything. We're a team, remember.'

From the clock tower above us, a bell rings. Daff pulls out her phone and sighs when she sees the time.

'Come on, we'd better get over to your uncle's. They'll all be wondering where we are.'

'Yeah, you're right. Let's go.' I stand up and give my eyes a final wipe, feeling just about ready to go through the wake all over again.

We walk out of the churchyard hand in hand, and I take a last glance back at Mum's gravestone on the way. It feels like we said goodbye properly this time.

We step through the iron gates to find that the street outside – which was previously chock-a-block with friends' and relatives' cars – is now pretty much deserted. There's only one car left in sight: down the far end of the street, a dark red estate, half hidden beneath a huge overhanging beech tree. Behind the windscreen, I can make out a figure in the driver's seat – a man, I think, his head bowed so that his face is hidden.

I feel something spasm inside me. Panic? Maybe even excitement? Because I'm pretty sure I recognise him, despite the fact that I haven't seen him in years.

I step off the pavement, into the road, to squint harder at the red car. To make sure.

'Who is that?' Daphne asks.

'I think …' I say, feeling my heart begin to hammer, 'I think it's my dad.'

Chapter Thirty-Four

'Your ... Shit, Ben, are you sure?' Daff is staring at me, wide-eyed.

'Pretty sure,' I say, although I am now completely positive.

'He wasn't in the church, though, was he?' Daff says. 'I mean, you didn't mention seeing him.'

'No, no. He wasn't there.'

My mind is throbbing with questions. He must have been here, on this street, the first time around, too. It's not difficult to work out how I missed him then: I hurried straight out of the churchyard as soon as the funeral was over, when the road was still full of cars, and stormed off in the opposite direction.

What's more difficult to work out is *why* he's here. Why would you bother coming to a funeral if you weren't even going to show your face in the church?

Daff looks at the car again, and then back at me. 'So what do you want to do?' she asks. 'Because whatever it is ... I'm with you.'

I run a hand through my hair and shrug. 'I'll go and speak to him, I guess. But I think it's best if I do it on my own, if that's OK?'

She looks at me, her forehead wrinkled with concern. 'Yeah, of course. If you're sure?'

'I am. Definitely. You head over to Simon's, and tell them all I'll be there in a bit. You can just say I … went for a walk or something. Needed some time to myself.'

'OK.'

I give her a hug, and when we break off, she says, 'Are you sure you're all right with this?'

'Yeah, honestly, I promise. I'll see you there. I love you.'

'Love you too.' She smiles.

I start heading slowly towards the car, watching as the man at the wheel becomes gradually clearer through the glass.

I can hear my heart pounding in my ears. I have no idea what to say to him. No idea what he will say to me. I haven't seen him since I was – what, thirteen years old?

After he moved out, I'd still visit him occasionally, spending the odd awkward weekend at the flat he shared with Clara, the woman he'd left us for. But these trips dwindled with every passing year, until – just before my fourteenth birthday – he told me he was moving out of London and up to Norfolk.

He promised to keep in touch, but there were no calls, no surprise drop-ins. Throughout my teens, despite Mum's muttered warnings, I tried in vain to arrange trips up to see him, but they'd always be knocked back or cancelled at the last minute because he was too busy. Eventually I gave up trying.

He still sent birthday cards – glossy and expensive, depicting *New Yorker* magazine covers or Jackson Pollock paintings. They had cheques tucked neatly inside, and were always signed *Patrick*, never *Dad*. But they stopped arriving when I was in my early twenties. I suppose when I hit twenty-one, he figured his job was done.

Over the years, I could never escape the feeling that all

this was my fault. I wasn't good enough somehow. It was as if he could already tell, even at thirteen, that I was a failure: that I wasn't worth bothering with. It sounds stupid, I know. But whenever things went wrong later in life, it never felt like a surprise, because I knew deep down that I was destined to become a screw-up, just as my dad had predicted.

I'm about thirty feet from him now. As I step towards the passenger side of the car, he finally looks up and spots me.

His face twitches with shock, and I realise that he hasn't simply been staring downwards – he's been crying.

I stand there for a second outside the car, my heart pumping as we watch each other through the glass. And then he scrubs a hand across his eyes, and reaches over to open the door.

I slide into the passenger seat. The car smells strongly of cigarettes and sharp, minty air freshener. It's so powerful, so overwhelmingly familiar, that I'm instantly nine years old again, in the back seat of our Volvo, watching the road signs fly past as Mum and Dad hiss at each other up front.

This car smells of him. How can you recognise someone's smell, but still feel like they're a total stranger?

He coughs roughly into his fist, and then sniffs. 'Ben.' He blinks at me and shakes his head. 'Jesus Christ. Look at you. You … you've changed.' He gives a quiet, unhappy laugh. 'Sorry, that's …' He tails off and turns his head to look straight ahead through the windscreen. 'I don't know what to say,' he mutters.

If he's shocked by my appearance, I'm just as surprised at how different he looks.

Whenever I've seen his photo in magazines, he's always been clean-shaven and smartly dressed. Right now, though, he's sporting a greyish-black stubbly beard and a ragged-looking woolly jumper and jeans. His hair is much greyer, too, and he seems thinner, the skin hanging more loosely around his neck. He looks about a million miles from the grinning, confident world-beater I remember as a kid. He just seems ... tired. Defeated.

The radio is burbling quietly between us, and he fiddles with it to switch it off. 'I didn't know whether to come in ... whether I'd be welcome,' he mumbles. I can hear the self-pity in his voice. 'Christ, Ben. I'm so sorry.'

He looks round at me and I have the sudden urge to say: *Sorry for what?* Sorry for Mum dying? Sorry for leaving us? Sorry for never once making an effort to be a proper father?

But then that old, awkward formality I felt around him as a kid creeps back in. It's like I'm twelve again, round at his and Clara's flat, sensing instinctively that I shouldn't rock the boat or cause any trouble. Otherwise he might not invite me back.

So I just shrug and mutter, 'That's OK.'

He stares down at his hands on his knees. 'I just got in the car this morning and started driving,' he says. 'I was going to come into the church, honestly I was. But then I got here, and I ...' He flaps a hand aimlessly. 'I couldn't. I don't really know why I'm even here,' he adds. 'It still doesn't seem real, all this. I'm supposed to be in New York right now, for the show. We've had to push the press night back and everything.'

Anger pulses through me, and I suddenly want to rip through that old, suffocating formality. I suddenly very much want to rock the boat. I look him straight in the eye, and before I lose my nerve, I say, 'No one asked you to be here.'

His mouth hangs half open for a second, and then he nods, scratching at his stubble.

'You've got every right to be upset,' he says finally. 'To be angry at me.'

'I'm *angry* because my mum's gone,' I say, feeling my vocal cords start to constrict and my voice to crack.

'You know, she meant something to me too, Ben,' he says. 'We were married eleven years. She was a big part of my life.' And the earnest, self-pitying, almost actorly expression on his face causes something inside me to snap.

'This isn't about *you*, Dad. This has nothing to do with *you*.'

The word 'Dad' dangles awkwardly in the air between us.

He picks up a squashed packet of Marlboro Reds from next to the gearstick. I notice his fingers are tinted yellow-brown at the tips. They're shaking ever so slightly as he pulls a cigarette out. He turns it between his fingers, but doesn't light it.

'How are you coping?' he asks. And then he shakes his head. 'Stupid fucking question. Sorry.' He closes his eyes and rubs the dark circles underneath them.

'I'm OK,' I tell him. 'Well, no, I'm not OK. But I suppose I'm coping. Trying to.'

'Good. That's good. And … I heard you got married.' He blinks. 'How's your wife doing?'

That nearly makes me laugh out loud. My own father doesn't know my wife's name. No reason why he should, I suppose.

'Daphne,' I say.

'Daphne. How is she?'

'She's OK. She's pretty much kept me together over the past couple of weeks. I don't know what I'd do without her.'

Despite everything, the truth of that statement hits me like a train.

'That's good.' Dad waves his lighter in front of me. 'Do you mind if I …?'

'No, go ahead.'

He rolls the window down and lights the cigarette, inhaling deeply.

'How's Bianca?' I ask him. Bianca was the woman he was with the last time we spoke on the phone. After Clara, there was Lucy, then Fay, then Bianca, each one a few years younger than the last.

He sucks on the cigarette and rubs at his stubble again. 'Bianca? Christ. No, that was years ago. Bianca's long gone.'

I nod. 'Right.'

He taps the cigarette ash out of the window and adds, 'A bit of a nightmare in the end, Bianca. Complete headcase. Not sure what I was thinking.'

He shoots me a kind of roguish half-smile, which withers pretty quickly when I don't return it. I have vague memories of him talking like this about all the women he dated after Mum. He would jokingly put them down; dismiss them as crazy or high-maintenance when the relationship failed. As a kid, I was impressed by it: it made him seem like this funny, swaggering man of the world.

It doesn't seem in the least bit funny now.

'No, I'm seeing someone else at the moment,' he continues, taking another drag on his Malboro. 'An actress from my play. Erin. She lives out in Brooklyn.'

I remember seeing the pictures of his play online: Erin was the lead role. Very attractive – and about my age, I reckon.

I watch him for a second, his cheeks hollowing as he sucks the cigarette. It strikes me suddenly that in the end, Mum was right. I only admired him because I didn't really know him. All I had was this *idea* of him – successful, talented, dating a string of younger and younger women. But here, now, that idea doesn't add up to anything. It certainly doesn't seem to have made him happy. He just seems lonely and confused and messed up.

I don't want to end up like that.

All these years, I've assumed it was predestined: my dad was a cheat, so I would end up cheating too. It almost became an excuse for what happened in Paris. I'd tell myself it wasn't my fault; it was written into my genetic code. But that's bullshit. I *chose* to sleep with Alice. And if I meet up with her for that drink in 2020, that'll be my choice too. I can't keep blaming all my mistakes and fears and failings on a father I don't even know. I didn't want to get married because I was afraid I'd turn into him. I wanted to have kids so that I could prove I wouldn't. He's coloured all my big life decisions, in one way or another. When really he's a total stranger.

It makes me flinch with shame that I thought I needed him to look up to, when I had Mum all along: a thousand times kinder, funnier, better.

He takes a final drag on his cigarette and flicks the butt out of the window.

'Where's the wake?' he asks.

'Simon's house. Come along, if you want.'

He glances at me. 'Do you want me to?'

'I don't mind either way.' And, honestly, I don't. I just want to get out of this car and back to Daphne.

He lays one hand on the steering wheel and nods. 'Well, I don't think it'd do anyone any good if I came.' Once again, I can hear the self-pity dripping from this statement, and it makes my skin crawl. I'm prone to self-pity too, and I hate myself for it. I must have got it from him, because I definitely didn't get it from Mum.

He sniffs and straightens his back against the seat. 'So, Ben, listen. If you need anything, or you want to meet up, or—'

'Well, you'll be in New York,' I interrupt.

'No … Well, yes, I will be. For the next few weeks. But I mean, you can call me if you like. I can give you my direct line.'

'Your direct line?' The phrase is so ridiculous it almost makes me laugh out loud. It's always been like this: me calling him, trying desperately to forge some kind of relationship. 'So, now Mum's gone, you're … stepping up, is that it?' I ask him. 'You're finally ready to be my dad?'

'No, I just …' He exhales heavily and starts chewing the nail on his little finger. It's the exact same thing I do when I'm anxious. Daff is constantly moaning at me about it, batting my hand away from my mouth.

'Look, I know I fucked up, Ben,' he says slowly. 'I made a hash of everything, especially with you. But after your mother and I split up, I did try to see you. I tried. But she didn't always make it easy.'

I keep my voice steady as I look him in the eye. 'I don't want to get into some big fight today. But if you blame my mum for anything, ever, then we won't speak again. OK?'

He rubs the back of his neck and nods. 'OK.'

I open the door and put one foot out onto the pavement.

'Take care of yourself, Ben,' he says.

'You too. Good luck with the play.'

He smiles at me sadly. 'I'll see you.'

I get out and shut the door behind me. I know there's a good chance that I will never see him again, and for the first time in my life, that doesn't make me feel bad or frightened or like a total failure. In fact, I don't really feel anything towards him at all.

I pull my coat collar up and walk into the whipping wind, listening to the big maroon Renault pull away behind me. It's a freezing December day, but the sun is beginning to creep shyly out from behind the clouds.

Suddenly the desire to see Daphne, to be with the people I really love, grips me so tightly that I break into a run.

Chapter Thirty-Five

The rest of the day is ... well, not good, obviously. But better.

I certainly get through the wake with a fair bit more poise and dignity and social interaction than I did last time. And by the time it's all over, and the black suit is off, and I'm lying in bed next to Daphne, I really feel like I have resolved something – with both my parents. Even if neither of them will ever know about it.

I can feel Daff's body start to relax as she drifts into sleep beside me. But my stomach is still churning like crazy. Not just because it's 11.49 p.m. and I have no clue where I'll find myself in ten minutes' time, but also because of everything I've realised or remembered or learned over the past few days.

That night in the bar at uni when I felt this instant connection with a girl I'd just met; that moment in the maze where I snapped the branch on purpose so she'd find me. The discovery that she'd given up her Rising Star evening to come and pick me up when I was down; the blinding misery I felt waking up in Alice's bed in Paris. Some of these memories have made me feel good; some have made me feel sick with shame and guilt. But all of them have served to reinforce one thing: it's always been Daphne.

Always.

I keep thinking of what I said to my dad back in the car: *She's pretty much kept me together over the past couple of weeks. I don't know what I'd do without her.* It's true. I would be lost if I didn't have Daff. I'd fall to pieces, I know I would. But that's not a relationship, is it? That's … dependency.

She said earlier, when we were sitting in the churchyard, that we were a team. Well, for years, she's been doing all the teamwork. If I want to be with her, I need to *earn* it. I have to stop taking her for granted and start pulling my weight.

I wasted so many years trying to salvage my relationship with my dad – a relationship that wasn't even worth saving. But my marriage to Daphne *is*. I've got to make things better. I know that now.

The clock on the bedroom wall now reads 11.54 p.m. I'm only two years away from the present at this moment. Will that be where I find myself in five minutes' time? My whole body tingles with excitement at the thought. I can't wait to get back to 2020 and start rebuilding my life.

The first step will be to have a perfect Christmas Day with Daff. And then, after that, look for a new job, maybe even restart the conversation about having kids … and who knows what else? For the first time in a long time, the future actually seems like an inviting prospect.

Daff wriggles next to me and nuzzles further into my neck.

I pull her close and kiss her cheek gently. 'Everything's going to be OK, Daff,' I whisper. 'I promise. I love you.'

'Love you too,' she murmurs. 'See you in the morning.'

On the wall, 11.57 becomes 11.58.

I hold my arm up so that my watch hovers right next to the clock in my eyeline, and wait for the time to match up.

Chapter Thirty-Six

I must have been subconsciously bracing myself for the hard wooden attic floor, because the soft mattress feels strangely disconcerting beneath me.

I know I've jumped again, because the dizziness and motion sickness are both in full effect. But when I open my eyes and sit up, I see I'm still in the same bed, in the same bedroom.

It's light outside now, though, and Daphne has disappeared. I can hear the gurgle and splutter of the coffee machine from downstairs. I reach across to the bedside table and open my phone. The date reads: 25 December 2020.

The realisation fizzes through me: I'm back. I'm definitely back.

But how did I get down from the attic? And when did Daff get home? There's a blank space between me falling asleep while poring over that stuff in the biscuit tin, and me waking up here now. And that blank space feels extremely unsettling.

The watch is still fixed tightly around my wrist, its hands stuck at one minute to midnight.

My heart starts hammering, but as I step out of bed, I decide to worry about filling in the gaps later. The only thing that matters right now is that I'm back, and I can start making things right with Daphne.

I get dressed quickly and head downstairs, but as I pass the living room, I spot the Christmas tree through the half-open door. It's fully decorated, with a stack of neatly wrapped presents underneath it. My heart sinks. Daff must have got up early to do the chores I was supposed to be doing last night. After everything I've just been through – and all my resolutions to make things better – are we right back where we were before? Am I about to walk into the kitchen and straight into another fight?

She's sitting at the kitchen table, reading something on her iPad, one hand clasped around a steaming cup of coffee. She's wearing pyjama bottoms and a T-shirt, her curly hair piled messily into a topknot on her head. The urge to go straight across and put my arms around her is almost overpowering, but she doesn't even look up as I walk in.

'Hey. Merry Christmas. There's coffee in the pot.'

'Ah, nice one. Merry Christmas …'

'Thanks for doing the tree. And the presents.' She looks up at me and gives me a quick, tight smile.

'I …' I stare at her, trying desperately to read her face for any traces of sarcasm or passive-aggression. There don't seem to be any. *Did* I do the tree and the presents? I have no memory of it. But chucking a few bits of tinsel up and not remembering certainly wouldn't be the weirdest thing that's happened over the past few days.

'No worries,' I say tentatively.

Instead of rolling her eyes, or yelling something along the

lines of 'I was being sarcastic, you selfish knob', Daff just smiles again and looks back down at the iPad. Something is definitely not right here. But still: I assumed an argument was on the cards, and it doesn't appear to be. So it's probably best to let the matter lie for now.

I pour myself a coffee and stand at the kitchen counter. She carries on reading in silence, and even though we're not in open verbal combat, I can tell the atmosphere is still definitely on the frosty side. Is this just about the fight we had on Christmas Eve, about me not coming to her work party? Or has something else happened that I can't remember?

I can't bear this grim, icy tension when all I want to do is hold her and tell her I'm sorry. Before I can weigh up whether this is actually a good idea or not, I'm rushing across the room to do it.

'Ben, what ...' She wriggles out of the hug, and looks at me with her brow furrowed. 'What are you doing?'

'I just wanted to give you a hug. Sorry.'

'No, it's fine. It's just ...' She tails off and shakes her head.

I step away from her. 'What's wrong?'

'Nothing.' She fiddles with her topknot, and avoids my eye. 'I've just got stuff on my mind, that's all.'

'About us?'

She gives a short, impatient sigh. 'About lots of things.'

I kneel down and take hold of her hand. I'm trying to keep my voice steady, but the words come gabbling out manically. 'Well, let's talk about it. We can sort it out. I'm sorry for how rubbish I've been lately. Whatever's gone wrong, we can fix it, and—'

I'm about to tell her how much I love her when she pulls

245

her hand away, cutting me off in mid-flow. 'Not right now. Let's just get through today. We can talk about everything else later.'

I'm desperate to put my arms back around her. To promise her that I've changed and everything's different now and it's all going to be OK. But I can tell this is definitely not the time. After all, she's put up with years of me acting like a selfish arsehole – sulking and moaning and clamming up. I can't expect everything to magically fall into place just because I appear to have woken up in an uncharacteristically upbeat mood.

It's actions that count, not words. I need to *prove* to her that I've changed, and I can't do that in five minutes.

I stand up and walk back over to the counter. I take a sip of my coffee, and ask, 'How was last night?'

'It was fine.' She swipes a finger across the iPad screen. 'Bit boring, but OK.'

'Any gossip? Anyone get off with anyone?'

She shrugs. 'Rich got very pissed and insisted we all try out Sarah's new karaoke machine. Nadia and I did "Push It" by Salt-N-Pepa. Went down pretty well. That was about as wild as it got, really. You didn't miss much.'

'You're not hung-over, then?'

She yawns, and covers her mouth with her wrist. 'No, just tired. What did you do?'

'I went out for a drink with Harv. Once I'd, erm, done the tree and stuff, obviously.'

'Oh, right.' She raises her eyebrows, her gaze still fixed firmly on the screen. 'I thought you'd stayed in for a drink.'

'How d'you mean?'

She flicks her eyes up to the kitchen counter and I turn around to look. The bottle of red wine I near-emptied before heading up to the attic sits there staring guiltily back at me.

Crap. I completely forgot about that.

'God, Daff, I'm so sorry. I'm an idiot. I had a couple of glasses when I came in. I don't know what I was thinking.'

She breathes out through her nose, irritably. 'You knew that was supposed to be for today.'

'I'll go out and get another one this morning, I promise.'

She just sighs and keeps swiping. So even though it turns out I *did* do the presents and tree, I still also necked that forty quid's worth of Haut-Médoc. I'm guessing one cancels the other out in Daphne's head. Which is fair enough, really.

And then I remember something. If I drank that bottle of wine, then I also surely sent that message to Alice. Which means I still have to cancel our meeting.

'Back in a sec,' I say.

I walk out of the kitchen and open Facebook on my phone. There it is: the message chain with Alice, ending with my most recent one arranging to meet up in four days' time. Cancelling on Christmas morning looks a bit weird, but there's no other option.

I start tapping out a message.

Hey, Alice – happy Christmas! I'm really sorry but something's come up for the 29th that I can't get out of, so I'll have to cancel our drink, I'm afraid. I'm not sure I'll be around much after that either to be honest. Sorry. Ben x

I reread the message and imagine Alice receiving it. There's no two ways about it: it looks pretty horrible. No actual explanation or reason for why I can't make our date. But I'm too frazzled to come up with a proper excuse, and the only thing that matters right now is getting out of it.

Without thinking any more about it, I hit send and slip the phone back in my pocket. Then I head back to the kitchen, fully intent on showing Daphne the best Christmas Day ever.

Chapter Thirty-Seven

'Right, I think I've got everything here: crisps, dips, beer, and orange squash for the kids. Plus a new bottle of wine that's one whole pound more expensive than the other one.'

I waggle the plastic bags triumphantly as I step back into the kitchen.

It's two hours later, and I've just been dispatched to the corner shop to pick up the last few things we need. Daff's family are currently en route, and all six of them should be arriving any minute: her mum, Clio, and dad, Michael, plus her sister Kat with her husband Joe and their twin sons Charlie and Fred.

Daff is squatting down, squinting into the oven at the turkey, the heat blasting her cheeks pink. The kitchen is hot and noisy and the food smells incredible. She wipes her eyes and shuts the oven door, and I can see she's fighting a smile as she turns around to face me.

'You specifically went out of your way to get a slightly more expensive bottle?'

'Yeah.' I take it out and show her. 'You said the one you bought was forty quid. This one was forty ninety-nine. It's a symbolic gesture. To show how sorry I am for drinking it.'

'Mmm. Ninety-nine pee's worth of apology. Nice.' She turns her attention back to chopping potatoes, but I can sense the frost in the air beginning to thaw.

I begin unpacking the bags, and as I dump the items on the counter, Daff reaches immediately for the tube of sour cream and chive Pringles. She pops it open and scoops out a fistful.

'Oi! Those are supposed to be for everyone.'

She scrunches her nose up and raises a hand to her brow. 'My head hurts, I need carbs,' she mutters, packing her mouth with crisps.

'I knew it!' I laugh. 'You *are* hung-over!'

She smiles, and covers her mouth to prevent Pringle detritus spilling out. 'Well, I'm surprised you're not too,' she says. 'To be honest, you seem weirdly sprightly for someone who drank a whole bottle of wine last night.'

'I *feel* weirdly sprightly.'

I'm well aware that I'm behaving oddly – in that I'm not being a sulky, uncooperative douche – but I can't help it. I feel almost childishly excited. The last time I can remember experiencing this kind of nervous, tingly anticipation was on Christmas Day when I was a kid. That infectious sense of knowing that the next few hours would bring nothing but good things.

I've spent the past few days constantly retracing old steps, and even though surprises have popped up along the way, I've always known roughly what was coming. Now, though, I have absolutely no idea. And it feels brilliant. Like I've been given a second chance. A blank slate.

I'm still having to fight the urge to tell Daphne how much I've changed, to promise her that things will be better from now on. But she's right: the first thing we need to do is get through today. Then, tomorrow, I can focus on rebuilding our relationship – being the kind of husband she deserves.

I finish unpacking the bags. 'Right. Shopping's done, turkey's in, veg are simmering.' I clap my hands together. 'What else can I do?'

Daff gives me the same look she's been giving me all morning; half pleased, half mildly bewildered. I am so different from the sullen grump she left at home last night that I wouldn't blame her for suspecting that some sort of *Invasion of the Body Snatchers* scenario had taken place.

'Well … You can give the table a wipe if you want,' she suggests. 'And then maybe hoover the living room?'

'On it.' I grab a cloth from the sink and start cleaning the table while Daff stirs the veg. She's listening to the radio on her laptop, and the opening violin strains of 'Gangsta's Paradise' by Coolio suddenly ring out.

'Oh, what a tune,' she says, through another mouthful of Pringles. Her fingers are coated with crisp dust, so she has to tap the volume up with her knuckles.

'A classic,' I say, nodding to the beat.

'I think I still know all the words to this.' She shakes her head. 'What a depressing use of brain space.'

'Go on then,' I say.

'What?'

'If you know all the words …'

She laughs and turns around to face me, and we are suddenly rapping Coolio's lyrics back and forth at each other, striking increasingly ridiculous poses with the oven gloves and the J-cloth.

At some point during the second verse, I'm seized by a rush of love so overwhelming that before I know it, I'm bolting across the room to wrap my arms around her.

She laughs into my chest. 'Oi. You cut me off mid-flow.'

'Sorry, it was just too much.'

'Told you I knew the words. I think I would make a *great* rapper, actually.'

'You really would. It's not too late. You should quit your job and go for it.'

I hug her tighter, and rest my chin on the top of her head. For a second, there's only the sound of water bubbling and the turkey sizzling and spitting in the oven.

And then Daff murmurs, 'I've missed this.'

'What?'

'This. Us. Just … being stupid. Having fun together.'

'Me too,' I say. I lean down and kiss her on the lips. The kind of kiss we had in the maze. The kind of kiss I haven't given her – in the present – for years. 'Things are going to change, Daff,' I whisper. 'I promise. *I'm* going to change.'

She laughs softly. 'What the hell happened last night? Did Harv give you a pep talk or something?'

I shake my head. I suddenly want to come out with it – tell her about everything I've just been through. But I know how utterly insane it will sound, and I don't want to risk ruining things just when they're starting to get better.

So all I say is: 'Nothing happened. It's just that before you left for that party last night, I felt like things were really bad between us.' She looks down at the floor, and I take this as agreement. 'I guess they've been bad for a while now,' I continue. 'It's all my fault, I know it is, and I'm so sorry. But honestly, Daff, I really feel like I've figured things out. I'm going to be less crap from now on, I promise you.'

She raises her eyebrows. She looks pleased, but not totally convinced. Which is fair enough. It's up to me to prove it to her.

The doorbell blasts out, and she breaks out of the hug.

'That'll be them.' She gives me another kiss. 'I'm glad you said all that. It feels like maybe we're finally on the same page.'

I feel my heart soar. 'We are. Honestly.'

The doorbell trills out again in five short, sharp blasts. Daff rolls her eyes. 'Bloody hell, are they letting the twins ring the bell?' She leaves the kitchen to go and let them in. As I follow her out, I absent-mindedly dip my hand into my pocket to check my phone.

I stop dead. There's a new Facebook message.

Hey Ben, I was really sorry to get this message. Are you sure you can't do 29th? I'll be around all that week, so eve of 28th or 30th could work too? I was really looking forward to seeing you. Was so good to catch up at the wedding and I felt we had more to say to each other. The truth is, I've missed you. What happened in Paris meant a lot to me, and I know it meant something to you too. Let me know about those other dates because I'd really like to see you again. Hope we can sort something. And Merry Christmas ... Alice xxx

I hear the front door open. The hallway is suddenly full of laughter and the excited squeal of children's voices. I stare down at the message again, feeling some unpleasant emotion I can't quite define.

I'm about to hit delete, but before I can, Daphne's five-year-old nephews come barrelling down the corridor towards me.

'Hey, you two! Merry Christmas!'

I slip the phone back into my pocket and bend down to hug them.

After lunch, we all stagger back through to the living room, drowsy from too much turkey and wine.

So far, the day has gone pretty much perfectly, apart from my making a slight hash of carving and having to be rescued midway through by Daff's dad. I think her family are just as surprised by my sudden buoyancy as she is; the last few times I've seen them, I've been typically downbeat. And the weird thing is, I'm not even having to try. I just feel good: totally positive about life for the first time in forever.

Every so often, Alice's message pops into my head, but I make a concerted effort to chuck it straight back out again. I've told myself to just ignore it. I've cancelled the date, that's the important thing. Now it's time to forget about Alice and focus on Daphne.

We all settle down in the living room to watch the carpet become a multicoloured sea of wrapping paper as Charlie and Fred tear their way through their presents.

Kat and Joe are slumped on the sofa next to me, while Daff sits with her mum and dad on the other one. Charlie and Fred have just uncovered our gifts to them – a pair of matching Nerf Zombie Strike FlipFury Blasters – and are scrambling to load them with foam bullets.

'These are BRILLIANT!' shouts Fred.

'I bet you can't hit me,' I say, and their eyes light up as they start chasing me round the room, firing wildly.

I'm hit again and again and I dramatically flop to the

ground to a backdrop of excited shrieks. The boys pile on top of me, and Daff's mum, Clio, laughs.

'You're so good with them, Ben. Isn't he good, Daphne?'

'Yes, Mum.' Daff sighs obediently, and we both exchange a grin. Clio, being Greek, is hilariously blunt. Within minutes of stepping through the door, she's usually asking when Daphne and I are going to give her some more grandchildren. To be honest, I'm surprised she hasn't broached the subject yet today.

Kat giggles as the twins continue to maul me on the carpet. 'Seriously, though, Ben, if you want to take them for a couple of days, please be our guest. We could do with a break.'

'Amen to that,' says Joe.

Clio clicks her tongue. 'Take yours? They should have some of their own!'

Everyone cracks up, and Daff's dad chuckles and shakes his head. 'Clio, honestly.'

This has been their dynamic as long as I've known them: Clio says crazy, forthright things and Michael (being English) feigns embarrassment on her behalf. It sounds weird, but it works. For some reason, they complement each other perfectly, and they're clearly still head over heels in love. I suddenly wish Mum was here too, to complete this family Christmas. She always got on brilliantly with Daphne's parents.

Clio thumps the sofa arm, refusing to be deterred. 'I'm serious!' she cries. 'When are you two going to give Charlie and Fred a little cousin?'

'All right, Mum, maybe leave it for today?' Daff says with a smile.

Clio flaps her hand in a vague gesture of comedic frustration, and the twins take this as a cue to launch a new assault on me. Under heavy fire from Nerf ammo, I scramble up from the floor. 'Right, you two, see if you can catch me!'

I leap over the sofa and sprint out into the corridor, the sound of little footsteps thundering behind me.

The three of us pile into the kitchen, where the twins unload their entire foam arsenal into my chest. I fall to the ground clutching my stomach as they leap on top of me.

'AGAIN! AGAIN! AGAIN!' Fred screams.

'In a minute!' I plead. 'Don't you guys want pudding?'

'YES!' they cry at the same time.

I load up bowls with ice cream and strawberries, and we take them back through to the living room.

Charlie barges the door open with the announcement: 'Ice cream!' But no one reacts. It feels like everyone has stopped talking the moment we enter, and there's a strange, stilted silence in the room.

'Ben. What is this?'

Daff stands up and comes towards me. Her eyes are glistening and her jaw is set tightly, like she's trying hard not to cry. I feel a sharp sting of panic in my chest. She's holding something in her hand. My phone. I pat my empty pocket instinctively. It must have slipped out while I was rolling around under Nerf fire.

'Ice cream!' Charlie shouts again, holding a bowl up to Daphne. Kat pulls him gently towards her. 'Not now, sweetheart.'

Her whole family is looking at me now, frowns plastered across their faces. My heart is thudding in my chest and my neck suddenly feels boiling hot.

'What's going on?' I say, even though, deep down, I think I know.

Daff says nothing. She just hands me my phone.

There on the screen is my entire message chain with Alice.

At the bottom, there's a new picture message, sent one minute ago. It shows the two of us in the photo booth at Marek's wedding, our eyes closed, our lips pressed together.

Chapter Thirty-Eight

I sit at a corner table in The Raven, two glasses of Guinness in front of me, trying very hard to ignore the glances I'm getting from the solo drinkers at the bar.

I'm not surprised they're staring. I must look an absolute state: red-eyed and tear-stained, as I sip my fourth pint in three hours. But fuck it: let them stare. Things can't be going too well for them either if they're sitting alone in a pub on Christmas Day.

I take a big gulp of Guinness and flinch as it washes stickily down my throat. My head is woozy, I'm definitely drunk, and all I want to do is stop thinking. But I can't. I can't get that look out of my head: the one on Daphne's face as she handed me the phone. The hurt shining in her brown eyes like she just couldn't believe this was happening. All those jokes she's made over the years about Alice fancying me. All the times I laughed along at them. The betrayal, the humiliation she must have felt reading those messages and seeing that picture. I can't even bear to think about it.

In that split second, the whole world crashed down around me. It felt a little like waking up after an 11.59 p.m. jump: the combination of confusion, dizziness and motion sickness, as if I'd just been swung around and then punched hard in the stomach.

Before all this time-travel madness began, I thought that maybe this was what I wanted. Up in the attic on Christmas Eve, I dreamed of a blank canvas, getting the chance to start all over again. I wondered if, maybe, Daphne and me splitting up might be for the best.

Well now I know: it's not. Not for me, anyway.

I can't bear the idea that I've lost her, and no matter how much I drink, the stabbing pain of it won't go away.

I take another sip and realise that I'm crying again, the tears dropping steadily onto the sticky table. I don't even bother to wipe my face. I can't find the strength to care about what I must look like.

'Are you all right, son?'

I look up, half expecting to see the watch-seller standing over me. But it's not him. Just another old bloke with a kindly smile.

'Yeah, I'm fine. Sorry. Thank you.'

He pats me on the arm and walks back to the bar.

The door opens and Harv enters in his comically huge parka, cold wind rushing in behind him. I scrub my eyes hard on my sleeve and try to pull myself together.

Harv's face is already etched with concern before he even spots me. Fair enough, really, since I wasn't clear about why I urgently needed to see him at 8 p.m. on Christmas Day, in the very same pub we met up in last night.

As he sits down, I slide the full pint towards him.

'Guinness?' He wrinkles his nose. 'Didn't we have this conversation yesterday?'

'Shit, yeah. Sorry. I forgot.'

He pushes the glass aside and looks at me. 'How many of these have you had?'

'This is my fourth.' I hiccup and taste cranberry sauce. I'm finding it very hard to focus. 'Sorry … I didn't drag you away from family stuff, did I?'

'No, I was coming back tonight anyway,' he says. 'My sister just dropped me off.'

'How was your Christmas? Are your mum and dad all right?'

He swats these questions away impatiently. 'Never mind all that. What the hell is going on, man? What are we doing here?'

I want to explain, but I'm worried I might start crying again. So instead I find Alice's message chain and slide my phone across the table.

Harv's brow gets progressively more furrowed and his eyes progressively more saucer-like as he scrolls down. By the time he reaches the photo-booth kiss picture, he looks like he's seen several ghosts.

He stares up at me. 'What the *fuck*?'

I nod.

'Alice? Alice-from-uni Alice?'

I nod again.

'When … when did this happen? How long has it been going on? And what does she mean about Paris? What happened in Paris?'

I opt to take a large gulp of Guinness rather than address any of these questions.

Harv is looking down at my phone again. 'So Daphne saw all this? The messages, the picture: everything?'

'Yep.' I take another swig to try and hold back the lump that's rising fast in my throat. 'The phone must have slipped out of my pocket. I tried to explain and apologise, but she just said she wanted me to leave. She said she needed to think. All her family were there too, and the way they looked at me …' I squeeze the bridge of my nose tightly and feel my voice starting to tremble. 'I can't bear the thought that I've hurt her. I've been such an idiot, Harv.'

'Mate …' He exhales and shakes his head. For a few seconds we sit in silence, listening to Shane MacGowan and Kirsty MacColl bicker on the stereo. I feel weirdly grateful to Harv for not judging me – or at least, not judging me out loud. Right now, I'm not sure I could take someone else's disdain on top of my own.

Finally he says: 'So, what … are you and Alice, like, a thing?'

'No! Not at all. I just … I don't know what I was thinking. I guess all this stuff happened because things between me and Daff have been bad for a while now. Maybe that's why I arranged to meet Alice in the first place – because I was thinking that Daff would be better off without me.'

Harv scratches his stubble and frowns. 'Well, that's pretty fucking patronising.'

'What? Why?'

'Because Daphne's a grown-up, Ben. She's not some weak, submissive idiot. It's up to her to decide whether she's better off without you. It's not your decision to make. If she's with you, then it's because she wants to be with you. Simple as that.'

I stare at him, letting the words settle inside my head. Even in my Guinness-fugged brain, I can see that he's absolutely right. Yet again I was shifting the responsibility for my actions off myself and onto someone else. I feel guilt and shame tag-team me sharply in the chest. 'You're right,' I murmur. 'You're totally right.'

'You don't have to sound so surprised,' Harv says sniffily. 'I do have my moments.' He picks up the full pint and takes a swig.

I can't stop myself smiling. 'I thought Guinness was worse for you than a Zinger Burger?'

He wipes his foamy top lip. 'These are extreme circum-stances.'

I almost laugh, before I remember just how extreme these circumstances are.

'So listen,' I say. 'Can I stay at yours tonight?'

'Yeah, man, of course. Stay for as long as you want.'

'Really? I'm not going to get in the way of you and your fitness instructor Tinder girl, am I?'

'Nah. I'm not sure that's a long-term thing anyway, to be honest.'

'OK. Thanks, man. Seriously. I really appreciate it.'

'No worries. Of course.'

I breathe out shakily and lean back in my chair. For Harv, it was only last night that we were sitting in this exact same spot while I wrestled internally with how to lay my emotions bare in front of him. This time, there's no need to wrestle. I'm drunk and broken and it all just spills out.

'What the fuck am I going to do, Harv?' I slur.

He shifts awkwardly in his seat. I can tell before he even opens his mouth that he's going to reach for the tried-and-tested banter to put out this fire. 'Come live with me permanently,' he deadpans. 'It'll be like old times. We'll get some goldfish, name them after rappers. Sit around playing FIFA all day in our pants. It'll be great.'

I attempt a laugh, but it gets swallowed by a strangled sob. I can feel my eyes starting to prickle again. I'm going to break down in front of him, and there's nothing I can do to stop it.

'I think my marriage is over,' I whisper. And as I hear myself say the words, the cold, hard reality of them hits me like a truck. All this jumping about through time has been for nothing. All it's done has made me realise how much I love Daphne. But now I'm here – back in the real world, where actions actually have consequences – and I've screwed it all up.

I've lost her. Maybe for good.

I put a hand over my eyes, but I can feel the tears leaking through my fingers.

'Sorry, man ...' I mutter.

I can't see Harv, but I feel him reach across and place a hand on my shoulder. 'Mate, don't be stupid,' he says quietly. 'This is you and Daphne. It can't be over. You're clearly meant to be together.'

That just makes the tears come even faster. 'You really think so?' I gulp.

'Of course.' He squeezes my shoulder. 'It's obvious. It always has been. You can totally save this. You just need to be sure that you actually want to.'

'I do,' I say. 'More than anything.'

'Well, why didn't you tell her, then?'

'Tell her what?'

'About Alice.'

I take my hand away from my face and look at him. 'Because ... Are you mad? You've just heard how she reacted when she found out.'

He nods. 'Yeah, because she found out. That's very different from you choosing to tell her. You say you want it to work, but if you're planning on keeping massive secrets from her, it's never going to, is it?'

I sniff loudly and stare into the dregs of my pint. 'No, I guess not.'

He takes another sip of his drink and wriggles in his chair again. 'You know,' he says, 'this whole thing is a bit like what happened with me and Liv.'

He's using that same forced-casual tone that Alice used in Paris when she was asking about me and Daphne. He's trying very hard to make out like this is just a casual statement; that it's no big deal. But I know full well that it is.

I clear my throat and push my pint away. 'How d'you mean?'

He avoids my eye, concentrates instead on spinning his beer mat. 'You know she went off with that guy, that *Made in Chelsea* dickhead?'

'Yeah.'

'Well, that had been going on for a while. She didn't tell me – I found out. Same as Daphne did. And that's ... Even though it was the worst I've ever felt, and the idea of losing her made me sick, I knew that it couldn't ever work if I didn't trust her. That's why you need to be totally honest with Daff. Tell her everything that happened – everything – and then tell her it won't ever happen again. And make sure that you mean it.' He takes another sip of Guinness and looks me straight in the eye. 'In the end, Liv wasn't worth fighting for, but Daphne definitely is. She's fucking brilliant. I've always said it.'

I blink and nod, feeling lighter suddenly. For the first time since I walked out of our flat three hours ago, I can see a tiny crack of light in the darkness. My heart is pumping, and I'm much more sober than I was a few seconds back. 'You're right,' I say. 'I have to fight for her. I just hope it's not too late.'

'It's not, mate.' Harv smiles. 'Trust me.'

He takes another swig of his pint. His cheeks are flushed – presumably from the novelty of us discussing something that actually matters for once. He slams the glass down and smacks his lips. 'God, I've missed Guinness. Vodka tonic really can't compete.'

I laugh. 'Harv, I've wanted to say for a while now that I'm really sorry about Liv. I feel like I was a shit friend to you throughout that whole time.'

He shakes his head. 'No, you weren't, man. I completely cut everyone off. I was trying so hard to blend in with her and her mates: going to those awful private members' clubs, listening to terrible house music. I was trying to be someone else, I guess. So it was my fault too.'

'Still, I should have tried harder to be there for you when it ended, and to chat to you about it. I'm sorry for that. But I'm just so glad that we …' I pause, because I can't think of any other way to finish this sentence than 'got back together'.

'Got back together?' Harv says with a grin.

'Yeah, exactly.'

'I'm glad too.'

We catch each other's eye and laugh. And just for a second, despite the fact that my entire life is lying in pieces around me, I actually feel good.

On the stereo, the Pogues give way to Slade, drawing a muted cheer from the old guys at the bar. 'We should talk about proper things more often,' I say to Harv. 'Not just football and hip hop.'

He narrows his eyes. 'Benjamin, there's nothing more proper on earth than football and hip hop.'

'True.' I spin my phone on the table and take a deep breath. 'So, do you think I should text Daff? Or call her?'

Harv takes a final sip of Guinness as he considers this. 'No. I reckon we should go back to mine so you can get your head straight, and then you should give her a call tomorrow.'

Tomorrow. For the first time in what feels like forever, I am actually going to have a tomorrow. I glance instinctively down at my watch. The main reason I picked this pub as our meeting place was the chance that I might see the watch-seller here again. This is where we first met in the real world, so surely there's a good chance I might see him here again now that I'm back.

But no: there's no sign of him. I guess his job – whatever the hell it was – is done.

'You haven't seen that old guy anywhere, have you?' I ask Harv absently as I scan the bar again. 'The one from last night?'

Harv frowns. 'Which old guy?'

'You know: the old guy with the beard.' I hold up my wrist. 'That weird bloke who gave me this watch.'

Harv shakes his head slowly. 'You've lost me there, Benjamin. You weren't even wearing that watch yesterday, were you? And we definitely didn't bump into any weird old guys with beards.'

'But you saw me talking to him …' I tail off as Harv's frown deepens. It's no surprise that he doesn't remember our time-jumping 2010 house call, but it's been less than twenty-four hours since he saw the watch-seller with his own eyes, in this very pub, in the real world.

Unless ...

Harv stands up. 'Come on, man. Let's get back to mine so I can make you some coffee. You're obviously more pissed than I thought. The only non-existent bearded bloke you should be talking about today is Santa Claus. Or Jesus, I suppose.'

I stand up with him, but my head is swimming.

I don't remember Daff coming home. I don't remember coming down from the attic. I don't remember doing the tree or the presents. And now Harv doesn't remember the watch-seller from last night, despite the fact that I am still wearing the watch.

What the *hell* is going on?

Harv pushes open the door, and I take one last look back at the bar before I follow him out into the freezing night air.

Chapter Thirty-Nine

We step outside the pub to see that the little square across the road is packed full of people. They spill out into the street on both sides, blocking our route.

At the centre of them, right in the middle of the square, a group of carol singers is belting out an enthusiastic rendition of 'God Rest Ye Merry, Gentlemen', and the crowd is bellowing along with gusto, sounding full to the brim with both festive cheer and copious mulled wine.

'Here we go,' Harv says, nudging my shoulder with his. 'This is exactly what we need – a bit of Christmas spirit.'

I'm about to protest – joining in with a load of drunk carollers is about the last thing on earth I feel like doing right now – but Harv is already crossing the road, making his way through the crowd towards them.

I follow him through the sea of Santa hats and hastily fashioned tinsel scarves, my brain still fizzing from our conversation in the pub. Once he finds a choice spot, Harv slings an arm around me and thwacks my shoulder repeatedly until I start singing along with him. And maybe it's the undeniable glow of festive goodwill in this square – or, more likely, the sight of my best mate gleefully strangling the high note on 'Oh-oh tidings of comfort and joy' – but for a few seconds, I actually find myself carried along by it all. For a brief moment, I almost lose myself.

And then I spot him.

He's standing right at the back of the group of carollers, singing at the top of his voice, even more enthusiastically and tunelessly than everyone else. As he catches my eye, he inclines his shaggy head and shoots me a wink.

My stomach performs several vigorous forward rolls. He doesn't look in the slightest bit different from when I last saw him, at Mum's funeral. He's still wearing the same shabby suit and garish reindeer speckled tie, and his tangle of grey-gold hair is as wild as ever.

Through the roar of confusion, I nudge Harv and indicate the watch-seller.

'Oh yeah.' Harv laughs. 'He's really going for it. Dude could give Brian Blessed a run for his money.'

There's not even a flicker of recognition in his face. He has clearly never seen this man before in his life – let alone in the past twenty-four hours.

Before I can process what this might mean, someone starts handing out Santa hats to the carollers. I watch the old man stick his on at a jaunty angle, still singing boisterously, and I'm struck once again by his resemblance to Grandad Jack.

The song comes to an end – the final protracted 'co-om-fort and joy' collapsing under the laughter of the performers – and the onlookers clap and cheer and stamp their feet as the singers take a mock-dramatic bow. A few Santa hats are thrown into the air, and people are hollering 'Merry Christmas!' over the applause. A few of the carollers weave straight in among us, shaking Salvation Army-branded tins, and before I know it, the watch-seller is right there.

'Any change, lads?' he asks brightly.

Harv digs into his pocket and slots in a pound coin. 'There you go, mate. Merry Christmas.'

'And to you too,' the old man twinkles.

'Good work on that tune. I was saying to my friend here, you've got a serious set of lungs on you.'

The watch-seller gives a warm chuckle at this. 'What I lack in capability, I feel I more than make up for in effort.'

'You definitely do.' Harv grins, and then glances back at the pub. 'Ben, can you hang on one sec? I'm just gonna nip back in for a wee.' He turns to the watch-seller. 'Long Tube journey, and I'm not used to drinking pints.'

The watch-seller laughs politely. 'No. You're a vodka and tonic man.'

'Er ... yeah,' Harv says, wrinkling his forehead. He gives me a confused look, and then walks off.

The old man smiles at me. 'You've managed to get him back on the black stuff, then?' He raises his eyebrows. 'That's the sign of a true friend: they'll abandon all dietary plans for you.'

I'm too desperate for answers to even acknowledge this remark. 'Look, can you please tell me what's going on?' I whisper urgently. 'Am I back in the real world or not?'

He readjusts his wonky Santa hat. 'I thought someone with your particular theatrical background might have realised that after Christmas past comes ... Christmas present.'

'Christmas *present*?' I repeat, stupidly.

I think of Marek's play – *The Carol Revisited*. His version of Christmas present involved Vinny Scrooge weeping uncontrollably as he watched a papier-mâché model of his own corpse being dumped in the harbour (a paddling pool) by rival gangsters.

But it was only a hallucination – a warning of what would come if he didn't change his ways …

'So today didn't really happen,' I say slowly, feeling a spark of hope ignite in my chest. 'Daff will have no memory of seeing those messages when I finally get back to reality. *If* I get back.' The hope gives way briefly to anger, and I look up at the old man. 'Or will I keep flitting about from one random moment to the next? No future, no consequences?'

The watch-seller smoothes his reindeer tie and chuckles. 'Oh, the future's on its way, my friend, don't you worry,' he says, his eyes twinkling. Before I can ask what he means by that, he adds, 'Just remember: "If you don't like your life, you can change it." H. G. Wells wrote that.'

'Really?' I say. 'He also wrote *The Time Machine*, didn't he? I guess that's why you're into him.'

He laughs – a hearty Grandad Jack laugh that sends another shiver of recognition down my spine. 'It's one of the reasons. Of course, *The Time Machine* is no *Groundhog Day*.'

I see my chance to ask the question that's been nagging at me for what feels like weeks. 'Listen, do we know each other? It's just that you remind me a lot of my grandad.'

The watch-seller twinkles at this, puffing his chest out and smirking. 'Good-looking fellow, I presume? No, I think I've just got one of those faces. People often remark on how similar I look to someone they know.'

'Oh. OK.'

I'm not entirely sure I believe him, but I can tell he's not going to be drawn any further. We stand in silence for a few seconds, while the crowd disperses around us. I feel the way I always feel in his presence: unreal. Like I've fallen through the cracks of reality and landed in some hidden pocket that no one else can see.

'Why can't you just tell me what's going on?' I ask finally.

'Because you'll find out soon enough,' he says.

'It really doesn't feel like it.'

Across the street, I see Harv re-emerging from the pub. I rub my eyes with the sleeve of my jacket. I feel more knackered than I have done all day.

The old man puts a wrinkled hand on my shoulder. 'Trust me,' he says kindly. 'You're nearly there.'

The sofa bed feels like it's made of broken coat hangers.

We've coaxed its rickety skeleton out from the depths of Harv's couch, and now the two of us are lying side by side on top of the duvet, eating Haribo Tangfastics and watching *Love Actually* on TV.

'The signs bit is coming up now,' Harv says, through a mouthful of heavily sugared gelatin.

'The signs bit?'

'Yeah, you know – when that *Walking Dead* guy goes round Keira Knightley's house with his creepy signs.' He takes another handful of sweets. 'I've always wondered – what would he have done if his mate had opened the door instead of Keira? He's literally standing there with a boom box and a shitload of signs about his wasted heart.

Obviously his mate would ask to see them, and then he's screwed, you know?'

I turn to look at him. 'How many times have you seen this film?'

His cheeks flush. 'Like, once … or, I don't know. Maybe twice. It's always on telly.'

He meets my eyes and we both start laughing.

After our deluge of emotional frankness in the pub, Harv seems to have adopted the firm position that breeziness and banter are now the way forward. Since we left the watch-seller in that square a few hours ago, he hasn't mentioned Daphne or Alice once. He obviously feels that the best method for keeping my mind off the horror show of my life is simply to act like nothing has happened: my marriage is not really on the brink of collapse, and this is just a normal Christmas Day like any other, ending as it always does with the two of us lying on a sofa bed watching a Richard Curtis film.

To be quite honest, I appreciate it. Not just because I'm too frazzled to talk any more about deep, serious, depressing stuff, but also because his tactic is more spot-on than he realises. Nothing *has* happened.

This is not reality.

Which means Daphne didn't see those texts, which means – surely – I have another chance to make things right. At the moment, that thought is the only thing keeping me going.

I flinch every time I remember the look on her face as she handed me my phone. I can't even bear to think of the hurt I've caused her. There has to be a way to mend this. There just has to be.

I lift my phone off the arm of the sofa. The time is 11.47 p.m.

In twelve minutes, all this will disappear, and even though I have no idea where or when I'll end up, I know that I have to find her. I have to tell her the truth – about everything. I have to somehow show her how much she means to me.

And preferably not by turning up on the doorstep with a load of creepy signs.

Harv stuffs another large fistful of sweets into his mouth. Clearly, that pint of Guinness was the beginning of a slippery slope, because we've now emptied a packet and a half of Haribo between us, in addition to the large kebab and chips we had on the Tube home.

If this was reality, I'd be considering staging an intervention.

I check my phone again: 11:48. It's like time is purposely slowing down, just to mess with me.

'Ben, come on,' Harv says quietly.

'What?'

He nods at the armrest. 'Stop looking at your phone. She's not going to text you now.'

'No. Yeah. I know.'

I lay it back down and we watch the *Walking Dead* guy doing his heart-warming stalker act in silence for a bit. And then, still looking at the TV, Harv suddenly says: 'You will be OK, man. Honestly. You and Daff, I mean.'

'Yeah.' I breathe out shakily. 'I hope so, but I'm not so sure.'

'Yeah, well, that's your natural pessimism talking,' he says. 'You need to tap into your inner optimist.'

'I don't think I've got one.'

'Well, fucking *get* one.' Harv mutes *Love Actually* and turns to look at me. 'Look, man, this situation is going to require some serious effort if you want to fix it. You screwed up big time.'

'Yeah, thanks, Harv. You don't need to remind me.'

'Well clearly I *do*, because you're not going to get Daphne back by wallowing in your own misery, are you? You have to believe in yourself a bit more, otherwise why the hell should she believe in you?'

I shrug. 'Self-belief doesn't exactly come naturally to me.'

He rolls his eyes. 'Self-pity, on the other hand, you've got coming out of your ears.'

The accuracy of this statement sends a shiver down my spine. I think of the funeral, of my dad's cloying self pity in the car. I can't give in to that side of myself. I have to be better. Not just for Daff, but for *me*.

Harv shuffles back against the cushions and continues. 'It's not going to be easy to win her trust back. It might be the hardest thing you ever do in your life. But isn't it worth the effort?'

'Of course it is. She ...' My voice catches in my throat. 'She's everything to me.'

Harv nods firmly. 'There you go then. Pep talk over.' He unmutes the TV. 'Now can we *please* get back to arguably the greatest cinematic achievement of the twenty-first century?'

Without thinking, I glance at my phone again: 11.52.

'Stop bloody doing that!' Harv snaps. 'Seriously – don't make me confiscate it.'

'Sorry. Sorry.'

He sighs. 'Tomorrow, Ben. You can sort all this out tomorrow.'

All I can do is pray that he's right. In eight minutes' time, maybe I'll get another chance. Maybe I'll wake up next to Daphne again, all ready to lay everything out there and try desperately to rebuild what I've nearly destroyed.

My heart soars at the thought as I count down the seconds in my head.

Chapter Forty

There's a high-pitched ringing sound, like a phone going off. Or an alarm.

I scramble upright, trying to calm my gasping breath, as the tinny noise continues to drill deep into my eardrums.

I'm in bed. At least, I think I am. Although it's a noticeably comfier one than Harv's sofa bed. My eyes are wide open, but it's pitch dark and I can't see a thing. The alarm is still going off, its cries for attention getting louder and more aggressive with every second.

I fumble blindly around me, trying to locate where it's coming from. My hand grasps something cold on the bedside table – an iPhone I don't recognise – and I shut the alarm off before dropping the phone back down. According to the flash of screen I caught a glimpse of, it's just after 9 a.m. And the date underneath said ...

No, hang on. That can't be right.

I go to pick up the phone again, but before I can, I feel movement beside me. The bed covers shifting as somebody turns over.

'Mmm. Morning, you,' a female voice mumbles. 'Merry Christmas.' An arm stretches out across my bare chest and a messy head of hair nuzzles underneath my chin.

I freeze. I know it's not Daphne. It's pitch dark, but somehow, I just know.

My heart is stampeding in my chest. I try to hack my sandpaper-dry throat clear, but I can't get any words out.

'Ben? Are you OK? You're shivering.'

The voice is harder now. It has an edge to it. I recognise it this time, and the shock hits me like a punch in the gut.

'What's wrong?'

I still can't quite get my mouth to emit any actual human words. I feel her sit up and reach across to the other side of the bed. A light comes on, and the sudden brightness forces my eyes shut.

'Oh my God, you look *awful*! You're white as a sheet!'

I try a few painful blinks, but as my surroundings swim gradually into focus, I find there is simply too much worrying information here to process. The first piece of worrying information is that I definitely do not recognise the bed or, indeed, bedroom I am currently in. The second, more worrying piece of information is that I definitely *do* recognise the half-naked woman sitting next to me.

All I can manage to say is: 'Alice …'

She wrinkles her forehead, and clambers out of bed. 'I'll go and get you some Nurofen. You *can't* be ill today, Ben. You seriously can't. It'll be so embarrassing.'

She wriggles into a dressing gown and clomps out of the room.

I lie in the unfamiliar bed, in the unfamiliar room, paralysed with panic. Alice was right: I really am shivering – trembling all over – and I can't seem to stop. I thought that by now I'd be used to it – the abrupt madness of finding myself suddenly transported to a different time and place. But this is something else. This is somewhere completely new, somewhere I've never been before.

I've only woken up next to Alice once in my entire life, and that was in her Paris flat.

This is not her Paris flat.

Which means …

I look down at my wrist to check the watch is still there. It very much is, the hands stuck in the exact same place. I reach slowly for the unfamiliar iPhone on the bedside table. I can hardly bring myself to touch the screen.

I must have imagined it. Surely.

I tap the phone tentatively with my thumb, and as the screen lights up, my stomach drops out from under me like I've just plunged into the first loop of a roller coaster.

The date reads: 25 December 2023.

I click the phone off and then on again. The date still reads 25 December 2023.

My heart is now beating so fast I think I might actually pass out. 'After Christmas past comes Christmas present,' the watch-seller told me outside the pub. But I never stopped to think about what comes after that …

On the chest of drawers opposite me, there's another phone charging – it must be Alice's. I run over to check the screen. The date reads: 25 December 2023.

There's no doubt about it: I am standing in a bedroom I don't recognise at just after 9 a.m. on Christmas morning three whole years into the future.

I drop back down onto the edge of the bed and put my head in my hands. The shock is so severe that I can't really feel anything – my whole body is numb, and my thought process currently resembles a fish on dry land, unable to do much more than just flap pointlessly from side to side.

Is this it? Is this where I've finally washed up? Have I just sleepwalked through three whole years of my life and ended up here, with Alice?

I can hear her footsteps pounding back down the hallway. The bedroom door opens and she sweeps in, holding a glass of water and two small white pills.

'God, you really don't look good. How do you feel?' She doesn't bother to wait for an answer, which is probably for the best since I'm unable to give one. Instead, she presses the glass and the pills into my hands, and says, 'Just take them, OK? I'm going to get breakfast started. They're going to be here at half eleven.' She snaps her fingers irritably in front of my face. 'Ben? OK?'

'Yeah, OK,' I croak.

And with that, she sweeps back out of the room.

It's still not fully light in the room, but even with the drawn curtains, I could tell how different she looks. Most obviously, her hair is much longer – the French Amélie bob she was still sporting at Marek's wedding is long gone, and her dark blonde locks now hang down past her shoulders.

I stare at the glass of water and the pills. My head is throbbing, and I do now genuinely feel a bit sick, so I decide it's probably a good idea to take them. As I chase them down with the lukewarm water, all that's going through my mind is: where is Daphne? What the hell happened to land me here?

I stand up unsteadily and pull some clothes on, before venturing out into the corridor, and the not-too-distant future.

Chapter Forty-One

At first sight, 2023 doesn't seem hugely different to 2020.

A quick glance through the upstairs window at the street below reveals a disappointing lack of hover cars, and there's not a single jetpack to be seen either. Closer inspection of the unfamiliar phone by my bed has revealed it to be an iPhone 13 – which would be quite exciting if it wasn't exactly the same as my old iPhone 8, albeit with a slightly shinier back.

Cars still can't hover, people still can't fly and Apple continues to massively rip us all off: clearly, three years is not sufficient time for the planet to undergo any genuinely seismic changes.

I creep down the stairs, which are lined with photos of Alice and people who are presumably members of Alice's family, and as I catch another glimpse of the street outside, I realise I have absolutely no idea where I am. Am I even still in London?

I check Google Maps on my trusty iPhone 13 to find that I'm currently in Hammersmith. Only a few miles from Daff's and my flat in Kensal Rise.

Which, surely, is no longer Daff's and my flat …

Panic ripples through me again. Is she there now? What is she doing?

I get the sudden urge to call her, but I'm instantly distracted from this idea by the sight of my reflection in the hallway mirror. I actually have to stop myself letting out an audible gasp as I see it. If the outside world appears unchanged, the same can definitely not be said for my face.

My hair has shuffled a good quarter-inch backwards on my forehead, and I'm sporting new wrinkles in places I didn't even know you could get them: the side of my nose, for instance. The patches of grey at my temples have extended their territory significantly, and most disturbingly, my eyebrow hair has taken on a vaguely owlish quality. A couple of strands are so long that they could almost be stretched out to meet my retreating hairline.

I am thirty-seven years old, and I very much look it.

I run a hand over my face. The world feels less real than it's ever felt, but it doesn't change the fact that this could be it: I could very well be back in reality right now. The thought makes my stomach flip. And then, from down the hall, I hear:

'Ben, come on! Breakfast!'

I tear myself away from my thirty-seven-year-old reflection and follow the sound of clinking plates down the corridor. As I push open the kitchen door, I see Alice at the counter, her back turned to me, pouring almond milk into a bowl of something that looks like it should be lining the floor of a hamster cage.

'Hey, you,' she says, without turning round. 'How are you feeling now?'

'Yeah, I'm—'

'Don't be ill, Ben, seriously,' she says, cutting me off. 'Not on Christmas Day. I want you on good form today, charming the pants off everyone.'

She spins around, holding the bowl of moist sawdust out to me, and prods me three times in the stomach: 'Don't. Be. Ill!' She's smiling, but her teeth are clenched, and those stomach prods were definitely straddling the border between playful and aggressive. Is she pretending to be annoyed, or is she actually annoyed? It's very hard to tell.

'OK?' she adds.

I nod. 'Yep. OK … No, I feel better already, actually.'

'Great. Good.' She sweeps back to the counter, and as she starts pulling spoons out of the cutlery drawer, I get the chance to take in her face properly. Like me, she's gained a couple more wrinkles, but she still looks great. Beautiful, even. Long hair really suits her.

None of which makes this situation feel any less terrifying or wrong.

'Back in a sec. I'm just going to wrap the last few presents.' She leaves the room, and I put the bowl down on the table and take the opportunity to have a look around my new home.

The first thing that catches my eye is a large black-and-white framed photograph of Alice and me. It's at the back of the room, hanging in pride of place behind the head of the table.

It must have been taken by a professional photographer, because the two of us are perfectly positioned – and possibly even artificially lit – in the middle of an outlandishly picturesque garden. Alice is sitting on a wicker chair wearing a long, flowing dress, and I'm standing next to her in a suit I don't recognise, my hand draped awkwardly on her shoulder. We are both smiling at the camera, but while Alice is managing to exude happiness and sophistication, I look like I am in genuine physical pain.

The whole thing is so ridiculous it almost makes me snort with laughter. I flash back suddenly to the attic on Christmas Eve 2020, when I saw that picture of myself in the university play programme. I didn't recognise the grinning, carefree nineteen-year-old in that photo, and I don't recognise the ludicrous, gurning thirty-seven-year-old in this one, either. There is no way I would ever pose for a photo like this – even if Daphne suggested it.

But the truth is, Daphne would never, *ever* suggest it.

The only photo of us on public display in our flat is frayed at the edges and dangling from a magnet on the fridge. It shows the two of us drunk and bent double with laughter at Bestival 2017 – her dressed as the Ultimate Warrior and me as Hulk Hogan. I love that photo.

As I stare at this gold-framed monstrosity on the wall, I can't help imagining Daff's reaction to it. I'm fairly sure it would involve a significant amount of giggling.

Who the hell have I become?

Next to the preposterous photo there is a calendar hanging on a little hook above the Wi-Fi box. I squint at it to see that it reaffirms the day and year, and that under today's date, someone – Alice – has written: *XMAS DRINKS DO!* and under tomorrow – Boxing Day – *LUNCH AT M&D's.*

Scanning down the calendar, I spot another entry, four days from today, on December 29th. There are only two words, with a flurry of red pen strokes surrounding them, as if they've just caught fire: *WEDDING PLANNER!*

My blood turns to ice.

I glance down at my left hand to see that my wedding ring has disappeared.

I am getting married to Alice. I am no longer married to Daphne and I am getting married to Alice.

The kitchen door swings opens and she comes back in, humming under her breath. 'OK, presents are done ... I need to ice the cake, and get the wine out. What are you going to wear, by the way, babe? Why don't you wear that shirt I like ...'

She tails off as she finally looks over at me.

'Ben, what are you doing?' she says sharply. 'Why are you looking at the calendar?'

'I just ... I was ... The wedding planner?'

I've been in the future for half an hour now, and I'm still yet to form a coherent sentence.

Alice's face falls and she puts a hand to her forehead. 'Ben, you are kidding, right? Tell me you're kidding. I told you about that appointment three days ago.' She shakes her head irritably. 'You probably just zoned out as usual, didn't you? God, you've been so out of it lately. I feel like I'm doing everything myself. Which is fine, obviously, as I don't think you'd be much use anyway.' She laughs to herself at this, and then whirs back into activity, pulling tin foil out of the cupboard and a large cake out of the fridge.

I get the sense that I am not really needed in this conversation – that Alice probably spends a lot of time talking *at* me, rather than *to* me.

'The wedding's only four months away, Ben,' she's saying. 'I really need you to engage a bit more, OK?'

'Yeah, of course,' I mumble.

Four months. In four months, I am marrying Alice.

She carries on. 'So, like I told you, this appointment is to talk about the flowers and the readings. And also the string quartet.'

I stare at her. 'The … string quartet?'

'Yes, the string quartet. I did tell you about that, too.' Her mouth curls up slightly at the side. 'It's funny, actually, Becks is going to be so pissed off that we've managed to book them. She wanted them for their wedding, but they couldn't do that date. She'll be *fuming*.' There's a gleeful snarkiness creeping into her voice: the same tone she used in Paris when she was slagging off her colleagues.

She glances at my bowl of cereal and sighs. 'Ben, you haven't even touched your breakfast. I know that stuff's not very nice, but we did say we'd do this wedding diet thing together.' She pushes the bowl across the table towards me. 'I also think we should go easy on the alcohol today,' she adds. 'Just a glass or two of wine. I know it's Christmas and everything, but if we're going to start trying straight after the wedding, then we both need to be on it as early as possible, health wise. Becky was saying she and Phil went fully teetotal six months before they even started trying. And they got pregnant after, like, two weeks.'

'Yeah … OK … Start trying?' In four months, Alice and I are going to start trying for a baby. I press my fingers gently against my eyelids.

'Babe, seriously, are you OK?' she says.

Babe. I don't remember Alice ever calling me that before. Daff and I used to cringe in unison whenever we heard couples call each other 'babe'.

Where is she? What the hell happened?

'Did you actually take those Nurofen?' Alice says. 'Because I really want you to be OK today.' She leans across the table, frowning. 'Oh, and while I'm thinking about it, maybe don't say anything today about what you told me last week, OK?'

I shake my head. 'What did I tell you last week?'

She rolls her eyes. 'The thing about teaching. About wanting to quit Wyndham's and retrain as a teacher.'

'Retrain as a teacher?' I try to process this statement, but my head is suddenly full of Mum. She always told me I'd make a good teacher. 'You don't fancy following in your mother's footsteps?' she used to joke. But I was too busy trying to follow in my father's.

'I just don't want you to say anything about it in front of Becky and Phil and everyone,' Alice says. 'Not until we've talked about it a bit more. I told Becks you'd only leave Wyndham's if you found something a bit more … you know, lucrative. I mean, teaching's OK, but it's not exactly up there on the wow factor, is it? It's more something you do when you can't do anything else.'

My throat tightens as I picture Mum: the passion with which she used to talk about her job. She'd come home at the end of every term laden down with bottles of wine and boxes of chocolates, stacks of cards from parents and pupils alike – *Thank you so much! Best Teacher Ever! Couldn't have done it without you!*

The cards kept coming long after the pupils had left school – decades after, sometimes. More than one ended with the simple statement: *You changed my life.*

Alice is looking at me, concern stamped firmly across her face. 'I just think you should hang on at Wyndham's a little bit longer, babe,' she says. 'I know it's boring at the moment, and I know management consultancy is not fully your thing, but Dad's positive that a better position will open up in the next six months or so.'

I remember Alice telling me her dad was a management consultant. And now, apparently, I am one too.

I need to get out of this flat. My head is fizzing and my stomach is churning and the Nurofen has done precisely sod all. I need to be outside. I need to be alone. I need to think seriously about what the hell is happening here.

'What time is everyone coming again?' I say, standing up.

'Half eleven,' Alice says. 'Why?'

'I just wanted to ...' I rack my brain for an excuse, and feel my phone through my pocket. 'I was just gonna call Harv quickly. To say happy Christmas and stuff.'

She flinches. 'Harvey? What, why? You haven't spoken to him in years.'

I squeeze the bridge of my nose tightly. 'What?'

'Well, unless you've spoken to him more recently but haven't told me about it. *Have* you spoken to him?'

There's no time to think about this right now. I just need to get outside. 'No, I've just been ... thinking lately about getting back in touch with him,' I stammer. 'So I thought I'd give him a call today.'

'Ben, are you kidding?' Alice snaps. 'You know how weird he was about me and you getting together. He told you that you should try and get back with Daphne after you broke up, for Christ's sake! I thought we agreed it was probably best if you didn't see him any more.'

Did I really agree to that? I look back at the black-and-white photo and see my own stupid face grimacing back at me. What have I turned into? Am I really the sort of person who'll ditch his best mate just because his fiancée tells him to?

'You're confusing me now, Ben,' Alice says. 'And this is really not a good day for it.'

'I know, I'm sorry.' I start towards the kitchen door. 'I still don't feel great, to be honest. I think I might just nip out for a walk around the block, just to get some air.'

She sighs. 'Right, well, don't be too long. I still need your help with stuff.'

I bolt down the hallway, grabbing a jacket off the banister and heading straight for the front door. It feels like the walls are closing in around me. I can't shake that image of my face in the photo, my mouth twisted painfully into a fake smile.

Once I'm outside in the freezing fresh air, I pull the iPhone 13 out of my pocket and scroll through the address book.

Before I can get to Harv, though, I find Daphne.

Chapter Forty-Two

It's the same number.

I tap on the thumbnail-sized profile picture next to her name to enlarge it. My stomach drops when I realise it shows two people, arms wrapped around each other's shoulders in front of a beach sunset. I recognise Daff instantly from her curly black hair, but the photo has been taken from so far away that I can't make out the man's face under his sun hat.

It is definitely a man, though.

She's with someone new. She might even be married to him.

Heart thumping, I go into my messages and scroll down to see that my last contact with her was in June 2022 – a year and a half ago. I'd sent a long, slightly desperate-sounding text full of questions – *How are you? How's the job going? Hope your mum and dad are well?* – and Daff had replied with one short, simple sentence: *Yeah, all OK, thanks – hope you are too.*

Scrolling further back, I can see that I'd fired off two similar messages four and five months before the last one. Daphne hadn't even replied to those.

I stare out at the unfamiliar street in front of me. My life has turned upside down. I'm now hiding away messages from Daff, hoping that Alice won't find them.

Not that there's anything to hide: Daphne clearly has no desire to see me or hear from me. The realisation hits me with a dull thud. There's no second chance: I have lost her. I try to hold on to Harv's advice about my inner optimist, but the words seem meaningless now. I can't imagine my life without her in it.

My thumb hovers over her profile picture. I'm desperate to speak to her, to find out what happened between us – when and how and why we broke up. But the blurry face of that man beside her stops me from making the call. Am I really going to be able to cope with the answers to these questions?

I hear the front door open behind me. 'Ben? Seriously? I *said* I needed you!'

Over the next two hours, I shadow Alice around the flat like a robot butler, assisting her clumsily with the icing of cakes, chilling of cava and plumping of cushions. In a weird way, it's actually nice to be bossed about – to not have to think for myself – as it stops my brain constantly spinning back to Daphne. That said, as half eleven approaches, a new kind of panic starts to creep in.

It's the idea of not knowing what's coming. It felt exciting yesterday – in 2020 – before Daff found those messages, but now it just fills me with a clammy sense of dread. I have no idea who is about to arrive at our place, how I might know them, what I should say to them …

'Ben?'

Alice snaps me out of this thought by glaring pointedly at the cushion I'm gently pummelling. 'You've already done that one. Twice.'

'Sorry.'

Chores finally completed, we head back up to the bedroom, where Alice suggests – fairly firmly – that I opt for a blue-and-pink gingham shirt and cream chinos: a combination that makes me look like a Tory MP on holiday.

Once this David Cameron cosplay has been approved, Alice shoos me out again so she can select her own outfit. Without her monitoring my every move, I can finally do what I've been dying to do ever since I woke up – snoop through the entire flat and try to piece together the last three years of my life.

If I wasn't so utterly freaked out, it might almost be exciting. I feel like an amnesiac in a film: sneaking through the apartment digging for clues, reassembling the jigsaw of my past. Like Guy Pearce in *Memento*. Or a less attractive Goldie Hawn in *Overboard*.

The first thing that strikes me as I take a proper look around is the almost total lack of Christmas decorations. Mum and Daphne both went nuts with the tinsel dissemination at this time of year, and as a result I've spent nearly every December of my life in a house bursting with festive colour. Here, though – just like in Alice's Paris flat – the only acknowledgement to the time of year is a smallish Christmas tree in the corner of the living room, decorated sparsely with a length of thick white tinsel that could easily double as a feather boa, and a few grapefruit-sized gold and silver baubles. The tree's general vibe is expensive, stylish and somehow vaguely aloof. If this tree was a human being, it would be Anna Wintour.

The rest of the room resembles a page torn from a glossy design magazine: a minimalist blend of chrome and glass. There are two shallow grey sofas that look like they've been lifted from a *Mad Men* set, and a sleek coffee table with a book full of Banksy murals lying open on it.

The whole place has the feel of a trendy Soho hotel: nice for a cocktail or a posh dinner, but not the sort of place you'd actually want to *live*.

And yet ... here I am.

I creep back upstairs, past the bathroom, where I *think* I catch a glimpse of matching his-and-hers towelling robes – but I'm too traumatised to actually go in and check. At the very back of the flat, I come across a cramped, cluttered box room that appears to be my office. Hidden among the vacuum-packed mountains of Alice's clothes, there's a little wooden desk with a laptop on it, which displays my email inbox. It's a work account, and as I scroll through, I find nothing but incomprehensible management consultancy-themed messages, most of them branded with screaming red exclamation marks. I can feel my blood pressure rise just looking at them.

Is this really what I do now? How have I not had at least one heart attack?

I try reading one of the emails, but I understand roughly one word in six. In the desk drawer, though, I discover something else entirely. Underneath another sheaf of terrifying business papers, there's a slim cardboard folder containing a brochure for a company called Those Who Can. Flicking through, I see that it's advertising a year-long paid course to train as a secondary school teacher. There are forms inside it – pages and pages of complex forms – and by the look of it, I'm about three quarters of the way through filling them out.

Future Me is obviously serious about this – about teaching

– and for the first time, I feel a glow of pride at what I've become, rather than the usual blend of shame and embarrassment.

My throat tightens as I catch a glimpse of one of my longer answers on the form: *I'm attracted to teaching because of my mum*, the paragraph begins. But before the memories of her can take hold, the doorbell sounds.

I slam the drawer shut as I see Alice whisk down the stairs in a long dark blue dress, and all of a sudden the hallway is filled with loud voices and the frantic *plap* of cheek-kissing.

'Hello! Hello! Happy Christmas!' I hear her cry merrily. And then, less merrily: 'Ben! They're *here*!'

I walk downstairs to see a stupidly good-looking couple beaming back at me. They look like something out of an IKEA advert. The man is in jeans and rolled-up shirt sleeves, salt-and-pepper stubble covering his Captain America jawline. The woman is all golden hair and gleaming teeth and a very un-December tan. She is also heavily pregnant.

'Ben! Happy Christmas! How *are* you?'

She pulls me in and pecks me on both cheeks over the exercise ball of her stomach.

'Oops – belly bump!' she laughs. 'Sorry, I can't help it these days!'

'Yeah, watch out, mate,' the man grins. 'The little bastard's kicking like mad at the moment – you're liable to get a boot to the chest if you go anywhere near her.'

The woman sticks her bottom lip out, mock angry. 'Phil! Please don't call our son a little bastard.'

'Sorry, sorry …' The man holds his hands up. 'I meant *big* bastard – if he's anything like his old man!'

They both bray with laughter at this, and I decide that either the standard of comedy has dropped significantly in 2023, or these people are absolutely dreadful.

'Anyway, merry Christmas, fella,' the man says, slapping me hard on the back. 'Good to see you.'

Alice is standing with her hands on her hips, staring at the woman in awe.

'Honestly, Becks, you're glowing! Isn't she glowing, Ben?'

'Yes, you are,' I say. 'You're glowing.'

Becks gives a satisfied squeal and flaps at our compliments with both hands. As she follows Alice through to the living room, the man – Phil – leans in to me and whispers, 'This'll be your life in a few months, buddy. Zero sex and constantly getting your ear chewed off about swollen ankles. Don't say I didn't warn you!'

He shoots me an unpleasant grin, and I'm reminded strongly of Jonno from *Thump*.

In the living room, we stand in a circle beside the Anna Wintour tree, which looks on disdainfully while Alice passes round a tray of vol-au-vents.

'Oh God, you are brilliant, Ali,' Becky says through a mouthful of pastry flakes. 'Did you really make these?'

Alice flushes. 'No, they're er ... they're Waitrose, actually.'

'Aw.' Becky tilts her head and smiles. 'Oh well. Still yummy!'

We all murmur in agreement, and I swear I see Alice's left eye twitch slightly as she takes the tray back.

'Drop of cava?' she asks, holding up the bottle.

'Bubbles?' Phil smacks his palms together. 'Fuck yes!'

Becky places a hand on her stomach. 'Just water for me, Ali.'

'Oh babe, really?' Alice frowns. 'They say you can have one little glass, don't they?'

Becks smiles at her kindly: a primary school teacher correcting a pupil. 'Yes, they do say that, but it just doesn't feel very *responsible*, if you know what I mean? When you guys are expecting, you'll understand.'

'Sure,' says Alice, through clenched teeth.

'Well, you can fill me up,' Phil chuckles. 'If the missus is eating for two, then I'm drinking for two!'

This is rewarded with another gale of laughter, and I suddenly wish Harv was here so I had someone to telekinetically cringe with. But in this reality, I haven't spoken to Harv in years. I've ditched my best friend for the world's most irritating couple.

'Well, cheers,' Phil says, as we all clink glasses. 'Christmas with mates instead of family is so the way forward.'

'Mmm,' Becky agrees. 'A year off from listening to Phil's granny rattle on about how much she hates everyone at her nursing home.'

Phil rolls his eyes. 'The old bird can talk for England, it's true.'

'Are you guys seeing your folks at all?' Becky asks Alice.

Alice nods. 'We're going up tomorrow.'

'Oh, lovely.' Becky pouts at me sadly. 'Aw, you must miss your mum terribly at this time of year, Ben?'

'Yes, I … Yeah.' I scratch the back of my neck. 'Christmas was always—'

'So, how's the wedding prep going?' she asks, turning to Alice.

'Good! So good!' Alice trills. 'I meant to tell you: we had a bit of luck with that string quartet. They're available! Oceano Strings!' She wrinkles her forehead. 'I think maybe you guys were thinking about them for your wedding, weren't you?' She looks genuinely unsure, and despite everything, I can't help marvelling at the performance. She's definitely matured as an actor since *The Carol Revisited*.

Becky's eyes are seething above her rictus grin. 'Oh. Wow. Amazing! Yeah, we did consider them, but I think in the end we just felt a DJ was a bit less … showy. A bit more *us*. Didn't we, Phil?'

'Yeah,' Phil agrees through a mouthful of vol-au-vent. 'He was a bloody good DJ, too, wasn't he?'

'Amazing,' says Alice.

'You know he did Dermot O'Leary's wedding?'

'Yes! Becks mentioned that. A few times.'

I watch Alice closely as she continues this passive-aggressive rally against the woman who is supposedly her best friend. And all the time, I can't help thinking: was she like this in Paris? Or at Marek's wedding?

I'm positive she wasn't like it at uni, when we both lived in scruffy hoodies and subsisted on roll-ups and sausage sandwiches. But having just relived Paris, I could definitely see glimpses of this new side of her: the snarkiness, the competitiveness, the fixation on work and money. But I guess, first time around – just like at the wedding – I was so totally, dumbly preoccupied by the fact that she seemed to fancy me. Everything else had just been background noise against all her arm touches and smiles.

Now, though, that attraction seems to have been replaced by irritation and frustration and boredom. She's marrying me – she wants to start trying for a baby with me – but she doesn't seem to actually *like* me.

It makes me long for Daphne in a way that is physically pain-ful. For her goofiness and her genuineness and her … Just *her*.

We all sit down on the *Mad Men* sofas – girls on one, boys on the other – and as Becks and Alice continue their game of fixed-grin verbal tennis, Phil asks me, 'How's work then, mate?'

'It's, erm …' I think of the swarm of red exclamation marks in my inbox. 'Stressful.'

Phil snorts loudly. 'Fuck off. You're shagging the boss's daughter! You could take a dump in the boardroom and probably still be in line for a promotion.' He reaches across me to top up his glass. 'You know, I've got mates who'd *kill* to work at Wyndham's. You should see their faces when I tell them you just breezed in there with sod-all experience.' He clinks my glass with his. 'Jammy bastard.'

I nod. 'Yeah. I suppose I am.'

'I've heard they're a pretty mad bunch over there. Big ses-sions at lunchtime and all that. Is it a laugh? I bet it's a fucking good laugh.'

'Yes, it is,' I say. 'It's a really great laugh.'

I can feel myself starting to sweat with anxiety now, because what am I going to do if he keeps probing? I have no idea what I even *do* at this Wyndham's place, much less the names of my apparently mad and hilarious co-workers. If I can't provide answers to the most basic questions about my job, it's going to look more than a little odd. I'm going to have to feign some sort of recent head injury or something.

I feel an overpowering urge to get out of this room, but before I can think of an excuse, the doorbell sounds again and Alice jumps to her feet.

'Ooh, that'll be Marek and Dipal!'

Chapter Forty-Three

'Marek?' I say.

Alice frowns down at me. 'Yes, Marek. What is wrong with you today?'

'No, nothing. Sorry.'

She goes out to answer the door, and Phil thumps me on the back. 'Wedding's not for four months, and they're already bickering like a married couple!'

'*Are* you OK, Ben?' Becky asks, leaning forward from her sofa. 'You do look a little peaky.'

'Yeah, I'm fine,' I say. 'Just ... tired.'

'Merry Christmas, fuckos!'

'Marek!' Becky squeals, and suddenly, the director, writer and star of *The Carol Revisited* is standing right in front of me, pumping my hand. His hair is still as wild as it was at his wedding three and a half years ago, but it's now almost entirely grey to match his neatly trimmed goatee beard. He's wearing a thick black polo neck and clear-framed glasses, looking like a bizarre mash-up of David Brent, Richard Ayoade and Steve Jobs.

His wife Dipal – Dee – pecks me hurriedly on both cheeks before shrieking and running across to manhandle Becky's bump.

Marek accepts a glass of Cava from Alice. 'So. How are you then, Benjamin?' he asks me.

'Good, thanks,' I lie. 'You?'

He nods, swallowing a large gulp of wine. 'Yup. Tons of directing gigs at the mo, so it's busy, busy, busy. But that's how we like it.'

In 2023, Marek is apparently exploring previously uncharted levels of pretentiousness by referring to himself in the majestic plural.

'Saw your latest masterpiece on telly last night, mate,' Phil laughs, putting on a jokey All-American accent. 'McCain Oven Chips: for a happy, healthy family!'

Marek smiles back tightly, and I get the impression that Alice v Becky won't be the only passive-aggressive grudge match on today's docket.

'No, fair play, not exactly Oscar-winning fodder,' he says with his jaw clenched. 'Still, I got a fucking good pay cheque for it, which I can use to fund something a little more creatively nourishing, if you know what I mean. That's how it works in this industry,' he adds snootily. 'One for them, one for you.'

'It's been more like twenty for them, none for you, hasn't it, mate?' Phil chuckles, to snickering laughter from Becky and Alice.

Marek soaks up their giggles with apparent good humour, and answers with a question of his own. 'And how's the fascinating world of accountancy then, Philip? Sitting behind a desk tapping away at your calculator: sounds fucking mind-blowing.'

Phil grins and punches Marek's shoulder. 'Whatever, mate.'

Becky squeezes Dee's arm. 'Oh, I love it when the boys go all alpha.'

There's more laughter at this – from 'the boys', too – and I see Marek smirk as he reaches for a vol-au-vent.

It's weird, really, how little he's changed since uni. That spark and arrogance he had at nineteen are still very much there, despite the fact that he clearly hasn't lived up to his own – and everyone else's – expectations. At York, the one thing we all knew for certain was that Marek would go on to be a superstar. The next Tarantino, the next Shane Meadows – at the very least, the next Guy Ritchie. The next *someone*, anyway.

After he graduated, though, nothing seemed to quite fall into place. Film school turned out to be a dead end, so he went into advertising. It was supposed to be a stopgap: a way to earn a bit of cash to fund his own independent movies. As the years went by, he clung to this idea tightly, retaining the dress sense and swagger of a critically acclaimed auteur when he was actually spending most of his time directing fast-food commercials. At his wedding, back in 2020, he was quick to tell me he was 'making shitloads' doing this kind of work, but I could tell that his guard was up. He was spiky and defensive about it; like he suspected I might be about to remind him of our student days, when he used to swan into pubs drunkenly bellowing that Bill Hicks line: 'If anyone here is in advertising or marketing ... kill yourself.'

I guess none of us turned out how we thought we would at nineteen. We all made mistakes and concessions and wrong turnings.

I realise I've zoned out slightly, and as I tune back into the conversation, I find that the chat about my and Alice's wedding has now somehow segued into the story of how Phil proposed to Becky. It's an anecdote everyone here is clearly already familiar with, but you can tell the protagonists get a massive kick out of rehashing it.

'Show them the photo again, Phil!' Becky squeals.

'There you go.' Phil passes me his iPhone – an iPhone 14, I notice – and I squint down at the picture. It's taken from far away, like a long-lens paparazzi shot, and it shows Phil and Becky on a swanky-looking speedboat. He's down on one knee holding a velvet box open as Becky does her best Macaulay Culkin in *Home Alone* impression: shrieking with both hands clasped to her face.

'Where were you again?' I ask Phil.

'Cancún, mate,' he says smugly.

'Right, yeah. So who took the photo?'

'They've told you this so many times, Ben,' Alice mutters.

'I'd hired a guy beforehand,' Phil explains. 'Gave the doorman at our hotel twenty pesos to snap a few pics with my Nikon as soon as I got down on one knee.'

I look at Becky. 'So the whole day, there was a random bloke on the shore watching you through a camera without you knowing about it?'

'Yes!' Becky tilts her head at Phil. 'It's *so* romantic, isn't it?'

Everyone murmurs in agreement, although 'romantic' isn't exactly the word I'd use. It sounds like the kind of stunt the *Walking Dead* guy might pull if there's ever a *Love Actually* sequel.

'How did *you* pop the question again, Ben?' Marek asks me.

Becky claps her hands. 'Oh yes! I *love* this story.'

All five of them are staring at me now, their smiles withering fast as I gape back in silent panic.

'Ha! He can't bloody remember!' Phil booms.

'I, er … No, of course I can … I just …' I can feel myself going bright red. I glance over at Alice. 'You tell the story so much better, babe.'

Babe. What the hell is happening to me?

Confusion and fury are fighting for territory in Alice's eyes, but she manages to compose herself. 'What is my fiancé *like*, honestly?' There's a tinkle of polite laughter. She continues. 'Well … we were in New York, on Broadway, about to go and see *Legally Blonde: The Musical*, and Ben did this whole sweet little routine, pretending to bend down and tie his shoelaces, and then suddenly he was looking up at me and holding a box …'

'Aw,' says Dee.

'Bless,' says Becky.

'Classic,' says Phil.

Alice nods. 'Yeah. It was a total surprise, and I just—'

'Oh come on, Ali,' Becky scoffs. 'You'd been dropping hints for *months.*'

There's laughter again at this, though you can feel the tension in it.

'No I hadn't!' Alice says, her voice suddenly a pitch higher. 'Had I, babe?'

She looks at me and I shake my head. 'No, not at all. Babe.'

'I was totally surprised,' she says again.

'I think we all were!' Phil nudges me with his shoulder. 'We thought you were still moping over your ex!'

This time, there's no laughter.

Dee looks at the floor. Marek coughs.

'Phil,' Becky says. But you can see a smile flickering on her lips.

'Sorry.' Phil holds his hands up. 'It was just a joke. Backfired!'
Alice laughs tightly. 'No, it's fine.'

'It's fine,' I agree, though it is currently taking everything I've got not to grab Phil by his Ralph Lauren shirt and *demand* that he expand on that comment. What did it mean? How did I get from 'moping' over Daphne to proposing to Alice on Broadway?

'Anyway. Such a romantic story,' Dee says finally.

'So sweet,' Becky agrees, the ghost of a smirk still lingering.

'Anywhere I can smoke, Alice?' Marek asks, jiggling a packet of cigarettes.

Becky clasps her bump protectively, and Alice frowns. I'm guessing her Parisian Gauloises-puffing days are now long behind her. 'You can go out in the garden if you like,' she tells him.

I see my chance for some fresh air, and a much-needed break from this dystopian nightmare.

'Hang on, Marek … I'll keep you company.'

We stand shivering in the little back garden as Marek lights his cigarette.

'Do you want one?' he says, offering me the pack.

'No. Actually … yeah. All right.' I haven't smoked in about fifteen years, but right now, I feel like I need one.

He gives me a strange look as he hands it over and lights it. We both exhale and watch the smoke drift up towards the white-grey sky.

'God, Phil can be such a dickhead sometimes, don't you think?' Marek says.

'Er, yeah, I guess.' *Still moping over your ex.* What *did* he mean by that?

'I honestly don't know how you can see those two all the time. I'd go mental.'

'Yeah …' I shrug. 'They're not so bad.' Why the hell am I defending them? I take another puff. The cigarette is making me nauseous. I don't know why I even asked for it. I feel like I'm not fully in control of my own actions. I wonder if I can just drop it on the floor. Would Marek notice?

He continues with what seems to be a pre-prepared monologue. 'Just annoys me, that's all. It's so frustrating to talk about your work with people who have no idea what it's like to be creative. Like, the stuff we're doing right now with McCain is actually pretty ground-breaking. No one's ever been this irreverent and playful and just fucking … *surreal* in the history of oven-chip marketing. We're in totally unexplored territory here. So it pisses me off that Phil thinks he can just belittle my work like that when he doesn't have a clue what he's talking about.' He exhales another plume of smoke and looks at me. 'I mean, you get it because you're … Well, you were sort of a writer, weren't you? For a bit. Or you tried to be.'

'Uh huh.' At another time, in another life, this jab would probably have stung. But right now, I hardly feel it. I hardly feel anything.

I have to find out more about what Phil said. How long exactly was I moping over Daphne? Does Marek know what happened between us?

'The guy's a fucking accountant,' Marek sighs. 'It's like: mate, just because your career's unbelievably dull doesn't mean you have to shit on everyone else's.'

'Yeah.' I can't take this any longer, and before I know what I'm doing, I force out what I hope is a casual chuckle. 'Hey, it was funny what Phil said back there. About me moping over Daphne!'

Marek looks at the floor. 'Ha. Yeah.' A pause while he takes a drag on his Camel Blue. 'Well. You did mope about a fair bit by the sound of it. But Alice got her way in the end!'

'How d'you mean?' I ask.

I'm aware that I'm now staring at him with what is probably an unsettling intensity. But I'm beyond caring how mad or odd I must look. I just need answers.

Marek clears his throat and fidgets on the spot. 'No, nothing. Just ... I think when you and Daphne split up, and then Alice moved back down from Manchester, we all thought that the two of you would probably get together. I mean, we all know she's got serious staying power, that girl. Plus, she'd only split up with Seb a few months earlier, too, so y'know ...' He grins. 'She was obviously on the lookout for a new fiancé. She ground you down eventually!'

He nudges me with his elbow as he says it: it's clearly meant as a joke. But like every other comment at this godawful party, it feels like there's something darker lurking behind it.

Is that actually what happened? When I saw her at Marek's wedding, Alice had just split up with Seb, the bloke she was about to marry up in Manchester. Was she scrambling for a replacement and I just happened to be there?

I feel light-headed all of a sudden. I have to see Daphne. I just have to.

I put a hand against the wall to steady myself.

'Ben? You all right?' Marek is frowning at me. 'You dropped your cigarette.'

'Oh, shit. Sorry.'

''S'OK ...' He takes a final drag on his and then squashes it under his shoe. 'Are you still in touch with Daphne?' he asks suddenly.

I shake my head.

'I always liked her,' Marek says simply. 'She was ... nice.' It's the first time he's sounded genuine all morning, and it tears something open inside me. How can I see her? I *have* to see her.

He opens the door and steps back into the flat. 'Still. You and Alice got there in the end, eh?'

Chapter Forty-Four

Over the next few hours, the urge to speak to Daphne – to just hear her voice – snowballs into a kind of desperation.

I'm torn between the agonising desire to call her and the awful fear of what she might say when she answers. *If* she answers: that text message exchange shows she's clearly in no hurry to speak to me.

In some ways, then, it's a blessing that I don't even get the chance to try.

As soon as Marek and I re-enter the living room, we are shuffled straight into our coats and out of the front door. Since Christmas lunch is – as Alice points out – 'a total ball-ache to cook', it transpires that we've booked a table for six at a posh gastropub on the cusp of Queen's Park.

Twenty minutes later, we're there: settling down in the oak-panelled back room in front of a roaring log fire, plates of steaming roast goose with all the trimmings being set down before us. The red wine starts flowing freely, and as midday bleeds into late afternoon, any hope I had of nipping away to phone Daphne fades into the ether.

The conversation over lunch is less a discussion and more a Royal Rumble of one-upmanship. Becky and Dee sweetly tell Alice that she *must* visit this new restaurant in Soho, because 'anyone who's anyone' has been there – including the two of them. Becky delivers a long monologue about the best nurseries and school catchment areas, and when Dee and Alice offer differing opinions, she politely suggests that her research might be a little fuller because she's actually expecting.

Phil and Marek trade consistent blows too, their voices getting louder as the empty wine bottles stack up. Phil 'seriously cannot believe' that Marek has never been to South America – he and Becky spent three weeks in Argentina last summer, and it was 'iconic'. Marek retaliates with a blitzkrieg of name-dropping: he had an 'epic' meeting last week about shooting a soft drink campaign with Tim Henman ('a bloody good guy'). Plus an encouraging Skype call about a cufflink commercial with Piers Morgan, who apparently is surprisingly down-to-earth.

As the meal goes on, I watch them all closely – my new partner and my new friends – and it strikes me that they're not really talking to each other; they're just taking it in turns to speak, each gearing up for their latest pitch about why they've got the best job, or the best house, or the best taste in restaurants or TV shows or holidays.

The scariest thing is that Alice is competing the hardest. She interrupts excitedly whenever she can trump an anecdote, and twitches with annoyance whenever someone trumps one of hers.

I do my best to make an effort and join in, but it gets harder and harder as the afternoon draws on. Not just because my thoughts keep flying back to Daphne, but also because Alice seems to jump on pretty much every comment I make, either dismissing it out of hand or using it as a springboard to wring a laugh from the others.

At one point, Phil presses me for further information on Wyndham's, and I mumble something neutral about how I'm 'getting along OK there'. Alice cuts in sharply and snaps, 'Don't be *stupid*, Ben, you're doing amazingly.' She turns to Becky and Dee: 'Dad says he's actually in line for a promotion pretty soon.'

Phil smirks at this. '*Dad* says ...' he chuckles under his breath.

Alice shoots me an irritated glance before turning away again. She seems to take my self-deprecation as a personal slight, as if it reflects badly on her. It's like she wants our friends to believe I'm a success because it makes her a success for being with me.

On the other hand, though, she also seems to relish any chance to put me down in front of them. When Marek starts laying into some 'massively pretentious' new novel he's reading, Alice groans and looks over at me.

'Oh my God, Ben, do you remember *your* novel?' She puts her head in her hands, miming utter mortification.

'That bad, was it?' Phil booms over the laughter.

Alice sets her teeth and winces at me. 'Sorry, babe. I'm being mean. But it *was* a bit cringe.'

'No, it's true,' I say quietly. 'It was pretty terrible.'

'Aw, sweet that you let her see it, though,' Dee says, reading my mind – although I'd have swapped the word 'sweet' for 'insane'.

Alice adopts a cartoonish expression of guilt. 'Actually ... I just found it in one of his boxes when we moved into the flat.'

She grimaces. 'He came into the room and found me laughing my head off reading it.' A beat, and then: 'It *wasn't* a comedy.'

Laughter rings around the table, and I do my best to add mine to it.

'Good thing you found your niche in the end, Ben,' Marek chuckles. 'I'd say management consultants earn a few bob more than wannabe novelists.'

Alice nods. 'Mmm. And press-release writers, thank God.'

There's more laughter at this – though mostly from Alice and Marek. It's strange: I'm only starting to remember it now, but during the first term at uni, the two of them used to do this a lot. Team up to take casual swipes at me after a few drinks in the student bar. We were a tight little trio, and I was usually the butt of our jokes. It was another reason I felt so much more comfortable with Daphne and Harv from the second term onwards.

Pretty soon, our plates are taken away and heaps of steaming Christmas pudding are set down in their place. As the meal comes to an end, I lapse into silence, nodding at whatever's being said while getting steadily drunker and drunker. I can see Alice's glare sharpening every time I refill my glass, and I remember her comment earlier about how we should take it easy on the alcohol. But I can't bring myself to stop. The thought that this might be it – that this might be my life from now on – sits like a lead weight on my shoulders. I can almost feel myself sinking into the ground as I contemplate it.

There must be another way. There must be a way back.

By the time we stagger out of the pub, the white sun is beginning to sink into the horizon.

Decked out in thick scarves and woolly hats, we meander slowly through Queen's Park, trying to work off the goose and gravy. Phil leads the way, stumbling slightly from his excessive wine intake while outlining his New Year's resolution to buy a sailboat. Becky looks distinctly unimpressed – by either his nautical ambitions or his drunkenness, or both.

My head is fuzzy from too much booze, and I realise with a lurch that this route through the park is one Daff and I used to take occasionally on weekends, just after we'd bought our flat in Kensal Rise. We'd wander hand in hand through the trees and read our books on the grass, or sit and people-watch on the bandstand.

I'm lingering at the rear of the pack, lost in these memories, only half listening to Alice telling everyone about the second series of some *Game of Thrones* prequel we've apparently started watching – 'Ben can't stand it, but I'm hooked. Aren't I, babe?' – when suddenly a bright red rubber ball stops us all in our tracks.

It skitters across the grass in front of us, followed a split second later by a shaggy-haired miniature Schnauzer, which scoops it up in its slobbery jaws and beams at us triumphantly.

'God, I wish people would learn to control their dogs,' Becky tuts.

I glance in the direction it came from, and in an instant, my wine-fugged head is clear, and my heartbeat has tripled in speed.

On the other side of the park, a scruffy-bearded man in a shabby-looking suit is waving at us.

'Yeah, OK, mate, chill out,' Phil mutters, waving back. 'Apology accepted.'

That lead weight on my shoulders has disappeared, and my whole body is suddenly alive with hope. He's here!

I glance around frantically for somewhere – anywhere – I might be able to talk to him privately, but the others keep walking on. The little dog stays rooted to the spot, staring up at me with its tail wagging. I get the strange impression that it won't move until I start walking with it.

'Hey – I'll catch you guys up,' I blurt.

Alice turns around. 'What?'

'I've just seen someone I know. From work. I should go and say merry Christmas. I'll catch up with you in a sec.'

Alice appears faintly appalled by this suggestion, but makes no effort to stop me. 'All right … fine. We'll meet you by the bandstand.'

'OK.'

It's all I can do to stop myself sprinting in the watch-seller's direction. I set off speed-walking as a compromise, and the Schnauzer begins trotting along next to me, panting happily. The watch-seller is wearing his usual crumpled Grandad Jack grin, and as I approach, he raises a hand in cheery salute.

'Lovely day for a Christmas stroll!' He nods in the direction of Alice and the others. 'They seem like a friendly bunch.'

'Look, what the hell is—' I begin, but he holds up a finger to stop me.

'Just a moment.'

He wrangles the ball from the Schnauzer's mouth and hurls it back across the park – with impressive force for a man who could well be pushing seventy. The little dog blazes after it, yelping with delight, and the old man watches it go with a fond smile.

'He gets rather fidgety if we stand around talking. Now then …' He pats my shoulder gently, and we set off on the Schnauzer's trail. 'What do you think?' He glances around the park. 'Is it everything you hoped for?'

I ignore this question and instead vent the thought that's been gnawing at me all day. 'This isn't it, is it? This isn't really where I end up?'

The old man shrugs. 'Why not? It's what you wanted, isn't it? That night in the pub, the night I met you, this was exactly where you were heading. You've just arrived a little earlier than expected, that's all.'

I stop dead and stare at him. Any trace of hope I felt is starting to disappear with the fading sunlight. 'So you're telling me this *is* the final stop?' I say breathlessly.

'Your life is the decisions you make,' the watch-seller says with his trademark infuriating vagueness. 'Those decisions have led you here.'

It doesn't compute somehow. My brain won't let it. 'But … I can't be stuck here!' I'm shouting now. People are starting to stare. 'There has to be a way back!'

The old man tugs at his beard thoughtfully. 'But do you want a way back? You know as well as I do what you were thinking on Christmas Eve 2020: that you'd made all the wrong choices, taken the wrong path. Perhaps this is the right one.'

'This is *not* the right path!' I yell.

'How do you know?' He looks genuinely curious as he asks this, his blue eyes narrowed, his shaggy head tilted.

I feel the desperation boiling up inside me. 'Because I'm not in love with Alice! I'm in love with Daphne! She's …' My throat tightens and I find I can't shout any more. 'She's my home,' I say quietly. 'I have to get back to her. I just have to. If I could only see her, talk to her, just for a minute ...' My eyes are stinging now, and I rub a hand across them. 'I just ... I just want to find out what happened. I want to find out if she's OK.'

The old man takes this in silently as the Schnauzer comes trotting back over with the red ball.

He reaches down to pet the dog.

'OK ,' he says softly. And then he glances at something – or someone – behind me.

I turn to follow his gaze, and the whole world starts to blur at the edges.

Chapter Forty-Five

Daphne is not alone.

That's the first thing I notice. There's someone sitting beside her on the bench on the other side of the park.

He's too far away for me to see him clearly, but I know instantly who he is, and suddenly the identity of that sun-hatted man in her profile picture seems agonisingly, gut-wrenchingly obvious.

The old man says something that I don't catch, because I am on autopilot now: walking away from him, moving towards the bench. I feel like I'm in a snow globe that's been shaken violently. I want to stop walking, but I can't. I have to get closer. I have to know.

They're sitting together, talking animatedly. I can't tell if they're holding hands, but they might be. Daphne is turned away from me; I haven't even seen her face yet.

And as I get closer, all I can think is: I made this happen. *Your life is the decisions you make*. Well, this was my decision. The worst one I ever made.

Suddenly Rich turns and looks in my direction. Panic rushes through me, freezing me to the spot. I see him mutter something, and then Daphne looks round too, eyes wide, palms out in a what-are-the-chances gesture.

They both stand up, and in the few seconds it takes me to reach them, my whole body clenches so hard I'm surprised it doesn't shatter.

'Hey,' Daphne says. 'This is weird. Merry Christmas.'

Her hair is pulled into a ponytail, and her cheeks and the tip of her nose have been brushed pink by the chilly air. She's wearing a smart black coat I don't recognise and a brick-red scarf wrapped loosely around her neck. She doesn't look a day older than when I last saw her. In fact, she looks so beautiful I actually have to glance away.

'Merry Christmas,' I say, somehow.

Rich eyes me warily and gives a curt nod. 'Merry Christmas, mate.'

'It's been ages.' Daphne smiles. Fucking hell, her smile. She hugs herself tightly against the cold wind. 'So ... how are you, Ben? What are you doing here?' She glances around. 'Are you by yourself?'

I swallow hard and do everything I can to keep my voice steady. 'No. Alice is ...' I nod in the direction of the bandstand.

'Oh, OK. Is she all right?'

'Yeah, she's ... good.'

'Good. And hey – congratulations are in order, right?' She taps her gloved ring finger. 'Saw her posts on Facebook.'

'Oh. Yeah. Thanks.'

'Yeah, nice one, mate.' Rich gives another unsmiling nod. 'Congrats.'

He seems obviously on edge – like he's more than ready to thump me if I come one step closer. But Daff ... Daff doesn't seem fazed. It's almost like we're work colleagues who've bumped into each other randomly, and she's obliged to go through the awkward motions of small talk.

I don't know how I was expecting her to react. I suppose I imagined her breaking down in tears, or screaming at me, or calling me every name under the sun. Whatever I imagined, this is a million times worse.

It's like she hardly even knows me.

'So …' Rich shifts from one foot to the other. 'We'd better be heading back, actually, mate. Only came out to get a bit of a breather from Daphne's lot.'

'Oi.' Daff rolls her eyes at him. She looks half annoyed, half amused. It's a look I remember well, and it blows yet another hole straight through me. 'My mum's been on the sherry,' she deadpans. 'You remember how she gets. Very … Greek.'

'Yeah,' I say. 'I remember.'

I must be staring at her too hard now, because she glances down at the ground, and Rich slinks a protective arm around her waist. The sight makes my stomach flip.

He *has* aged since I last saw him, but maddeningly, he actually looks better for it. Back in 2020, he was lean and skinny and almost boyish, but he must have been hitting the gym hard, because he's now filled out into a proper, handsome, sturdy *man*. He has Phil's salt-and-pepper stubble, as well as his apparently immovable hairline. There is no denying it: he and Daff make a very good-looking couple. The realisation is like a punch in the gut.

My eyes drift back to her. I can't help it. Is she happy with him? Is this what she wants? Is she happier than she was with me? My head is throbbing with so many questions, but just

318

as I take a breath to steady myself, Rich clears his throat and gives Daphne a look.

'Well,' she says. 'It was good to see you, Ben. Really. Take care of yourself, OK?'

'You too,' is all I can manage.

She looks me straight in the eyes then, and in that moment, I see it. Something flashes between us. Pain, maybe – the same hurt I saw shining in her eyes when she found those messages from Alice. Or it might even be regret for what we've lost. For what I caused us to lose.

Whatever it is, it's only there for a second before it fades away.

'See you, then,' she says. Rich nods goodbye too, and then the two of them walk away, towards the park's exit, Rich's arm still fixed tightly around Daphne's waist.

The pain of it is real – physical – like a blade in my chest. I can feel my eyes beginning to sting. I have to get out of here.

I turn and start walking, and as I stare straight ahead, I see that the watch-seller and his dog have both disappeared.

Chapter Forty-Six

Christmas Day 2023 is finally crawling to a close.

It's approaching midnight now, and we're back home, in our bedroom. Alice sits at the dressing table in her nightie, rubbing various powerfully scented creams into her face. I lie on the bed behind her feeling ... not much of anything, really. Just hollow and wrung-out: half wanting this day to end, half terrified of what might come next.

The rest of the evening passed in an unreal fog, as if I was observing everything from behind smudged glass. Everyone came back to ours for coffee and cake, and I went through the motions as best I could. But it felt – it feels – like something has broken inside me. I can't stop thinking about that look in Daphne's eyes as we said goodbye. That flicker of sadness that told me she was still hurting too.

'We need to be on the road tomorrow by half nine latest,' Alice says. 'Boxing Day traffic is always horrendous, and you know how annoying my dad is about lateness.' She tuts at my silence, and catches my eye in the mirror. 'Ben? OK? Half nine latest?'

'Yep, sure.'

'So that means getting up about half seven, eight?'

'OK.'

She spins round to face me. 'And try not to be so *down* about Wyndham's tomorrow, OK? Because Dad's obviously going to ask how it's going. It was so embarrassing, you just sort of muttering vaguely about it in front of Phil and everyone. You should be proud to work there. I mean, isn't it better than what you were doing before?'

'Yeah, it is.' I nod. 'Sorry – I don't mean to be down on it.'

'It's a *good* job, Ben.'

'I know. I'm grateful for it. I'll be on better form tomorrow, I promise. I've just been feeling sort of spaced out all day. Maybe I'll take another Nurofen.'

'Well, take *something*.' She turns back to the mirror, snapping the lid off another pot of cream. 'I don't know what's up with you, honestly …'

I shake my head. I don't know either. I feel completely cut loose – like I'm sinking slowly into deep, dark water.

I have no idea what's coming next: will I just keep jumping forward at random? Will I wake up next on my wedding day to Alice, and then on our honeymoon? And if so, when will it stop? What if I just keep hurtling randomly from month to month, year to year, deeper and deeper into a life I don't even want?

The thought makes me giddy, like peering off the edge of a skyscraper.

On the other hand, what if the watch-seller was right? I wanted all this to happen back in 2020; this was where my life was heading. *Your life is the decisions you make*, he said. So maybe this is it now: this is reality, and I really *will* wake up tomorrow, bright and early, ready to drive up to Alice's parents. And then it'll be the wedding planner on the 29th, and back to work on the 3rd, and I'll somehow have to keep going. Keep living this life, day after day, trying to make the best of it.

If that's the case, then one thing's for certain: I'll have to bite the bullet and tell Alice how I feel.

It's not fair to stay with her – to *marry* her – when I'm still in love with someone else. She'll be upset, of course, but it will be for the best in the end, for both of us. I don't believe she's truly in love with me either. I can feel that she isn't. Maybe she's just scared of falling too far behind Becky and Dee in the life-goals stakes.

The question is, though: what will I do after that? Daphne has moved on. She's with someone else now; it wouldn't be fair for me to try and ruin that for her too. No, I had my chance with her. I had hundreds of chances. I blew them all.

The future stretches out ahead of me, blank and unknowable, just like it did all those years ago in the maze at uni. But this time it doesn't fill me with excitement; only with a hopeless, dizzying dread.

Alice screws the lid back on her final pot of cream and climbs into bed next to me. She lets out a tired sigh. 'Well. It was a good day in the end, wasn't it?'

'Yeah. It was.'

'Although Becks was a bit much at lunch, don't you think?'

'How do you mean?'

'Just going on about the baby *all* the time. After a while, it's like: OK, we get it. You know?'

'Yeah.'

She reaches across to switch off the light, and I think suddenly about Daphne and her best mate, Jamila; the way they are together. The absolute polar opposite of Alice and Becky. I'll never forget coming home from a night out a few weeks after we got married to find them both sprawled drunkenly on our sofa holding bags of frozen peas to their shoulders. It transpired they'd cricked their necks dancing far too energetically to the song 'Whip My Hair' by Willow Smith. I remember them groaning with laughter as they told me about it. I don't think it's possible to love anyone more than I loved Daphne at that moment.

In the darkness, Alice flips her pillow over. 'Please don't be weird with my parents tomorrow, OK? Just try and be … normal.'

'OK.'

'And definitely don't say anything to Dad about the teaching thing.'

'I won't.'

She sighs again and rolls over, turning her back to me. 'OK. Night, babe.'

'Night.'

On the bedside table, my iPhone 13 tells me it's just turned 11.58 p.m. For some mad reason, I decide to see if I can hold my breath for the next sixty seconds. As though maybe, if I manage it, I'll somehow beat the system: make myself jump again, but this time back into the past.

Just as I'm about to explode, 11.58 becomes 11.59.

I breathe out raggedly. I'm still here.

This is it. This is the rest of my life.

Alice mutters something and turns over.

'What was that?'

'I said: what's that noise?' she mumbles.

I listen carefully. 'It's, erm … I think it's …'

I hold my wrist up to my ear.

The watch has started ticking.

Chapter Forty-Seven

For years, when I was a kid, I used to have this recurring dream.

I'm in my bedroom at home – *home* home, Mum's home – and the doorbell rings. I run out of my room and down the corridor, and as I get to the top of the stairs, I can see the outline of a person behind the stained-glass panel on the front door.

I jump onto the banister and slide down gracefully, but as I approach the door, I still can't make out the figure behind the glass. I reach up to open the latch, and then … nothing.

Either I'd wake up, or the dream would just fizzle out.

I started having this dream when I was about ten, soon after my dad left, so it doesn't exactly take Sigmund Freud to figure out that it might have been about him; about me wishing desperately that he would come back.

Anyway, it's a dream I haven't had – haven't even thought about – for decades.

Until now.

As soon as I raise the ticking watch to my ear, everything goes dark, and there I am again: in my bedroom at home, hearing the doorbell ring out downstairs.

As usual, I sprint out and see that shadow behind the glass. And as usual, I slide down the banister and run towards the door. But this time the figure is clearer – I can make out that he's wearing a blue suit and some kind of colourful tie – and the dream holds together even as I reach up and place my hand on the latch.

But when I open the door, there's no one there. It's not even my front door – it's the door to another room entirely, a room I don't recognise, dingy and grey and sparsely decorated, with two people sitting on a sofa in the centre.

I realise instantly what I'm looking at, and even though part of me somehow knows this is a dream, the shock is still visceral.

It's me, as an old man, and Alice as an old woman.

We're sitting at opposite ends of the couch – so far apart that we might be strangers – our heads bent, not speaking.

I cry out – I'm not sure what I say – but Old Me looks up suddenly, and I feel the same jolt of panic as when Rich glanced round to see me in the park. This time, though, it's not the shock of being spotted; it's horror at the expression etched deep into my weathered old face. My eyes are glazed and vacant. I look tired and broken and defeated.

And that's when the dream finally buckles and comes apart, the room starts collapsing piece by piece, crumbling and dissolving and melting until there's nothing left except …

'Ben? Ben … Are you awake?'

Chapter Forty-Eight

'Ben?'

I try to lift my head, but I can't; it's too heavy.

I'm lying down, my face pressed against a hard surface, and my whole body feels brittle and stiff, like I haven't moved in days.

There's no motion sickness or dizziness like there usually is after a jump; it just feels like I've been asleep for about a decade, like my brain is floating slowly to the surface from the bottom of a deep, dark lake.

'Ben? What the hell?'

It's Daphne's voice. Oh my God, Daff …

Something ignites inside me, and I manage to wrench my eyelids open. My surroundings swim gradually into focus, and when I look up, she's standing over me, hands on hips, her face full of confusion and concern.

'Are you OK?' she says. 'What are you doing up here?'

A burst of pure happiness surges through me like electricity. I can't believe she's really here. A sound comes out of my mouth that is part gasp, part groan. Am I hallucinating? Am I still dreaming?

'Daff?' I croak dumbly.

'Were you *sleeping* up here?'

I stare around me, blinking stupidly against the light, my body still tense and heavy but starting to fizz with the exhilaration of what I think I'm seeing.

I'm … I'm in the attic. I'm with Daphne in the attic in our flat. Next to me, a biscuit tin lies open to reveal various items: a ticket stub, a tattered programme for a play, and a fake plastic revolver.

Relief crashes over me in a tidal wave, and I stare up at Daff in joyous disbelief, my heart battering against my ribcage.

'Ben … Hey – what are you doing?'

I have no control over what I'm doing, and before I know it, I've wobbled to my feet and pulled her towards me in a tight, breathless hug.

'Oh Daff …' I stammer. 'Oh my God … I can't believe it … I can't believe you're really here!'

'What … What is going on, Ben? What's *happened*?'

I'm vaguely aware that I'm crying now – tears spilling hotly down my cheeks, soaking into her hair as I hold her – but I can't help it. I thought I'd never see her again. I thought I'd lost her.

'I thought I'd …' I try to tell her, but the words collapse under a sob.

'All right, Ben, seriously, this is getting weird now. What is going on?'

She pulls away and holds me at arm's length, looking even more perplexed than she did before. My God, she's beautiful. With another rush of euphoria, I realise she is wearing the exact same shirt and jeans she was wearing on Christmas Eve 2020, before I went to meet Harv in the pub. I'm still not entirely sure whether this is all real or I'm imagining it. I feel like at any moment the whole scene might crumble and dissolve, just like that room did in the dream. I can't bear the thought of her disappearing, and I'm about to take her in my arms again when she spots the biscuit tin next to me.

Her worried frown morphs slowly into a surprised smile. 'Oh my God ...' She kneels down, laughing softly. 'Why were you looking through this old stuff?' She picks up the gun and the programme. 'Haven't seen these in years ...'

I want to reach out for her again, so badly, but instead I hear myself say, 'I can't believe you kept it all ...'

She raises her eyebrows. 'Yeah, well, there's more where that came from.' She reaches into the box behind me to dig out another, larger tin. Then she pulls the lid off and holds it out so I can see what's inside.

The electric charge pulses through me again as I process what I'm looking at. Among the various letters and postcards and photos, four items stand out: a fully opened advent calendar featuring twenty-four pictures of Larisa Oleynik; a chunky glass award that says *RISING STAR* across the bottom; a cheap snow globe depicting the Dodo Manège in Paris; and a delicate dried white lily plucked from a funeral wreath.

I try to work some moisture into my parched mouth. Daff takes the award out and turns it over slowly in her hands. 'I don't think I ever even told you about this ...' She looks at me and sighs. 'So, is this really how you've spent the whole evening? Getting pissed and maudlin and taking a trip down memory lane? I notice the tree still hasn't been done ...'

Without thinking, I pull her towards me again, the breath

exploding out of me as I take in her feel and her smell. She smells like her. She smells like home. 'Oh my God, Daff,' I whisper into her neck. 'I missed you so much.'

'Oh-kay.' She laughs uncertainly. 'I was gone all of five hours, Ben. How much have you had to drink exactly?'

I move back and look at her. 'What day is it?'

She laughs wearily at the question, and slips her phone out of her pocket. 'Well, since you ask, it's actually Christmas Day. Five past midnight on Christmas Day, to be exact.'

She holds up the phone. The date reads: 25 December 2020.

'Merry Christmas,' she says.

'Merry Christmas,' I murmur back, and I can feel something swelling to bursting point in my chest now, because I know that it's true: I've been given a second chance. I don't know how or why, but I've never felt so grateful for anything in my entire life.

'Is that new?'

She's looking down at my wrist. The watch reads five minutes past midnight. I lift it to my ear. It's still ticking steadily. Does that mean my journey is over? I'm finally back where I'm meant to be?

I look up at Daff. I can't blow this. I know exactly what I have to do now.

'It was … a present,' I say slowly. 'From Harv.'

Daff stands up and dusts herself off. 'OK, well come on,' she says. 'We can put all this stuff back in the morning. Let's go to bed now.'

'No, Daff … wait.'

She sighs. 'Ben, please. It's been a pretty exhausting day all round. And now I come back and you're drunk and being weird and—'

I cut her off, desperately. 'I'm sorry, I'm sorry. But I'm not drunk, I promise.'

'There's a nearly empty wine bottle downstairs that would suggest otherwise.'

'I know, but …' I can feel the words boiling up inside me, rushing to get out. 'Listen, Daff, there's something I want to tell you – something I *need* to tell you – and I know that it's Christmas and it's late and this is not exactly the ideal place or time for a big, serious talk, but this is the most important thing I'll ever say. And I just please – *please* – need you to hear me out while I say it.'

Over the course of this manic gabbled statement, the look of mild irritation on Daff's face has transformed into one of genuine concern. She stares at me now, her eyes wide, almost fearful.

'What?' she says hesitantly. 'What is it?'

I take her hand and guide her gently back down to sit on the floor opposite me. And as I look deep into her big hazelnut-brown eyes, it all comes flooding back – everything I've just been through.

That instant spark between us in the bar after the play, and the realisation in the maze that I'd *made* her find me. The memory of her and Mum looking at me fondly across the dinner table. The shame of knowing she gave up her Rising Star evening to come home and comfort me, then the night of the pantomime, when we ate turkey sandwiches and retraced the early days of our relationship. The searing guilt and regret over what happened with Alice in Paris. The way Daff was there for me at Mum's funeral – the way she's *always* been there for me, no matter what. And then the sickening, hopeless terror I felt in 2023, knowing I'd lost her forever.

And finally, that piece of advice Harv gave me as I lay on his sofa bed with my life in tatters: *It's not going to be easy to win her trust back. It might be the hardest thing you ever do in your life. But isn't it worth the effort?*

This is my last chance. I can't risk losing her again. I just can't. This is the right thing to do – even if it ruins everything.

'Ben?' Daphne urges, her eyes searching mine. 'What is it?'

I swallow the lump that's rising steadily in my throat. 'I just … There are some things I need to tell you. But before I do, I want to say sorry. For how I've been over the past couple of years – and before that, to be honest. I'm so sorry. You're … Daff, you're the best thing that's ever happened to me, and I love you so, so much.'

Her beautiful face is still etched with anxiety. 'I … love you too,' she says tentatively.

'OK … Well, here goes.'

And right there in the attic, just after midnight on Christmas Day, I take a deep breath and tell Daphne the truth. About everything.

I tell her what I said to Mum before she died, and how the guilt of it has eaten into me ever since. I tell her I'm sorry for pushing her away in the months and years after Mum's death. I tell her I should have let us grieve together, but I was too stupid and selfish and shattered to realise it. I tell her about my dad, too: how I've spent years either worrying that I'll turn into him, or desperately wanting to prove him wrong for abandoning me. I tell her that all my fears and doubts about work and marriage and having kids were linked to him leaving, and it's a mess I've spent twenty-five years trying to untangle, but I think I'm finally free of it now.

And Daff cries and kisses me and tells me it's OK and she understands and she's so happy that I've told her all this. And it's the greatest feeling in the world, being held by her like this, but somehow I manage to pull away, because there's more I need to say, and if I get too comfortable in her arms, then maybe I won't say it.

So next, I tell her what happened in Paris with Alice. I tell her how I felt afterwards, how guilty and how sick. Then I tell her what happened at Marek's wedding in that photo booth. I tell her it was Alice who kissed me, and not the other way round, but I'm honest about the fact that I didn't push her away either. I show her the messages on my phone. I tell her I was planning to meet Alice in four days' time, but that I am going to cancel that meeting. Because I understand now that if I go ahead with it, I'll be ruining the best thing that ever happened to me, and I'll spend the rest of my life hating myself for it. I tell her I'm sorry and that I've been a total fucking idiot. I promise her that nothing like this will ever happen again – and I truly, *truly* mean it.

I tell her I will do everything I can to make things better, because she is my wife, and she is the person I love most in the entire world, and that's the only thing in this life I'm genuinely sure of, and I know I can make her happy again if she'll give me another chance.

The words pour out of me uncontrollably, and even though I burn with shame at most of them, and it rips me apart to see how much they hurt Daphne, it's a relief to finally have them out there. It's a relief to finally be honest with her.

*

The hours afterwards pass in a blizzard of tears and anger and disbelief. I've said everything I needed to say, and so, for the rest of the night, I listen.

Daff is quiet at first. She seems almost dazed, shaking her head like she's still processing everything I've told her. But as she starts talking, the fire rises in her, and the fury and the pain come spilling out. She cries and she shouts at me, and I take it, because it's exactly what I deserve, and I can't bear to see the hurt I've caused her. Through jagged tears, she tells me how lonely she's felt over the past few years, how agonising it's been to feel that we're drifting apart without either of us even acknowledging it.

At one point, with anger flashing in her eyes, she tells me that Rich has hinted several times that he's interested in her, but even when things were at their worst between us, she never dreamed of letting anything happen.

This vaporises what little strength I have left, and all I can do is cry breathlessly, just repeating how sorry I am, over and over again, like a broken record.

We move from room to room in the flat, alternately crying and talking and shouting, until finally, as the sun starts to come up outside, we're left sitting in silent, broken exhaustion at opposite ends of the living room sofa.

Daff goes upstairs and packs a bag. She tells me she's going to her parents' and she needs some time to think about everything. I tell her that of course that's fine, she should take as long as she wants.

And then she leaves, and she doesn't come back.

Chapter Forty-Nine

The undecorated Christmas tree stares back at me from the other side of the living room. It seems mildly insane to suspect an inanimate object of taunting me, but that's what it feels like.

According to my watch, it's now half past ten in the morning, and outside, I can hear the cheery sounds of Christmas Day whirring into action: kids laughing, dogs barking, car boots being opened and loaded with presents. Neighbours calling 'Merry Christmas!' as they pass each other in the street.

And here I am: alone in my flat with the curtains drawn, two biscuit tins full of keepsakes open on the sofa beside me. I'm not sure why I even brought them down. To remind myself of what Daff and I have been through? To convince myself that we'll be OK in the end?

She's been gone a few hours now, and even though I haven't slept a wink all night, I don't feel in the slightest bit tired. I don't know what I feel really. Devastated at hurting her, of course. Heartbroken that she's gone. Terrified because I don't know when – *if* – she'll come back.

But as crazy as it sounds, I also feel a weird kind of peaceful stillness. Everything is out in the open now; both of us have been completely honest with each other for the first time in years. I've finally owned up to my mistakes, to the hurt that they've caused, and now I can focus on trying to make up for them.

When Daff walked out of the door, a horrible feeling swept through me that maybe that glimpse of my Christmas future had been real. That by telling her about Paris and everything else, I had set in motion a timeline that would lead me, inevitably, to Alice and Marek and Phil and Becky and Wyndham's.

But as soon as that thought arose, I swept it away. That's not how I'll end up. I just know it. I've spent too long drifting, allowing myself to be a passenger in my own life, blaming other people for the mistakes I make. It's not Daff's fault or Alice's fault or my dad's fault that I screwed up; it's mine. I'm the one in control here. I need to remember that.

If you don't like your life, you can change it.

The watch-seller was right about that – and he was right about something else, too. All that hopping about through Christmases past, present and future did make me realise once and for all what I really wanted.

Daphne.

It's always been her, and it always will be. Even if I never get to hold her or kiss her or even see her again, at least I know now for sure. That's why I *have* to fight for her, even if it takes everything I've got. If she says it's over, I will accept that – I'll have to – but I need to try. I need to prove to her that I've changed, that I can be the kind of husband she deserves.

My phone rattles on top of the biscuit tin: a message from Alice. I switch it off. I can deal with that later. I sent her a text an hour ago, cancelling our drink on the 29th and apologising for everything: for what happened in Paris, and afterwards, and at Marek's wedding. I told her that I was still in love with Daphne and I was going to do everything I could to make it work between us. Whatever Alice has said in reply, this – today – will be the last time we speak.

I glance down at my watch again. It's hard to stop looking at it: the novelty of seeing the thing actually ticking after all this time. I wonder if I'll ever see the watch-seller again. Or whether he was telling the truth when I asked him about his resemblance to my grandad Jack. A mad thought suddenly surfaces that maybe he *was* my grandad Jack, sent back to earth from God-knows-where to look out for me. Probably best to sweep that one away too. I'm not sure I'll ever find out the truth. Either way, I feel an overwhelming rush of gratitude towards him. Despite his maddening tendency towards vagueness, I've learned so much on this journey he sent me on: about myself, about the world, about how to love and how to show love. Part of me keeps wondering if I just dreamed the whole thing, but deep down, I know it all happened. I can't explain why; I just know.

A car engine starts up outside, and its radio bursts into life midway through 'I Wish It Could Be Christmas Everyday'. I can hear the family inside singing along as they drive off. For some reason, the sound fills me with an intense sadness. My family was Mum and Daphne. One is gone and now the other might be too.

Those old feelings of self-pity start to stir inside me again: the childish sense of injustice, the inclination to hide away, feeling sorry for myself, getting angry at things I can't define and forces I can't see.

I have to fight that. Another nugget of Harv-brand wisdom

pops into my head: *You're not going to get Daphne back by wallowing in your own misery, are you? You have to believe in yourself a bit more.*

He said it off the cuff, I think – out of sheer frustration with my moaning – but for some reason, it gives me strength. I *can* do this. I can be a better man. I can make Mum proud, make Daphne proud, make myself proud.

I take a deep breath and stand up, and as I pull the curtains open, sunlight floods the room. The sky is a clear blue, and it's cold, crisp and bright outside: a beautiful Christmas Day.

I seal the lids back on the biscuit tins. Enough digging through the past. It's the present that matters now. As I take them back up to the attic and tidy up the mess I made, I spot something else: the box of Christmas tree decorations. I did promise Daphne I'd put them up. And even if it's way too late, it's about time I started keeping my promises.

Downstairs, in the sun-soaked living room, I open the box and start stringing tinsel and fairy lights around the tree's branches in much the same haphazard way I remember Mum doing when I was a kid.

I know it's not much, and there's no one else here to see it, but still … It feels like the first step on a long road ahead.

Chapter Fifty

The kettle's boiling, the bacon's sizzling and the scrambled eggs have just hit that split-second sweet spot between too runny and too firm.

I dish the food out onto two plates, humming along to 'Jingle Bell Rock', which is currently thumping out of the radio on top of the fridge. Moving quickly around the tinsel-lined kitchen, I plunge the cafetière and pour two cups of fresh hot coffee, as well as two glasses of freshly squeezed orange juice. I arrange everything neatly on the trays and stand back to admire my work: perfect.

I flick the radio off, but just as I'm about to head up to the bedroom, I wonder if, actually, I should let her sleep in a bit longer.

I look down at my watch – *the* watch – which is somehow still ticking faultlessly after all this time. It's not even eight yet, and we were out late last night. Well, late for us, anyway.

For the first time in ages, I'm hung-over – that eggnog brandy was lethal – but I just can't sleep in these days. In my freelance years, I'd sometimes stay in bed until mid-morning, trying to summon the resolve to get up and get on with things. Now, though, I have to be up at 6.30 on the dot most days, and the routine has installed a sort of internal alarm clock within me. Not that I need it: starting the day is something I genuinely look forward to now.

These last few months have been maybe the happiest of my whole life, which is crazy, really, when I think back to how this year started. On Christmas Day 2020, I would never have imagined that next Christmas could look like this. Not for the first time this year, I'm struck by how incredibly lucky I am.

I pick up the trays. I'll just go up and see if she's awake.

I walk slowly out of the kitchen, trying not to spill anything, and as I pass the living room, I see the Christmas tree. It's heaving under countless layers of multicoloured ornaments, and I can't help smiling as I remember the chic, scarcely decorated tree that greeted me in that unfamiliar flat on Christmas Day 2023. If that was the Anna Wintour of Christmas trees, then this one is probably the Dame Edna Everage. And let's be honest, Dame Edna is the look every decent Christmas tree should aspire to.

I tiptoe up the stairs, balancing the trays precariously as I go. Holly and ivy and tinsel have been draped at random around every photo or painting on the staircase, and right at the top, a combination of all three frames my favourite picture. It's one I found recently while going through some of Mum's stuff. It's of me, Daphne and Mum, huddled up in coats and scarves, in Queen's Park on Christmas Eve 2011. We're all mugging cheerfully at the camera, our cheeks pink from the cold, arms flung around each other's shoulders.

On the wall at the end of the landing, just outside our

bedroom, there's another picture I discovered in the same box. This one's of Mum and her dad – Grandad Jack – on the beach at Whitley Bay. Mum must be about nineteen. She's grinning, a towel around her shoulders, while Grandad stands next to her, beaming, his blue eyes twinkling. This photo always makes me smile when I see it.

I nudge the bedroom door open with my shoulder, trying to be as quiet as possible in case she's still asleep. But she's not. She's sitting up in bed, reading a book. Her curly black hair is piled messily on top of her head, and she's wearing my faded *Rick and Morty* T-shirt as a pyjama top.

For just a moment, I stand in the doorway looking at her, the heavy trays balanced in my hands.

Daff. Sometimes I still can't believe that she's back here with me.

When she walked out of this flat a year ago to the day, I honestly thought I'd lost her. She stayed put at her parents' house for weeks, and we talked only on the phone: sporadically at first, and then more frequently – long, fraught conversations about things we'd never really spoken about before. I listened as she told me how isolated she'd been feeling over the past few years, how she felt she couldn't get through to me, and how – even before I told her about Alice – she'd been questioning whether or not we were really meant to be together. It was hard to hear. Horrible, even. But she also told me that despite all this, she'd never stopped loving me, and I saw there was still hope.

At her suggestion, I tried grief counselling – to finally talk properly to a professional about what happened with Mum. I was hesitant at first, but honestly, it's been one of the best things I've ever done. I can feel myself starting to let go of stuff that's gnawed at me for years – stuff from even before Mum died. I'm learning that it's OK to miss her so badly that it hurts, but it shouldn't stop me letting in the people I love.

Gradually, as winter turned into spring and we began to meet up in person again, I think Daff started to see a genuine change in me. A change I was only just beginning to recognise myself. She started to truly believe that I'd never lie to her, or keep anything from her again. She started to forgive me.

And then, a few months ago, just after I started the new job, she moved back in.

I'd be lying if I said it's been plain sailing from then on. It hasn't. It's still tough. In fact, it turned out Harv was right when he said that regaining Daff's trust would be the hardest thing I'd ever have to do. I still don't know if I've fully achieved it. But we've learned to communicate with total honesty now, and because of that, it feels like we're in a better place than we have ever been.

And today, we're going to tell everyone the news. The news that we're still reeling from ourselves …

The floorboards squeak under me suddenly, and I realise I've been standing here looking at Daff for a period of time that may have slipped beyond romantic, and into *Walking-Dead*-guy-in-*Love-Actually* territory. As I enter the room, she looks up and gives me the full wattage of her incredible smile.

'There you are. I wondered where you'd …' And then she spots the trays. 'Oh my God. No. Way.'

I nod. 'Way. Oh yes. Surprise Christmas breakfast in bed.'

She puts her book down, shaking her head. 'I mean … this is next-level. Does this even happen in real life? I thought it was just a sitcoms-and-films thing.'

'What can I say? I'm just a really, really great guy.'

She nods solemnly. 'That does appear to be the case.'

I lay the tray down with a flourish across her lap, and she laughs. 'Thank you.' She takes my hand and squeezes it. 'Seriously, this is lovely.'

I squeeze back. 'No worries. How are you feeling?'

She picks up a rasher of crispy bacon and bites off the end. 'Mmm. Good.'

'You, or the bacon?'

She laughs. 'Both. The bacon and I are both great.'

'Good.' I slide into bed next to her, settling my own tray on top of the duvet.

'The bigger question,' Daff says, a smile playing on her lips, 'is how are *you* feeling?'

I wince. 'Was I that bad last night?'

She grins. 'No, you were great! My colleagues all loved you. I think everyone was a bit weirded out by how great you were, to be honest. After previous work Christmas Eve dos.'

'I know, I know. Don't remind me.'

She lays her head on my shoulder. 'I loved seeing you talking to them all about the teaching stuff.'

'Ha. I hope I didn't ramble on too much.'

'No! I can't tell you how amazing it is to see you actually being *proud* of what you're doing. And you were so funny with Nadia and Sarah.' She kisses my neck and looks up at me. 'You weren't faking, right? You did genuinely enjoy yourself?'

I put my arm around her. 'Yeah. I genuinely did.'

I mean it, too. Daff's annual Christmas Eve work do used to instil a pathetic sort of dread in me. I'd worry about it for weeks beforehand, certain that everyone there would be secretly looking down on me, or wondering what Daff was still doing with me. But last night, none of those thoughts even crossed my mind. For the first time, I found I was able to just relax and have fun.

'I'll be honest, though, I am a bit hung-over,' I add, yawning widely. 'You don't mind that I ended up having a few, do you?'

'I was mortified,' she deadpans. 'No, of course not. It's weird, actually: I don't miss drinking at all. Yet, anyway. And it's so funny being sober at these things; watching everyone else get progressively more pissed around you.'

I laugh. 'So what do you remember from last night that I might've drunkenly forgotten?'

'Well ...' She chews a mouthful of scrambled egg thoughtfully. 'You and Rich doing karaoke together was an obvious highlight.'

'Well I remember *that*, yeah.'

'I don't think anyone will ever forget it. Nads filmed the whole thing, by the way.' She taps her phone on the table. 'It's already on the work WhatsApp.'

'Glad to hear it. Who knew Rich knows all the words to "Gettin' Jiggy wit It"? I swear he didn't look at the screen once.'

Daff grins as she takes a sip of coffee. 'Hey – did you talk to his new girlfriend? Miranda?'

'Yeah, a little bit. She seems nice.'

'*So* hot.' She shakes her head in disbelief. 'Even hotter than his last one.'

I load my fork up with bacon. 'The first thing Rich said to me last night, before he even said hello, was that Miranda had once auditioned to be in a Corrs tribute band, but she'd been rejected for being – and this is a direct quote – "too good-looking".'

Daff splutters into her orange juice. 'Ah, Rich. His heart's in the right place, but he really is a ridiculous man.'

A few months ago, a comment like that would probably have had me searching Daff's expression carefully for any trace of hidden meaning. It would have sent my brain wheeling back to that day in the park at Christmas 2023 – the image of Rich's arm slinking around her waist. Now, though, it doesn't even make me flinch.

It doesn't bother me when Daff and Rich work late together, or go out to plays or screenings, just the two of them. Because I know that I love her and she loves me. I believe in us completely.

I guess Harv was right in the end: all I needed was a little less self-pity and a little more self-belief.

We sit for a few seconds in contented silence, sipping our coffee, watching the sunlight filter in between the curtains.

'When's your Christmas thing with the teaching lot again?' Daff asks.

'The twenty-ninth,' I tell her. 'It'd be great if you wanted to come too.'

'Yeah. I'm seeing the girls that night, but maybe we can come along for a drink later.'

'Definitely – anyone's welcome. I've invited Harv, too.'

She nudges me with her elbow. 'You still trying to set him up with the Iron Woman?'

I laugh. 'Can you please not call her that? It makes her sound like Margaret Thatcher.'

'Sorry. I'm only joking – you know I love Isha.'

'Yeah, well, the feeling's mutual. She's always banging on about how great you are. Anyway, I do think she and Harv would be good together.'

She nods. 'I think you're right.'

Isha (aka the Iron Woman) is one of many new mates I made on the Those Who Can teacher training course earlier this year. She's brilliant: smart and funny and – incredibly – perhaps even more fitness-obsessed than Harv. She ticks off a different triathlon pretty much every weekend, and since she's recently single, I've been talking Harv up to her at every given opportunity.

Daff takes a last sip of coffee and plonks her mug on the bedside table. 'I still can't believe that by this time next year you'll be Mr Hazeley.'

I lean into her, kissing her hair. 'Oi, don't jinx it. I've still got the exams to get through.'

She smiles at me. 'Come on, Ben … You know you're good at it.'

I shrug, but I can't help smiling back. I *am* good at it, I think.

I'm now four months into my stint as a teaching assistant at a local comprehensive, and the first time I stood up in front of a class, it was like something finally clicked. The lesson was Year 11 English, and I had to suppress my shock when I saw the book we'd be dissecting: *The History of Mr Polly* by H. G. Wells. A book that contains the line: '*If you don't like your life, you can change it.*'

Anyway, it's early days, but I love it. I really do. By next summer – exam results pending – I'll be a fully qualified teacher. The idea makes me tingle with excitement.

Daff finishes her last bit of bacon and sets her tray aside. 'Well, that was outrageous. Thanks very much.'

'No worries,' I say. 'Although I am kind of disappointed that you're still eating normal food. I thought you were supposed to be having weird cravings by now. I'm quite looking forward to knocking you up pilchards with raspberry jam, or whatever.'

She smiles at me, her brown eyes sparkling. 'You've been reading those leaflets the doctor gave us, then?'

'Erm, to be honest, I think I'm getting this from an episode of *Friends* where Phoebe was pregnant.'

'Excellent.' She nods. 'Good to know you're taking this whole experience seriously.'

I lay my tray aside too, and cuddle up to her. 'So … how are we going to do it today, then?'

Daff shrugs. 'I think we should just do it when everyone's arrived. All my lot, and your uncle and aunt and cousins and everyone. Harv and Jamila are coming for drinks at eleven-ish, so they should still be here too. We can tell them all at once.' She pounds her fist into her palm. 'Maximum impact.'

I kiss her shoulder. 'Your mum is going to lose her mind.'

'I know,' she laughs. 'I'm genuinely worried. I think we should hide all breakable objects.'

'We should do that anyway, with your nephews coming.'

She kisses me on the forehead. 'I wish your mum was here today,' she says suddenly. 'So much.'

'I know,' I say quietly. 'I've been thinking about her a lot since we found out.'

We lie there for a minute, forehead to forehead. I wonder if it will ever get easier – missing Mum. Probably not. But at least I've let Daff in properly this time. Now at least we can miss her together.

Daff sighs and says, 'Well. It's been a pretty weird year, hasn't it?'

I laugh. 'It really has.' I lay a hand gently on her stomach.

'And next year's going to be even weirder,' she says. 'I mean, there's a person in there.' She pokes her belly. 'An actual person.'

'Bernard,' I say.

'Yep. Little Bernie.'

'The B Man.'

She nuzzles into my neck. 'You know we have to think of some proper names soon, right? Bernard's fine for a bump, but I'm not sure about it for our actual child.'

'What, even if it's a girl?'

'Even if it's a girl.'

'OK,' I say. 'I'll brainstorm.'

I've been thinking lately about Jack, if it's a boy. I haven't told Daff yet. Maybe I'll pitch it in the new year.

The whole thing still doesn't seem real, to be honest. When Daff missed her period back in October, we hadn't even restarted the conversation about having kids. We were still trying to find our way back into married life. But I knew for certain it was what I wanted. A family with Daphne: the thought made me explode with joy. And when she told me it was what she wanted too ... Well, put it this way, I was unable to form a coherent sentence for a good few hours.

She places her hand on top of mine, and I hear the soft clink of our wedding rings touching.

'I love you, Daff,' I tell her.

'I love you too. And hey – we haven't even said it yet.' She smiles at me: her wide, bright, beautiful smile. 'Merry Christmas.'

'Oh yeah. Merry Christmas.'

We kiss for a while, our fingers interlocked on her tummy, and I find myself hard pressed to remember a moment when I have ever felt happier.

Our families and our best mates will all be here in a few hours, and over a glass of champagne, we're going to let them know we're expecting.

Today is going to be a very good day.

'All right,' I say finally, climbing back out of bed and collecting the trays. 'You stay put. I'm on turkey duty, gravy duty and trying-to-get-rid-of-this-hangover duty. Do we have any Nurofen?'

'Under the sink in the bathroom.' She sits up and wriggles out of the duvet. 'I'll come down and give you a hand with everything.'

'No way,' I tell her, mock-sternly. 'You're not lifting a finger today.'

She laughs. 'You can save that attitude for the third trimester, when I'm genuinely losing my mind.' She walks around the bed and takes my hand. 'Come on, let's do it together. That's the best way.'

Down in the kitchen, we switch the radio on to hear Michael Bublé warbling about what he wants for Christmas. We start chatting and laughing as we pull out spices and chopping boards and everything else we need to prepare our slap-up festive lunch.

I am nervous, to be honest. About everything: about being

a good husband and a good dad and a good teacher. It's daunting. It's scary.

But I also can't wait.

Daphne's right: we'll do it together. All of it. That's the best way.

Epilogue

'Time for one more?'

Harv raises his empty vodka glass at me hopefully.

I check my watch. 'Nah, it's after eight, I'd better be off,' I tell him. 'Sorry. Daff's on her own and I told her I wouldn't be too late.'

He rolls his eyes. 'Mate, she probably *wants* some time on her own! In, like, ten days, she'll never be on her own again. Neither will you.'

'I'm having a kid, Harv, I'm not grafting on a Siamese twin.'

'Still. This is your last opportunity for some actual me time. Or *you* time. Or … You know what I mean.'

I laugh. 'Yeah, I do. But still, I'd better get back.'

Harv sighs as we stand and take our glasses back to the bar. 'I thought this was supposed to be a celebration,' he moans. 'You're now officially qualified to shout at children in exchange for money. We should be out tearing it up.'

I called him on the spur of the moment, as soon as I walked out of the final interview. I was still dazed at being officially offered the job I've been training to do for the last ten months.

When the new term starts in September, I will be an English teacher – and a Year 7 form tutor – at Belmont Comprehensive School, Willesden.

It feels absolutely amazing.

We've just spent a very pleasant couple of hours toasting the news in a little pub next to Harv's new office in Bloomsbury, but now I'm eager to get back to Daff. She's always telling me not to worry, but I can't help it. Plus, I just like coming home to her.

When we step outside the pub, it's still very much T-shirt weather, the sun blazing brightly in the clear blue sky.

'You heading back to yours?' I ask Harv.

He shakes his head. 'Nope – staying at Isha's tonight.'

'Ah, right.' I grin at him. 'I still can't believe it's been six months now. Honestly, I'm the greatest matchmaker of all time. This must be how Paddy McGuinness feels whenever there's a *Take Me Out* wedding.'

'Who said anything about weddings?' I swear I see Harv blush as he fights back a sheepish smile. Have I tapped into something he's genuinely thinking about?

Before I can probe any further, he starts walking. 'OK,' he says, 'by the time we get to the Tube, we have to name every Premier League top scorer since 1993. Without googling.'

'Right.' I nod, feeling a powerfully simplistic delight at the task in hand.

As we turn the corner, though, we pass a street sign that reads *Foster Road*, and out of nowhere, a strange electric shiver passes through me. Like I've just remembered I was supposed to do something important, but I can't recall what …

Harv is striding along with his lips pursed. 'OK …'93 …

Well, it's got to be Alan Shearer, hasn't it? Or maybe whats-hisface … the guy that tried to be a rapper for a bit … Andy Cole! Or hang on, maybe …' He breaks off mid-sentence. 'Wow. Pretty weird place.'

I stand frozen to the spot beside him, my mouth hanging open as I stare up at the building in front of us: a squat red-brick house with an uneven roof and a precariously wonky chimney. It's almost like it's been dropped onto this street by mistake – one snaggled tooth in an otherwise perfect mouth.

'Sort of a Harry Potter vibe,' Harv says. 'Who d'you think lives there?'

I'm barely listening. Heart pounding, I take my watch off and examine the back of the face. The inscription reads: *15 Foster Road, Bloomsbury, WC1A.*

It never once crossed my mind to come back here. In fact, I realise now that this is the first time I've actually thought about 15 Foster Road, Bloomsbury, since being here in 2010.

It's like that whole afternoon had been wiped from my memory until now.

That strange sense of unreality sweeps through me: the same feeling I used to get in the watch-seller's presence. Like I'd slipped off the grid somehow, into a secret corner no one else could see.

'Can I just check something?' I murmur.

I walk across the road to the bottom of the little flight of steps that lead up to the bright purple door. The gold number 15 glints sharply in the sunlight.

'What are you doing?' Harv asks, arriving next to me. 'Do you know who lives here?'

'Not exactly, but—'

Before I can finish the sentence, the purple door opens, and a man and woman step out. They're about my age, chatting breezily to one another, the man carrying a buggy with a very cute baby in it. They give us a friendly smile as they pass.

For a second, I hear nothing except my heart beating.

'Did you know them?' Harv asks.

'No, I just …' I stare at the purple door. It's just somebody's home. But still, somehow, I *know* I was here. I know that the watch-seller was real. Because the changes he wrought in me are real.

I glance down at my watch and feel a warm glow pass through me as I see the hands ticking steadily. I fix it back around my wrist.

'Come on, man,' I say to Harv. 'Let's go home.'

And I turn and walk away, my best mate beside me, under the fading summer sun, back to Daphne, back to the next chapter of our life together.

Acknowledgements

First and foremost, a massive thank you to the mighty Emily Kitchin, who is not only a brilliant editor, but also a master plotter, indefatigable great-idea generator and highly skilled de-italiciser. Thank you so much for everything, Emily – I owe you many, many drinks...

Big thanks also to: everyone at HQ, Kirsty McLachlan and all at DGA, Rachel Leyshon, Lucy Ivison, Anne-Sophie Jahn and Ersi Sotiropoulos. Thanks to my parents and my brother. Thanks to my friends, in particular the ones from whom I shamelessly borrowed names, traits, jokes or anecdotes to put in this book. Including but not limited to: Carolina Demopoulos, Harvey Horner, Jeremy Stubbings, Susan Simmonds, Daphne Koutsafti, Robin Pasricha, Rob Ellen, Chris Carroll and Neil Redford.

I wrote big chunks of *All About Us* at two fantastic writers' residences in Greece – the House of Literature in Paros and the International Writers' & Translators' Centre of Rhodes. Thank you very much to everyone at both, and in particular to Eleftheria Binikou at the IWTCR.

And thank you to Charles Dickens for the loan of his story structure. Thanks, Charles.

Author Q&A with Tom Ellen

Can you tell us about your inspiration for writing *All About Us?*

I think everyone can relate to those 'What if...' moments in life – times you look back and wonder, 'If I did such-and-such differently, what would my life look like now?'. That was the initial inspiration for *All About Us* – the concept of being able to *actually* revisit a few of those moments. If you could go back five, ten, fifteen years, what would you change – and why? Aside from its magical, time travel elements, though, the book is also a romantic comedy at heart, and I've always loved romcoms, so ultimately I just wanted to write a funny, romantic book that encompassed lots of other themes I'm also interested in: family dynamics, grief, toxic masculinity. I should also mention that Dickens' *A Christmas Carol* was a pretty major inspiration for *All About Us*, since I – ahem – 'borrowed' the basic time-hopping structure from that excellent novel!

Is there a character in the book you connected with most deeply?

Ben is probably the closest to me – in terms of both his good and bad points. Like him, I'm definitely prone to being a bit over-anxious and mawkish, but hopefully I share some of his more positive characteristics too! Aside from him, though, the character of Daphne is based on my girlfriend, and Ben's best mate Harv is a kind of amalgam of lots of my closest friends, so I definitely connected to those two very deeply as well.

Do you have a favourite scene in the book – past, present or future?

I really enjoyed writing the early chapters when Ben wakes up to find himself back in the past for the first time. It was fun to channel that feeling of *what-on-earth-is-happening-here* craziness as he realises he has somehow jumped back fifteen years. Plus, that section is all set at the University of York – where I studied – so it was very nostalgic to write about drinking Snakebite Black in the college bar, playing Sardines in the campus maze and acting in (usually extremely poor quality) student plays – all things I genuinely did during my time there!

Some of the scenes between Ben and his mum are hugely emotional. How did it feel to write those?

I loved writing them. I hope they come across as moving and tender, but I also wanted them to be humorous, as I think Ben's mum is one of the funniest characters in the book, and

I really enjoyed writing her dialogue for that reason. Those scenes were also some of the most difficult to write, though, because it's so tough to imagine how you'd feel if you'd lost someone you were so close to, and then you were miraculously given the chance the see them again one last time! I wanted Ben to be completely overwhelmed by this bittersweet sensation of seeing his beloved mum again, but also of being reminded how much he misses her now she's gone.

The theme of toxic masculinity, and of how men don't feel that it's 'manly' to show their emotions, is a strong one in the book. Did you always set out to explore this?

Yes, absolutely. I've always been interested in that idea that 'banter' is basically how men communicate. I'm quite lucky in that I can actually talk to most of my male friends about that kind of stuff, but I think it's still very tough for a lot of men, so I was interested to explore that. There's a scene early on in the book where Ben's chatting to Harv and unwittingly puts on a 'comedy' accent when he confesses to feeling depressed. That's something I've definitely noticed in myself and my own friends: the idea of not wanting to dampen the mood, or of feeling awkward and embarrassed to admit that something's wrong.

Can you tell us what your favourite Christmas films are? We certainly hope that *Love Actually* features!

Love Actually is indeed up there, but I'd say *The Muppet Christmas Carol* probably pips it to the post for me. A great film and arguably Michael Caine's finest hour (don't @ me). *Home Alone* is definitely in the mix, too. There is also a long-standing debate about whether or not *Die Hard* counts as a 'Christmas film' – and I'm very much of the opinion that it does – so that's probably up there for me, as well.

Do you like to read books in a similar area to *All About Us*, or watch TV dramas to get ideas? Can you recommend any to us?

Yes! I really like Mike Gayle's and Marian Keyes' books, plus lots of other authors writing in a funny, clever, interesting way about modern relationships: Holly Bourne, David Nicholls, Kiley Reid, Beth O'Leary, Lisa Owens, Josie Silver. I am a big fan of funny novels in general, so for comic inspiration I'll most often go back to stuff by Flann O'Brien, Sue Townsend and Dan Rhodes.

What does your typical writing day look like?

I usually like to go out to a library to write, rather than staying at home, as I tend to get much more done that way. But if that's not possible, the first half-hour of my writing day will traditionally be given over to intense procrastination – probably tinkering pointlessly with my fantasy football team – before actually getting down to doing some work. I find I'm most productive in the morning, and I tend to work best if I set myself a concrete goal for the day – i.e. to finish a particular chapter, or hit a certain word count. My typical writing day will also involve *at least* six cups of tea and probably some Haribo.

Do you have any tips for aspiring writers?

My main tip would be to enter writing competitions! When you're starting out as a writer, the hardest thing can be just FINISHING something, so competitions are a brilliant way to impose a deadline on yourself and get to the end of a draft. I started out writing Young Adult books, and my co-author Lucy Ivison and I decided to enter our first book into *The Times*/Chicken House children's fiction competition. We were both working full-time, and it was so hard to motivate ourselves to write on the weekends and in the evenings after work, but the contest's looming deadline gave us a reason to keep going. We would tell each other, 'We HAVE to get this finished in time for that competition', and honestly I think that's the only reason we got it done! We ended up making the shortlist, and although we didn't win, the book was still published anyway. So, I'd really advise having a search for any contests that cater for the kind of book you want to write, and then putting that deadline in your calendar as a goal to finish it by. You've got nothing to lose and so much to gain!

Can you tell us what you're working on next?

I'm working on another novel for HQ called *The Start of You and Me*, which is inspired by volunteer work that I do on a crisis telephone helpline. It's another uplifting romantic comedy, and you can read an extract right after this very interview! Aside from that, I'm finishing up an illustrated children's book – based on some cartoon characters I invented when I was about nine – which should be out some time in 2021!

Did you fall in love with *All About Us?*

Read on for an extract from Tom Ellen's
uplifting and emotional new novel,
The Start of You and Me.

WILL

It could be him.

That's the thought running through my brain in this dingy little ground floor office, as the phone bursts into life for the first time this evening. It's a ridiculous thought, but it's there all the same.

It's always there.

I push aside my Tupperware containing tonight's dinner – a gluey clump of leftover tuna pasta – and feel my chest tighten as I lift the receiver: 'Hello, Green Shoots?'

'Oh... Hi. Sorry. Hi.'

The tightness slackens. It's a woman's voice. A voice I'm pretty sure I haven't heard before. She sounds almost surprised that someone has answered.

'Hi,' I say. 'How are you doing tonight?'

'Sorry,' she repeats. 'This is weird. I don't really know why I'm calling, actually.'

'That's OK.'

You hear this pretty often: new callers apologising for having the audacity to phone up a crisis line. For having the nerve to feel desperate or lonely or sad. For having the *sheer brass neck* to admit that they're in pain. Always makes me wonder how many people have chosen not to reach out for exactly that reason. How many lives have been derailed or ruined or even lost because people were too... *British* to seek help.

'So, how are you feeling?' I ask again. The line crackles as the woman sighs into her phone.

'I'm just, erm... Not brilliant, to be honest.'

'I'm sorry to hear that.'

'Well, thanks.' The woman gives a forced laugh. She's got a nice voice – husky and full of humour, the ghost of a Northern accent just audible. She sounds around about my age, though obviously I can't tell for sure.

'This is stupid, really,' she says. 'There are people with actual problems trying to get through to you and I'm calling up because of an Instagram comment about my boobs.'

There's a short pause – during which I try to work out if she just said what I think she just said – and then the line is flooded with a sound that could either be laughter or crying. Possibly a mixture of the two.

'I, erm...' I don't really know what to say, to be honest. They don't exactly prepare you for this kind of comment in training. I briefly consider typing 'Instagram boobs' into the computer's advice search bar, but decide against it. It probably wouldn't be a great look if anyone here keeps track of the Internet history.

The snuffling dies out suddenly, and the woman's voice is so quiet I can barely hear it. 'Sorry,' she says. 'I don't know what's wrong with me.'

'Just because you're not feeling brilliant it doesn't mean there's anything wrong with you,' I say. 'We all feel not-brilliant every now and then.'

'Yeah.' The woman sighs. I hear her take a large gulp of something, and then the clink of glass as she puts it back down. 'But lately it's all the time,' she says. 'And I can't even really put my finger on why. Nothing big has even happened.'

'I'm guessing something must have happened, or you wouldn't be calling?'

'Yeah... Well, like I say, it's stupid. A friend left a comment on my Instagram and it just made me realise how much I miss her.'

'Does she live far away?' I ask.

The woman laughs – a genuine laugh this time; nothing forced about it. 'No. She lives ten minutes from my flat. I see her all the time. It's just that she's married now, and she's got a husband and a baby... And obviously I love her husband and her baby – to bits – but... it's not the same any more. I miss the 'old' her, I suppose. Which is technically the 'young' her. Well, you know what I mean. And it's like that with most of my friends. They're all in couples now and they've got such different lives...'

'Mm-hmm, I understand.' Like a lot of first-time callers, I can sense this is someone that just needs to *vent*. To open a valve and let out the thoughts that have been pinballing madly around her head for God knows how long.

She carries on. 'It's like... I realise that their families are the most important things in their lives right now. So I just feel that if I ever want to talk to them about my stuff, about what's going on with *me*... I know they won't fully be present, you know? Because whatever it is, it couldn't possibly be as important as their child or their marriage. And I can tell they feel guilty too, because they think I'm being left behind and I'm going to end up on my own. Which, don't get me wrong, I wouldn't really mind. I like being on my own. But I don't want to be... lonely.' The word catches in her throat and she breaks off. The phone feels hot against my ear. 'I'm constantly surrounded by people,' she says. 'My friends and my family and my colleagues. But, still, that's how I feel. I feel lonely.'

She cuts off suddenly, almost breathless. 'Sorry. God. Actually hearing myself say this stuff out loud makes me realise how selfish and spoiled it all sounds. Talk about First World problems.'

'Not at all,' I say. 'Not in the slightest.' And I mean it. After six years of doing this, I can tell when someone is genuinely suffering.

'You're being far too nice,' she laughs. 'If you think I'm a dick, you can just tell me I'm a dick. I honestly won't mind.'

I can't help laughing too. 'I don't think I'm technically allowed to tell you you're a dick, actually. That's not really what this helpline is for.'

'Right. I guess it would go against company policy to tell callers that they're dicks.'

'It would almost certainly be frowned upon, yeah.'

We both laugh this time. It's weird. It feels sort of... comfortable. I've felt many different emotions listening to callers over these past few years, but 'comfortable' has never been one of them.

'Maybe,' the woman says, 'there's a gap in the market for a helpline where someone just calls you a dick and tells you to get on with it. You babble on about your so-called problems, and at the end they just say: "Yeah, get your shit together and stop being a dick." I actually think that'd be quite effective.'

I should really stop laughing so much. I have no idea what this person is going through – maybe she's deflecting her pain with humour, using it as a defence mechanism to hide how much she's really struggling. The problem is, she is undeniably pretty funny. I clear my throat and try to be a bit more professional.

'For what it's worth, you wouldn't believe the number of calls we get from people in a very similar position to yourself, who are feeling the exact same thing.'

'Right,' she says. 'So, I'm not a dick; I'm just staggeringly unoriginal.'

'Exactly.'

More laughter – from both of us.

I hear her take another sip of her drink. 'God, this is so weird. This is the most honest conversation I've had in months, and it's with someone I can't see and whose name I don't even know. What does that say about me?'

'It says that you're feeling low and you made the right decision to reach out for help,' I say, firmly. 'And as for names, if you like, you can call me Jack.'

She laughs softly. 'So I'm guessing your name's *not* Jack, then?

'Well, we use "safe names" on this line. It just makes things...'

'Safer?'

'Yeah.'

'OK. Well... Can I tell you my name?' she asks.

'Of course, if you want to. And if you don't want to that's fine, too.'

'Hmm.' I hear the rustle of the phone shifting as she moves around. I suddenly wonder where she is. What she looks like. 'Maybe I'll give myself a safe name as well.'

'If you like.'

'OK.' There's a pause. 'You can call me Pia.'

'OK, Pia,' I say. 'Nice to meet you, Pia.'

'Nice to meet you too, Jack.'

The computer fades into sleep mode and in the black screen I catch my own reflection – a silly grin plastered across my face. Weird. Can't remember the last time I saw myself smile.

For a second, neither of us says anything. And then:

'I broke up with my fiancé,' she says. 'Four months ago.'

'OK...'

Even after six years, I can't help fighting the urge to say 'I'm sorry' in response to a comment like this. The first thing we were taught in training was not to express any opinion or judgement whatsoever when a caller says something along these lines. It makes sense, I guess: somebody calls up and tells you their mum has just died, you say, 'Oh, I'm sorry to hear that,' and then they tell you that their mum abused them or neglected them or abandoned them. By expressing sadness or regret, you're making the caller feel worse about the fact that they may have mixed emotions about their mother's death.

Basically, we're supposed to stay neutral until we have all the information. Which, in practice, is much harder than it sounds. Still, I manage to wrestle down my natural human instinct to offer condolence and instead say, 'And how did that make you feel?'

I hear her take a breath as she considers this. 'I felt awful because I'd hurt him, and he didn't deserve to be hurt. And I felt bad because my mum and my sister and all my friends thought I was *insane* to break off an engagement aged thirty-three. But despite all that, I felt glad that I didn't have to marry him.'

I nod. 'It sounds like the right decision, then?'

'Maybe. Sometimes it doesn't feel like the right decision.'

'How did you meet?'

Not sure where that came from. I feel a giddy – and slightly pathetic – thrill at having asked a direct question, which strictly speaking we're not supposed to do on this line. We're meant to stick to 'open-ended' questions – 'How did that make you feel?', 'Can you tell me more about that?' – rather than digging into specific facts or details. I suddenly hope Carole, Green Shoots' director, doesn't monitor these calls, or I'm sure to be in for a strongly worded email.

Either way, Pia doesn't seem to mind.

'We met on Tinder', she says, inflating the last word with about six heavily-sighed Ns. 'I know, right – how original. But I liked him straight away. And we were good together, I think. He made me laugh and he was kind, and – honestly – when my dad died last year, he was the one who kept me from falling apart completely.'

I swallow another 'I'm sorry'.

She carries on. 'I love him so much for that. I always will. But I just wasn't ever... *in love* with him, no matter how hard I tried to be. It feels horrible to say that, but it's true. And when he proposed, I thought...' She breaks off. I imagine her shaking her head, staring down at the floor. 'I don't know what

I thought, really. That I didn't want to hurt him by saying no? That maybe I would grow to fall in love with him. That my mum would be off-her-nut delighted, and it's not often I get the chance to make her feel like that. Maybe even because all my friends were getting married and having kids, and I didn't want to be left behind. Pathetic to admit it, but there it is.'

'It's not pathetic at all. I get it. So, what caused you to break it off?'

Another direct question. I'm a maverick. A rebel! I'm the James Dean of telephone crisis lines.

'Well, Dom kept saying, "We should get a date in the diary", "We should start looking at venues", and I just kept telling him, "Ah, there's no rush, let's take it slowly". Then, one evening, I came home from work early and he'd left his laptop open on the kitchen table. There was this Word document on there – five pages long... It was his speech for the wedding. We didn't even have a date set and he'd already written his speech. And it was so... so *lovely*.' Her voice quivers and breaks on the word. She takes a shaky breath. 'He deserves someone who feels the same way. And seeing that speech made me realise: this is real. This will be the rest of our lives, unless I do something to stop it. And then he came downstairs, and I told him I wasn't sure I wanted to marry him. And his face just...'

She is crying now – little gulps between each word. My neck feels hot suddenly, and I notice that I'm twisting the phone cord so tightly my knuckles are white. 'He didn't deserve that,' she whispers. 'He didn't deserve what I did to him. I just feel like such an awful person.'

'But you can't...' My voice comes out croaky, and I swallow

hard and start again. 'Pia, if it wasn't meant to be, then he will thank you in the long run. You have to remember that.'

'But it's been four months and he's still suffering,' she sniffs. 'And I am too. It's like my life is on pause while everyone else is fast-forwarding. I just keep thinking: Who the hell do I think I am, waiting around for some fantasy person who won't ever show up? Maybe this is as good as it gets, so why can't I be like everybody else, and just... settle?'

'Look... I can't say what you should or shouldn't do,' I tell her. 'But from what you've told me, I don't think you're an awful person. Not in the slightest.'

She sniffs again and says, 'Well. Thank you.' And then she lets out a gasp that lands halfway between anger and relief. 'God, it feels good to actually talk about this. I don't really have anyone I can speak to about it properly.'

'That's what we're here for,' I say.

'What do you think, though, Jack?' She coughs, and suddenly I can hear the smile back in her voice. 'Did I make the right decision? I mean, you're the expert.'

I play along, but I'm smiling too. 'Not at all, actually, Pia. I'm just a volunteer, and I've known you for all of about nine minutes, so I definitely can't go making any sweeping judgements on your life. The whole point of this line is to listen without judgement.'

'Oh, OK. I get it... So you're like a kind of phone Beefeater?'

An extremely inelegant snort-laugh splutters out of me. 'A what?'

'Beefeaters aren't supposed to react, are they, no matter what you do in front of them. I remember my dad taking us to see them when we were kids, and me and my sister would jump about, sticking our tongues out at them, and they had to stay totally composed and professional. So – that's you. You're a phone Beefeater. No matter what I say, you can't react.'

My grin stretches even wider. 'Couldn't have put it better myself.'

'OK'. There's another weirdly comfortable pause. Then she takes a deep breath and says, 'Well. I'd better go – there must be other people trying to get through to you.'

'How are you feeling now?' I ask.

'Better than I was when I called. So that's something.'

'That's very good to hear.'

'Thank you, Jack. It was really nice talking to you.'

'You're welcome, Pia. You too. And you can call again, you know. Any time between 1 p.m. and 11 p.m. – someone will be here.'

'OK, thanks. Maybe I will.'

I suddenly very much don't want her to hang up. I don't know why, but I just want to talk to her – to listen to her talk – for just a little longer.

'Bye, then,' she says.

'Bye.'

Then the dial tone is drilling into my ear, and I'm sitting here wondering why my heart seems to be beating slightly faster than usual.

WILL

Friday, 4th March

I'm still thinking about Pia's call at half seven the next morning, as I stumble bleary-eyed onto the Hammersmith & City line.

I navigate the carriage's complex obstacle course of takeaway trays and discarded *Evening Standards* and slump down into a free seat. It's weird – this used to happen all the time when I started volunteering at Green Shoots. Every call I got would stay with me for days afterwards. I couldn't help imagining the caller's life in intricate detail; colouring in all the bits they hadn't told me. I'd picture them at work or at college or at home – nailing on a brave face for friends and family, pretending everything was fine, and all the time holding this secret pain in their chest or their head or their heart, or wherever it was their particular pain was located.

I'd even project the callers onto strangers, people I passed in the street. The woman who barely made eye contact as she served me in Tesco could be the same woman who'd tearfully told me of her husband's suspected affair the night before. The teenager who barged past me onto the bus might be the same frightened kid who'd confessed he was too scared to come out to his right-wing Christian parents.

It seemed like this incredible – and incredibly strange – privilege; to see into someone's life for just a brief moment, to have them tell you things they wouldn't even tell their closest friends. Things they maybe wouldn't tell anyone.

Better than I was when I called. That's how Pia said she was feeling before she put the phone down. I think about how she sounded when she said it, and for the first time in a long time, I feel... OK. Like I'm doing something good.

One of our regular callers, Eric, has this tradition before he hangs up of telling me he's 'so grateful' for the helpline and I'm such a 'good lad' for doing what I do. From reading the logbook and all the email chains, I know it's not just me he says this to: he signs off with this same monologue to all the volunteers.

It's sweet, but it always makes me flinch when I hear it. Because he doesn't know why I'm doing this. Not really. He thinks I'm a 'good lad' – giving up my spare time to help others. He doesn't know what made me sign up, what keeps me coming back. Occasionally, I get the mad urge to tell him why I really do it. To hear his voice buckle under the disappointment.

But then there are calls like Pia's, last night, and I think... Maybe I *am* doing something good. Even if I'm doing it for selfish reasons. Maybe I am making some sort of difference.

Better than I was when I called. I wonder where she is right now.

The Tube driver's voice crackles suddenly through the speaker, making everyone look up, wincing, from their phones.

374

I look up too, and as I do I catch eyes with two blokes sitting across from me. Their gazes scatter as soon as I notice them. They look at each other, lips bitten, eyebrows raised in amusement.

I feel a horrible churning in the pit of my stomach. I pick up a half-shredded *Metro* from the seat next to me, holding it slightly higher than necessary to mask my face, like a crap spy in a crap spy movie.

I can hear them whispering over the whirr of the train. This is pathetic. I'm being ridiculous. I'm being paranoid.

But they do fit the exact profile of the 0.0001 per cent of people in this city that might recognise me – i.e. men, maybe a couple of years younger than I am, with shoulder-length hair and wrist tattoos now half-hidden by freshly ironed office shirts. Indie kids all grown up.

The train hisses into Great Portland Street.

'Sorry, mate. 'Scuse me?'

I focus hard on a '60-second interview' with Paul Chuckle and try to block out the hot thudding in my ears.

'Sorry? Mate?'

I lower the paper to see them both staring at me. 'Yes?'

'You're not... Did you used to be in a band?'

My throat is dry suddenly. I attempt a smile. 'Yeah.'

'I knew it!' The first bloke slaps his knee in delight. 'I knew I recognised him!' He nudges his mate. 'Didn't I say it was him?'

His mate just shrugs. 'I've never even heard of him.'

Before everything happened, back when I was a different person, I used to daydream about what it would be like to get recognised in public by strangers. I used to pine for the attention – the furtive glances, spreading smiles, looks of embarrassed awe. Now I realise it just means people talking about you as if you weren't there – like you're a Madame Tussauds waxwork, or something.

The truth is: I am the absolute worst kind of 'famous' – recognisable only to a tiny handful of people, all of whom probably think I'm an utter knob.

The first bloke turns back to me with a broad grin. 'I think I saw you lot at Reading in like... 2014?'

'2015,' I say, the memory of it flashing into my head. That intern from Universal chopping coke on the airbed in her tent. Powder bouncing everywhere, all of us laughing. So out of it I could hardly breathe. Backstage, Joe, quieter than normal. Me, telling him to stop being so miserable. Telling him we'd finally made it. I remember taking my shirt off onstage, swinging it around my head like the worst cliché of a rock star. It's still on YouTube, I think. The shame and the guilt heat my whole body instantly.

I need to get out of this carriage.

'Yeah, 2015, that was it!' says the Grown-Up Indie Kid. 'You guys were... all right.'

'Cheers.' That's probably as accurate a summary of our band as you'll ever hear, to be fair.

I grip the handrail, ready to stand up. Need to get out of here.

'So, what happened, then?' the GUIK asks, waving a hand at my general appearance, as if to say: 'Why are you slouched on the Hammersmith & City line at half seven in the morning, rather than jet skiing with Bono and Liam Gallagher in the Seychelles?'

The thumping in my ears is louder than ever. I can't think about this now. I can't. 'I just...' The words congeal in my throat. Joe, backstage, quieter than normal. The memory of it grips me around the neck.

I shake my head. Get to my feet. 'Sorry, this is my stop, actually. Nice to meet you, though.' I can feel the sweat prickling on my forehead.

Why won't this fucking train *stop*?

The GUIK is up now too, his hand on my shoulder. 'No worries, man. Can I get a quick photo, though? I've got a mate who used to be really into your group – he'll think it's hilarious.'

Turn away, head throbbing. 'Sorry, this is my stop.' I can just keep repeating that until the doors open. The train bursts out of the tunnel, finally, the signs for Euston Square flashing past in a reddish-blue blur.

I hear him sit back down, muttering, 'Fucking prick. Who does he think he is?'

The doors hiss open and I stagger out onto the platform, gulping the dirty air. My face is boiling, the blood thundering in my ears. Joe, backstage, quieter than normal.

I never even asked him if he was all right.

I look round as the train moves off to see the GUIK holding his phone up at me, smirking. The camera flash stings my eyes through the window.

I swipe yet more *Metros* off the hard plastic bench and wait for the next train. It's not for ten minutes. I'm going to be late for work now.

For some reason I think of Pia again. How her call had made me feel like I was OK, even if just for a few hours.

But I am not OK. I am very far from it.

ONE PLACE. MANY STORIES

Bold, innovative and
empowering publishing.

FOLLOW US ON:

@HQStories